C210275

CW01426489

WB

Nottinghamshire County Council

Please return / renew by the last date shown.

D&P/4261/4.12

BOUNTIFUL FAMINE

A Novel

Sheg Aranmolate

*****

"The greatest threat to freedom is the absence of criticism."

WOLE SOYINKA | NIGERIAN LITERATURE NOBLE LAUREATE

INSPIVIA
BOOKS

An Inspivia, Incorporated *Company.*

This is a work of fiction. The names, characters, places and incidents are the product of the author's imagination or are used fictitiously. Any resemblance to actual events, locales, or persons, living or dead, is entirely coincidental.

Inspivia Books
Memphis, Tennessee, United States of America.
www.inspiviabooks.com

Bountiful Famine: A Novel
© Copyright 2011 by Inspivia Books.
Chief Editor – Petroula Dorset
Author Photograph – Tyler Andrews
Cover Designer – Sheg Aranmolate
Cover Editor – Steven Danielson
Cover Image – Bethany Haley

All rights reserved. No part of this book can be used or reproduced, in part or in whole, by any means, by anyone, without written permission from Sheg Aranmolate or Inspivia Books.

For permission to reproduce the information in this book for commercial purposes or redistribution, please e-mail: copyright@inspivia.com

To contact the author, Sheg Aranmolate:
authors@inspivia.com

ISBN-10: 0-615-54651-X
ISBN-13: 978-0-615-54651-3

LIBRARY OF CONGRESS CONTROL NUMBER: 2011919020
Aranmolate, Sheg
Bountiful Famine/Sheg Aranmolate—2011 Inspivia Books

INSPIVIA
BOOKS

This Inspivia Books Paperback Edition December 2011
Inspivia Books is a trademark of Inspivia, Inc.
Printed in the United States of America

For more information about this book and the author:
www.bountifulfamine.com

REVIEWS *for* iACTUATE:

"The author blends inspirational themes that keep readers engaged in... self reflection. ...greatly needed."
—The Tennessee Tribune.

"It's amazing to me how a young man of Sheg's age can be so wise beyond his years. I just love it!"
—Tuwanda Coleman, News Channel 5 - Talk of the Town.

"... [An] effective and simple tool to live a full and inspired life."
—The Tennessean.

"A must read... for inspiration and motivation by a bright new talent...the perfect gift."
—Bookman/Bookwoman Reviews.

"...Aranmolate's book blends stories and themes."
—Nashville City Paper.

TABLE OF CONTENTS:

Dedication: I

Acknowledgement: II

Foreword: III

DEDICATION:

I dedicate this book to the loved ones in my life: Dad, Mum, Lewa, Nilaja, Funke, Korede, Funmi and Fola.

I appreciate you for the encouragements and for inspiring me to follow my dreams.

I AM THANKFUL

ACKNOWLEDGEMENTS:

First and foremost, I thank the Almighty for giving me the strength and knowledge to write such a great book. I thank my family and friends for their encouragement, support, and efforts in helping me make this book a reality.

I thank my friend and graphics designer, Steven Danielson, for all his pointers and help with designing the book cover. I thank my Italian friend and fellow writer, Philippe Ziglioli, for his insight and for proof-reading the book. I thank my editor, Petroula Dorset, and her husband, Daniel Dorset, for all their effort, helpful comments and criticisms.

I AM GRATEFUL

FOREWORD:

Reason is the natural order of truth; but imagination is the organ of meaning.

C. S. Lewis.

.

1

CHAPTER ONE:

✳

"A chicken that keeps scratching the dung-hill will soon find the mother's thigh bones."
African Proverb

The young boy was suddenly awakened from his slumber by a cold drift that made the minute hairs on his skin stand erect. He couldn't remember what he was dreaming about this time, but it surely wasn't one of those dreams that most people long to remember. He was lying in an uncomfortable position in a strange and foreign environment. He tried to open his eyes to get a glance at his present milieu, but he was unable. His eyelids felt too heavy to be lifted. He tried moving his hands and legs, but they seemed bound. He began to feel a burning sensation in his face; the ominously familiar, coppery taste of fresh blood filled his mouth.

Where am I?

Why is there blood in my mouth?

The young boy rolled his tongue across his teeth, inspecting his oral cavity for signs of damage. He felt a gap between his right molars; it was evident that he had lost at least one tooth. He felt weak all over as though intoxicated by a sedative concoction. He was nauseous and the constant unpleasant smell of rotten fish didn't help to alleviate his queasiness. The young boy began to struggle in the dark, hoping to loosen the restraining forces. However, after a futile struggle that lasted for a few frustrating minutes he came to the daunting realization that he was trapped. He knew that he was enclosed in a wooden box because of the hollow sounds he heard each time his legs hit the sides. His heart raced with ferocity and cold sweat seeped out of his forehead, trickling down into his ears. The boy wanted to shout, but his lips were so parched that he couldn't part them.

Where am I?

What's going on?

Have I been drugged?

As the young boy lay in his new sarcophagus trying to figure out the conditions that led to his dreadful situation, he was suddenly disturbed by a creeping sensation on his bare feet.

Oh, what's going on?

The creeping sensation intensified and rapidly ascended from his toes towards his ankle and then up his legs.

"Insects!" He mumbled, losing his initial calm.

I've been drugged and buried alive with insects?

I'm going to die with insects.

No! No! No!

He screamed in his mind and began to cry. The young boy wiggled his bound feet, hitting them several times against both sides of the barrier, hoping to crush whatever was crawling up his legs. His actions paid off and the crawling stopped. He was relieved because he feared insects, especially large ones.

I need to get out of here!

I need to get out of here!

He repeated this to himself like a sacred chant. The young boy tried to concoct an escape strategy, but his claustrophobia was taking a huge toll on his mental capabilities. His muscles tightened, his breath shortened, and his body temperature dropped as if he was drowning in a cold lake. He began to shiver and shake. His mind drifted in and out of reality as a series of vivid chronological black and white images of his past flashed before his mind's eye. Initially, they were images of himself as a baby crying, then as a boy strolling through a *maize* plantation, and finally as a teenager running along a dusty meandering clay path. In this trance he continued to run along the familiar pathway, when out of the blue he saw himself walking untroubled through a forest. The deep green leaves on the trees varied in shape and size, and a large number of the trees were adorned with colorful flowers that wrapped around the trunk, giving the forest a mystical feel. The air had a subtle aroma of carefully blended exotic spices. The young boy gazed up through the dense vegetation towards the bright blue sky. The rays of sunlight combined with the mist, producing thousands of tiny colorful speckles that beamed with transient luminescence. It was a remarkable sight. He shifted his gaze from the sky towards the moist earth. The entire forest floor was adorned with exotic plants and the most beautiful flower combinations he had ever seen.

How weird is this?

What a bizarre transition!

Is this the spirit world that Papa always talked about?

The young boy didn't know why he was walking forward nor did he know his final destination. Nevertheless, he continued on his expedition towards the unknown, untroubled and unhurried and trying not to trample upon the flowers. Out of the faint banter between the leaves and the wind, the young boy suddenly heard a tune that caught his attention. He slowed his pace and gave the melody his attention. It was a familiar tune, but at that moment he couldn't remember where or when he had heard it. Shifting his gaze quickly from tree to tree, he scanned his environment for the source. Behold, after probing for few seconds, he spotted the artist a few feet from where he was standing. It was his favorite bird, the colorful *African-ringnecked* parakeet, singing on a short tree branch. He stopped in his tracks, fixed his gaze towards the tree branch, and smiled. Captivated by the sweet melodies and possessed by intense fascination, the young boy dashed through the thicket towards the bird, abandoning his prior caution for the flora below. After sprinting for a few seconds, he got to the base of the tree and greedily stretched out his hand to grab the creature. All of a sudden, a peculiar incident unfolded before his eyes; the pretty and surprisingly calm little bird transformed into a large *African-grey* parrot with bright yellow eyes. Scared and confused, the young boy retracted his hand and slowly walked backwards away from the tree. The bird simply stared at the young boy as he took each step. After his fifth step backwards, the passive bird squealed, flapped its large wings and flew with aggression from the tree branch towards the boy. The boy, instead of running away, froze with terror and stared at his airborne assailant. When the bird's claws were only a few inches from the boy's face, it shrieked out two words that sent chills down the boy's spine and instantly returned him to his original state of apprehension.

"Remember ÉDUJTNIAS!" The parrot wailed.

The young boy repeated those words several times, trying to find a connection. Suddenly, it hit him. He remembered *Édujtnias* and the series of events and circumstances beyond his control that led up to his painful incapacitation.

Who is this young boy? What is so intriguing about him?

For starters, his name is *Nadus* and he was a captive.

2

CHAPTER TWO:

🕉🕉

"A man who pays respect to the great paves the way for his own greatness."
African Proverb

The young boy's story began early one morning during the dry season, which is characterized by the absence of rain and the presence of hot dry winds. It was one of those mornings when failing leaves hung dearly for life on tree branches, commencing the slow metamorphosis that *Mother-nature* deemed a necessary means to an end. Many had turned and many more were still turning from the green hue that confers plants with life to a darkish yellow gloom. Piles of detached comrades accumulated at the base of the village trees. Hushed whimpers of fallen leaves calling up to their relatives high up could be heard as they were carried away by the northern gust. The infamous *agama* lizards that are known for terrorizing inattentive grasshoppers, as well as the hoppers were fast asleep. It was the time when the castoffs of daylight come out from hiding to play. Stray dogs, egocentric cats, blind bats, meandering serpents and all that enjoy darkness were alert, roaming the village like vagabonds.

The young boy was lying in bed, a large rectangular grass sleeping mat that once belonged to his late mother, *Etiovl'detoc*. Legs crossed and arms behind his head, he stared at the ceiling. This is an appropriate starting point for his story, because for him waking was a reference point that signified a fresh start with countless possibilities. This particular morning, he was experiencing another episode of insomnia. Lately, he had been awakened hours before dawn by strange dreams. It used to be that he never paid attention to his dreams and consequently forgot them. However, having been roused on several occasions by the same strange dreams, he decided to heed them in hopes of finding a connection. Nadus shared the hut with his entire family: *Nineb*, his middle aged father, and *Tpyge*, his older brother. The size of his family was small in comparison to their neighbors whose families had six children on average. This was because the young boy's mother, according to his father, died during childbirth, and the couple had lost three children before Tpyge's birth; the first child was a miscarriage and the other two succumbed to disease.

Nineb loved his wife dearly and he always kept her picture by his bedside. Small, square and wooden, it was the only framed picture the family possessed. It wasn't one of those fancy picture frames embellished with intricate designs of masquerades and animals. It was simple, but to Nineb it was perfect. It housed a colored picture of Etiovl'detoc smiling in a vibrant white, blue and black tie-dyed cotton *kaftan* attire with front slits, matching embroidery and a matching head-wrap that was elegantly tied to the side. She wore no makeup, except a touch of black eye shadow around her kind oval eyes. Her slender neck was ornamented with a white *cowrie* shell and black stone necklace that was beaded on a leather rope, accentuating her caramel skin. Matching earrings hung delicately from her ear lobes, harmonizing her majestic appearance. No one denied that Etiovl'detoc was a pretty woman. The picture was taken a few hours before one of their happiest moments together, the marriage between Nineb and Etiovl'detoc; her departure was particularly difficult for Nineb.

For several years, he struggled with the elements of sadness and on several occasions cried in silence, pondering on their misfortune and the reasons why his best friend was prematurely taken away from him, leaving him to care for two infants. However, as the boys grew older and Nineb saw several features of his wife in their faces and mannerisms, his struggle was easier. Nineb was fond of his sons and thankful to have them. He wanted to provide them with a happy, comfortable life. As a result, he farmed harder and fished longer than his peers who usually called it a day at sunset. He even tried befriending other women, hoping to find a new wife to provide his boys with a mother's touch, but it never worked out. Nineb couldn't for one day stop thinking about Etiovl'detoc. He was in love and too attached to her memories that he always found flaws in every other woman. After several failed attempts with three ostensibly suitable women, he concluded that his wife couldn't be replaced. He stopped searching and vowed not to remarry, bestowing the motherly care of his boys to his younger sister *Aybil*, who lived nearby.

The interior of their round mud hut was typical for their village, furnished by necessity rather than aesthetic. There were three sleeping mats arranged side by side in the center of the circular room, each with thick cotton sleeping covers. Nineb slept on the larger middle mat, whereas Tpyge slept on the left mat and Nadus on the right mat. An aged wooden drawer for storing their few clothes was to the right of the door, while a wooden cupboard for storing their cooking utensils and cutleries was to the left. A small round slab with two calabashes on the top and three simple wooden stools bordering it were to the right of the mats, between the cupboard and a large clay water pot. On the far side of the mats were several miscellaneous items neatly placed on the hard clay floor: three gourds, three brooms, two cutlasses, two kerosene lanterns, one hoe, several old hardcover books stacked in a pile, and a small fruit basket containing a few guavas, mangoes, and unripe plantains. A small square window, positioned six feet from the floor faced the door, bringing in sunshine by day and moonlight by night. The dimensions of the room were small. Nevertheless, for them it was cozy, neat, and comfortable; they were content.

For the past several months, the entire village had been suffering from a rather arid season; the young boy's father and the other farmers had been unhappy with the drought and were scared of a possible famine, but this morning was special—it was drizzling! Nadus switched his position and was lying on his stomach. He glanced through the open window into the dark, staring at the tiny droplets shimmer in front of the full moon as they fell to the desiccated soil. Nadus always found solace in the moon because the dark shadows on it resembled a mother carefully holding her baby.

"Ah, ah! Finally, Papa will be very pleased." Nadus whispered with excitement towards the light showers. "Yes, he will."

The young boy was hopeful that the showers would emancipate his people from some of the constraints that kept them in a constant state of paucity. The drizzle became stronger, and the repetitive staccato of the drops on the thatched roof seemed to syncopate with the boy's hairs rising in waves as the cool breeze blew across his skin. It was soothing and Nadus adjusted his sleeping cover to accommodate the cooler temperature; he continued to admire the lit moon and the surrounding dark rain clouds. He was relaxed and grateful for the downpour, but wary about the inevitable rise in mosquitoes, nuisances to bare skin. Tpyge always snored when he slept and on that day, he was sleeping on his back with one leg tucked under the other. One hand rested on his navel while his other arm was wrapped around his head; his older brother was an acrobatic sleeper who frequently tossed and turned. His father in contrast was not a snorer and he only repositioned himself after Tpyge shifted the dynamics by encroaching on his mat. Nineb was slender and muscular and he stood five feet, ten inches from the ground. His bearded face was hardened from work and the sun, but pleasant in appearance. His hands were strong, his palms calloused from long hours on the farm, and his feet cracked from arduous walks and struggles in life. Nadus knew he should get more sleep before the roosters began to crow but he just couldn't go back to the land of dreams. He wasn't feeling scared or anxious, at least he didn't believe he was; he tried squeezing his eyes together and ignoring his thoughts, but that didn't help either. He was wide awake. The young boy smiled and accepted his defeat to insomnia. He proceeded to encourage his imagination, musing over his prior fear of the dark and tricks of the mind; he recalled when he used to be terrified of monsters and the day he wet himself because he was too frightened to walk outside to urinate.

❀

CHAPTER TWO

On that day, Nadus was awakened in the middle of the night by the *Nimaidi*, a large and fierce monster that according to the villagers eats scared little boys. The young boy was terrified by the fiend standing by the door and he closed his eyes in hopes of avoiding detection. Unfortunately for him, he couldn't shut his bladder as firmly as he shut his eyes. He ended up wetting himself and having to lie quietly in the mess until his father woke up and discovered that he was also soaked.

"Nadus! Tpyge! Wake up!" Standing at the edge of his mat and close to the boys' feet, Nineb called out twice in an authoritative voice.

Right away the shirtless boys sprang up to their feet like startled cats, leaving their respective sleeping covers on the mats.

"Yes Papa. Good morning," they both said in accordance.

"Yes! Good morning to you too. Did you both sleep well?" their father asked.

"Yes we slept well, Papa." Tpyge nodded and looked at Nadus for confirmation.

"Yes Papa!" Nadus bobbed his head in agreement.

"I'm glad to hear that," their father said. "So tell me, which of you boys made the mess?"

"What mess are you talking about Papa?" Tpyge replied. "I don't know what you're talking about." Shrugging his shoulders, he gave his younger brother a puzzled look as he spoke, "Nadus, did you make a mess? Do you know what Papa is talking about?"

"I don't know," Nadus responded with a nervous expression.

Their father looked at both of them; his eyebrows arched. "Come on boys. I don't have to speak with my entire mouth. There are only two of you. Are you trying to tell me that neither of you knows who wet the mat?"

"Oh, wet the mat?" Tpyge felt his brown khaki shorts with both hands. Then he walked closer to his younger brother who was standing to his side and felt his black cotton shorts. He quickly retracted his hand and laughed. "Papa, I think we know who made the mess. It's Nadus! Feel him

Papa, he is soaking wet." Tpyge chuckled. "Don't you think you're a little too old to be wetting the bed?" he asked as he continued to laugh.

"Nadus?" his father interjected. "Did you wet the bed?"

Nadus was ashamed and he couldn't look his father in the eyes. He slowly responded with fear in his voice. "Yes Papa. I wet the bed."

"Tell me Nadus, why didn't you admit to making a mess when I first asked you?" his father asked in a stern voice. "I'm sure you knew what I was talking about. No?"

"Yes Papa. I guessed as much. I was afraid. I'm sorry. I didn't mean to wet the bed. I swear Papa!" Nadus replied in tears. "I didn't want to be punished."

"And what makes you think that denial would prevent you from being punished?" his father asked in a softer voice.

"I don't know why I did, Papa." Nadus replied.

"That's ok my son. Look, I'm your father and I know you very well. I already knew it was you, Nadus. Look, you're not very good at hiding your emotions. I mean, it was written all over your face. I wanted to see if you would own up to your mistakes and I'm glad you did," he added as he walked closer to Nadus.

He hugged his son and patted his head. "We all make mistakes in life." He cleared his throat. "You need to realize that there's nothing wrong in making mistakes. However, when you deny your mistakes and refuse to learn from them, you're doing yourself wrong! Do you understand me?"

"Yes Papa I do. Thank you. I'm sorry," Nadus responded in relief.

"And that goes to you as well," their father pointed to Tpyge who was clearly holding back his amusement.

"Yes Papa," he replied and then burst out laughing. "Nadus come on! How are you going to wet your bed? You're no longer a child. That's something Aunt Aybil's baby would do, not a grown boy like yourself. Papa, don't encourage him to wet the bed," Tpyge said. "I'm going to tell all the girls in your school that you're a bedwetter. Now I have something against you!" Tpyge laughed as he pointed at his brother's wet shorts.

"Ok Tpyge. That's enough. Stop making fun of your brother and I don't want you blackmailing him either. Do you understand me?" their father spoke with a hint of reproach. "Ok you boys go clean up and get ready. Tpyge, we have a long day ahead of us on the farm. Nadus you need to get ready for school."

Unfortunately for Nadus, Tpyge didn't let it go. On several occasions, he joked about the bedwetting episode and poked fun at Nadus in front of friends. A few months later, Nadus was once again awakened by the Nimaidi, but instead of taking his chances and enduring another episode of being the laughing stock, he decided to confront one of his fears. He stood up and like a lithe cheetah cautiously watching its prey, he tiptoed in the dark towards the intruder. His heart rate intensified, his pupils dilated, and his palms sweated; his body was ready for the unexpected. A few feet from the mysterious entity, lightning struck and the true identity of the fiend was revealed. It was his father's shirt and trousers hanging on the wall, swaying from the draft that seeped through the crevices in the door. Nadus was relieved by the revelation, but felt silly for letting his fears get the best of him. Thereafter, whenever he needed to make water in the middle of the night, he didn't hesitate to dash to the door.

❈

Nadus continued to lie in bed. He was still tired, but his mind wouldn't give in. He had once read in a book that counting a herd of jumping goats could help with sleep. Consequently, he imagined himself amongst a herd of goats that differed from the ones in his village. These ones were plump with large protruding bellies, and they were struggling to jump over a short wooden fence. The thought was humorous and it made the young boy chuckle. He disregarded the counting idea and decided to make better use of his wakefulness. He thought about the day ahead and some of his chores: feeding the chickens, milking the goats, washing clothes in the stream, cleaning the hut, attending school, class assignments, and caring for his friend *Dahc*, a brown *African-bush* dog. Although he had a long day ahead, Nadus was glad and even grateful that he didn't have to work long laborious hours like his brother. Though only four years older, upon graduating from primary school Tpyge decided to join their father on the farm, where they both worked from sunrise to sunset every day, except on Sunday when they worked till midday. Nadus couldn't understand why Tpyge would forgo attending secondary school in exchange for farm work.

"Nadus, I'm a man now and I drink palm-wine with real men." Tpyge would brag on occasions, referring to the other farmers and fishermen.

On the other hand, Tpyge had always struggled with school work and barely graduated. His gifts were different. He could tie a tight knot, make toys from scrap, climb almost any tree, navigate through the forest, and he was ambidextrous, favoring the left hand more. He was also strong and resilient for his age. Their father, though, never formally educated, valued the principles of learning. He used to joke that if he had been given a chance, he would have been an "animal doctor," as he would say, because of his fondness for the wild. Over time, he had learned to accept his circumstance and worked hard as a farmer and fisherman, skills he had learned from his father, *Acirfa*, who had learned them in turn from his father. Nineb was familiar with the struggles of the farm and the river, as well as the lifelong thoughts of regret towards a lost dream. He strived to break that perpetual cycle and wanted all his children to be educated and to have the life he never had. He was adamant about this decision, despite Tpyge's reluctance toward academics and overt exuberance towards farm work. Nevertheless, their father made sure that Tpyge at least completed his primary school education.

Nadus, on the contrary, was fonder of school and he did well in mathematics and the sciences. Nineb was so pleased of his son's academic talents that he would buy random hardcover books whenever he went to the market to sell his crops. He picked books based on the colorfulness of their covers and would ask Nadus to read them to him. For that reason, their book collection covered a wide variety of subject matters, including romance, mystery, economics, grooming-etiquettes and even advanced-astrophysics. Nadus enjoyed reading to his father and sometimes his brother on Sundays. At times when he didn't understand the content of a particular book, he would make up stories and act like he was reading. However, he underestimated his father's attention to detail. One day, he repeated a similar story to his father from a different book with a different cover. His father smiled and told him that he had heard the same story about the greedy boy and the diamonds from another book titled Imperialism and Neocolonialism. Nadus was embarrassed. Smiling as he turned the pages, he denied the accusation and told his father that he was reading directly from the book. He claimed that the story was popular and that different versions with alternate endings existed in several other books. Nineb was wary of Nadus's claim. Nevertheless, he admired his son's creativity and decided to be gullible at that moment. He smiled again, patted his son on the back, and listened ardently to the story.

Nineb tried not to impose any of his aspirations on his boys because he knew they both had unique paths towards their destinies. However, like any good father, he wanted to support and encourage them to maximize their potential. He knew that Tpyge was technical and good with his hands. As a result, he felt Tpyge would make a fine automobile mechanic like the young men he saw in the big city, wearing blue overalls and whistling as they repaired fancy cars. On several occasions, he tried convincing his son to desert the farm and pursue that possibility, but his pleas fell on deaf ears. Tpyge was unwilling to compromise, a trait he inherited from his grandfather. Nadus, on the other hand, was good at remembering words and was compassionate like his mother. Nineb felt Nadus would make a fine medical doctor, a profession he highly respected. He believed doctors were ordained to serve the needs of the poor and alleviate the suffering of the weak. This perspective developed in him as a young man after his ordeal with an excruciating stomach ache that kept him bedridden for months. Nineb had tried waiting it out—to allow his body to heal itself but the pain persisted. Then, he tried eating several fruits and drinking a variety of herbal concoctions. He still had no luck. Finally, one of Nineb's older brothers, *Anahg*, had overheard that some foreign doctors were in the neighboring village helping the sick. Scared of losing his brother, he decided to walk for several miles to the other village. When he got there, he was able to beg and convince one of them to drive down with him to his village.

When the doctor walked in the hut and made contact with Nineb, he immediately noticed her presence. She looked at him, knelt down by his mat, touched his forehead with her palm, and then smiled. She had bright white teeth and her hair was pulled back; her flawless skin radiated in the sunlight, perfectly complimenting her warm and welcoming aura. She was wearing a white coat and over her shoulder was a black rectangular bag with a faded but visible red cross on its side. She carefully unzipped the bag as if cautious about fragile items inside that might drop to the floor. She rummaged through the several medical supplies in the bag and pulled out a stethoscope, a small white notepad, and a flashlight. She took his pulse, and then listened to his heart sounds and his lung capacity. She gently touched both sides of Nineb's cheeks with her fingers and signaled to him to open his mouth. He slowly opened his mouth and she inspected his oral cavity with the flash light. She took some notes on the pad and smiled. Then, she put her things back into the bag and pulled out a small clear plastic bag from one of the side pockets on the bag. The plastic bag had a few muddled inscriptions on it and it contained several oval orange tablets.

"Make sure he takes two of these tablets in the morning and in the evening with water. After he eats! It is very important that he eats. Also make sure he takes every single tablet. That is also very important." The doctor spoke in a motherly but foreign accent. Anahg, who was standing by the edge of the mat, nodded and continued to stare at the doctor's actions with a blatant look of bewilderment.

Two days after Nineb started taking the medication, the pain stopped and he felt much better. Thereafter, he frequently prayed for the angel in the white coat who saved his life. He also prayed that his son Nadus would be ordained, so that he could help the sick and prevent the death of loved ones, like his wife who died because there was no medical doctor in the village when she went into labor. He was initially bitter about such unfairness, but he reasoned that it was destined to happen and he would see his beloved Etiovl'detoc again.

Outside, adjacent to the window of the mud hut, the old rooster sleeping on the slender branch of the aged guava tree was awakened by its internal clock. The partially blind fowl opened its eyes and wobbled its head as if shaking off the effects of sleep. It rose to an erect position, shook its feathers, raised it wings and its head, and then commenced its only morning duty, crowing! After hearing the rooster, Nadus pulled the sleeping covers away from his face and sighed.

Another day begins!

He continued to lie in bed, expecting to hear his father's deep voice. On this day, it was his brother who was the first of the two to wake. Upon arousing, Tpyge moaned and coughed. He stood up from his mat, raised his hands above his head and stretched till a couple of his joints popped. He yawned, rubbed his eyes with his hand and scratched his bare stomach; the moon was hidden behind the dark clouds and Tpyge had to interrupt his routine to orient himself to the dark. With both arms stretched out, he maneuvered towards the other side of the room, trying not to lose his footing along the way. A couple of steps later, his finger tips came in contact with a moist and rugged surface. He took another step forward before squatting and exploring the floor with both hands.

"Where did these stupid matches run to now?" Tpyge whispered with a hint of impatience as he ransacked through the miscellaneous items resting on the floor: the lanterns, the farming tools, the fruit basket, and the books. "If I remember correctly, the matches were sitting right here yesterday," he referred to the top of the book stack. His full bladder was beginning to sting and that made him petulant. He hurriedly searched the floor again, but he still couldn't find the matches.

Tpyge resigned to failure and decided to forgo his search. However, as he turned around to walk blindly towards the door, his bare feet came in contact with a small object that produced a familiar sound, the rattling of match sticks in a box. During his search, Tpyge was so preoccupied by his prior convictions, as is typical of human nature, that he failed to find the matches directly in front of him at first. Nevertheless, he was pleased by his find and he bent down to pick it. He held the box firmly in his hand and carefully opened it. Pulling out a match with his left hand, he struck it twice against the side of the box. Instantly, a small flare brightened his vicinity and filled the air with a mild odor of burnt sulfur. He knelt to move the flame towards the floor and picked up one of the hurricane lanterns. Placing the lantern and then the match box on the topmost book in the stack, he opened the transparent glass globe with the metal lever and lit the wick before blowing out the matchstick. The room was dim. Tpyge looked at his family before walking outside to ease himself. A few minutes later, he walked back into the room with the lantern and a small calabash of water. He then proceeded towards his father, who was still dreaming about his true love, and placed the calabash on the floor by his father.

He tapped the sleeping man twice on the shoulder. "Papa, Papa! It's me, Tpyge." His father mumbled and switched his sleeping position to get more comfortable. "Papa, wake up! We need to get ready for the day. Wake up." Tpyge tapped his father as he called out; he knew his father had to wake up soon, and he had a strong inclination to yell and strike him harder. However, because their culture considered it highly disrespectful for a child to yell at elders, he controlled himself a little.

"Papa! Wake up!" he uttered, striking his father harder.

The louder tone worked. His father opened his eyes and through his bleary view he saw his eldest son smiling. Without delay, like a resting warrior geared for battle, he sprang up to a sitting position.

"Thank you my son," Nineb said groggily, his voice still asleep. "I was so tired and I was dreaming about..." He stopped short in his sentence and covered his mouth, trying to conceal a yawn. He put his hands behind his back and stretched. Smiling, Nineb wiped his watery eyes with both hands and placed them on his son's shoulders. "Thank you again son. I'm awake now!" He took the calabash from his son and stood to his feet.

Nineb walked towards the corner of the hut towards a small stash of old plastic bags bearing logos of foreign supermarkets. Placing the calabash on the floor, he rummaged through one of the bags and pulled out three chewing sticks. Nineb placed one in his mouth and began to chew on it, cleaning his teeth in the process.

He turned around. "Take," he said. "Take one. Go wake your brother and give this to him," he handed the sticks to Tpyge. "You both need to get ready for the day."

Tpyge nodded and responded. "Yes, Papa."

He walked over to his brother and as he was about to shake him, Nadus uttered "I'm awake!"

3

CHAPTER THREE:

☒

"Rain beats a leopard's skin, but it does not wash out the spots."
African Proverb

Nadus walked outside with a chewing stick in his mouth, an empty calabash in one hand, and a lantern in the other. His nakedness was covered by a green flowery cloth that wrapped around his waist and flowed down to his ankle. His chest was bare and his feet were protected from the elements by worn-out leather slippers whose soles clapped with each step as if applauding the very act of walking. It was partially dark, but at the visible horizon the morning sun was slowly showing its dominance over the moon. The air smelled like fresh rain and the parched soil was still preoccupied with satisfying its thirst. The young boy walked with caution through the muck towards the barn, a small rectangular mud hut that was positioned a yard away and perpendicular to their residence. The barn housed two goats, four chickens, one hare, and his canine friend Dahc, the designated night sentinel who was rescued as a puppy in the nearby forest. After safely arriving at the front of the edifice without slipping, Nadus wiped the mud buildup from under his slippers on the gravel that beautified the doorway. He tried to enter the barn quietly without making noise, but the rusty door made from old sheets of galvanized iron nailed on planks didn't cooperate. The clanking startled the caged birds. As a result, they began to fidget, crowing and walking with haste in their elevated cubic rattan cages. Dahc in response barked and dashed towards the entrance. His greenish-yellow eyes glistened in the dark; his pricked up ears, tensed muscles, and exposed razor-sharp teeth were all synchronized to ward off intruders and trespassers.

"Dahc! Ah, come on boy. It's me," Nadus raised the lantern higher to reveal his face.

Recognizing his master's voice, the dog relaxed and dropped his ears before bowing in submission; he wagged his tail with excitement and walked up towards Nadus.

"That's a good boy. Did you sleep well?" Nadus placed the lantern on the floor that was sparsely covered with dried elephant grass. He gave his dog a quick stroke on his back and face. "Yes, that's a good boy, I bet you slept well."

The hungry and upset fowls continued their morning rants, revealing the brilliant acoustic properties of the mud walls and the thatched roof. Nadus ignored them. Instead, he picked up the lantern and proceeded towards the two tethered *African Pygmy* goats. Dahc tagged behind. The bigger male goat was alert, standing on all hooves. The female goat, on the other hand, was lying on her side, chewing on grass and enjoying the symphony. The young boy placed the calabash on a small wall shelf; he then hung the lantern on a long nail embedded in the wall directly above the goats, partially illuminating the area. This freed up his hands, allowing him to tend to the animals. Nadus hissed and snapped his fingers towards his companion. Excited by this simple gesture, Dahc wagged his tail and lifted his front legs from the floor, placing them on Nadus's thigh.

"Come on now. Easy boy! Are you trying to take off my wrapper?" He laughed at Dahc as he readjusted the wrapper around his waist. He patted his dog on the head and proceeded towards the corner of the room, where two hemp bags rested against the wall. The larger of the two contained dried yam flakes for the mammals; the other bag contained a mixture of dried corn, beans and millet grains for the birds. Nadus untied the rope on the larger, less compact bag and proceeded with a generous scoop.

CHAPTER THREE

The young boy walked back to the goats with a salvaged milk container full of yam flakes, trying not to spill the feed. He slowly began to pour the flakes into the feeding trough. "Here you go," he said in a drawn-out manner, belying his fatigue caused by waking up early before school to tend to his farm duties. The two ruminants rushed towards the large circular plastic bowl and began to feast, butting horns as they contended for the best share. In the rectangular cage opposite to the goats one of the rarest and most endangered animals in the world, the *Bushman* hare, was preparing for sleep. Neither Nineb nor Tpyge nor Nadus knew the rarity of the shy nocturnal creature they had in their possession. Nevertheless, they all knew that there was something special about it. Unlike the other hares in and around their village, this one had a black stripe running from the corner of its mouth to its cheek, brown body fur, cream-colored fur on its throat and belly, a pale brown woolly tail with a hint of black towards the tip, and large clubbed hind paws. According to Nineb, the discovery of this intriguing creature was "unintentional but divine."

A while back, Nineb and his favorite brother Anahg went on a hunting trip in the nearby plains. Both men, although incredibly close, hadn't seen each other in years. Anahg had moved to the big city in hope of improving his circumstances, leaving behind his wife and five children, a tough decision for a young father. This expedition, unlike many others, was fueled by brotherhood bonding rather than by survival; the men wanted to share their triumphs and successes. On that day the men were dressed alike. The brothers were shirtless, wearing mud-soiled khaki shorts with visible stitch marks that complemented the brown worn-out leather sandals on their feet. A wooden bow carved out from the resilient *Baobab* tree slung across each of their backs, while a water gourd hung across each chest. Around their waists they each carried a sharp machete and a narrow leather quiver containing a few arrows.

"My brother! I'm so happy to see you after all this time," Nineb said. "It has surely been a while. So, tell me, how have you been?" Nineb asked as they walked across the shallow ditch in the north that separated their village from the wilderness.

"Not too bad brother. I can't complain about the complainable. Over the few years, I have come to learn that there's no point in doing such a thing," Anahg adjusted the machete on his waist.

"Ah! Yes, you may have a point there," Nineb interjected, gently stroking his beard. "You can't complain about the complainable? Interesting! But you know that there are times in life when we just need to let it out. I mean, simply complain. Don't you think?"

"Are you asking me what I think about complaining?" Anahg asked.

"Sure. What do you think?"

"I think complaining is a sign of weakness, especially when it comes from a man." Anahg responded.

"I must disagree with you. I personally believe people, both men and women, complain because they want others to share their pain. Think about it! Our people celebrate the great harvest at the end of the farming season because we want others to rejoice our bountifulness. Correct?"

"Yes, for the most part."

"Eh! For the most part," Nineb chortled. "Okay, for the most part also, many of us at times of failure and disappointments, instead of celebrating with our friends and family, we complain and act unkindly towards them. I don't think it's because we're bad people, but it's because we want to get a different perspective on our situation and on life.

"A different perspective on life? What do you mean by that?" Anahg smiled. "Are you saying that we complain to get a different perspective?"

"Absolutely! Tell me honestly my brother why don't you invite people over to eat when your crops fail?"

"Well, when crops fail there's no food to cook, right?" Anahg chuckled.

"Nice one!" Nineb also laughed. "Okay tell me, at times when you do have food, but happen to be upset, why don't you invite people over?"

"Let's see," Anahg stroked his bearded face. "Because I'm too upset to share and I don't want to be bothered?"

"You're too funny, but that's exactly my point. When we're upset or disappointed, we act differently and usually keep to ourselves. However, when given a chance we complain to inform others that we're not happy. In a way, you can say that we complain to get attention from people. Does that make sense to you?"

"It makes sense, I suppose. We complain to inform people that there is something wrong and hope they hear us out," Anahg replied.

"Yes, that's my point. Well, this doesn't mean that it's acceptable for anyone to complain all the time. I just feel that occasionally complaining is normal and it doesn't always show a sign of weakness in a person."

"Good thought. I see that you haven't changed one bit. You're still Nineb, the child who always tries to question everything."

"I suppose some things just don't change."

"True son of the land!" Anahg praised Nineb and tapped him on the back. "Remember when everyone used to call you that name years ago because of your intense love for nature?"

"Anahg, we haven't seen each other in a while, but surely it hasn't been that long. How can I ever forget that name? I remember when you first started calling me that and you knew I didn't like it. I begged you to stop, but that didn't happen. In fact it only got worse. Not only did you keep calling me that, but everyone else started calling me that as well. So I just accepted the name and decided to take it as a complement. Now, I even tease my sons with the name every now and then."

"Good move on your part," his brother laughed. "You know we were crazy kids. It was fun though? No?"

"Definitely," Nineb replied.

"But I must say that you surely did have a thing for nature. You were one special boy and there were times when I wished I had your curiosity for the world."

"But wait now, you get to experience a different part of the world. The big city!"

"If you say so," Anahg responded apathetically. "Anyway, how are you keeping up, especially with your boys?"

"It's not easy, but I'm doing my best. I mean, it's not the same without their mother."

"I bet! I battle with a similar feeling as well. I feel like they're growing up without a father. I sometimes even feel like I don't know my children. Nini, they're growing up without my presence."

"Nini? I haven't had anyone call me that in a long while. You are surely stirring up old memories."

Anahg paused before turning to his brother and offering a smile. "Talk about memories! Remember that one time when *Mama* was very angry with us because we took out the largest piece of meat from the stew and took tiny bites from it?"

"You mean stole the piece of meat and took large bites from it," Nineb chuckled as he picked a few pebbles from the ground. "Yes, Mama was furious that day. We were lucky that Papa was away fishing or else we would have been seriously punished."

"I really do miss those old times. You know that many of the memories we shared when we were young, both good and bad, have helped me get through many tough times. They remind me that I'm human and I have lived a good life with people who care about my wellbeing." Anahg confessed as they trekked across the green plains towards the woods.

"Yes, I do miss many of our memories, Anahg."

"I can say that our memories make life worth living," Anahg replied.

"True say! What fun times we had when we were young. It's so crazy how fast life comes at you. Once, we were carefree and we had no worries as long as we completed our chores. Then all of a sudden we have our family to care for." Nineb threw some pebbles towards the sky.

"Very true." Anahg shook his head as if suddenly realizing truth in the statement.

"However, to be honest," Nineb sighed, "I can't imagine living without my boys. During those days when I don't get to see them because I'm at the farm all day, I feel bad. Just like you said, it seems like they're growing up without me."

"At least you get to see them often. I don't get to enjoy that luxury. It's been a couple years for me."

"I understand your heart." Nineb consoled his brother.

"I mean, they've all grown. Have you seen my oldest son, *Uassib*? He is practically a man now. His voice is so deep and he is almost my height. I mean, he grew like elephant grass."

"Yes, your son has some height on him."

"I'm very proud of him." Anahg nodded. "He surely has my personality and good looks. Don't you think?"

"Personality maybe, but I don't know about your good looks," Nineb laughed. "Jokes apart, I must agree, Uassib is now a fine young man. You might want to start looking for a wife for him."

"True indeed! My son's about ripe for a wife, but right now I can hardly send enough money to his mother, not to mention paying his dowry. I suppose he can start saving up on his own. Remember when I first saw *Suitiruam* and I started saving money because I wanted to marry her?"

"Very true, very true my brother." Nineb concurred. "You acted like a scared chicken around her."

"Aaah! Look who's talking!" Anahg hissed. "I remember the first time you saw Etiovl'detoc at the market square and you begged me for money, so that you could buy all the fruits in her basket. Don't even get me started." He quipped with a smile.

"You surely got me on that. I still miss her dearly and sometimes wish she were here. So tell me brother, what's new with you? You have to tell me more about the big city. How's city life? I bet it must be amazing!"

"So many questions, but very few answers. The city is all right."

"All right? What do you mean by that?"

"To be honest, there isn't really anything special about the city. It can actually be very tough and lonely out there. Trust me! See, at least in our village we have each other. In the city, it's every man for himself and that can be very depressing!"

"Depressing? Isn't that an overstatement? But life here in our village is tough. We don't have electricity or easy access to clean water. I mean we have to walk for miles to get water, food is not always abundant, and obtaining medical treatment is an ordeal that can take days. I hear you city people have all those things readily available."

"Trust me having problems is human. Human beings, regardless, of their conditions or environment will always have problems of the mind. Nineb, I can honestly say that I've seen some the happiest people in the world right here in our village, not in the big city."

"I don't understand you," Nineb said with a puzzled look. "I always thought that life in our village would be happier and more productive if we had all those amenities of the city."

"More productive? Well, maybe. Probably! But definitely not happier. Happiness, my brother, depends on how we feel about ourselves, not what we have in our possession. I was once naïve and I honestly thought that when I got to the big city all my problems would be solved. Oh, I was wrong!"

"What do you mean by that?" His brother asked innocently.

"I have seen things, Nineb, and I have experienced pain and rejection in the city," Anahg stared at his hands and gently rubbed them as if trying to remove a stain. He raised his head and looked at his brother. "With new possessions come new problems of the mind. In the big city, people are told that the more you get the better your life becomes. As a result everyone is trying to get more, even at the expense of the less-fortunate, and at times when you just can't get more you are made to feel like one of the destitute. I have even seen people become so enslaved by their possessions that they killed themselves in times of loss."

"What! Killed themselves over their possessions?" Nineb asked with a look of bewilderment.

"Yes! As crazy as it sounds, some people in the city have killed themselves over their possessions."

"Unbelievable! How can people become so ungrateful?"

"No, no, Nineb. Let's not judge their actions. It takes a strong mind to resist and overcome the many pressures of the city, and some people are just too fragile. They need others," he said with a pleasant smile. "My brother, don't make the same mistake and think that riches or new amenities would bring you happiness because you would be disappointed. See, the concept of happiness is like a delicious meal and our possessions are like different food ingredients." Anahg paused and cleared his throat.

Nineb laughed and interjected. "Anahg, are you hungry or something? I honestly don't see the connection."

"Ah! Okay. I guessed as much." Anahg replied. "Let me clarify myself. Take your favorite *fufu*, which is made solely from two food ingredients, cassava flour and hot water." He showed Nineb his first two right fingers. "Now if you decided to add another ingredient to fufu, say, salted palm-oil, you might enhance the appearance and the taste, right?"

His brother nodded reluctantly in agreement.

"Now if you went further and decided to add more ingredients, say, sugar and groundnuts, to fufu, it will probably change the taste, right?"

"Ugh! That sounds disgusting," Nineb frowned. "Why would anyone ever want to add anything to fufu? It's perfect just the way it is!"

"Exactly my point! I think you get my point about happiness. Having more or adding more doesn't always make things better, it can actually make it worse." Anahg beamed with satisfaction as he spoke.

Nineb comprehended his brother's point of view and thanked him for the insight. Sweating profusely, the two young men decided to stop for a bit under a large tree to rest their aching feet and hide from the blazing sun. Standing side by side with their backs against the uneven tree trunk, they wiped their clammy faces with the back of their hands and then quenched their thirst with several gulps from their gourds. Nineb sighed before taking in a deep breath of fresh air; he closed his eyes to reflect and better savor the moment. As the young farmer began to ponder on their prior conversation, Anahg abruptly interrupted him.

"Hey, Nineb," his brother tapped him repeatedly on the shoulders and spoke in a hushed voice, "quick! Look over there."

"Yes, what's going on?" Nineb slowly opened his eyes.

"Quiet," Anahg placed his fingers over his brother's lips. "Look over there by the bushes."

Feeding off the excitement in Anahg's eyes and following the direction of his stretched out arm, Nineb looked towards the dried-out shrub by the oak tree.

"I don't see a thing," Nineb whispered as they both crouched.

"Look closely. Don't you see it? It's moving."

Using his hand as an eyeshade, Nineb strained his eyes.

"I don't see anything."

"Are you sure about that?"

"No, I don't see anything," Nineb replied with disappointment in his voice. "Oh, wait!" he added. "Oh, yes I see it now. It's moving. What do you think we should do?"

"I think we go for it. First we should both go in opposite directions. I'll stand by that tree over there and you by that one. Then, on my signal we will both run toward the bush so that we can corner it before it can run away. Okay?" Anahg pointed and then sketched out his strategy on the dirt with a dried stick.

His younger brother took a mouthful of air and responded. "Okay, but what if it sees us and runs towards the forest, what do we do?"

"I'll shoot it and if I miss, you should be ready to fire as well, and if all fails, we'll have to chase it into the forest. Agreed?"

"Yes, agreed." Nineb patted his palms on the dusty ground.

"Great, let's do this." Anahg grimaced and spat on their secret plot.

The men removed their bows with grace, quickly placed the vane of their arrows on the taut rope, and positioned the shaft on the bow between their fingers. They began to creep through the grass, moving away from each other. A few feet apart, Nineb had a thought.

"Anahg! Anahg, wait!" he looked back and whispered.

Anahg turned towards his brother with a look of confusion. "What's the problem?"

"You didn't say what your signal was going to be." Nineb replied.

"Yes, great question. Sorry, I forget to tell you. When you get there, signal with your hands. I'll whistle and then we attack," he winked.

Avoiding detection, the stealthy men reached their respective posts. Hidden under the shade behind the tree and its surrounding vegetation, Anahg was in close proximity to their prey. He continued to crouch with one knee planted into the soil and the other facing the hare; his heart was beating faster, pumping nutrient-rich blood to his brain and extremities. He felt alive once again. Unaware of the apparent conspiracy, the animal continued to feast on the tuberous root as Nineb positioned himself behind a large rock and prepared for the ambush. The young farmer slowly raised his hand and signaled to his brother. Anahg knew it was time. Gripping the bow and the arrow with one hand, he placed two fingers on his lips. As he was about to whistle, he suddenly realized why he was so miserable working as a porter at the hotel; the job was a poor fit and he felt no sense of identity or purpose. He wasn't meant to be stationary, opening doors and smiling at strangers and pretending to be excited; he was supposed to be *alfresco*, in the wilderness, battling the unpredictable. Anahg's mind drifted back and he whistled, triggering Nineb and the hare into motion. Arrows drawn, the men dashed towards the frightened animal, hollering and chanting as they advanced. The hare, dazed by the element of surprise, paused and stared at the advancing assailants as if trying to assess the best escape strategy. Then, as Nineb had predicted, it proceeded towards the dense forest, hopping quickly in a zigzag manner across the plains.

"Quick Nineb, get ready." His brother exclaimed as he released the stretched out string. "Get it!"

The taut twine returned to its original position, transmitting most of its energy into the arrow and dissipating the rest in the resonance and harmonic motion of the vibrating string. Spinning rapidly, the arrow flew through the air with a parabolic trajectory and landed an inch from the hare's hind foot. Although skillful, Anahg was rusty as archery requires constant practice for proficiency and he couldn't apply himself in the city.

"Nineb, now!" Anahg yelled out as he tried to catch his breath.

Still running with all his might, Nineb studied the animal, analyzing its zigzagging trail across the meadow. He reasoned that if fired the arrow towards the left as soon as the hare leaped to the right, he had a good chance. He followed his insight and released the arrow.

"Yes!" His brother blurted out. "You got it. Nice!"

The arrow landed on the hare, penetrating its left thigh. The animal shrilled and continued to leap towards the dense forest in a slower pace. Seizing the opportunity, Anahg knelt down and released "the killer shot" into the air. As though understanding its assailant's thought process, the hare halted abruptly and changed its direction before increasing its pace and nose-diving into a thicket; the arrow didn't accomplish its mission.

"No!" Anahg yelled. "Quick, don't let it go."

"Okay, I'm on it," Nineb withdrew his machete and pursued the long-eared mammal.

The men dashed into the murky forest, running up the lush, hilly terrain and clearing the way with their blades. Nineb was in the lead.

"I think it went this way," Nineb stopped and pointed to a faint trail on the grass.

Anahg walked closer to his brother and squatted; he touched the wet maroon stain and felt the texture with his fingers. He then smelled it and tasted it.

"It's blood. Fresh blood." He spat repeatedly to the side. "Yes, it went this way. It's close by and probably over there." Anahg grunted as he rose to his feet and pointed towards one of the few enduring terrestrial giants, the *Afrormosia* tree.

The weather was hot and windless and the forest was losing vital light as the sun prepared to entrust the day to the moon. Above the ground, occasional sounds and echoes of flapping wings, singing birds and loud primates tree-hopping formed an ensemble whose inharmonious tunes resonated amongst the ancient trees. The famished men walked through the forest, studying the integrity of the plants as they searched for their fare. Three yards from the large greenish-brown mildewed trunk, they noticed a sudden movement in the surrounding bush.

"Right there," Nineb grabbed his brother on the shoulders. "Did you hear that?"

"Yes, I saw it move." Anahg continued to gaze at the lower left corner of the tree.

The bush shook again.

"Okay brother. I'll head there and chase it out," Nineb whispered as he began to walk forward with his machete leading the way. "Have your arrow ready, just in case it tries to escape." He looked back at his brother.

Anahg affirmed with a thumbs-up and withdrew his bow. Nineb nodded and continued to walk furtively through the undergrowth towards the dancing plant. A minute later, he arrived at the base of the tree and wavered for a bit to study the unusual movements. As soon as he raised his weapon to strike, a pair of eyes emerged from the scrub that aroused that primal, instinctual feeling experienced by all in anticipation of danger—fright! On impulse, the young farmer swung his machete towards the encroaching beast, scattering several bits of shredded leaves into the air; he then turned around swiftly and ran for cover.

"Leopard! Leopard, Anahg! Quick, fire!" Nineb shouted with terror in his voice, stumbling as he sprinted.

His brother didn't waste any time and released two arrows almost simultaneously towards the black-spotted cat. The first arrow glided through the air, swooshing past Nineb and barely grazing the attacker's tawny coat. The second arrow, on the contrary, hit the mark. However, because it was fired right after the first shot and before the twine could fully recoil, its momentum was greatly reduced. As a consequence, the second shot wasn't powerful enough to slay the beast. The arrow landed momentarily on the leopard's muscular chest, startling it and causing it to growl. The injured cat slowed, but having set its eye on Nineb the leopard wasn't deterred in its pursuit; the hunter was now the hunted, an inevitable cycle that endows a state of balance in the world.

"Quick Nineb! Run the other way towards the water!" Anahg shouted, referring to the west as he ran towards the eastern part of the forest.

Moving as fast as his legs could carry him, Nineb dashed through the forest, hurdling over several fallen tree branches that barricaded his path towards refuge. On a typical day, he would have interacted with the diverse populace of the jungle, studying their ethological and botanical properties. However, he was too preoccupied with the motions and his unreal thoughts that he was apathetic to the surrounding splendor. Nineb continued to run through the forest, desperately trying to dodge many of the slender branches that whipped his face along the way. The leopard, also tired of being flogged, jumped up on a nearby, sturdy branch and continued the hunt. The wild cat was in its favorite predatory element, hidden in the trees and bestowed with aerial advantage. Noticing the sudden shift in the cat's movements, Nineb realized that his assailer was above and could pounce down at any moment. Nevertheless, he was still hopeful and didn't give up. In no time, he heard the soothing sounds of flowing water and saw the rock face ahead—his goal was in view. This realization boosted his morale and he responded by increasing his pace and stride. His actions paid off; he arrived at the edge of the cliff and took a leap into the running waters just as the leopard jumped off the tree.

"Yes! I did it!" he cried out as he took the plunge.

His voice was bursting with emotions and its resonating high decibels scared many nearby birds out of their nests. Nineb landed with both legs and as expected he was pulled to the bottom of the shallow stream by his weight. The sole of his sandals made full contact with the muddy floor, swirling up loose dirt and clouding up the surrounding water. The impact of the fall temporarily threw him into a state of confusion, but the loud sounds of rapidly popping air bubbles and the cold, fast-flowing water revived him. Desperate for oxygen, he opened his eyes to the turbid aquatic situation and stretched out his legs like a leaping toad as he swam up to the top. As soon as he surfaced from the water, Nineb exclaimed and then took a deep breath, filling up his lungs with fresh, moistened air. He surveyed his environment and noticed that he was facing the lower-western region of the forest, drifting with the downstream current.

"The leopard!" Nineb spat as he fought to catch his breath. "Where?" His spirit was disturbed by the thoughts of his prior predicament with the wild beast; he turned around and fixed his eyes on leopard up on the cliff. Upon realizing that the man had survived the fall and was staring back with fearful eyes, the crouching beast jumped into the water to continue the chase. The animal's actions astonished and startled the young farmer, forcing him to revaluate his prior misconception about leopards; the leopard, although preferring to keep its coat dry, didn't fear running water and was a powerful swimmer.

"No! No! You're not supposed to..." Nineb blurted out as he took in unwanted gulps of water.

All of a sudden, the simple act of swimming became difficult for him. He struggled and stroked harder through the waves, but his increased tempo didn't translate into increased progress; he had lost his cool and coordination. The gritty leopard, although slowed by the currents, was closing the gap, and that thought made Nineb fretful. He allowed doubt to set in.

What if I don't make it?

What if this is the end?

Oh, my promise to Etiovl'detoc.

I have failed you, my love.

I have failed my boys.

Short of breath, he arrived at the shallow end of the stream. His hands and knees pressing on fine gravel, he crawled out of the water and took to his feet, running into the dense vegetation with no apparent strategy. His clothes were drenched and the added weight in his khaki shorts and the slipperiness of his mud-covered sandals reduced his swiftness. Nineb paused and thought about climbing one of the trees, but he recalled that leopards are excellent climbers, capable of capturing even the "masters of the tree"—monkeys! The cascade of trampled plants and approaching footfalls of the growling beast became more evident; the attacker was closing in. Nineb fought his anxiety and dashed further into the forest, hoping for a divine intervention. Arriving at a grass-covered hilly terrain that impeded his apparent escape, he was crushed and felt like all his hard work was in vain. He looked around for a split second and concluded that he was cornered in a dead end—there was no way forward! He turned around and saw the leopard a few yards away, slowly approaching and licking its lips as though trying to relish the moment.

Fixing his eyes on the large cat, Nineb felt his waist and his quiver, and realized that he had lost his machete and all his arrows. He was without a weapon in a time of distress. Like many, he relied on his physical abilities and his possessions to overcome adversity, but in that instant he felt completely stripped-down. He realized that he had been living a some-what prideful illusion that he could always control the outcome of his circumstances with his actions. Humbled by the realization, he continued to stare at the hungry leopard, thinking about his legacy: honesty, integri-ty, and steadfastness. However, at that very moment he wasn't following all of his doctrines; he was about to give up his gift of existence without a fight. The idea of letting down his family, especially his boys, actuated him. Wasting no time, Nineb withdrew his bow from his back and broke it into two with his knee. Holding the splintered halves in his right hand, he squatted and picked up a moistened rock from the ground; he had improvised and he didn't feel so helpless. Adrenaline coursing through his arteries like the waters up east, his senses were stimulated and heigh-tened. The thoughts of the unforeseen stirred Nineb's heart and widened his nostrils; he was ready for the inevitable encounter. Noticing the sud-den change in the man's demeanor, the leopard paused in its tracks. It growled and moved its head obliquely from side to side as though cau-tious of the change. The cat growled again, but Nineb didn't falter.

"Come on! I'm Nineb, the son of Acirfa!" he shouted, pointing and wav-ing the splintered wood towards the beast. "I'm ready for you!"

The leopard driven by necessity and the man ignited by survival were about to clash when an unexpected sound halted their actions like a refe-ree's call. It was the familiar screech of a frightened hare. The injured hare with the cream-colored fur on its throat hopped out from behind a nearby tree and screeched again. The hare's erratic behavior distracted the man and the beast, diverting their attention and causing them to look away in unison. The leopard, bewildered by the noise, turned towards the hare with ravenous intentions. Seizing the golden opportunity, Nineb grabbed onto a protruding region on the rugged vertical terrain and be-gan to climb up the moist, grass-covered hill; realizing that its initial prey was harder to reach, the opportunistic predator chased after the bleeding hare with the arrow lodged in its thigh. Nineb climbed up in haste, gauging his footing to avoid a mistake that could send him to rock bottom. Approaching the apex of the twenty-foot elevation, he turned his head to catch a glance at the two wild animals. The leopard was chasing the hobbling hare towards the northern part of the forest across a patch of green undergrowth and it was closing in rapidly. Nineb got to the top, and instead of continuing his getaway he stood by the edge to get a better view of the scenario unfolding before his eyes. He was so intrigued and he focused most of his attention on the hare. The young farmer couldn't comprehend why the hare had sacrificed itself for him, considering the fact that he injured it. Nevertheless, he was grateful, but sympathetic as he saw the leopard open its mouth to lock its sharp teeth on the hare.

"Oh, how sad!" Nineb swallowed his saliva and closed his eyes as he dropped his head in reverence.

The young man heard harsh rustlings of broken stems followed by a sudden thump and then a short-lived scream.

"What in the…" he opened his eyes.

There was a large hole in the verdant ground and the hare was close to the boundary, entangled in a mass of twining plants. Nineb watched from the distance as the small animal shrieked and struggled for several futile minutes. It was stuck, ensnared in the flexible thorny stems of the "tree-climber" and it appeared that the cat had fallen and was trapped in the pit. The sun was sinking below the horizon and dusk was quickly encroaching. Thoughts of his previous encounter flashed through his head as the young farmer stood to a more erect position; he geared himself up to find his brother and avoid another escapade. However, he just couldn't ignore the pleas of the injured hare.

Run towards the stream and be home in no time.

Before the other night animals come out!

No! No!

That's not right.

I can't just leave it there to bleed to death!

Or be eaten by an owl or wild dogs.

The farmer sighed and rubbed his eyes with the back of his hand. "But it saved my life!" Nineb whispered.

So what?

It didn't save my life.

Climbing the hill saved my life!

"If it wasn't for the hare, I wouldn't have been able to climb the hill."

What if the leopard isn't trapped and it attacks me again?

I can't afford to risk this chance.

Nineb battled with his conscience. Embracing his empathetic side and allowing it to reign over his judgment, he climbed down and picked up the halved bow. He then walked with caution towards the opening in the ground, wary about his decision and the lurking beast. The closer he got to the hare the stronger it struggled. However, realizing that its actions were inflicting more pain with little success, the hare stopped struggling and watched helplessly. Nineb got close to the edge of the pit. Positioning himself for the unexpected, he peeked inside in the hole. At first glance, he didn't see anything, only dirt, twigs, and fresh leaves and grass. The suspense scared him. Fearing a potential ambush, he looked into the pit again and was appeased. He saw the leopard lying on its side; its head turned upwards as if looking towards the sky and its legs spread apart as though still in motion. Its eyes were partially closed and its flaccid tongue was lolling out of its mouth. Blanketed with heaps of dirt and leaves, a sharp stick protruded from its chest, obstructing the flow of its last few breaths; it was the piteous sight of a fallen warrior. Nineb dropped his weapon on the ground and removed the small gourd from across his chest. He opened it, took a gulp of water, gargled and spat to his side, away from the hare. He then crouched and looked at the slain beast.

"Great leopard, I thank you because you have taught me well," he said. "Once again, I have come to realize that I'm a man with many weaknesses. May your fierce spirit return peacefully and safely to the land of our ancestors!" He sprinkled the cat three times to show his last respect.

CHAPTER THREE

The leopard growled softly and exhaled its final breath of life. Nineb then approached the hare and the injured creature wiggled harder in response, driving more thorns into its blood-stained fur.

"Stop, stop! It's okay!" he said. "You're just hurting yourself that way." He hunkered down and raised his hands to disentangle the hare.

In an attempt to move its head away, the hare continued to struggle.

"No! Stop! Stop, I'm sorry for hurting you. I promise! I'm not going to hurt you again. You have my word on that," he said in a softer tone as he pulled off some of the spines. "If you continue to shake this way, you're only going to hurt yourself and make things harder."

The animal, as though understanding the human language, stopped shaking and became passive. With care, Nineb removed the thorns from around the hare's face and neck, releasing its head and allowing the animal to breathe freely.

"That's good," he said. "Don't you feel a lot better now?" Nineb asked as he inspected the hare's fur for additional cuts.

Nineb saw a few contusions caused by the friction between the thorny stems and its fur. Nonetheless, he decided not to untie the hare until he had removed the arrow from the terrified animal.

"Okay! Now, we need to get that out of your leg before you bleed to death."

Nineb stood up and walked around the undergrowth, searching for one of the many healing plants found in the forest. He was in luck. A few yards away, he spotted a cluster of short plants with small white teeth and flecks on their green, succulent, serrated stem surfaces. It was the *Aloe vera*, well-known amongst his people for its many antiseptic, healing and soothing properties. Nineb grabbed onto one of the thick, fleshy stems and broke it off. Then, he plucked off several leaves from surrounding plants. He walked back to the hare, squatted, and placed the Aloe vera stem and the broad leaves on the ground. He picked up his broken bow and removed the twine, wrapping it loosely around his right hand.

"Alright! This is going to hurt. So be ready," Nineb grabbed onto the hare's left thigh.

He placed the twine just above the broken arrow and began to wrap it tightly around, forming a rough tourniquet; the animal twitched.

"I'm not trying to hurt you, just trying to help. It will soon be over."

Nineb applied additional pressure with one hand and quickly pulled out the broken arrow with his other hand. The hare shrieked in pain and retracted its leg. Nineb picked up the Aloe vera stem and squeezed it, releasing its sticky content into the gash. He picked up three broad leaves from the ground and folded them together. Then, he squirted some of the gel on it. Holding the hare's foot, he placed the leaves over the cut and wrapped it tightly around its thigh with the overhanging twine from the tourniquet.

"See, that's it! We're all done. Now, I'll release you from this mess and you can be free to roam the wild," Nineb said as he removed the spines ensnaring the hare, trying not to prick his fingers in the process.

"Alright! You're free as a bird," he smiled. "I bet you have a family of hares waiting for you. Don't you? For me, I have two lovely boys. Honestly, I don't know if you knew about this pit, but I thank you for distracting the leopard and I hope I've been able to return the favor," he patted the hare on its head. "It's already dark now! So you better run off before the other dangerous animals come out," he added.

The hare didn't run; it just stared at Nineb, sucking its front teeth.

"I'm serious! I'm about to leave you and I won't be able to protect you from owls. So go! Leave! Run!" Somewhat perplexed by the animal's odd behavior, Nineb walked towards the hare, stomping his feet in hopes of scaring it into motion.

As Nineb neared the creature it hopped a few yards away. However, as soon as he turned around and began to walk back towards the stream, the hare quietly followed him. Shortly afterwards, Anahg and two other men, an old man and his son, came trotting along through the forest towards Nineb. They were chanting and singing warrior songs with their machetes drawn; in their hands, they each carried a burning torch.

"Nineb! Nineb! Is that you?" His brother raised his torch and called out, trying to get a better view of the figure in the distance.

"Anahg?" Recognizing the voice, Nineb shouted back. "Yes, it's me!"

The brothers picked up their pace and met halfway while the two other men lagged behind.

"Oh, my brother! I'm so happy to see you. I feared the worst had happened, especially when I saw this by the cliff." Anahg handed the machete to his brother. He grabbed Nineb by the shoulders and shook him, revealing his joy to see his comrade in arms.

"Oh, thank you! I needed this," Nineb took the machete and inspected it as though it were brand-new. "Anahg," he continued, looking up at his brother, "it was crazy. I don't even know where to start."

"Sure, I bet! Being chased by a leopard will make anyone's day a little crazy. No?" His brother said with a bit of laughter.

"Hey, you think?" Nineb also laughed. "It was more than just that, the stream, the hare. I don't even know where to start."

"Really! More than just being chased?" Anahg looked intrigued. "Okay, tell me all about it later. But for now, all that matters is that you're alive and unharmed. I honestly couldn't imagine facing your boys to tell them that something bad happened to you. Anyway, you look like you could use something in your stomach," he tapped his brother on the side of his abdomen. Anahg removed a large mango from his pocket and handed it to Nineb. "Plucked this one on our way, just in case I had to offer it to the leopard in exchange for you," he joked.

Nineb took the ripe fruit and began to devour it. "Ah, thank you! Great decision on your part!" he added with a mouthful smile.

Shortly after, the old man and his son joined the joyful reunion between the brothers and became acquainted with Nineb. Anahg met them along the way as he sprinted through the forest towards the village; they were descendants of *Abmumul*, great hunters of the forest.

"We're glad that you're alive and well. The forest, especially at these late hours, can be a dangerous place for anyone, even for the most skilled of men," the old hunter spoke with a raspy voice as he looked at the surrounding trees.

"Yes! We're happy to see you. My father is correct! The forest can be a very dangerous place," the middle-aged man added as he put away his machete. "When your brother approached us and said you were being chased into the forest by a leopard, we were very worried. See, if you don't already know, leopards are one of the strongest and swiftest forest hunters, capable of quickly attacking and even dragging large animals up trees. I mean animals twice their weight." The hunter spoke with his hands in an animated manner.

Nineb bowed his head towards the old man and his son. "I thank you for your sincere concern and effort. I truly appreciate it."

"Young man, you shouldn't be thanking us. We haven't done anything, only our duty as human beings to help those in need. You should thank the heavens because only a few men," he paused, "trained warriors, have single-handedly outsmarted and escaped a leopard in the forest. Your ancestors must be watching over you!" The old man slowly touched three long, diagonal scars across his chest. "Well, having said that!" He sighed. "We need to be on our way before the flames attract unwanted guests."

"So tell me, my friend, how did you manage to escape the mighty leopard?" His son interjected with a hint of envy in his voice.

Nineb looked at him, smiling as he shook his head. "With all due respect, I didn't escape the leopard. The leopard escaped me."

"Huh? What do you mean by that? The leopard escaped me?" The man was puzzled by the answer. "Come on! Tell us how you did it."

Also confused by the statement, Anahg butted in. "Hey, I'm sure my brother is probably just …"

The old man interrupted their conversation. "Quiet, quiet! Something is following us." He turned around swiftly and pointed his torch towards the ground with his machete ready to strike.

In response, the men withdrew their respective weapons and turned around for another potential challenge.

"Ah! How convenient?! *Bushmeat!*" Anahg dashed towards the *leporid* a few feet away.

The farmer, surprised to see the hare again, dropped his machete and chased after his brother. "No, Anahg!" Nineb stopped him just before he struck the animal with his blade.

"Nineb! It's going to run away!" Anahg struggled to free his wrist from his brother's grip. "What's wrong with you?"

"No! There's nothing wrong with me. This animal saved my life!"

"Saved your life? Are you drunk or something?"

"No, I'm not and yes, it saved my life. Let's go. I'll tell you all about it."

Anahg lowered the blade with reluctance and then noticed the leaves around the hare's leg. "What's all this? What's going on, Nineb?" He gave his brother a bewildered and confused look.

Nineb sighed and began to talk. Ignoring their prior vigilance, the curious men gathered around the farmer and the feeble creature, enclosing them in a triangle. Resting his weight on his knee, Nineb stroked the hare as he told them the details: the leopard, the stream, the hill and the injured hare. Upon hearing the full account, the men, with the exception of the old hunter, were in doubt; they didn't understand the significance of Nineb's encounter and they wanted proof.

"Take us to the leopard." The middle-aged man uttered. "I want to see it for myself!"

"It's back this way." Nineb pointed to the northern part of the forest.

The young farmer picked up the injured hare and guided the skeptics through the woodland towards the opening in the ground; the old man simply accompanied them through the woods.

"Incredible! It's lying in there!" Anahg couldn't control his excitement; he began to skip as he pointed to the lifeless beast. "It's in there!"

"I don't understand and this doesn't make any sense! Why would an injured animal risk its life for the person who hurt it? And how could the leopard, an animal so intelligent and so formidable, fall victim to such an obvious trap?" the middle-aged man thought aloud.

"Yes, I don't know." Anahg added. "Maybe it was frightened out of the bushes by, say, a snake? Or maybe the sight of the leopard made it cry?"

"No, that doesn't make sense either! It could have run the other way!" The middle-aged man pointed to his left.

Nineb, who was still holding the hare, watched and listened to Anahg and the hunter debate over the motives of the animals; the old man, on the other hand, closed his eyes and didn't say a word.

"My sons!" the old hunter eventually spoke, revealing his watery eyes to the arguers. "There are times in life when we experience events that seem irrational or unexplainable. During those unique moments instead of trying to disprove or question them, we should be thankful and embrace their very essence—in so doing we're more likely to find many more answers to the questions we seek from life," the old hunter said as he walked towards the two men, placing his arms over their shoulders. "It's all about sacrifice! That's why the hare's actions seem irrational. You know, when a person willingly gives up his or her life for someone else that can be a tough concept to swallow, especially for an outsider looking in. Many of us might never understand the driving force for such actions, and some might even view it as rash or foolish. But, in the grand scheme of things the act of sacrificing, or at least the act of giving up one's life for others, is a basic human duty that's going to happen if we like it or not!"

"What do you mean by that?" Anahg asked solemnly. Several times in the city, he had battled with the notion of sacrifice.

"I don't understand you, my son! Are you asking about willingly giving up one's life, or if it's going to happen regardless?"

"Well! Oh, okay!" Anahg stuttered. "Both, actually!"

"Okay, the act of choosing—notice I use the word choice—to give up one's life or comfort to relieve other people's suffering is a divine human quality that is rewarded through external memories and the impacts on those people. Do you understand?" The old man looked at the three men.

The men glanced at each other with strained expressions and nodded.

"In regards to my earlier statement about sacrificing being a basic duty required by all to fulfill, this is what I mean. Every day I wake and realize that I'm still aging, evident from my hair." The old man touched his bushy gray locks. "Aging is an unavoidable process in life, and sooner or later I'll have to leave to the land of our ancestors to make room for the unborn! Now, suppose we all lived forever, then in no time there'll be no more room for the young to grow. Things would be very hostile and self-centered! It would be an every man for himself scenario! Thankfully, nature wouldn't allow this to happen. No! No!" he shook his head, "There has to be balance in the world. As a result, you can say that life is taken from one person to give life to another—all for balance and the greater good. Like it or not!" He smiled and revealed his crooked brown teeth.

"Does that only apply to old people?" Nineb dropped the hare to the ground. "What about the young who didn't have a chance to live a full life before passing away? That doesn't sound fair at all to me!" Nineb asked the old man as memories of his late wife and children flooded his head.

"Who didn't have a chance to live life?" The old man scratched his full gray beard. "I don't think anyone has the right to say such a thing because we don't know that for a fact."

The three men looked at each other again, slightly confused.

"What I mean is that many of us feel that we know what's best for others and how their lives would have turned out, when in truth we don't have a clue. In a way, we make these self-driven assumptions."

"How so?" Nineb interjected. "Assumptions?"

"Okay, you're men of the field and you know that it takes some men days to learn certain skills and others months or even years. Right, no?"

"Yes! You're right." Nineb replied. "For example, my oldest son, Tpyge, learned how to weave a basket in about two days, but it took his younger brother Nadus several weeks."

"Good analogy, Nineb! That's similar to the different amounts of times we have on earth! Some people accomplish their purpose and destiny faster than others, in shorter amounts of time. Regardless of the duration, they lived a life, which in itself is very special," the old man looked at Nineb. "You need to realize that no life is wasted. Every human being has a purpose, something he or she is meant to teach the world. Sadly, many of us with the loss of a loved one get so caught up in the act of mourning that we fail to appreciate, celebrate, and even learn from their presence on earth."

"Wow! I never thought about it like that!"

"You're truly a wise man," Anahg said.

"Pardon me. But father, are you saying that this animal," the middle-aged hunter pointed at the injured hare, "decided to sacrifice itself for the one who injured it?"

"No, my son! I didn't say that the hare decided. What I said or at least tried to say is that the hare's actions is similar to the idea of sacrifice and that is, or should I say *might*, be the reason why its actions seem irrational. However, one thing that I've come to learn over the years is that if you take care of Mother-nature, she, in return, will take care of you! And that just might be the reason why the hare cried out."

"What about the leopard?" Nineb asked.

"Now, as for the formidable leopard, it teaches us an important lesson in life, that we always have to be cautious of the way we carry ourselves and treat others, because no matter how strong, rich or powerful we might become in life, one simple slip-up can cost us everything and bring us down to our destruction, just like that leopard."

"Very true! Thank you for the teachings," Nineb bowed his head.

"As I have said before, you don't have to thank me. Thank the heavens and your ancestors for the favor. I'm only fulfilling my purpose," the old man walked closer to Nineb and pulled out a palm kernel from the leather pouch across his waist. He bit into the red flesh and squeezed it until there was a visible oil droplet on the kernel. Then, he used it to draw on Nineb's chest. "Only a few men have faced the great leopard in the forest and survived! You're favored by your ancestors and by Mother-nature. You should be thankful to the heavens and continually care for our Mother-nature," he said as he completed the drawing of the five-pointed star. "Important, you have to let go of the past, hold onto the present, and look forward to the future. Your family needs you, young one!" the old hunter turned to Anahg. "You too, your wife and children need you!"

Later on, the four men gathered together once more and thanked the heavens for everything, but especially for the nutrition the meat of the leopard would provide for their respective families. They shared the wild beast amongst themselves, offering Nineb the pelt and the largest portion before parting ways. Happy to be alive, the young farmer took the hare along with his prize to his home and celebrated with his family. This is the "intriguing story" of how the peculiar creature found its home in their barn and became acquainted with Nadus.

4

CHAPTER FOUR:

"Do not look where you fell, but where you slipped."
African Proverb

Nadus walked over to the wooden cage that housed the hare and inspected its exterior for discrepancies. It all checked out; everything on the outside looked the same and there was no cause for alarm. Inside the large cage, he saw the hare sleeping in the corner with its head buried in the bedding away from him, occasionally shaking its fuzzy tail. The hairless, scarred area on its leg often reminded the young boy of his father's intriguing story and subsequent lectures.

"Tpyge! Nadus! Why isn't there enough food in here?" Nineb cried out one day as he pointed to the cage. "Didn't you hear me before? This hare was sent to us by the heavens and we need to care for it! Make sure it's comfortable." Their father had scolded them on several occasions, holding his left earlobe as he waved his index finger.

"Yes, Papa! We hear you. We won't let it happen again." Nadus and his brother both responded, reiterating the same shame-tinged chorus.

As a result, the boys, mainly Nadus, had to cater to the hare on a daily basis, and as with most children there were days when they questioned and even despised their father's fondness towards the animal. Nadus refocused his thoughts and continued his morning chores. He checked the bedding in the cage, the feed and the water trough. A few barely visible patches of urine were scattered over the bedding and at the right of the cage was a small cluster of soft droppings. The hare was good with food and water, and he didn't have to change its bedding that morning. Over the years, Nadus had come to learn that the hare produced two different types of droppings, *cecotrope* and *fecal* droppings. The fecal droppings were hard, round, and used on their farm as manure. The cecotrope, on the other hand, were softer, smaller, and high in nutrients; the hare ate them afterwards. Nadus walked back to the corner of the room, opened the smaller bag of feed, and took a scoop with the corroded can. He then proceeded towards the two birdcages beside the hare and checked for eggs before showering the restless chickens with an abundance of breakfast. The birds, already eager for their meal, clucked aloud as the grains scattered all over their feathers and cages; they immediately began to stuff their beaks. Nadus was excited because his chores, at least in the barn, were almost completed. He placed the container back into the large bag, patted his dog and stood up from his hunkered position. Then, he proceeded towards the small, square window to his left. He was about to unbolt it, to reduce the stuffiness and invite some of the morning radiance, when he thought of the hare and its nocturnal habits.

Oh, yeah!

I better cover it before Papa gives me one of his talks.

He smiled and walked back towards the hare. Picking up an old, dark cotton sheet from the floor and quickly unfolding it, he covered the cage and protected the slumbering animal from daylight. The young boy then commenced his previous plan and opened the window. The rusty hinges creaked and the panes swung away from the frame, brightening up the room. Instantly, the dust particles and loose feathers lingering in the air were exposed in the beam that radiated through the opening in the mud walls; the odor in the shed was altered to an uneven blend of fresh rain, chicken droppings and smelly goats.

"Oh, that's more like it." Nadus took in a whiff of the day and sighed. "That's much better!"

He walked towards the goats, picked up the lantern hanging on the wall, and blew out the flames. He squatted and unknotted the ropes that tethered the ruminants to the buried plank, occasionally using his teeth to aid the process. He picked up the calabash from the shelf with one hand and the hurricane lantern from the floor with the other, suspending it over his forearm. Then, still using his right hand, he grabbed the loose ropes and guided the goats outside towards the withered tree, opposite their hut and the shed. Nadus placed the items on the moist soil to firmly secure the pygmy goats to the tree trunk. Afterwards, he held the female by her miniature horns and grabbed the calabash as he knelt, placing it directly under her breast. He then began to squeeze and pull on its long teats. Having being subjected to the same, uneasy routine on several occasions, the fragile female had learned to be compliant and didn't resist; the male and the dog were simply spectators, observing the usual. The young boy began to milk the goat and a stream of warm, nutritious liquid jetted out of the animal into the calabash. His mouth began to water and his stomach grumbled; he was hungry—very hungry!

Ah yes!

This is my chance to get more!

Nadus looked at the bowl of milk and just couldn't resist its appeal. He released his grip on the goat and picked up the calabash, staring at the cloudy bubbles as he swallowed his saliva.

Yes, I know!

I shouldn't, but I'm hungry.

Only one sip!

I'm the one getting the milk.

I can always just get some more from the goat.

He put the calabash to his lips and took a quick gulp; he sighed as the milk was so delicious and refreshing.

I promise.

Just one more!

After that I will take it inside.

The young boy took three more gulps, and as he stared at the residual hoping to justify a fifth guzzle his brother's loud voice interrupted him.

"Nadus," his brother called out. "Nadus!"

"Yes? What's the matter?" the young boy mumbled, quickly wiping his lips and turning around towards his older brother.

"What are you doing there? Come on, hurry up! We need the milk and breakfast is almost ready."

"Oh yes, I'm almost done milking the goat. I'll bring it in very soon."

"Okay, that's fine. Just hurry up, we need to leave for the farm soon," Tpyge walked back towards the hut and just before he entered the room, he turned around, "Yes, also Papa wants you to take a bath today!"

"Okay Tpyge, I hear you!" Nadus replied with a low disgruntled tone, revealing the obvious; he wasn't fond of cold baths in the morning.

He milked the goat some more and quickly but cautiously walked back towards their hut with the lantern and the half-full calabash in his hands, trying not to slip or spill some of the precious liquid. Wagging his brown, stubby tail, Dahc followed his master towards the delicious smell. After delivering the produce, the young boy walked outside alone. This time, however, he was wearing a pair of mismatched rubber slippers and a tattered towel wrapped around his waist that barely reached his knees. With both palms placed under the base, Nadus carried a plastic bucket filled with four pints of rainwater. Floating and rocking on its surface was a small gourd containing his bathing supplies: a bar of *Ose dudu*, African black soap, made from plant ashes, palm-oil and cocoa butter; an amber sponge obtained from the dried fibrous interior of the *Luffa cylindrica* fruit; and a porous stone for exfoliating cracked soles. He walked around the side of the hut towards a cluster of banana trees by the shed. Resting the green bucket on the ground, he plucked a large banana leaf, placed it beside the bucket, and removed his towel, hanging it on one of the trees. Due to the scarceness of water in the village, the act of bathing was considered a luxury for the young boy and the other inhabitants; it required skill, frugality and patience.

The weather was still cool from the early morning's downpour and it wasn't uncomfortable. Regardless, Nadus didn't enjoy being naked outside, especially when the sun was out for fear of being spotted by one of the girls in his school. He hurriedly began to bathe. He picked up the gourd and placed the porous rock on the leaf lying on the ground. Then he took a scoop of the water with the gourd, lathered the sponge and began to scrub himself all over; this was the easy part. The harder part was getting most of the soap off his body without using water. Using the side of his palms, Nadus began to scrape off the excess foam, trying to ignore the stinging sensation in his eyes. After removing a considerable amount of the brownish froth, he poured the remaining water over himself, skillfully rinsing the sponge at the same time. The morning breeze embraced Nadus and he shivered as goose bumps arose on his skin. He grabbed his towel and dried himself in haste. Even though bathing reminded him of the idea of redemption, that the unclean can be made clean again, he still wasn't fond of cold baths, and he was glad it was over. Stirred by hunger pangs, Nadus gathered up his things and darted into the hut towards the wooden dresser in the corner of the room. He pulled out the bottom shelf and picked out his only school uniform: a pair of faded green shorts and a dull white short-sleeve shirt.

"Nadus! Nadus! Are you putting on makeup or something? We're not going to the festival at least not today. Come on, get dressed! The food is getting cold. Quick now! Sharp, sharp!" his father teased.

"I'm almost done. I just need to..." he rubbed shea butter over his ashy face. "I'm done. Honest Papa! I just need to put my clothes on now," he looked at his father as he applied the lotion to his arms and legs.

His starved father and brother briefly looked at each other, smirking and shaking their heads in amusement. A few minutes later, Nadus was dressed and joined his family at the circular wooden slab, taking a seat on the last of the three stools with short legs. They held hands, bowed their heads and thanked their ancestors and the heavens for the food and good health. They unclasped their hands and washed their right hands in the small calabash resting on the table. Their father, being the oldest, was the first to wash his hand, followed by Tpyge and finally Nadus. Although favoring his left hand, Tpyge couldn't use it to eat or for many other tasks as it was considered disrespectful. Using their hands, they began to down their meal, which consisted of boiled cassava, *akara*—fried bean cakes, salted palm-oil, and milk. Their breakfast, though simple in preparation and appearance wasn't simplistic. Cassava provided them with carbohydrates for energy; beans and goat milk supplied protein, and the palm-oil contained vitamins, minerals and oils. They rarely ate red meat or poultry at breakfast or during any other meal as it was scarce and expensive; it was enjoyed only on certain occasions like weddings and funerals. However, from time to time they ate the eggs from their chickens. Breakfast was important to them because it was typically their only meal of the day; it symbolized the concept of family and togetherness and it offered them another chance to create new pleasurable memories before heading out to the unpredictable world.

"So Nadus, tell me what's going on today in school?" his brother asked, chewing and smacking his lips loudly.

"Well it's..." Nadus paused; raising his finger towards his brother, he chewed on his food and continued. "Yes, you know, it's the last week of school before the break and that's really nice."

Tpyge took a piece of cassava from the largest calabash and dipped it into the smallest calabash containing the palm-oil. "No, I don't know!" he laughed. "Why do you always say 'you know' all the time like I know? I don't know! I was talking about class. What classes do you have today?"

"Oh that's what you mean. Of course, you know!" Nadus smiled.

"Nadus are you trying to be funny? Now! Because if that's what you're trying to do, then I must say that your joke is dry. It's so dry that the food in my mouth is boiling hot," Tpyge pointed to the food in his mouth.

"Huh? Joke? What are you talking about? Mouth is boiling?"

"I mean your joke about 'you know' is so dry. Very dry indeed, that it's making the food in my mouth so hot that it's boiling."

"Oh yeah! That's deep!" Nadus responded in a prolonged manner as though bedazzled by his brother's answer. "Wow!"

Their straight-faced father couldn't resist the contagiousness of their hilarious behaviors and started laughing as well.

"That was a terrible comeback," Nadus continued. "I must say! That was bad, just bad! A joke that makes you think too much is definitely not a joke. It's more like a riddle, if anything. I meant you know or at least should know the schedule because you graduated from there."

"Hey, hey, do I smell jealousy around here little brother?"

"Nope, I can only smell the akara that I'm about to put in my mouth," Nadus ate the bean cake in his hand. "I'm not jealous! It was just too bad for me to think about such a thing as jealousy," He chewed as he spoke.

"Hold up now! Have some respect for your elders. Boy, oh boy! Have you lost it? Come on! Admit it and accept the fact that you love my funny jokes," Tpyge chuckled as he handed over a calabash to his brother.

"Okay brother! If you say so," Nadus took a sip of the goat milk, rolling his eyes and rinsing his mouth.

"So tell me Nadus, does Mr. *Ohtosel* still teach Math?"

"Most definitely! He still teaches Algebra and Trigonometry and the man is still as strong and strict as ever!"

"Really?" Tpyge turned to his brother as food crumbs were propelled from his mouth. "Goodness! I hate that man so much!"

"Tpyge!" their father interjected. "Don't say you hate anyone!"

"But Papa that man is so wicked. He used to beat us every time we got the math problems wrong. I can't understand the idea of beating and punishing a person for having a hard time learning. Isn't that the whole idea of learning—to better understand something that you don't know?"

"Yes I understand! First of all, hate is a strong word that you don't just throw around whenever you're upset or angered by someone. Secondly, you can't measure hatred; just like love, you can't hate a person a little bit or more because once and if you truly hate that person," he paused, "you hate them and everything that comes with hatred applies. Tell me Tpyge, if you saw him stranded and injured in the woods would you just abandon him or walk away if he called out to you?"

"Come on Papa! I wouldn't do such a thing. I'll help him or get help!"

"Well, I'm glad to hear those words. This shows you don't hate him. You more likely dislike his actions towards you."

"Thanks Papa. I suppose so!"

"Yes! Listen to Papa, don't say that!" Nadus teased his brother.

"Hey, you!" Tpyge pointed to Nadus with a half-eaten piece of akara in his hand. "Shut up! What do you know?"

Nadus chuckled. "Well I know for a fact that I don't hate him like you."

Tpyge mimicked his brother, repeating his last statement as he made silly faces and spoke with a funny, high-pitched tone of voice. "Oh shut up Nadus! Stop acting like a do-gooder. Please don't make me remind you of the day you got smacked at the back of your head by the headmaster," he continued in his normal voice. "I remember you were jumping like a goat and crying like a baby. Ow, ow! Cry baby!" He laughed, flapping his hands like a bird and rubbing his eyes as though wiping off tears.

Tpyge's theatrical performance and intense facial expressions were priceless; it made all three of them erupt in laughter.

"You got me on…" Still laughing, Nadus choked on his words and food. "Got me on that one…" His eyes became bloodshot and he began to cough.

"Okay boys! That's enough talk for the entire day. What did I tell you about eating and laughing?" their father stood and tapped his son on the back with a guilty countenance.

Nadus covered his mouth and nose with his hand. Then, he forcefully expelled air from his lungs through his nose, clearing his air passages and propelling tiny food particles onto his palms.

"Aaah!" He blinked and then rubbed his hand on his shorts. "Yes Papa. I'm fine. Thank you!" he slowly chewed on the rest of his food. "And yes Tpyge! Thank you also for your concern."

"You know it." Tpyge winked and continued to laugh. "You're always welcome!"

"Okay boys! That's enough," their father said in a more authoritative voice as he washed his hand. He turned to Tpyge and passed him the calabash. "Wash your hands and go get ready. We need to be on our way."

"Yes Papa." Acknowledging his father's seriousness, Tpyge stood to his feet and took the calabash with his greasy right hand—never with his preferred, unsoiled, left hand.

Tpyge washed his hand and passed the calabash to Nadus. Then, he proceeded to the corner of the room and started gathering their farming tools: three machetes, two hoes and a short-handled rake. Nadus, on the other hand, cleared the table and wiped off the food crumbs and oil stains from its surface with a moistened rag.

"Okay Nadus!" his father said as he slung a water gourd and a leather pouch containing a few fruits across his hairy chest. "Your brother and myself are about to leave for the farm. The dirty clothes are over there," he pointed to a small heap of clothes on the floor. "Be sure to have them washed before you go to school. Okay?"

"Yes Papa! I'll do that."

"Thank you son! Well, as always, have a good day at school and learn something new."

"Yes. Thank you, Papa. I'll learn something. You have a good day at the farm. You too, Tpyge." Nadus sat on his heels and began to pile the dirty calabashes in the corner of the room.

"Thanks! I'll do my best and try not to get flogged again today. Okay? I don't want to be embarrassed by one 'dancing chicken' for a brother." He laughed as he placed the sack containing the tools over his shoulder.

Nadus chuckled, "I'll do my best to make you proud! Bye now and take care brother."

"Bye! Take care little brother!" Tpyge replied.

"Okay we are off. We'll see you later in the day, and may the heavens be with us all!" their father said as he walked out of the door with Tpyge.

Nadus stood up and walked towards the pile of soiled garments in the center of the room. He began to sort through the clothes, separating them by size and color. Abruptly, his brother began to call on him from outside.

"Hey Nadus! Come outside. Your friend is waiting for you."

"Ah thanks! I'm coming—on my way out!" Nadus shouted back.

He gathered the clothes and stuffed them in a plastic bag. He slipped on his rubber sandals and grabbed his frayed notebook and pencil from the top of the dresser. Nadus stuck the pencil into his folded book and tucked the notepad under his armpit. He picked up the plastic bag and walked out of the door with his dog, set for another day. Nadus bolted the door to prevent strangers, mostly strays, from drifting into their humble abode. Once, he accidently left the door unlatched and the draft pushed it wide open, inviting a lost dog and several agama lizards into their hut. His father was upset that time because the dog chewed and urinated on his mat; the lizards, on the contrary, were just a pain to chase out.

"Nadus, Nadus! Let's go. I'm sure you don't want us to be late. Do you Nadus?" his friend spoke in a loud voice as he strolled towards the young boy and kicked loose pebbles with his sandals.

Disturbed by the shooting stones, Dahc bolted towards the intruder, barking and frequently looking back as if waiting for approval to attack.

"Nadus!" his friend yelled. "Back off! Back off! Nadus, make sure your crazy dog doesn't bite me. Back off!" he stomped his feet repeatedly and swung his fists in the air like an awkward boxer.

Dahc wasn't startled by the boy's gestures. Instead, the dog stood his ground and was aggravated, looking fiercer and barking louder. Nadus turned around and saw his hysterical friend a few yards away; his father and brother, in contrast, were in the distance with their back turned, departing towards the dawning horizon. The rising sun put their silhouettes in sharp relief against the wide landscape. Off to the right, Nadus noticed some plumes of smoke coming from the direction of the city. Odd as they were, Nadus had more important things to worry about, like joining up with his pal and departing together for the long journey to their school.

The young boy was clearly amused by his two friends. "Hey *Idnurub!*" he laughed as he walked towards the rivals, "haven't you learned by now that stomping your feet like that wouldn't make things any better?"

"Nadus, it's not funny!" His friend spat nervously. "Come on now. Call off your crazy dog."

"Now why should I do such a boring thing when I'm having so much fun watching you two?" Nadus's eyes were widened with mischief.

"Nadus! Have you lost it? Call off your dog!"

"Okay, just this once!" Nadus replied. "Dahc! Hey boy, over here!" He tapped his folded notebook on his thigh.

The obedient canine stopped barking; he wagged his tail, and walked towards Nadus, turning around a few times and growling.

"That's a good boy!" Nadus squatted and stroked Dahc's slobbery face. "Yes, that's a good boy! Don't mind that guy."

"Hey Nadus, cut it out. Come on! We need to leave now or else we'll be late, and I don't want to be punished." Idnurub beckoned with his skinny chapped hands.

"Alright, alright Idnurub! I'm coming." Nadus stood up. "Alright Dahc! You be good and watch them, okay?" He pointed to the goats tethered by the tree. "I'll see you later in the evening. You be a good boy." the young boy stared at his dog as he walked backwards towards his schoolmate.

Wanting to be part of the pack, Dahc sat on his hind legs and wagged his tail in the dirt, whining in sadness as his master walked away. As soon as Nadus turned his back, Dahc dogged after the two boys.

"Hey, hey!" Idnurub turned around and exclaimed. "It's your crazy dog again!" He pointed at the canine.

"No Dahc!" Nadus faced his dog and pointed in reprimand. "You know better."

Upon hearing his master's admonitions, the dog lowered his head and warily looked up at Nadus.

"You can't come along with me to the stream and you definitely can't come with me to school. You need to stay at home and watch the hut, the barn and especially the goats—they need you here. Okay?"

Dahc whined, turned around and ambled towards the hut as Nadus hustled back to his impatient colleague.

CHAPTER FOUR

"Nadus, we need to hurry if we want to make it to the stream and still get to school on time."

"Okay! You're right." Nadus looked over his shoulder at his dog.

They increased their pace along the reddish-brown muddy path. The plastic bags in their hands swung from side to side, colliding repeatedly with their thighs—competing in resonance with the soles of their sandals smacking and welting the wet ground. The young boys raced to complete the imminent five mile journey to the village stream.

"Wait Nadus! Wait, that's enough!" Idnurub exclaimed, "Nadus, we really need to..." he stooped over with his hands on his knees, panting and sweating heavily as he tried to catch his breath. "Oh, we need to stop for a few. But, ugh, I feel like throwing up. I can't run any longer."

Nadus, who was a yard ahead, turned around and continued to jog on the same spot, in a small puddle. "Idnurub! What's the matter with you?" Nadus showed off his stamina. "We've only been running for two miles and I know you can do better than that. Weren't you the one complaining about being late to school? Come on! Don't be lazy." Nadus added as he walked towards his friend and clapped his hands.

Idnurub looked up with bloodshot eyes and a weary countenance. "Yes Nadus! You know that on a good day I could run five miles nonstop, but..." He patted his chest with his fist and coughed. Afterwards, he spat greenish-yellow phlegm towards the grass and continued talking. "I haven't had anything to eat since yesterday afternoon when we ate those oranges and fried crickets. I'm so weak! I feel faint and my stomach is cramping," Idnurub held his abdomen, wheezing and blinking his eyes.

Nadus realized his classmate's distress and was consumed with guilt for being so critical, especially since he was, in contrast, satiated and full of energy. "Oh my! I'm sorry to hear that. What happened? Why have you not eaten since yesterday?"

"Well..." Idnurub replied.

"Goodness, I can only imagine it." Nadus interjected as he recalled his hunger pangs from earlier. "You must be in pain! How are you feeling?"

"Oh well... Yes, my belly still hurts a bit and I'm a little dizzy, but I feel much better now. I just need a minute to catch my breath."

"No worries! Take your time." Nadus squatted in front of his friend. "Tell me again, why haven't you eaten since yesterday afternoon?"

"You know ever since father left us, things have been really tough and my mother can barely feed us. Now to make things even worse, she's very sick and we can't even afford to get her medicines."

"Oh, I didn't know." Nadus grimaced. "I'm so sorry to hear that!"

"It's okay! Thanks." Idnurub sighed and spat again. "Yesterday we ran out of food, except for a small bag of beans that we'll cook later tonight. I don't know how we're going to survive with the drought—foodstuffs are just so expensive!"

"Very true!" Nadus nodded. "Yes, I understand."

"Oh, that's right. You know what I'm talking about." Idnurub raised his upper body to a more erect position. "Your father's a farmer."

"Yeah, on few occasions I have overheard him talk about the rain and the failing crops. Well, at least there's some hope—it rained last night," Nadus replied.

"I hope so too. It has been tough lately!"

"Idnurub! I'm really sorry about your mother. I hope she gets better and I hope things turn out for the best." Nadus looked at his friend as he untied his plastic bag and searched through it. Seconds later, he pulled out two small globular fruits, rubbed them on his shirt and handed them to his classmate. "Hey, this is all I have on me. Take it and hope it makes you feel better and reduces your dizziness."

"Alright, guavas! For me? Really?" Idnurub took the yellow fruits and gobbled them, ensuring that nothing was wasted.

Nadus smiled and watched his friend as he retied the bag.

"Thank you so much. I needed that!" Idnurub picked out guava seeds from his teeth with his dirty fingernails. "I feel so much better and I could use a drink of water right now. But, we better start moving or else."

"No, we can wait a few minutes," Nadus chimed in. "Seriously, we'll just have to chat less at the stream and wash the clothes faster. It's okay!"

"No, I feel much better. Let's go!" Idnurub spoke with added energy in his voice. "Let's go."

"Okay then!" Nadus blew his nose. "Let's get going."

"Alright!"

CHAPTER FOUR

The boys continued their journey along the road towards the village stream. This time, however, they weren't jogging, but speed walking.

5

CHAPTER FIVE:

❧

"Character is like smoke, it cannot be hidden."
African Proverb

The boys hadn't traveled far before the bright morning sun was out of hiding and the added luminosity seemed to seduce the villagers, mostly the young women, towards the pathway. The women, young and old alike, with their long, beautiful multihued tie-dye wrappers around their bosoms and the outsized baskets balanced on their heads drifted onto the path like *Papaw* leaves floating on a pond. A flock of curious chickens unearthing the moist soil for breakfast scurried in several directions as three neatly dressed men sped by on vintage bicycles. They were headed to the city for work. Angry outbursts of upset fowls, sounds of tire treads gliding through puddles, the melodic hymns of cheerful women along with the laughter of their toddlers chasing after every cyclist brought the meandering village road to a bustle. The boys continued walking, paying little attention to the shifting surroundings.

"Hey! Hey! Idnurub, Nadus! Is that you?"

The boys were surprised to hear their names and they both turned around, wearing curious facial expressions. In the distance, approaching them on a black rusty bicycle, was a boy in his teens, smiling and waving.

"Hey *Ituobijd*!" They chorused, waving and gleaming with excitement.

Ituobijd responded by flicking the bell on his bicycle a few times and pedaling faster. Moments later, he was a few feet away and he began to apply the brakes, watchful of the slippery ground and the added weight of the stacks of bananas fastened to the rear carrier. The boys, wanting to avoid a collision, jumped towards the side of the road.

"You see all the trouble I have to go through just to stop and chat with you." Ituobijd laughed as he steered the handlebar and maneuvered the bicycle to a stop beside the schoolboys. "It's good to see you little rascals again." He planted one leg in the ground, while the other remained on the pedal.

"Oh yes, it's good to see you Ituobijd. It's been a while since we've watched one of your crazy football games," Nadus replied. "So how have you been? Do you still get to play often?"

"That's right. Wow, the way you move the ball. I mean you dribble the ball so fast that some players trip and fall flat on their face. Incredible!" Idnurub exclaimed.

Ituobijd laughed, wiping his lips with the back of his hand. "You little rascals," he smiled and nudged Nadus. "I don't know why you always say this. To be honest I'm just an average player having fun with the sport," Ituobijd was flattered and his large oval eyes beamed with rekindled excitement.

"No, no! You're a great player," Nadus said.

"Yes, you're the best player I've ever watched and wish I could someday learn to play football like you," Idnurub interjected again with ardent admiration in his voice.

"You're both too kind. Thanks for the compliments. How have I been?" Ituobijd hesitated and then shrugged, "I've been good I suppose. Busy! I've just been working a lot lately and don't get to play often. How about you? What are you up to these days? Staying out of trouble I hope."

The boys looked at each other and gave out a mischievous laugh.

"Oh yes," Nadus giggled. "We've been good and staying out of trouble."

"What's so funny? Why are you both laughing? I don't remember saying or telling you a joke of some sort." Ituobijd frowned as he fought off some of the pestering morning flies circling his face, enticed by the sweet scent of fresh bananas.

"Oh nothing, we're just laughing." Nadus chuckled. "It's not you."

"Yes honest." Idnurub echoed. "Honestly."

"Come on you. Tell me why you're laughing. Sharp sharp now! Don't make me knock your coconut heads before I get an answer."

The young boys continued to laugh.

"Ah Ituobijd, please don't do that! Don't knock my head! I just got it shaved yesterday evening," Idnurub rubbed his flaky scalp and sloughed dandruff onto his shoulders.

"Then, you better start talking." Ituobijd grabbed Idnurub by the ear, "or else I'll twist it off. I'm not joking. I'll pull it so hard you'll feel like it's about to be ripped off your coconut head. Well," he paused and sighed, "that's if you don't start talking."

"Ouch, ouch my ear!" Idnurub gave out an exaggerated cry. "Come on Ituobijd, don't squeeze my ear," he pouted and turned his head towards his side. "Why not his?" He pointed at Nadus. "Why don't you squeeze his ear? At least he's the one who first started laughing."

"Geez Idnurub!" Nadus shook his head. "Whatever happened to the old times when friends stick up for each other?" The young boy shrugged and revealed his palms as though expecting a gift.

"Whatever, Nadus! Are you sticking up for me?"

"Perhaps you have a point there," Ituobijd let go of Idnurub. "Nadus, I'll just have to twist your ear as well." The farmer stretched out his dry, weathered hand towards Nadus who was standing beside his classmate.

"Nah uh! You're not going to twist my ear." Nadus leaped backwards.

"Oh you think you're so fast, uh? You know, if I didn't have to balance this bicycle I would have your ears in my hand."

"Ha hah, well you can't catch me. Can't get me!" Nadus grimaced, making funny faces and stomping his feet in the grass. "Wait, wait, a minute," Nadus stood in contemplation and held his ears, "that doesn't even make sense! How in the world are you going to hold both ears with one hand?" he stared at his fingers as though they were foreign objects. "I mean, your hand isn't much bigger than mine." Nadus spread out his fingers, showed off his palm, and continued his prior gestures.

"Boy! Honestly you're so lucky," Ituobijd pointed and waved his index finger at Nadus, "that I don't have time to park this bicycle and chase you down. If I did you wouldn't have that smirk on your face."

"You know, perhaps you should stop," Idnurub sensed the rising tide in Ituobijd's voice.

"Sure, if you say. Yes, if you say so." Nadus beckoned and responded by increasing the rhythm of his uncoordinated dance. "Come on now!"

Suddenly there was a low thump on the ground followed by the utterance of a few bitter curses and a mixture of laughs. While performing as a motley fool, Nadus had stepped on a heap of slick, dead grass. He slipped and was sent into the air. He landed first on his buttocks and then on his back with his legs wobbling for a few seconds like those of a powerless cockroach turned upside-down.

"Ha Nadus! You see what I was saying? Oh my..." Idnurub pointed at his classmate and continued to laugh. His squinty eyes were full of tears.

"I think," Ituobijd snorted, "seriously I think. Oh gosh, I can't breathe." He closed his eyes and gripped the rusty handlebar. "Seriously though," the farmer added as his laughter subsided, "you see that's why there's the old saying to always respect elders. It's because of times like this."

"Yes. Always respect your elders Mister Nadus! Now who's laughing? Surely it isn't you," Idnurub smiled with his hands in his pockets and his legs crossed.

"Sure! Go ahead, I see how it is. Laugh! Keep laughing. Ha ha! Yes, it's so funny," Nadus slowly rose to his feet and wiped his elbows.

The back of his shorts and shirt were splotched with green and brown stains, souvenirs from his recent fall. He wasn't too pleased with failure and he was upset, embarrassed and his throat burned. At that moment, like many people, he failed to appreciate being alive and uninjured.

"That was nice! I haven't laughed this hard in a while. At least I don't seem to remember when I laughed this hard," Ituobijd sighed. "One of the luxuries I miss from not being in school anymore."

"Well, I don't think you're missing much," Idnurub replied.

"He's right you know. You're not missing much at all," Nadus chimed in. His recent humiliating tumble had lent a softer cadence to his speech.

"You're both saying that just because you're still in school. Trust me! I really mean it. Trust me, enjoy it, enjoy every moment in school because life after school doesn't get any easier."

"Sounds like you've forgotten how miserable it feels like to be in that school," Idnurub replied. "Wait! Just think about it for a bit. You're telling me that you miss the many assignments, the long treks early in the morning, and getting flogged and punished by teachers? Oh, no, no! Not me! I don't think I'll ever miss it. I'd rather be on the farm working and drinking palm-wine with men!"

"Palm-wine?" Ituobijd shook his head. "Is that what you think it's all about?"

"Of course not! I know it's not all about drinking, but the farmers sure get to drink the freshest palm-wine, right from the source," Idnurub replied.

"Ah, I once felt like that and I don't think you know how hard it is to work on the farm, especially when the soil is hardened from the drought. Boy, its hard work! It's many times harder than reading poems or solving math problems. Look at my hand, I mean," he licked his chapped lips and revealed his blistered palm to the boys. "Solving math problems, at least for me, was easy! Way easier than having to spend many hours bent over plowing and pulling weeds in the blazing sun. As the wise folks say, you really don't appreciate what you have until it's gone."

"Thanks Ituobijd. I see your point. Tpyge tells me how hard it is and that's probably why he's always tired," Nadus concurred.

"Your brother is so right. It's no joking matter."

"Okay thank you Ituobijd," Idnurub said. "But I don't know. I really don't know. Sometimes I feel if I quit school today and worked on the farm I'd be able to provide for my family and my mother wouldn't have to suffer so much pain. Good enough reason, eh?"

"Idnurub you're young and you have your entire life to work. Take my advice if you can. Stay in school, it's a lot easier. Besides, while in school you often get to play football with the other boys. Don't you? Now that's something I miss very much."

"Yes, guess you're right. It's just hard sometimes," Idnurub grumbled.

"Hang in there. It's really not that bad." He looked at his wristwatch. "Anyway, I better get back on the road. I think I've wasted enough time for one day with you rascals. But I say that it was worth every minute. Nadus you're something else, a real character indeed!" Ituobijd nodded and placed his leg on the pedal.

"Sure thing, I'm glad you enjoyed the time," Nadus replied.

"Thanks for the advice," Idnurub added.

"Alright, I'm off!" the farmer saluted and rode off on his bicycle.

A few feet away from the boys, Ituobijd braked abruptly. "Hey, okay, wait a minute, come here. Quick, quick before I forget okay?" he turned around, yelling and beckoning with his free hand.

A little surprised, the schoolmates dashed towards their caller.

"What, what? What's the matter?" they both chorused.

"No, it's nothing serious. I just wanted to know though. Why were you laughing earlier? I just want to know, trust me. I'll not be mad or upset."

"Oh!" Nadus smiled and looked at his colleague. "Well, okay I give up! I was laughing, actually we were laughing because you made that face."

"What face?" the young farmer asked with a curious mug.

"You know that face you normally make when..."

"Yes, the funny face!" Idnurub interrupted.

"Wait, what funny face are you talking about?"

"You know the face you make like this." Nadus frowned, pouted his lips, and voluntarily twitched his left eye.

"What the heck?" Ituobijd laughed out. "That's the face? You're saying I make that face when I talk?"

The young boys nodded.

"My goodness, incredible! That's one ugly look! No wonder all the village girls don't want to talk to me. I must be scaring them away. I mean that face will even scare me. You boys are still rascals, always rascals."

"Come on now! We can't both be lying to you," Idnurub replied.

"Oh really?" Ituobijd scoffed. "You can't both be lying?"

"You do sometimes, honest! You make that face when you talk." Idnurub also frowned and pouted his lips, mimicking his friend and revealing his version of the questionable expression.

"Oh no! Idnurub that's not even the same face he just made. Ah bah! That's way uglier than his. You're killing me with these faces," the young farmer lamented and his whimpers made the boys laugh.

Ituobijd couldn't resist the contagious grins. He became infected and joined the schoolmates for another round of rib-stifling laughs.

"Oh my God! This is too much. This is too much laughing for one day." Ituobijd covered his mouth, coughed and wiped his hand on his khaki shorts. "You boys have really made my day. You know what?" He touched his face and cheeks, "I'll pay more attention to this face thing you both talk about and make it a little less scary! Who knows maybe this will make me more attractive, no?"

"Oh yes, definitely!" Idnurub stretched his arms over his head. "Sure."

Nadus rolled his eyes and spoke with a hint of friendly sarcasm. "I agree, most definitely agree!"

"You're both very silly you know. You're actually admitting that I need some help, eh? And I scare away the girls with my looks. Well, I suppose the truth hurts sometimes. I guess."

"Ah, come on Ituobijd we didn't say that. We wouldn't say such a thing to hurt your feelings," Nadus replied.

"Sure, I should've known better. What was I even thinking?" Ituobijd tapped his forehead. "You boys will never say such a terrible thing." The farmer laughed again. "Anyway, I better leave now before I get you two in more trouble at school."

"Yes, you're right. Idnurub! What do you think?"

The boy didn't respond.

"Idnurub?" Nadus looked at his friend and nudged him.

"Oh yes." Idnurub looked up, swallowed his saliva and continued to stare at the bananas fastened to the rear carrier. "That's a good idea." He was distracted and his stomach grumbled.

"Don't you think you've looked at those bananas long enough?" Ituobijd chuckled, briefly examining the fruits before fixing his gaze on the hungry boy. "I swear if you look at them any longer they'll all go bad."

"Oh you're right! Actually, I'm sorry, sorry. I was just admiring them." Idnurub looked at Ituobijd. "They're just so beautiful!"

"Huh? What are you talking about? They are beautiful?" Nadus asked as he examined his elbow for bruises. "Idnurub are you okay?"

"Huh, yes—they are! They are so beautiful," Idnurub stuttered again.

"Is that your way of asking for one? Hah!" Ituobijd smiled. "Because it isn't working, at least, not on me!"

"No, no not at all! That's not what I'm trying to do." Idnurub waved his hands in denial.

"Are you sure? Are you sure you don't want one?" the young farmer asked as he plucked one from the bunch. "Oh yum-yum, they're pretty tasty you know. You sure you don't want one?" The older boy offered the banana.

"No, it's okay. Seriously, I was just admiring them. No, it's okay. Thank you." Idnurub slowed his speech as he rocked his head from side to side, acting as though hypnotized by the banana in Ituobijd's hand.

"Okay then. I'll just have to give it to Nadus. Hey Nadus, you want it?"

"Well, sure if he doesn't want it. Yes, I'll take it." Nadus took a step forward and stretched out his hands.

"Wait wait, I change my mind!" Idnurub exclaimed as Ituobijd handed the banana to Nadus. "I want it. Please I'm hungry, please give it to me."

"Oh now you want it, eh?" Ituobijd smiled. "I'm sorry but I just gave it to Nadus and it's up to him to decide if he wants to give it back. What do you say Nadus? Do you want to give it back?"

"Nadus please, I'm hungry," Idnurub pleaded.

Nadus stared at the large, appetizing banana in his hand; he looked up and was greeted by his friend's sad face. "You know what?" Nadus sighed. "It's okay. You can have it. I'll be fine without it, besides you haven't eaten since yesterday. Here, go ahead."

"Wait Nadus, don't worry yourself! I'll just give him another one." The farmer plucked another banana from the bunch. "Just for next time, for future sake, when you really really want something and someone offers it to you, go for it as that chance might never come again."

"I know. You're right." Idnurub peeled the banana with haste and took a large bite. "Thank you! This is so delicious," he mumbled.

"Yes thank you! It's nice—pretty tasty." Nadus added.

"No worries. You boys earned it. I had a great time talking to you rascals. You two together for some strange reason make great jesters. Just like that time during the big match," the older boy laughed. "Remember? The day you two changed the mood of the entire village and made everyone, well, run?"

"How can we ever forget?" Nadus scratched his head. "It was awful!"

"Yes, I won't say all that either but it was a memorable day." Idnurub grunted as he tossed the banana peel into the bush.

"It was pretty funny! Anyway, I really have to get going now." Ituobijd glanced at his bicycle, inspecting the tires and the rear carrier. "You two, make sure you don't go out looking for trouble, okay?"

"Oh yes! Sure we won't," they spoke over each other.

"Good! Well I'm off!"

"Okay, thanks! Bye," Nadus said.

"Yes, thanks for the bananas. Take care Ituobijd."

"Sure, you're welcome. Take care boys. Bye!"

The farmer got on his vintage bicycle and rode off, trailing behind the other workers. The schoolmates, on the other hand, continued their trek towards the stream. They were excited about their brief encounter with the farmer as it brought back old memories—most significantly the unforgettable football match with the city boys!

6

CHAPTER SIX:

"Great fires erupt from tiny sparks."
African Proverb

The weather was typical and it wasn't the most desirable, especially for the highly anticipated football match. It was hot, dry and the breeze was sluggish. Nevertheless, it was preferable to playing on one of those scorching and humid days when the face smolders and sweat refuses to evaporate from the skin. On that day, once every year, before heading to the field for the match, the entire village gathered in the public square to celebrate *Itegneres*, the festival of life, art and creativity. Many villagers believed the Itegneres festival began in ancient times and marked the day King *Airegin*, the great benevolent sovereign, ended the feud amongst his three sons, *Aburoy*, *Obgi*, and *Asuah*. Others claimed it commemorated the agreement between King *Aertire* and King *Aipoihte* to end the long war that spanned three decades and claimed thousands of innocent lives. A couple of the villagers even believed it was formed by the deity to remind humans to always celebrate their unique talents and individuality. Although the true origin of Itegneres remained a mystery, during the yearly celebration the festivity, fervor, and unity amongst the dwellers was undeniable. It was a brilliant display of pageantry, grace and beauty.

"Excuse me please! Excuse me ma'—excuse me sir, coming through, coming through!" Nadus and his best friend, like fishes swimming against forceful currents, shoved their way through the boisterous throng towards the center of the public square.

"Where do you think you're going? Stop right there! Think you're the only one who wants to see the dancers, huh? No! No! You're not going anywhere." A short, stocky man with broad shoulders yelled, raising his elbows as the boys tried to pass.

The man's loud voice and obstructive gesture caught the attention of nearby spectators, swaying many of them to become less receptive to the boys. Nadus and Idnurub, on the other hand, were undeterred by the uninviting people; they just ducked, crawled and wiggled their way through the crowd. Having encountered additional resistance along the way and endured a few slaps and kicks from uncompromising and chastising individuals, their juvenile persistence paid off as they reached the front of the line.

"Yes, we made it, awesome! Nadus, we made it." Idnurub exclaimed as he staggered to his feet and dusted his knees.

"Yes, it's great! This is just great! Look, we made it just in time. It's just about to start." Nadus dusted his knees and pointed at the large wooden podium a few yards away, covered with beautiful blue, green, yellow and red organza and decorated with many different beads and sculptures.

Shortly after, a lanky, man with long dreadlocks, an unkempt beard, a slightly humped back, and surprisingly smooth skin slowly walked onto the podium. He wore a white robe adorned with simple black embroidery across the chest and his aged face was painted in stripes with white clay. Around his neck were numerous strings of white and black beads, and in one hand, he carried a tambourine and in the other he carried a polished stick for support. His name was *Alednam*; he was the oracle, the diviner and the herbalist, known by many of the villagers as the "wise one."

"My people welcome! It is time." The oracle stood in the center of the platform, cleared his throat and spoke with a baritone voice.

As set forth by tradition and to prevent a bad omen, the oracle had to bless and thank the heavens before any ceremony in the village could commence. However, due to all the commotion, a handful of the spectators didn't notice him on the podium nor did they hear him speak.

"My people!" the oracle spoke in a louder voice. Then, he began to shake the tambourine rapidly and continuously. The clang of the thin metallic disks caught the attention of the crowd and silenced them.

"My people!" The old man stopped shaking the wooden percussion instrument and repeated himself in the same tone of voice.

This time, however, he was received by the entire crowd.

"*Alednam! Alednam! Alednam! Wise one!*"

They cheered hysterically, clapping and whistling.

"Welcome my people!" the oracle exclaimed as he limped towards the edge of the podium. "It is time for us to celebrate the beauty and talents of our people, the unique talents with which the heavens have blessed us. It is time for us to come together," the old man raised his cane towards the sky, "as one! Let today, this festival, be yet another reminder that we, the people of *Htraete Nalpruo*, can be united as one! Let today be yet another reminder that we can leave our differences behind and focus on our similarities as human beings, as brother and sister! Dear children of Mother-nature! As our ancestors have said that one piece of firewood is easy to break, but a bundle is many times harder to break, even for the giants of men! So let us come together today as a bundle of people willing to celebrate our great ancestors, willing to celebrate life. My people! My people." The oracle smiled and tapped his cane on the wooden platform.

The crowd, responding to his words and gestures, cheered for several minutes. As the roar of the animated crowd dampened, the oracle turned to his side, winked and signaled with his cane. Before long, three women with identical features darted towards him. The three women, *Eiln*, *Izebmaz*, and *Regin*, were clothed in sparkling brown and gold satin wrapped around their bosoms. They had skillfully braided hair, flawless skin, and dazzling oval eyes; their beautiful faces were painted with white and yellow plant dye, their plump necks, wrists and ankles were heavily adorned with amber beads, and they each carried a calabash in their hands. The three women were called the "gorgeous triplets" by the villagers because of their stunning looks, curvy figures, kind hearts, and bubbly personalities. They were also the youngest daughters of the king and were desired by many of the village men, young and old alike. The triplets knelt in reverence. The oracle waved the tambourine towards his right, signaling to his apprentice. Without delay, a tall, muscular, bare-chested man ran towards the oracle, bowed and took the tambourine with both hands. The apprentice, like the oracle, was also adorned with several strings of white and black beads around his neck. However, unlike the old man who wore a robe and whose face was painted in stripes, the apprentice had only a white wrapper around his waist, and his face and upper body were dotted with clay, signifying his apprenticeship to the oracle.

"I thank the heavens and our ancestors for giving me another chance to bless this wonderful ceremony." Alednam hobbled towards the kneeling sisters and withdrew a large, white feather from the rope fastened around his waist. "I'm old, but look at them! Aren't they all so young and beautiful?" The oracle patted the triplets three times on the head with the feather.

The excited boys in the crowd, including Nadus and Idnurub, along with all the aroused men whistled and hollered their approval. The oracle stepped away from the princesses. Facing the crowd, he placed his cane and feather on the floor. Then, with both eyes closed, he raised his empty hands, palms wide open, as though lifting a large, invisible object. The women, still kneeling behind the oracle, understood his simple gestures and responded. They rose to their feet and opened the large calabashes in unison. Each calabash housed two gourds, each containing one of six vital ceremonial items: palm-oil, honey, kola nut, salt, *hepper* pepper, and palm-wine. These essential foods, although commonplace in the village, possessed significant cultural and theological importance to the villagers. The red, greasy palm-oil symbolized the universal emollient to life's problems. Honey, viscous and sweet, recalled comfort and relief during life's pleasurable moments. The hard, bitter, and invigorating kola nut was a corollary to the motivating effects of life's difficult experiences. Salt, the universal food seasoner and preserver, adds zest and liveliness to life. Hepper pepper, commonly called "alligator pepper" by the villagers because its seeds have a rough, papery covering reminiscent of the back of an alligator, spices up and intensifies life. The sweet, sour, and intoxicating palm-wine represented the duality of life's sweet and sour experiences as well as the need to always enjoy life's pleasures in moderation. The oracle turned around, walked back to the princesses and inspected the contents of the calabashes. Then, he looked at the young women, nodded and smiled, revealing his aged teeth. The triplets nodded and smiled in return. The old man visited each gourd and placed some of the contents of each one into his mouth, one after the other, without swallowing. He closed his eyes and chewed on the victuals as though trying to savor the complex flavors. Suddenly, he opened his eyes wide as if in a trance and sprayed the masticated food towards the audience. Then, he exclaimed. "May the heavens and our great ancestors bless us!"

"*Rufradevas Enoeraew! So be it!*" the crowd shouted.

"Bless us with good health, bless us with good weather!"

"*Rufradevas Enoeraew!*"

"Bless us with long life and prosperity!"

"*Rufradevas Enoeraew!*"

"Grant us victory in today's football match! Let the festival begin!"

"*Rufradevas Enoeraew! So be it!*" the audience raised their arms wildly and stomped their feet. "*So be it!*"

Following his compendious sermon, the oracle waved at the sea of people, picked up his belongings and hobbled off the platform towards his apprentice. As soon as he vacated the stage, the princesses covered their calabashes and followed the oracle, walking off in the opposite direction. Shortly after the triplets departed the stage, four barefoot men, each wearing identical multicolored sleeveless shirts with matching hats and baggy trousers, stormed out from behind the podium and stationed themselves in front of the crowd. Their mere appearance excited many of the viewers as they began to cheer at the top of their lungs. Slung across their shoulders, they each carried a *Djembe*, a large, goblet-shaped handdrum that, according to legend, was originally crafted by the deity from the trunk of the sacred *Afzelia* tree and the hide of a *Gebraffe*, the mythical crossbreed between a giraffe and zebra. The men, *Ituk, Opal, Ukina*, and *Alef*, were famous percussionists, capable of manipulating the pitch and controlling the tempo of their drums to the extent that they often used them to converse and relay cryptic messages to trained listeners over great distances. Standing side by side like warriors in an arena, the primed drummers faced the enthusiastic crowd and all together, with their bare hands, they struck the stretched membrane swiftly. Alternating between their left-handed and right-handed strokes on the successive beats, they instantly fed the hungry villagers with a stimulating, musical repast. The celebrities played the distinct tune wholeheartedly for several minutes, further stirring the crowd into a state of bliss. At the end of their short musical piece, they raised their heads towards the light-blue sky and yodeled, fluctuating between their normal and falsetto voices.

Their loud, distinct howls penetrated the crowd like powerful, unseen forces, swaying many of them, mostly the ardent admirers, into a wild bustle like tree branches flapping in a windstorm. The action of the men, however, wasn't just a means to excite the audience or to flaunt their impressive range and powerful vocal cords. It had a unique purpose; it was an elaborate signal. Without delay, from both sides of the podium like water jetting out of two identical cracks in a clay pot, a troop of acrobats streamed out, running, tumbling, and yodeling. The dancers, physically fit and full of life, faced the audience and gracefully assembled in a circular formation beside the drummers. They were all dressed alike and according to their sexes. The barefoot women were clothed in scarlet, tie-dye wrappers individually fastened around their hips and bosoms, revealing their bare shoulders and navels. They wore large earrings and identical headdresses, and their necks, wrists, and ankles were embellished with several strings of matching red and yellow beads. The men, on the other hand, were less elaborate in appearance. They were also barefoot and clothed in scarlet, tie-dye wrappers fastened around their waists. However, they were bare-chested and didn't wear any of the fancy jewelry and accessories that beautified their female counterparts. The drummers again began to play their instruments with added passion. The dancers countered, intensifying their vocals and erupting in a vivid display of

strength, agility and devotedness. The crowd reacted, dancing and singing along to the anthem. Nadus and his friend stared with a feeling of
awe. It was their first time watching women dancers so closely that they
caught whiffs of their sweet perfumes every time they swung their hips
and moved their bodies with grace; their hearts throbbed with boyish
excitement as they relished the truly surreal experience.

"Yes! Yes! They're coming. Nadus they're coming." Idnurub grabbed
his friend by the shoulders, jumping and pointing to his side.

"What?" Nadus replied on impulse without switching his gaze. "Huh?"

He was still intrigued and preoccupied with the female dancers.

"Nadus! I'm serious, look now! They're coming!" Idnurub yelled again
as he shoved his friend.

"What? What are you talking about?" Nadus frowned and looked in
his friend's direction. "Who's coming?"

"You see them?" Idnurub asked. "You see them?"

"Oh, yes! Nice!" Nadus sounded more enthusiastic. "Oh, look at them!
Yes, I see them. They're coming, just great!" He pointed and jumped with
excitement.

In the distance, as the musicians doled out more improvised beats
and the dancers continued to entertain the villagers with their energetic
performance, King *Akniyos Ebehca* and his chiefs approached on elegantly decorated horses. The king and his twelve chiefs, six to his right and six
to his left, were dressed in wide, long, flowing satin robes decorated with
intricate embroidery. The six chiefs on his right side wore white robes
adorned with black embroidery and rode on white horses; the other six,
clothed in black robes adorned with white embroidery, rode on black
horses. The king's appearance, in contrast, was a fusion of the two groups
of influential men. His striped black and white regal attire was decorated
with more intensive silver embroidery; his horse was a very rare black
and white mix that resembled a *Zorse*, the offspring of a zebra stallion
and a horse mare. On his head, he wore an ornamental jeweled headdress
made from pure gold and lined with fine silk, signifying his noble sove-
reignty. Around his neck and wrist, he wore several strings of large gold

and silver beads, and his feet were protected from the elements with well-polished, handcrafted sandals. In his right hand, he carried a wooden staff embellished with elaborate carvings that denoted his status and royal ancestry. Walking beside the king and the chieftains were the stoic *Snoitandetinu*, the tall, muscular and highly-trained royal guards sworn to death with the sole responsibility of protecting the king from harm. The guards, although curiously large and conspicuous in stature, were always required to wear attire suitable to their surroundings or the occasion. On that day, they were bare-chested like the male dancers, clothed with dark-green tie-dye wrappers fastened around their waists, and on their feet they wore simple black leather sandals. For protection, they carried either a leather scabbard around their waist that housed a sword, or carried a bow and a leather quiver with several arrows across their chest. Strategically positioned around the king and his chiefs, the formidable men were primed, alert and ready for the unpredictable.

A few yards in front of the king, the mysterious and revered *Orajnami-lik* masqueraders sang, danced hysterically and moved zigzag across the path like dried shrubs spiraling in whirlwinds. Their scheduled performance, with the exception of the football match, was the highlight of the Itegneres festival. The visages and ornamentation of the masqueraders were peculiar and flamboyant beside the other participants in the ceremony. Their faces were concealed with large, colorful wooden masks that were carved to resemble the skulls of wild beasts. Every one of them was covered from head to toe with colorful, patterned, and textured costumes, graced with flowers, leaves, feathers, animal hide, and miniature clay sculptures—representative of the fluid and amorphous nature of the deity. In their gloved hands they each carried freshly cut bamboo that they waved in a combative fashion as though fighting off invisible forces, and often used to flog unsuspecting bystanders and "the evildoers" in the crowd. The true identities of the masqueraders were unknown. However, many of the villagers believed they were actual spirits of their ancestors veiled behind the elaborate costumes because of their detailed understanding of the audience and their ability to invoke supernatural powers. Others believed they were humans possessed with the spirits of the ancestors, and a few believed they were simply people who had undergone extensive training to gain the knowledge and earn the privilege of performing as masqueraders. Regardless of their personal convictions, the entire village respected the Orajnamilik for their clairvoyance and ability to delight viewers with their spectacular performances. Adhering to the schedule, the dancers concluded their recitation and briskly vacated the scene, leaving the drummers behind.

"Idnurub, they're here!" Nadus whispered in his friend's ear and covertly pointed at the Orajnamilik a few feet away.

The masqueraders stopped dancing abruptly and stood still in front of the crowd as though lifeless. The lively swarm in reverence became silent with the exception of a few coughs and murmurs.

"Oh yes I know! I see them too." Idnurub nodded, replying in a hushed voice. "They're so different up close. I think they're very scary looking."

Nadus concurred with a subtle glint in his eyes. The young boy and his friend were thrilled about the upcoming performance, but they were terrified of the Orajnamilik. In synchrony, their eyes widened, their pupils dilated, their palms became sweaty, and their heartbeats doubled in rate. The boys couldn't hide their nervousness.

The king and his chiefs halted near the wooden platform, and with the assistance of the royal guards they descended from their horses. Without ado, the percussionists rolled their drums and the town crier, a short and round man with an amicable face, ran onto the podium. Standing by the edge, he smiled, cleared his throat and briefly adjusted his simple long robe. He rubbed his large belly habitually and made an announcement.

"People, my beautiful people of Htraete Nalpruo!" the crier shouted.

"*Yes!!!*" the crowd replied.

"As the oracle said, the heavens have blessed us today, on this day!" the crier continued. "Please help me welcome and greet our most beloved highness and respected ruler, the great King Akniyos Ebehca!" The jovial man bowed and with both hands pointed to the king by the base of the podium. Then, he clapped repeatedly and walked off the stage in haste.

Yes!!!

King Akniyos Ebehca!!

Our great ruler!

The greatest!

We love you!

The crowd applauded and cheered. The musicians once again played their drums and the villagers joined them, singing the sacred, royal song.

Heaven bless us as we stand

Bless the king of our land

Bless him with wealth

Always with health

Make him so stealth

The keeper of our land

We're all made from sand

Heaven bless us as we stand

In a majestic fashion, the king and his twelve chieftains walked up the ramp onto the podium and faced the ebullient crowd. In accordance to custom and in deference, the chiefs took two steps back from their superior. They removed their noble hats and bowed their heads. The citizens emulated the village elders; the men removed their hats and every man, woman and child bowed to the king who stood before the crowd.

"My people, people of Htraete Nalpruo! I thank you so much! I thank our oracle, Papa Alednam, for blessing this event and I thank you all for coming out on this glorious day." The king greeted the villagers, waving the royal staff above his head like a newly awarded trophy. "It's always a great honor to be called your leader, your king." He paused for a moment. "I feel very privileged to be celebrating Itegneres with you and I'm deeply humbled to be here, standing at a place where our great ancestors and my forefathers stood and delegated." The king looked down and pointed to his feet. "This festival is very important to me, to all of us! Why?" He smiled and briefly inspected his staff. "Just think about it for a moment," he stared at the audience. "Should we all conclude that we gathered here today, in this moment in time, as a result of mere circumstances or is it because strong patronage actuated us to the crossroads of our village, to celebrate our customs and culture?"

"*No! No! It's not!*" the crowd responded.

"Or is it simply all this fine food and fresh palm-wine over here that made us gather in the square today to celebrate?" The king pointed to the stacks of yams, mangoes, tomatoes, green vegetables and several gourds of palm-wine arranged on the podium like several miniature mountains.

"*Ah! No! No! Never!*" the villagers laughed.

"But the foodstuffs are surely fresh, no? I just thank the keeper of our land for blessing us this year with fertile soil and ample rain." The king walked over to the pile, picked up a large, ripe mango and smelled it.

"*Football!*" a couple boys in the audience shouted.

"What? What did they say? I didn't hear correctly." The king placed the fruit back in the pile and looked towards the multitude.

"*They said 'football!'*" Nadus, Idnurub and few other schoolboys replied, cheering, clapping and whistling.

"Oh yes, the football match afterwards! Yes, that's very important to you boys." The king smiled and pointed at Nadus and his friend. Immediately, a few of the audience members in front turned and looked at the two scruffy schoolboys.

The boys noticed the sudden attention and fidgeted. From left to right, they looked bashfully at the lookers; their heartbeats increased and their palms sweated again from the embarrassment.

"Okay now, on a serious note, you're right," the sovereign continued. "It's surely no mere or trivial coincidence. Our deity, in great anticipation of this occasion, cleared a path through all primordial chaos and etched a way through time, through the core of our momentary existence, for us to be reunited here today as one. However, I must emphasize again that it's not just by my doing alone that I stand here before you and you stand here before me! It is due to the inevitability of divine sequences of events, events that are greater than all of us! We're truly blessed people! Blessed enough to be alive and in good health, exempt from the suffering and bitter consequences of gravely diseased and warring nations!"

"*Yes oh! We're blessed!*" The villager sang with joy in their voices.

"I'm simply a humble messenger, grateful to be part of such a symbolic encounter, and I thank our great deity for my strength, health, intellect and creative muse. With the blessings of the heavens, today at Itegneres, we affirm our old traditions and mark new beginnings. We mark the undeniable truth that every one of us is creative and has a purpose in the world, some obvious and some, well, not so visible to the naked eye." The king pointed to his eyes. "Nevertheless, we're all endowed with a divine purpose to positively impact humanity. Sadly, however, some of us abandon these gifts, these precious talents, and like neglected teeth," the king opened his mouth and shined his white teeth to the audience, "we allow them to waste away to the point that they lose their viability, their function and become nuisances to us and to others. We play a significant role in an ongoing story. A story so short and yet so long, a story about beauty, victory and unity between persons with an end that I pray we never witness and naively hope never comes to pass. It is the story of a new generation of people, bound by familial ties and once greatly divided by ignorance and distanced by animosities. It's the cheerful story of citizens who made a conscious decision to forgo their superficial differences and embrace their commonalities to become adept forgers of peace and justice, and liberators from old and demoralizing ways and values. It is the beautiful story of the people of Htraete Nalpruo!"

Yes!

Yes, oh!

Heaven bless the king!

King Akniyos Ebehca!

"Though the history of our people is deeply rooted and trails behind many generations, we're still a growing nation with many youthful tendencies. However, it is time, time for us to discard our childish ideas, mannerisms and ways, and embrace a new sense of maturity and responsibility. It's time for us to be conservative of the natural resources endowed to us by the deity, conserve and not waste! We need to care for

Mother-nature if we want her to take care of us. Remember that our life on earth is borrowed and nothing in this world truly belongs to us.

It is important for us to always be thankful and always be appreciative of our circumstances in life. On this blessed day, my people, we all gather here under the protection of the deity to proclaim our affirmation that we firmly choose bravery over fear, togetherness over conflict, joy over grief, and mostly importantly love over hatred. Let us fix our eyes towards the sunny horizon at times when our lives are rocked by life's raging sea and our families are tried by life's tribulations. Let us cast the seeds of hope into the winds of opportunity and realize that our deity's grace and benevolence is upon us, shielding and protecting us each day.

May we continue to prosper for many generations to come and may our children's children enjoy a better tomorrow! Dear citizens of Htraete Nalpruo, I thank you! May the heavens continue to bless us and guide us! Rufradevas Enoeraew! Let the celebrations of our ancestors continue!"

The ruler bowed and waved his hand cordially to his people. The villagers were wowed by his eloquence and were briefly silenced.

Rufradevas Enoeraew!

King Akniyos Ebehca!

Heaven bless the king!

The audience cheered and rejoiced, hailing their ruler. King Akniyos Ebehca turned around and his wide, loose robe swooshed through the air. He walked towards his throne, a large, polished chair that was meticulously carved from aged wood, cushioned with organza, and decorated with an assortment of colorful beads and shells. The intricate design of the throne along with the numerous carvings engraved on its surface was redolent of the king's long heritage and power over his people. The headrest of the throne was carved to resemble the head of the majestic lion, king of the jungle. The armrest was shaped like the sharp talons of the hawk, chief of the skies, and its wide legs were lined with the leather and burnished teeth of the ferocious Nile crocodile, ruler of many waters. The king took a seat and the chieftains followed. The revered men sat on their respective chairs beside their leader. The six chairs to the right and left of the throne formed an arc and their proximity to the king was based on the ranks of the chiefs, from highest to lowest, analogous to their previous riding positions. As the dignitaries situated themselves, several of the royal servants ran onto the podium, each carrying either a large fan made from ostrich feathers, a large colorful umbrella or a calabash filled with washed and freshly cut fruits. The servants with the fans and umbrellas positioned themselves behind the dignitaries; they opened the large umbrellas and began to fan them. The servants with the calabashes, in contrast, kneeled before the elders and served them first before serving the king, a simple gesture that guaranteed the fruits were tasteful and were not poisoned.

Shortly after, as the crowd continued to chant praises, six men ran out from behind the podium and joined the drummers. They were dressed like the drummers; three of them carried wooden flutes and the others carried large gongs. The percussionists played their instruments again, yodeled another tune, and began to sing. The men with the gongs struck the metal plates repeatedly with their drumsticks and the flutists played their high-pitched woodwind instruments with fervor. Immediately, the catatonic Orajnamilik sprung back to life, screeched and danced wildly, beginning their famed performance. The villagers, reacting to the sudden change, sang louder and danced with their hands in the air. The masqueraders joined the villagers, singing with loud but muffled voices and dancing to the fast paced music doled out by the musicians. The Orajnamilik lifted themselves up from the ground and flipped high in unison, twisting and singing in midair. As soon as they landed, the masqueraders, still chanting, kneeled and then stood up. They drew large, cryptic symbols in the dirt with their bamboo and continued to dance at incredibly quick speeds. They repeated the unique set of acrobatic maneuvers for several minutes without slowing down or showing any signs of fatigue. Without prior notice, the masqueraders stopped dancing and as though berserk, they jumped repeatedly and spun around on the same spot, chanting and singing in a language that was foreign to the villagers. Soon after, they stopped, paused, dropped their sticks and began to roll on the ground in different directions, hissing and curling like infuriated snakes.

"*Orajnamilik! Spirits of our ancestors!*" The villagers chanted, clapping to the music and the masqueraders rolling in the dirt.

The villagers believed the Orajnamilik masqueraders were conjured into deep trances by their magical incantations and rolled vigorously as they battled bad spirits lingering in the crowd and vicinity. The masqueraders, just as suddenly as they started rolling, stood up and continued their energetic dance, dusting off their colorful costumes in the process. Shortly after, several boys dressed and dotted like the oracle's apprentice ran out from behind the large podium that elevated the dignitaries. They were acolytes, young pupils of the oracle, and they each carried two fire torches in their hands. Since infancy, these well-nourished boys, based on their birthmarks and star divination, were handed over by their parents to live and learn under the oracle's protection and strict guardianship. From an early age, they were taught about the importance of virtue and compassion, the consequences of evil and sin, and the healing properties and preparation of many sacred forest herbs. Upon reaching adulthood, depending on their acquisition of the information and based on the divine prophecy of the deity, the boys either graduated to become junior apprentices of the oracle or were released from the academy and allowed to join the general public. The acolytes were a great source of fascination and admiration to many of the village boys, Nadus and Idnurub included. The young attendants ran towards the Orajnamilik and handed them the fire torches with caution before running back towards the podium. Each masquerader was given four torches and without delay, they all began to juggle the sticks of fire, throwing them up in the air and catching them as they performed complex acrobatic acts. The spectators were amazed and many of them, like thirsty gazelles struggling at a crowded oasis, tried to squeeze their way to the front to get a better view. The people already at the frontline, on the other hand, were prevented from further encroaching onto the dusty dance floor by the hefty royal guards.

"Oh! Oh! That's so brilliant, unbelievable!" Idnurub covered his mouth with his fist and pretended to bite it hard. He then grabbed Nadus by the shoulders with his other hand. "Oh, did you just see that?" The schoolboy pointed to one of the masqueraders in the far corner. "Nadus look, *he* just

BOUNTIFUL FAMINE – A NOVEL

did a back flip and now he's doing a front flip! Huh eh, ah oh wow! He did it! Nadus, he did it!" Idnurub tightened his grip on his friend's shoulder. "He's still catching the torches. Incredible! That's just too much!"

"Yes, that's nice! Not too bad, I guess," Nadus responded with less fervor. "Sure, it's okay."

Unlike his friend and the other villagers, Nadus wasn't at the front of the line solely for his entertainment; he was also there to learn. With the diligence and zeal of a scholar, he studied the complex motions of the fire torches as well as the different acrobatic maneuvers of the Orajnamilik.

"You're kidding me? Yes, you're joking! What?" Idnurub lamented with his hands spread out. "That's not just okay! That's phenomenal!"

"Sure, sure if you say!" Nadus raised his eyebrows. "Sure, it's phenomenal." Nadus briefly looked at his friend, sounding even less convincing. The young boy was so engrossed by his interest for juggling and tumbling that he appeared nonchalant.

7

CHAPTER SEVEN:

"The market is not attended from a single road."
African Proverb

The source of the young boy's unusual curiosity dated a few years back to his brief encounter with a jovial beggar. On that day, Nadus was working at the village marketplace with his father and older brother, selling tubers of yam that they had harvested from their modest farm. The marketplace, like the world, was a very rowdy place filled with admirers, competitors and detractors alike. As a result, many of the market veterans had come to learn the three vital skills required for success: effective guarding, calculated flattery and strategic peddling. Nineb, Tpyge and Nadus divided those duties, based on their personal qualities. His father, strong and fairly tall, guarded the stack of yams and the money box from damage and theft. Tpyge with his charm and good looks grabbed the attention of distracted customers and smooth talked them. Nadus, on the other hand, being the youngest simply stood by his brother and carried a few tubers, occasionally peddling them and hoping his smiles would win their hearts. The customers weren't falling for it. Nadus wasn't the most skilled salesman, not like his brother; he was better off with the books.

"Hey, excuse me madam!" Tpyge called out several times and signaled without aim to the crowd. "Hey, there! Excuse me madam!"

Shortly after, a woman stopped walking, turned around and scanned her vicinity for the caller. She was holding a toddler by the hand. On her back, tightly secured by a dull yet flowery wrapper, she carried a sleeping baby. Noticing the woman and reading her social cues, Tpyge smiled and waved again. She was a potential client and point of sale.

"Wait, wait! Can I talk to you for just a minute?" Tpyge beckoned as he trotted towards her. She noticed him and responded with a baffled look.

"Yes, can I ask you a question?" Tpyge smiled, standing a foot away.

"Yes? Do I know you?" the woman asked bluntly.

"No, no! Well..." he paused, "maybe you do know me. I don't know. My name is Tpyge. I'm a humble farmer and a handsome one. No?" he laughed.

"What? Oh, oh I see." the woman laughed. "Well, I don't know you and I don't think you're very humble."

"I hope you didn't take me serious, did you?" the older boy asked.

"Serious about what? About being handsome, or the farmer part?" She looked bashfully at Tpyge; he was slightly taller and charming.

"What do you think?" He smiled again as he looked into her eyes. "You tell me."

"Is this why you called me? Just to ask me this question? Please I have a lot to do today so I'll be on my way." She rolled her eyes and turned around to leave.

"No, wait, wait!" Tpyge patted her on the shoulders. "Wait."

The woman looked at the young cultivator and frowned.

"I think you're pretty. No kidding!"

"Really? Oh!" She was taken aback by his remark. "You think?"

"Yes!" Tpyge nodded. "I know you are."

"Well, thank you!" The lady smiled and briefly touched her hair and cheeks, further revealing her appreciation and shyness. "That's very nice of you."

She was beautiful, slender and looked fairly young, perhaps just a few years older than Tpyge. However, the growing lines around her eyes and her sunken cheeks, revealed forced maturity and the pressures of parenthood.

"You're welcome! I better let you go now." The young farmer added.

She nodded. "Yes, I better be on my way. I have a lot of chores today."

"So why are you here in the market?" Tpyge asked a genuine question.

"Well, I have to buy some food for my children," She looked down and pulled her little girl closer, "and their father, my husband." she hesitated and answered with a hint of reluctance.

"Oh okay." Tpyge looked at the little girl and waved. "That's fine! Hey, would you like to buy some fresh yams?" Tpyge slid his catchphrase into the conversation. "I just harvested them yesterday. They're fresh, very tasty. You could use them to make yam porridge for your family today."

"Well, I wasn't planning on making porridge today. But..."

The lady had let down her guard; she was willing but hesitant. From experience and from studying body languages, the farmer knew his time was limited. He needed to act quickly before she changed her mind.

"Nadus!" Tpyge turned towards his brother and beckoned. "Nadus, come here. Quick!" The young boy didn't respond or answer.

"Please do pardon me! I'll be right back." Tpyge bowed and smiled at the lady before dashing towards his distracted sales associate.

"Nadus!" Tpyge grabbed his brother by the arm and shook him.

"Huh?" Nadus looked up at his brother. "Yes?"

"Nadus, what's wrong with you? You're supposed to pay attention." He lowered his voice. "Quick, come with me now. That woman over there is about to buy some yams."

"Really? I'm very sorry, I was just looking at-" Nadus pointed towards the fish sellers in the corner.

"Save the conversation for later. Quick, grab the yams and follow me! Let's go." Tpyge snapped his fingers and clapped.

Tpyge ran back to the lady and resumed his conversation. With both hands, Nadus picked up the three tubers from the dusty, trash-littered ground and walked towards the customer as fast as he could.

"Sorry, that's Nadus, my kid brother." Tpyge pointed to the young boy who was a few feet away, clumsily dodging the busy traffic of marketers. He was struggling with the yams in his hand and trying to avoid contact with his skin; yam peels make the skin itch with the exception of the skin over the palm.

"He seems to have his hands full. No, not at all. It's okay," the lady replied, smiling as she watched Nadus draw closer.

Shortly after, the young boy joined the conversation.

"Hello, good day!" Nadus bowed his head, squatted and dropped the tubers on the ground. "Here! Which one would you like?" He looked up and smiled at the woman as he tapped the yams with his fingers.

"So which one would you like, eh?" Tpyge scratched his cheeks and interjected with the evident impatience of an eager salesman.

"They all look nice!" she replied. "Well! Can I see that one please?" The lady pointed to the smallest of the three.

"Oh, sure you can! Of course!" Tpyge picked up the yam and handed it to her. "What do you think? Fresh, eh?"

"Wait, let's see." The woman held the tuber with care and inspected it for blemishes. "Okay, how much for it?" She looked at Tpyge.

"How much are you willing to pay?" Tpyge replied. "Look at it first. I'm sure you wouldn't find anything wrong with it. Honest, how much can you pay?"

As Tpyge and the shopper bargained and debated the freshness of the yams, Nadus fixed his eyes on his prior diversion, the old man by the noisy and smelly fish mongers. Through the multitude of eager buyers and sellers, Nadus had noticed three unique qualities of this man that aroused curiosity: his heavily wrinkled skin, a pleasant demeanor and unusual strength for his age. Sitting on a dirty, plastic crate, the man looked frail, his arms were thin, his stomach was sunken and his ribs were visible. He wore a dirty hat on his bald head and his nakedness was concealed by tattered, plaid trousers. On his feet he wore leather shoes that appeared just as old and worn as the man and he didn't have a walking cane. On the ground, to his left there was a bottle of water and a small calabash with few coins in it; on his right side, there was a small, aged basket filled with several unripe fruits. The old man was singing and clapping. He greeted every passerby and begged for alms, raising his calabash and jingling the few coins. Most of the patrons were oblivious to his pleas and didn't even acknowledge his presence; they were too busy with life. Others looked at him with pity, shook their heads and walked away without stopping or saying a word. These folks were aware of his needs. However, they were too ashamed of his appearance that they quickly thought of reasons why they couldn't help him. Only a handful of the people walking by greeted him and offered some change. Nadus continued to stare at the man with intense fascination and several questions and thoughts flooded his head.

What's so funny?

Does he have a family?

Where are his children?

They're just ignoring him!

What song is he even singing?

Why are those boys laughing at him?

Why aren't those people helping him?

Why is he still smiling at those people?

Through his naive eyes, Nadus couldn't comprehend such unfairness and couldn't understand why such a pleasant old man was in such a deplorable condition. The young boy wanted to talk to the beggar and have his many questions answered but he couldn't. He had to pay attention to his father's warnings about talking to strangers, especially in the market.

"Nadus! Hey, listen!" Tpyge looked at his brother. "I'm sorry! Okay, as I was saying that sounds like a good price for two." The older boy continued his discussion with the lady. "You can have those, the two large ones. See, I told you I'll give you a good deal."

"Thank you." The lady smiled. "Can you pack them for me? I have to be on my way now." She waved her hands as she spoke. "It's getting late."

"Sure thing! No problem." Tpyge pulled out a wrinkled bag from his pocket and straightened it. "Nadus can you hand me those two?"

"Okay." Nadus picked each yam tuber and handed it to his brother.

The older boy took the yams, placed them in the plastic bag, tied it and handed it over. The lady took the bag and placed it on the ground, securing it between her feet. Then, using her fingers and teeth, she unfastened a small knot on the tip of her wrapper that was close to her bosom. She opened her secret makeshift-purse that was popular amongst the village women. It was a convenient and secure way for them to carry money around in the market. All they had to do was stack their coins, place them on the hem of the wrapper, tie them up, and tuck it close to their breast, a place where men weren't allowed to touch in public. Unlike with purses, they didn't have to worry about pickpockets slashing or snatching them. The woman counted a few coins and placed it in Tpyge's palm. He immediately put the money in his shorts and smiled.

"Thank you for your time. I hope your family really enjoys the yams."

"Yes, I hope we do," the woman replied as she hid her money. "It was nice to meet you, Tippikee? What's your name again?" She smiled.

The older boy giggled. "It's Tpyge!" he pointed to his chest. "And that's my brother, Nadus." He pointed to the young boy who was still squatting.

"Well, it was very nice to meet you and your brother. Goodbye now!"

"Goodbye. Thank you." Tpyge replied.

"Goodbye!" Nadus echoed as he rose to his feet.

She held her daughter's hand and walked away, quickly blending into the bustling crowd.

"See Nadus, now that's how you sell some yams." Tpyge upraised his palm. Responding to the gesture, Nadus also raised his palm and slapped his brother's palm. "That's right! Learn from the best," Tpyge added.

"Yes, yes, I know you're so good at it." Nadus sounded a little let down.

"What can I say? I guess it's just a gift of mine. Yes!" Tpyge bragged.

"You're right. A gift that you have and I don't." Nadus frowned.

"Of course you know I'm right!" Tpyge winked. "Okay, now we need to get back to work, I'm going to look for another customer to buy this last piece. You stay here and I'll call you when I need you. Okay?"

Nadus nodded in accordance.

"Please pay attention this time, okay?" Tpyge pointed in reprimand.

Nadus looked at his brother and nodded again.

"Great!" Tpyge walked away and began to call on customers.

Without delay, Nadus turned his attention back to the beggar. The old man was still sitting on the crate, singing joyfully. This time, however, he had stopped clapping and was adeptly juggling five unripe oranges. Nadus gawked; he was intrigued by the way the old man, with little effort, threw the oranges into the air and caught them simultaneously and continuously. It was his first time watching a skilled juggler up close. On many occasions, Nadus had overheard his brother and his friends argue about the masqueraders and how they juggled. However, because Nadus wasn't old enough and mostly because his father feared he might get injured by the rowdy celebrators, he wasn't allowed to attend Itegneres. Still juggling and singing, the beggar stood up from his seat and began to skip and dance. His sudden acrobatic gestures caught the attention of a few onlookers, but not for long. These people stopped for a bit and kept on walking. Nadus, on the other hand, was filled with awe, and he wanted to get a better view of the act. Ignoring his father's advice, Nadus picked up the yam from the ground and like a vulture attracted to the sight and smell of carrion walked towards the man. Before long, he was standing in front of the man and was greeted by buzzing flies and the stench of rotting fish offal littered on the ground.

It stinks.

The flies, yuck!

Nadus observed the juggler for a moment and was deep in thought. A few seconds passed and the old man noticed his young visitor; he smiled, stopped dancing and stepped up his juggling. He picked up two additional oranges from the aged basket, juggling a total of seven oranges at once.

The young boy was flabbergasted and remained speechless with his eyes and mouth wide open.

"Well, hello there little man!" the man spoke after several minutes in a coarse but kind voice. "You might want to close your mouth," he laughed. "Those flies can be very aggressive and you don't want them getting into your mouth." The old man stopped juggling and with the finesse of a proficient performer, he dropped the fruits back into the basket, one after the other. "So how are you doing today?"

Nadus closed his mouth and blinked but didn't answer.

"O-kay!" the man said in a drawn-out manner. He sighed, sat on the small crate, stretched his back and cracked his fingers. "Alright, what can I do for you young man?" Using the back of his hand, he wiped the sweat off his sunburned face. Then, he looked up at Nadus as he opened his water bottle. "I'm sure you didn't come here just to stand here. Did you?"

Nadus shook his head.

"Okay. Are you lost or do you want some water?" The man took a gulp and offered his bottle. "I don't have any food to give you."

Nadus shook his head again. "No thank you sir! I'm not thirsty."

"Ah, you speak!" The man grinned. "Okay, so tell me young lad, what's your name?"

"How did you do that?" Nadus asked timidly as he dropped the yam to the ground and stared at the basket. "How did you throw those oranges so high and catch them so fast without dropping them?" The young boy pointed to the green fruits and looked at the old man.

"Ha, you mean how do I juggle?" The old beggar chuckled and coughed. "I figured that's why you came over. You want to know how I juggle. Is that right?"

The young boy nodded. "Yes sir."

"Okay, I'll tell you how, but you didn't answer my last question. I think it will be polite for me to at least know the name of my new pupil. What's your name young lad?"

"It's Na..." The young boy hesitated.

He remembered his father's warnings.

Don't talk to strangers!

Don't tell them your name or where you live!

Most especially, don't eat or drink anything they give you!

"What's the matter? Are you scared of me?" The man looked at Nadus; his yellow eyes were teary, narrow and full of experience.

"Yes sir! No sir, just a little sir!" Nadus stammered. "My father warned me not to talk to strangers or even tell them my name."

"You're right." The beggar slowly rocked his head back and forth. "Yes, I'm indeed a stranger and I'm grateful for your company," he continued. "Not too many people notice me here and only a few take the time to talk to me. I'm thankful and your father taught you well. He must care about you very much." The old man rubbed his aged hands together. "I respect your decision and you don't have to tell me your name. I'll just call you, young lad. Is that okay with you?"

Nadus nodded. "Yessir! That's okay with me."

"Good! Okay now, young lad! The very first thing you need to learn is throwing in an arc. Pick four oranges and throw two to me, okay?"

"Yes sir." Nadus nodded, picked the fruits from the basket and tossed two to the man.

"Great! You have quite a steady throw for a young man. I can already tell you'll make a fine juggler someday."

"Really? Think so?" Nadus exclaimed and his face lit up like a bulb.

"Of course, young lad, I know you can. Always believe in yourself. No matter what!" The man spoke from experience; harsh life had taught him the power and importance of hope.

"Thank you, sir! I just don't know if I could. It seems really hard."

"No! You know looks can be deceiving." The man groaned as he stood to his feet. "My body isn't the way it used to be, you know." He rubbed his elbow and stretched his arm out towards the young boy; his rough and candid face didn't hide any of the pain and discomfort that he was feeling. "My joints and bones hurt and sometimes it burns and sometimes in the mornings, especially during the dry season. It feels like there's broken glass stuck in there."

"I'm sorry sir." Nadus took a few steps forward. "I would have never known from the way you smiled and danced."

"You know what lad, smile at every chance."

"Why?"

"Well, because a smile, a simple smile, baffles an approaching frown and uplifts a saddened heart. It also makes you glow and it increases your face value." The man giggled and revealed his gapped, brown teeth. "Now about dancing, I actually don't feel so much pain when I clap or move my body like before. It's only when I stop that it begins to hurt."

"I'm so sorry sir. Can I help?"

"No, I'm fine!" The man smiled and straightened his back. "I'm used to it. Okay, back to teaching you how to throw in an arc. Watch me closely; start with one orange in each hand." He held the fruits in both hands and watched Nadus. "Good, just like that! Then, you toss the ball in your right hand to your left hand, in an arc, to your eye level. Okay, give it a try."

The young boy looked at the oranges; he shook his hands as if ready but didn't throw the fruits.

"Go ahead, give it a try. Would you?"

"Excuse me sir! What's throwing in an arc?" Nadus looked at the man, feeling a little stupid.

"Oh pardon me. It's my mistake, I forgot to tell you. I'm surely a terrible teacher! An arc is curved in shape." The man pulled out a small stone from his pocket and drew a half circle in the dirt. "See? That's an arc," he continued as he stood up. "Just throw it like a curve to eye level. When it gets to your eye, the highest point, it forms an arc. Go ahead, give it a try."

Nadus watched closely as the man threw the fruit from his right hand to his left hand. Imitating him, Nadus also threw the oranges into the air. He fumbled and dropped them. He tried again with no luck; the oranges fell to the ground. "I can't do it, it's too hard," the young boy whined.

"Throw it again. Juggling isn't hard, anyone can juggle. In fact, everyone in this market is juggling," the old man said patiently.

"What do you mean sir? You're the only one I see throwing oranges in the air. I don't understand you." Nadus looked around, turning in circles.

The man nodded. "Indeed, I'm the only one throwing oranges. That's true, but I'm not the only one juggling! See that woman over there selling tomatoes?" The man pointed towards his left. "Or that gentleman over there, walking quickly? And that boy in the blue shorts! Over there?"

"Yessir, I see all of them." Nadus was even more confused.

"Good. They're all juggling something in life," the old man said. "Ideas, insecurities, chores, sadness, emotions, problems..." he mumbled.

"Huh, I don't get you sir," Nadus said candidly.

"Ah, it's okay, it's okay. You're still a child who hasn't watched or experienced many acts in the play of life. You'll understand what I mean the older you get." He winked. "Okay young lad, try throwing in an arc again."

Nadus nodded and threw the orange. This time, he caught it with his left hand but the fruit didn't hold for long before falling.

"Ugh, I can't do it!" Nadus dropped his arms in defeat. "It's too hard."

"Young lad, you're already giving up after three tries? Well, I would have thought differently about you." The man scratched his bushy moustache. "I mean, the way you stared for several minutes, looked like you had the drive. Well, I suppose I was wrong about you and we'll just call it quits." The old man looked away as though ashamed of Nadus and began to pack up his belongings.

"No, please wait! Please don't stop." Nadus pleaded and desperation gushed through his voice. "Okay, I'll try again, I promise! Please sir don't stop teaching me how."

The beggar turned around; he looked at Nadus and he could read the young boy's sincerity. He knew the amount of humbleness and courage required to beg someone for help, especially in times of despair.

"Please sir." The young boy's eyes and face roused compassion.

"Alright, alright! I'll still teach you but you need to focus and let go of your fears and doubts. To be good at anything in life, not just at juggling, you need to think like a person driven by impulses, but then act and behave like a person with forethought. Now try it again and don't worry if it falls! Remember, you didn't learn to walk or even see overnight." The old man rubbed his eyes. "Some things in life take time to grow and mature."

Nadus, focusing and fighting his many distracting thoughts, propelled the orange out of his hand. Wobbling a bit and tracking the fruit with his eyes, he caught the ball with his other hand and held it securely.

"Good job. You did it! See, it isn't as hard as it seems."

"Yessir." Nadus was proud of himself.

"Now throw one of the two oranges in your left, still in an arc, to your right. Just like before, just with a different hand."

The young boy looked at the oranges and became a little nervous. Like many people faced with expectations and suddenly under pressure, he opened the door of doubt and welcomed in thoughts of failure.

I don't know if I can throw again!

I was perhaps just lucky last time!

What if it falls?

This time there are two oranges!

What'll the old man think of me?

It's heavier!

I can't do it!

"Focus young lad!" the beggar interjected. "Believe in yourself and be confident! Once you believe that you're a product of success, everything about you and everything you do in life, even your few misses becomes a form of success. Throw it!"

Nadus nodded, and without delay tossed it. The orange traveled with the parabolic projectile of a professional juggler and with the swiftness of a wild cat, Nadus caught the fruit firmly with his other hand.

"Yes!" the old man spat. "You're a natural! Ha! You've already learned the basics of juggling. Now, all you have to do is repeat those steps over and over again until your throws and catches improve; before long it will be as easy as say walking or drinking water." The beggar picked his bottle and took a gulp of water. "Ahh! Next, you can simply start adding more oranges as you get more comfortable—three, four and more!"

"That's it, really? That's all I need to know to juggle like you did?" The young boy was excited but a little disappointed; he didn't expect the instructions to be that simple.

"Yes, that's pretty much it."

"Ok sir! Thank you."

"Oh, yes, there's one more thing!" the beggar exclaimed.

"I knew there had to be more!" Nadus sounded excited and relieved.

"A common beginner's mistake is throwing two objects in the air at the same time, instead of one at a time. I'm not saying that you can't catch the two objects thrown together, it just makes things harder for you. Just like if you chased two rabbits in the forest at once, it will be very hard to catch either one, right." The beggar laughed. "One and then the other!"

"Yes, you're right about that!" Nadus laughed as he thought of the injured but swift hare sleeping in their barn. Then, he recalled his family in the marketplace and how he had wandered away from them; panic instantly overcame the young boy and his heart began to pound.

"Are you okay?" the beggar noticed and responded to the boy's sudden mood change. "Are you okay?"

"I'm so sorry sir, but I have to leave now!" Nadus dropped the oranges back into the basket. "I left my brother, Tpyge. Over there!" He turned and pointed to his right. "He must be looking for me. I must go now."

"Oh, I see, you should leave then. I don't want you getting into trouble with your father."

"Yes sir. Take care and I thank you for the lesson." Nadus bowed briefly and turned to leave. "Thank you again!"

"One more thing young lad," The old man added, "by the way, you just told me your brother's name, Tpyge, and I still don't know yours."

"Oh, it's Nadus, sir!" the young boy said as he walked away in a hurry.

"Great, Nadus! That's a good name. It was a pleasure to meet you! You take care and always believe in yourself." The old man smiled and waved. "Perhaps we'll cross paths again!"

Nadus fought his way back through the horde, searching for his older brother. Without warning, the young boy felt a tight grip on his arm that startled him.

"Nadus! Where've you been? I've been looking for you."

The young boy recognized the deep voice; it was his father's.

"I was talking..." Nadus stuttered.

Nadus turned around and locked eyes with Nineb; his palms sweated and his throat was burning hot. Shortly after, his brother appeared out of the crowd and he also didn't look too pleased.

"You were talking to who?" his father asked in a calm voice.

"Nadus, you were meant to stand by my side and help! Not wondering off!" Tpyge yelled. "Wait, you were talking?" The older boy paused and considered his father's question. "Who were you talking to?"

"I was talking to the old man," Nadus replied.

"You were talking to the old man?" his father and brother chorused.

"What old man?" his brother yelled. "Nadus this better not be one of the silly games you play."

"Tpyge, enough! You don't have to raise your voice at your brother."

"But Papa, I was..." the older boy was defensive.

"No buts, Tpyge! That's enough. Let him speak." Nineb pointed at his son in reproof. "Nadus, tell me. What old man are you talking about?"

"The old man, the beggar, standing by the fish." Nadus raised his head and looked at his father.

"Didn't Papa tell you not to talk to strangers?" Tpyge butted in.

"Why were you talking to this old beggar?" his father ignored Tpyge's commentary.

"He was juggling oranges and I wanted to..."

"Nadus, where's the yam?" Tpyge interrupted again.

"Oh no! The yam!" Nadus looked at his bare hands. Then, he looked at his family and tears filled his eyes.

"Nadus, where's the yam?" his father asked calmly.

"On the ground, I dropped it on the ground," Nadus replied as tears flowed down his cheeks. "I dropped it!"

"Where exactly did you drop it?" Nineb asked.

"I dropped it on the ground beside the beggar."

"Nadus! How can you do such a thing? What's wrong with you, huh?" For some reason, Tpyge was the most bitter of the three.

"Tpyge, don't raise your voice." Nineb looked at his older son. He placed his hands on Nadus's shoulder. "That's okay son. There's no reason to cry. Let's go find this old man you talk about and collect our yam."

"Okay Papa! I'm very sorry," Nadus said. "He's sitting over there."

The young boy led the way through the crowd towards the old beggar and his brother and father tagged along.

"Papa, he was standing right here." Nadus pointed to the ground and looked around. "Honest!"

"Nadus are you sure this is the place?" His father looked concerned. "I don't see any sign of him, just fish waste and many flies."

Nadus nodded. "Yes, this is where I was standing. Honest Papa!"

"This place is filthy," his brother grumbled. "I don't see this man and our yam is nowhere to be found."

"Nadus your brother is right, you know."

"You got scammed! You were tricked and the yam was taken right under your nose. Geez Nadus!" Tpyge spat and fended off a few flies trying to land on his face.

"No! I'm not making this up. The man was sitting right here and I was standing here." Nadus showed his father. "Papa, I'm sorry, please forgive me!" He became teary again.

"I know son, we all make mistakes and I forgive you. I trust you and I know you're not making this up. As your brother said, you probably got scammed. Now you see why I tell you to be careful when in the market."

"Yes Papa!" Nadus looked at the ground.

"I thank the heavens. It could have been worse, say you got kidnapped or hurt." Nineb patted his son on the back. "Next time, just don't leave your brother's sight and take my advice. Don't talk to strangers and if you really need to talk to someone you don't know, be sure to remain watchful, okay?"

"Yes Papa. I'm sorry."

"Yes Nadus, listen to Papa!" Tpyge scolded his brother.

"Tpyge, what's the problem? You seem to be taking the loss of the yam very personally. What's the matter with you? Are you hiding something from me or did that one tuber really mean so much to you?" Nineb smiled and held his son by the back of his neck. "What is it?"

"Come on Papa!" Tpyge twisted his neck to the side and removed his father's hand. "You know how much time and sweat I invested into those yams," Tpyge replied. "I don't get to play like him. Its work, work, work all day! Now Nadus lost the yam, the fruit of my hard work, while he was playing instead of working."

"Yes, I know my son. We both worked hard this season." Nineb patted his son's head. "You're a very hardworking man and I'm proud of you."

Tpyge looked at his father and cracked a small smile. "Thank you Papa!" It was his first smile since they found his younger brother.

"Okay boys, that's enough trouble for one day!" Nineb yawned as he placed his arms around the boys. "We found your brother, sold the yams, now it's time to go home."

Before long, Nadus and his family packed their belongings and left the marketplace for their humble home. The young boy was still perplexed about the sudden and mysterious disappearance of the old man and their yam. He was also a little disappointed that he didn't ask the old man for his name or ask if he had any family or children. Nevertheless, Nadus was happy and he didn't let the past get to him. He had apologized to his father for losing the yam and was forgiven. He at least told the old man his name and importantly he remembered the old man's advice about being a "product of success" and the idea of successful mistakes. As they trekked back, Nadus told his father and brother all the details of his odd encounter with the beggar and his newly acquired skill in juggling. They all laughed at the way Nadus painted his mental imagery and his facial expressions. Like any good family, they supported his ideas and listened to his accounts, even though they were full of doubt. For Nadus, watching and talking to the old man was one of the most enchanting performances and edifying conversations he had ever experienced. From that moment, despite his father's deep desire for him to go to school and learn a "respectable profession," Nadus decided he was going to become a juggler like the old man, a secret ambition that he kept to himself.

8

CHAPTER EIGHT:

ᛒ

"By persevering the egg walks on legs."
African Proverb

At the peak of the Itegneres festival, the Orajnamilik were in the full swing of things: chanting, dancing and entertaining the dignitaries and the villagers with their juggling and acrobatics. Like a trained hunter in the forest, Nadus watched the masqueraders as they ran across the dance floor. He continued to study their coordination and analyze their dexterity with the torches. The masqueraders were performing a novel juggling style that Nadus didn't quite understand and that bothered him.

They throw the torches and wait for two seconds.

Then spin around, back flip, catch the fire torch.

Actually, they wait three seconds and back flip.

Nadus couldn't decipher the technique.

Wait, wait, I just might be right!

No, I don't think that's it.

Frustration sprouted in his mind.

This is so difficult!

"Come on Nadus!" Idnurub yelled and interrupted his friend's train of thought. "Are you mad or something? How can you say such a thing? Actually, you know what?"

"What?" Nadus looked at his friend and frowned. "What do you know that I don't know?"

"I think you're just jealous!"

"Jealous?" Nadus laughed. "Jealous of what?"

"You're just jealous that you can't perform magic like the Orajnamilik. Nadus, look at the way they're moving, incredible! No human being can ever move like that!" Idnurub coughed repeatedly and spat. The dust was getting to his sensitive lungs. "There's no doubt that they're the spirits of our ancestors," he added in a raspy voice.

"Oh, wait, wait Idnurub!" Nadus scratched his head. "So you're telling me that it's a man over there!"

"Huh?" Idnurub looked at his friend.

"I mean, how do you even know it's a man? For all I care it could just as well be a woman. Idnurub is there something you know and you're not telling me?" Nadus rubbed his auricle and gave his friend a wry look.

"Huh? What man are you talking about, which man? I don't think I get you. You're confusing me." The boy's face showed his frustration and bewilderment.

"Weren't you the one who said that the masquerader was a man?"

"What, when? When did I say that? I remember just saying they're the spirits of our ancestors!"

"No before that!"

"When?"

You said 'he just did a back flip' and according to our grammar teacher the words 'his' and 'he' are used to describe a man. I lie?"

"Ah, ha, now I get you!" Idnurub sneezed and blew his nose. "You're so stupid you know, Mister know it all!" He hissed and laughed. "Well class, you also know that the words 'his' and 'he.'" Idnurub raised his hand and spoke in a forced deep voice, "a possessive pronoun can also be used to describe boys and due to my brilliance, those masqueraders could also be boys."

"That was good." Nadus grabbed his stomach as he laughed. "That was very funny, a good impression of him! He does talk like that! Seriously."

"Yes he does. He's too funny!"

"Okay, now based on that grammatical sentence," the young boy also deepened his voice, "we can conclude that those are some big boys dancing over there."

"Nadus!" Idnurub exclaimed as though suddenly in pain.

"What? What's biting your head?" Nadus smiled at his friend.

"Come on! We're not in class, I don't want to think about school or any more of that rubbish, for now! I'm enjoying myself. Anyway, you think you're so smooth, huh?"

"What are you talking about?"

"You're trying to avoid my question and not tell me that you're jealous of them." Idnurub nudged his friend.

"Please! I'm not jealous of anyone."

"Don't worry. I won't look at you any differently if you just admit that you're jealous. I'll still be your friend and I won't tell anyone that you're jealous of the Orajnamilik," Idnurub teased as he danced to the music.

"Didn't you just hear me?" Nadus spoke louder. "I'm not jealous!"

"Sure Nadus! I believe you."

"I'm serious! I'm jealous!"

"Of course, I knew you're jealous," Idnurub added as he giggled.

"I mean, I'm not jealous. Especially not jealous of those masqueraders just because they juggle." Nadus pointed to the Orajnamilik. "Anyway, it's not even magic, it's not real. In fact, you're crazy for thinking that's magic!" Nadus took a defensive stance.

"Nadus watch your mouth!" Idnurub covered his friend's mouth with his hand. "Hush, don't say that!" The boy spoke in a lower tone, "how can you say such a thing? You know they can hear us and they can read our minds!" He glanced at the masqueraders. "I don't want them coming over here and I surely don't want to get flogged."

"Well, I'm not lying and I'm serious about what I said, it's not magic! It's just a bunch of tricks. Did you even know that I can do a front flip and juggle also? Really, all you have to do is…"

Acting pompous and insecure, the young boy was about to brag about his endowed talents and disclose his secret aspirations.

"Please stop!" Idnurub covered his friend's mouth again. "You're playing with fire and I beg you to stop. Please don't disrespect them!"

"Idnurub, why are you begging me? I haven't done anything wrong!"

"Sure, okay I agree that you haven't done anything wrong but they're so close to us. I mean Nadus they're right there!"

"Okay, okay! Yes, yes Idnurub! You're right." Nadus rolled his eyes and rocked his head from side to side. "I suppose I better stop and be quiet before they hear us," he lowered his voice insincerely and smiled, "but all I'm saying is that flipping, like that, while juggling is pretty easy!" Nadus raised his voice again and pointed at the masqueraders. "Well it's not that easy I suppose but it's not as hard as you think. I'm not lying, all you have to do is sim-" Nadus swallowed his words and froze in fright.

Without warning, three Orajnamilik masqueraders strayed from the pack and like ravenous hyenas dashed towards the two schoolboys. They were chanting and waving their bamboo sticks as though ready to attack.

"Nadus! I told you to stop!" Idnurub clenched his teeth and fist.

Nadus didn't respond to his friend; he was momentarily arrested by anxiety and immobilized by catatonia. Like an encroaching tornado, the three masqueraders moved and planted themselves right in front of the terrified schoolboys. The villagers in the vicinity scrambled and quickly parted. Then, the masqueraders began to bang their sticks on the ground, beside the boys and close to their feet. Stupefied by the cacophony, Nadus didn't flinch. Idnurub, in contrast, trembled, cried and was so scared of the unexpected behavior that he accidentally wet himself. The masqueraders stopped and stared at the two boys, hovering over them and smelling them. They then focused their attention to Nadus, humming as they continued to stare into the young boy's eyes. Nadus didn't blink as he stared back at the masqueraders and for a fleeting second the young boy was visited by a sinister vision of a burning hut and crying villagers. Nadus finally nictated his watery eyes and the three masqueraders without delay began to dance and chant around Nadus like celebrators at a bonfire. They continued for a few minutes without touching or flogging the young boy and his friend as many of the villagers had expected they would; they retreated and joined the others on the dance floor. The audience mumbled and was astonished because the masqueraders rarely targeted people in the crowd, circled them and left without flogging them. Besides being expert jugglers and acrobats, the Orajnamilik were also skilled emotional investigators and like trained dogs were able to read people's actions and analyze subtle interpersonal cues not easily understood or interpreted. The masqueraders, simply by looking at people and the way they carried themselves, could tell if they were happy, angry, anxious, lying, scared, insecure or even "full of hate."

On most occasions, when surrounded by the daunting masqueraders, people have been known to tremble, weep, urinate, defecate and confess their bad deeds and crimes to humanity. The Orajnamilik, in a way, were strict and proactive judges. They sentenced wrongdoers right away, punished them and consequently "set them free" of their consuming guilt. Clemency was uncommon and on that day, their sudden change of heart was a mystery to the villagers. It could have been due to an extrasensory appeal from the oracle or a divine intervention by the deity or something special about the young boy. Notwithstanding, on that day and in the face of trial, Nadus recalled the beggar's advice and didn't flinch. As a result, he masked his underlying fears and became unreadable to the masqueraders. Before long, as the boys caught their breath and recuperated from their brief and shivery encounter, the Orajnamilik wrapped up their famed performance and filed off the dance floor, the same way they arrived. The musicians stopped playing their instruments and followed them. The town crier ran onto the podium and announced the end of the masquerade performance and the start of the "football celebration." As soon as he completed the message, the villagers cheered. The fleshy crier bowed and walked off the stage. The king and his chiefs stood up from their seats and also walked off the podium. They got on their horses and headed towards the grassy plains. Nadus, his friend and the jubilant villagers trailed behind the royal cavalry. They were singing and dancing and many of them waved fresh leaves in their hands.

9

CHAPTER NINE:

❧

"A fish is the last to acknowledge the existence of water."
African Proverb

The sun was resting behind a few satin clouds, ruffling through the pearl-colored sky. The temperature hadn't changed much; it was still very hot. However, the quiescent afternoon breeze had finally roused and was slowly cooling the villagers as they ascended up the steep, grass-covered hill. The top of the hill was flat and wide and marked the highest point in the village. As a result of the altitude and peculiar soil composition, the top of the hill nurtured a unique assortment of plants not found anywhere else in the area. The grass and the leaves on the few trees were deeper in color and contrast, endowing the scenery with a soothing green hue. Depending on the luminosity and the time of the day, the hilltop served as a multifunctional venue for several engagements. In the mornings, mostly during the dry season, it served as the training ground for the Snoitandetinu, the place where they learned, practiced and perfected their fighting and defensive tactics. In the afternoons, it was a great place for picnics and in the evenings, due to the elevation and remarkable view of the entire village, it was a popular romantic spot where young men took their dates to unwind and to look at the stars. Nevertheless, the hilltop was mostly known by the villagers as the battling arena for major football duels, the few matches that the king attended and in which every village boy dreamed of being the star player. The dignitaries and the royal guards reached the top first and without ado headed for the four trees, across and adjacent to the field, that served as the royal viewing booth. The dignitaries descended from their horses and took a seat on elegantly decorated benches positioned to shade them from sunlight. The guards tethered the animals to the tree trunks and then positioned themselves behind the dignitaries. The villagers, on the other hand, lined up around the rectangular field and continued to sing. Nadus and Idnurub, although still a little shaken up, squeezed their way again to the front of the line.

As always, the villagers were all excited and passionate about the appearance of their turf—to the point that some of them were angered by a few small brown patches of dead grass, blemishing the surface of the green playing field. Their intense passion might have stemmed from the fact that many of them, especially the older folks, were physically and financially involved in its construction. A few years back, during the Itegneres festival, the king cast his vision of building a "superior field" on the hilltop that could rival those found in the city. He had briefly explained the potential benefits: a tourist attraction, an entertainment venue and most significantly, community pride. Afterwards, he detailed the price tag and although the village still lacked many essential amenities, the villagers were more welcoming to the idea than they were to his previous proposal of building a well and a clinic. The citizens began to chip-in from their savings and many of them even assisted with the labor, including clearing the shrubs, walking several miles to the stream to fetch water and irrigate the grass, as well as guarding the site from vandalism. Mostly because of its natural topography and the deciduous grass that grew on the hilltop, the design and construction of the football field was quite simple. The city contractor only had to level the grass, paint the sidelines and erect the ready-made goal posts. It was the fastest "big project" ever built in the village, completed in a few months. At the following Itegneres festival, the field was officially launched and from that day forth the village acknowledged and observed the yearly "football celebration."

"Alright boys, gather around, gather around boys," the football coach yelled and beckoned to twelve football players, squatting and stretching by the sideline. "Quick, hurry and gather around, all of you in a circle!"

"*Yessir*!" the boys chorused and immediately joined their coach.

"Alright boys, listen up!" the tall, lanky man exclaimed as he joined the fraternal embrace. "Today is big for all of you, for all of us. The day has finally come for us to show our people what we're made of, the reason why we've been training for many months. How are you boys feeling?"

"*Good, coach*," the young players replied.

"I know you can do better than that!" the coach scolded them. "I said how are you feeling?" he asked in a louder tone.

"*Good, coach!!!*" the boys yelled.

"That's much better! Now I want to hear the excitement in your voice. So tell me, are you boys ready to do this, are you ready to win?"

"*Yes coach!!!*" they yelled.

"Can't hear you!" the coach stomped his feet on the grass as he spoke.

"*Yes coach!!!*" they roared and stomped their feet.

"That's more like it, much better! I hope you boys know," the football coach paused, "that I'm proud of you, very proud of your dedication and diligence and you have inspired me."

"*Thank you coach!!!*"

"You've once again showed me that boys with time and proper training do become men, and I'm proud to be in the midst of young men who challenged themselves to be better. It wasn't easy but you all did it! I saw the transformation of amateurs into professionals and I'm very pleased.

As your math instructor and football coach, you know I'm strict." The lanky man laughed with delight. "And some of you might even think that I'm wicked and evil. Regardless of your opinions, I can proudly say that I'm a man of principle and I know from experience that certain things in life are constant. For example, I know that 'two' plus 'three' equals 'five.' Similarly, I know that 'dedication' plus 'hard work' equals 'success.'

You boys have entrusted your talents in my care and at every practice you listened to me with diligence, took my advice and showed me dedication and perseverance."

The young football players nodded as though in contemplation.

"And because of this I want to thank you and let you know that there shouldn't be any reason why success isn't ours. I hope I have led you boys by example as I don't know any other means to lead but by example."

"Yes coach, you always do."

"Thank you coach!!!"

"Good, I'm glad! Now you'll need to keep your eyes on the prize." The coach disengaged himself from the huddle and pointed to his eyes. He then touched his forehead with both hands. "And that means winning this game! Yes!" He smacked his fists together, "It's not always about winning. Yes, I know that most games in life are lost, not won! However, today our opponents will not play by this rule and they will be concerned only with wearing you out and kicking as many goals in our net as possible. No! We can't let them do that to us! We need to hold them accountable for their actions, win this match!"

"Yes coach!!!"

"Boys, I mean," he smiled as he scratched his eyebrow, "if winning or losing wasn't so important in the game of football, there wouldn't be any reason or point keeping scores, right?"

"Yessir! Yes coach!!!" they yelled with the enthusiasm of young cadets.

"Good! Now, before we all get fired up and head to the field I want you all to promise me that you'll act like gentlemen. Observe the rules, play to victory and most importantly don't give in to any of their tactics or tricks, regardless if we're winning or losing! I want a fine game!"

"Yes coach!!!" the boys treaded their feet heavily and repeatedly.

"All our drills and intense training, you still remember our motto?"

"Yessir!!!"

"Okay, say it, let me hear it. Winning is..." The coach waved his fingers in the air as though painting.

"*Winning is a habit and so is losing!!!*" they yelled and brought their hands together, creating a single enormous clap.

"Boys, that's excellent! That's right, winning and losing are habits and like any habit they can be corrected. Just be sure to keep..."

The coach's motivating speech was interrupted by a loud and obnoxious honk, followed by the revving of an engine. The instructor raised his eyebrows and the entire team turned to their side and took a gander at the noisemaker. It was a medium-sized lorry, climbing up the rugged and winding hill. At the back and in the wooden carrier, the city football players and several of their supporters were sitting, standing and swaying as the vehicle struggled with the terrain; they were crammed together like cocoa seeds in a dry and shriveled pod. After a few huffing and puffing, the large metallic beast reached the top of the hill and was maneuvered to a stop. The driver, a tall and skinny man, opened the door, got down and inspected the tires. Then, he pulled out a cigarette and a lighter from his breast pocket, placed the butt on his lips and lit it. He took two puffs, exhaled and spat to the side.

"We're clear, all clear!" The gaunt man shouted, walking and banging the side of the lorry with his fist.

The passenger's door opened and a short, burly man with broad shoulders, a paunch and a trimmed mustache got down from the truck. He was wearing a black jockey cap, a green and white tracksuit and black running shoes. The man's face was lined with scars and his eyes were hidden from the sun by oversized aviator glasses, making him somewhat intimidating. His name was *Inas-Ahcaba*. He was the head coach who had earned a reputation of being a ruthless opportunist. The domineering man walked around to the back of the lorry, unlatched the wooden tailgate and beckoned to the football players.

"Get down, boys!" Insa-Ahcaba knocked on the tailgate and offered a scornful laugh. "It's time for us to teach these villagers a lesson in football! Sound good?" He smacked his lips and continued to chew his gum.

"*Yes!!! Yeah!!!*" the city boys roared from inside the truck.

The players immediately threw their duffle bags out of the lorry onto the ground and jumped down, one after the other.

"Hey, hey, watch it, careful as you jump! Do you understand me?" the coach lamented. "I can't afford to have any sprained ankles! I need all of you in optimal condition to give them a real flogging!" He turned around, lifted his glasses and frowned as he eyed the village team.

"*Yeah!!! Yes coach!!!*" the boys replied and their deep voices resonated across the field.

The village players stared at the city team and were bombarded with feelings of awe, admiration and panic. The city players looked much older; they were expressionless, taller, bigger and more muscular in stature. Unlike the village boys who wore old khaki shorts and tie-dyed tees, the city boys were clothed in custom uniforms that caught the eye. Every one of them, with the exception of their goalie, wore green spandex shorts and white jerseys with names and numbers printed on the back. They were sipping on bottled sugary beverages and were outfitted in the latest gear: black cleats, long white socks and shin-guards.

"Listen boys! We've trained too hard for this game," the village coach spoke after a few minutes of gawking; his voice was a little dry. "Don't let them intimidate you. Okay?"

"*Yesssir,*" the young players responded with less enthusiasm.

"What's the matter with you? Why don't you sound excited?"

The village players glanced at each other; they uttered a few mumbles but no audible response.

"Come on boys, speak up!"

One of the players raised his hand. "Excuse, sir! Mister Ohtosel."

"Yes *Ognoc* you have a question?" The coach pointed to the boy.

"Sir, I don't know if we can beat them, they all look like men," he stuttered. The boys looked at each other, mumbling and nodding their heads.

"Nonsense! Absolute nonsense!" the coach interjected. "We've worked too hard to let their show get to us. Listen to me," Ohtosel held his right earlobe and pointed with his other hand, "and listen to me good! You're the best of the best in our village." He pointed to his feet, "and every one of you standing here, earned your spot. I didn't just hand it you. Okay?"

"*Yessir,*" they answered back.

"Do you get me?"

"*Yessir!*"

"But coach, understand," the goalie raised his hand as though asking for clarification, "that we don't have the proper uniforms and equipments like them. They're so lucky."

"They're hairy men and they're drinking juices," another boy added.

"Oh, look at the way that they're kicking it up." A third player pointed to four of the city boys practicing and juggling a ball.

"Lucky? Lucky? Enough nonsense!" the coach interrupted his players. "Winners don't whine in the face of a challenge and you're all whining!" Ohtosel scuffed and his voice revealed his aggravation. "You've not even stepped foot on the field and you're already beating yourselves down. The inferior man blames others for his problems, while the superior one blames himself! Understood?"

"*Yes coach!*"

"You're not lucky to be here, representing our village, you're fortunate! And one thing I know for sure is that luck results when adequate practice meets chance, the right opportunity! You've all practiced hard and you all have the potential to win! But potential doesn't mean anything if you're not willing to do something with it. Am I clear?"

"*Yes coach!*" The boys sounded more excited.

"Recall what you've learned during practice and apply it. You're men now, not boys!!! Is that right?"

"*Yes coach!!!*" the village boys shouted.

"If there's anything in this world that I never ever want to be accused of doing, it's not doing my best!" Ohtosel exclaimed. "As your coach, I want you all to live by this standard and when you get on that field today, you give me…"

As the two coaches rallied their players and prepared their minds for the first forty-five minutes, the referee and the linesman walked to the center of the field. The two middle-aged men looked similar in appearance and were about the same height. They both carried a shiny metal whistle around their necks and wore black cleats, black shorts and nameless jerseys. The referee's jersey was striped with black and white lines while the linesman wore a solid black one. They were both from the city and had arrived in the lorry with the city team. Nevertheless, their affiliation with the city didn't compromise the integrity of the game as both men had taken oaths to disregard personal views and judge every game in a evenhanded manner. The officials formally shook hands and then the referee raised his right hand straight up and blew his whistle. Without delay, the two teams, standing on opposite sides, stepped onto the field and walked towards the center. The villagers cheered, clapped, whistled and began to mock the city team with satirical songs. The city boys, focused on their mission, tuned out the noise and continued to march with devotion. They were confident and it showed all over their stoic postures and expressions. Before long, the opposing teams were standing behind the officials, lined up and facing each other. The boys were all sweating, fidgeting and breathing heavily like combative rams about to butt horns. The straight-faced officials stood at ease and the referee placed his hands behind his back. The linesman, in contrast, held a leather ball in his arm and slung a white handkerchief over his shoulders.

"Captains, please step forward," the referee spoke in a distinct accent that was foreign to the village boys. Straight away, two tall boys stepped forward and shook hands with the two officials.

"I assume you both know the rules of the game and I expect you to respect them! Today we'll be playing an eight-versus-eight game and that means a lot of running. Your playing formation is at the full discretion of your coaches, you choose the position of the attackers, mid-fielders and defenders. Important! The ball should remain on the ground," he said in an authoritative tone and pointed to the grass, "at all times, except during a throw-in. None of you can touch the ball with your hands, of course with the exception of the goalkeepers." He nodded and looked at the captains. "Minimal body contact is permitted only when dribbling or struggling to gain possession of the ball. Let this be a warning to you, elbowing, punching, biting or scratching is unacceptable and depending on the severity will lead to a yellow or a red card and dismissal from the game! Understand?"

"Yes sir," the team captains replied.

"Now, off-sides aren't permitted. I don't want to see any of your players standing close to the posts just waiting to score a goal. I will penalize you! This game is called football. You should all be on your feet, kicking the ball and running around! Alright, I want you two to play fair and give me a clean game. The less rubbish the better! Do I make myself clear?"

"Yes sir."

"Okay! Any other questions before we start?"

"No sir." They shook their heads.

"All ready then!" The referee signaled to the linesman.

The linesman squatted and placed the ball on the white circle painted on the green grass, in the middle of the playing field.

Still standing upright, the referee put his hand into his breast pocket and pulled out a silver coin that shined in the sun. He inspected the metal piece and blew it a few times. He then rubbed it on his shirt and placed it in his palm. "Alright, I'll give the home team the honors to go first, heads or tails?" The referee looked at the village captain.

Ituobijd paused and looked at his rival. "I choose heads, sir." He nodded and licked his lips. "Yessir, I'll go with heads." He blinked and the side of his face twitched.

"Okay, let's see what we have here." The referee tossed the coin up in the air and caught it with his right hand. He placed the coin on the back of his hand and revealed it. "Heads it is!" he exclaimed. "Kickoff goes to the home team." Using both hands, he pointed to his side and the players assumed their respective positions on the field. Then, the referee blew his whistle and Ituobijd kicked the ball to his left. The match commenced and the villagers clapped, cheered and sang louder.

Go home!

Hey! Hey! City boys!

We're the Village people,

Singing songs of victory,

On the hills of glory!

Hey! Hey!

Six thousand voices,

Roaring us on to victory!

And if you are a City fan,

Surrender or you'll cry!

Go home!

The ball rolled on the plot and was received by the left-winger. The boy stopped the ball with his foot, pivoted, and began to run with it towards the opponent's goal post. He was short, skinny and very quick on his feet. In fact, he moved exactly as fast as the ball so that from a distance the white leather sphere appeared to be glued to his faded cleats. A midfielder and fullback from the city team like hungry beasts rushed to stop the ball's advance. The village boy anticipated their rush and abruptly stopped the ball as the two approached. With a flourish he nudged the ball to his left as if to sprint down the line but then with a flick of his toe tipped it just over their heads towards the middle of the field. As the winger's two opponents tried to change their direction, he slipped between them. The crowd's applause enveloped him as he drove towards the goal. He sidestepped the central midfielder with a zigzagging dribble, but the middle fullback quickly converged on him. The winger glanced up to see his options, four opponents were closing on him from all directions, so he knew a teammate had to be open. On the opposite side of the penalty area, the village team's right-winger waved his arms frantically. "Osaf! Cross it!"

Osaf-Anikrub saw the opportunity and didn't hesitate. He sent the ball over the heads of the fullbacks and it hit his teammate square in the chest. The right-winger settled the ball at his feet, but before he could take another touch he was muscled aside by the burly defender guarding him. The city team's defender tapped the ball up the field and then, with a deceptively graceful motion, sent the ball careening over the midline. The crowd booed in dismay as the ball flew through the air into the village team's half. Midfielders from both teams fought for position as they watched the ball fall towards them. As it neared the ground, the four players pushed each other and leaped together. The ball didn't make contact with their sweat covered heads and landed on the grass, bouncing and rolling off. Moving swiftly like a desert eagle and as though their lives were at stake, the boys dashed towards the round spinning object.

Of the four runners, the right-winger of the city team reached the ball first and tapped it slightly with his feet. The ball moved away and the stocky boy guided it with the tenacity of a rhinoceros. Quickly countering, the two village players, the center midfielder and center defender, increased their speeds and caught up. They tried to tackle him but fell short as they were no match to his heavy build and powerful ball-control. The stocky boy ran a little further, stopped the ball and then pointed to his left. He shouted and kicked the ball with the front of his boot, firing it into the air and towards his team's captain. The captain understood the tip and ran to his left to take delivery of the ball. He dribbled around the left defender and headed straight for the goalie. As soon as he entered the penalty box, the city captain paused for a half-second to set his feet and then fired a powerful, curving shot towards the left corner of the post. The goalie tracked the ball as he swiftly dove with his arms outstretched and landed hard on the grass. He rose to his feet and the villagers rejoiced. The boy had a grin on his face and he was holding the ball in his brown tattered gloves. It was his first save of the day and he had successfully thwarted his opponent's plan. As the crowd subdued their acclaims, the referee blew his whistle and the city players retreated back towards their half of the playing field. The goalkeeper walked out of the goal box, signaling and shouting to the defenders. He threw the ball to the right defender who kicked it up the sideline to the midfielder on his side. The midfielder trapped the ball and began to dribble it across the field. The villagers and their rivals, the city supporters, sang different and contrasting satirical songs about pride, winning and victory. Their glorious tunes brought the top of the hill to life and further pumped up the players.

The village midfielder was approached by two challengers that he swiftly and cleverly outsmarted with calculated stops and turns. He ran with the ball for a few feet and then kicked it to Osaf-Anikrub. The skinny boy arrested the ball and pinned it with his cleats. Before he could assign a task to the leather sphere, he was rushed and tackled by three players. The skinny boy tried to escape the evident ambush but ended up tripping and losing control of the ball. The city team was playing with aggression and leaving the village boys with no breathing room. The city right-defender ran with the ball and kicked it to his midfielder. The taller boy moved with the ball for a few yards before kicking it to the team captain, the striker. The captain took the ball and stormed towards the penalty box. He dribbled around the first defender in his path and passed the ball to his teammate. The left-winger moved the ball forward, turned to his right and touched it back through to the captain. It was a quick and seamless transaction; before long, he was in front of the goalpost, directly facing the goalie. The captain nudged the ball just a few inches forward and raised his right leg as though ready to nail the ball to the top-left corner of the post.

"Don't! Please don't fall for it." Nadus and Idnurub exclaimed, jumping and gesticulating with their hands.

Anxious and pressured, the goalie prematurely reacted. As soon as he dove, the captain fired a fast curve-ball to his right. The goalkeeper realized the ruse. In midair, he turned his head to watch helplessly as the ball slammed into the net.

"*Go, go goal! It's a goal!!!*" Grouped together and standing by the sideline, the city supporters screamed and jumped.

"That's right, I'm the captain!" the boy shouted as he dashed towards the sideline, stooping with his arms spread-out like a large bird.

The city captain stopped before reaching the white line and flipped backwards. As soon as his feet touched the ground, he kneeled, pointed to the crowd with both hands and pretended to be sobbing; all at once, he was surrounded and embraced by his elated teammates. The villagers booed and the city supporters sang aloud. A minute later, the referee was standing in the center of the field, wiping his perspiring forehead with a folded handkerchief. He placed the cloth back into his shorts, looked at the stopwatch slung around his neck and blew his whistle. The players heeded the signal, marching to their respective positions.

"Hey brothers," Ituobijd heaved a deep sigh and spoke, "we need to be more organized out there, make sure we don't act like chickens with no heads." He blew his nose and continued to walk. "Those boys are fast and they're playing big on the offensive, you know."

"Yes I know but to make things worse they're stronger and much bigger than us," Osaf-Anikrub added, "and they're not playing fair."

"Tell me about that! It's so hot and they probably have so much energy from their fancy drinks!" a second boy chimed in.

"What can I say, huh? Can't do anything about that—they're notorious for playing rough! Either way we have to listen to Coach and we can't allow them to get into our heads. It's important that we each know our positions so that we're spread out and have room for wide passes. Do you follow?"

"Yeah, okay sure!" the four players answered.

"Also don't forget that our positions aren't permanent, say you have the ball with no one covering you, don't feel the need to stop at the end of your zone. Just keep moving and continue to attack, one of us will surely cover you."

"Understood!" The right-winger stopped and tied his shoe lace.

"Likewise, if you're the nearest defender, closest to the ball, you have to pressure the player to release it, even if you're outside of your zone."

"Alright captain," the boys replied.

"Thank you! Remember, we play like gentlemen!" Ituobijd grasped the midfielder on his shoulders before jogging towards the referee.

The official placed the ball on the grass, positioned it on the white dot with his foot and blew his whistle. Ituobijd steered the ball forward and immediately kicked it back towards the midfielder. The other player received the ball gracefully but didn't spend much time with it.

"Enoel, take it!" The midfielder pointed and quickly sent the ball up in the air towards the right-winger.

Enoel-Arreis jumped up and caught the ball with his upper body. However, due to the force and impact of the shot, the ball didn't drop to his feet. Instead, it bounced off his chest and rolled away. Without wasting time, the right-winger pursued the ball and was instantly assailed by two opponents. Enoel-Arreis kept his cool and focused on his control of the ball. The first opponent dashed towards him and purposely slid on the grass with both feet forward. The malicious tactic didn't work as Enoel didn't trip; he simply dug his foot under the ball and raised it slightly off the ground. He jumped over the defender's legs and continued to run with the ball. Right away, the second opponent ran towards the right-winger, cut into his space with his hip and tried to steal the ball in the process. Enoel-Arreis lost his balance and control. The city player, without delay, took advantage of the situation and kicked the ball away. As the villagers hooted and hollered, the leather sphere like a frightened bird spun and flew through the dry air and past the sideline.

"Out of bounds!" The linesman threw his handkerchief on the ground, raised his hand and pointed to his left. "The ball goes to the village team."

The audience cheered. Enoel-Arreis ran towards the linesman and nodded as he took the ball from the official. Using both hands and standing on the sideline, he threw the leather sphere into the field towards Osaf-Anikrub. The left-winger caught the ball and passed it back to Enoel-Arreis who was already sprinting ahead. The right-winger didn't delay; he ran a few yards with the ball and then passed it to Ituobijd. The striker gladly accepted the ball; he took a quick breath and briefly surveyed his environment. Twelve seconds later, he had already dribbled through the two city defenders and was going in for kill.

"Stop him! He's coming!" The city goalie shouted and pointed as Ituobijd neared the post. "Stop him!"

The defenders, like wild dogs chasing a bush rat, gyrated, barked and pounced on the village captain. Ituobijd tried to outwit them but couldn't; they were faster, stronger and very aggressive. All of a sudden, the village captain fell to the ground, holding his face and grunting in pain. He had been elbowed in the chin by one of the hefty defenders. Nadus, his friend and the audience uttered choruses of disapproval; the referee and linesman left their positions and ran towards the scene.

"Are you okay?" The referee hunkered down and examined the boy's face. There was no blood, only a minor bruise. "Can you see me clearly?"

"Yessir, I can see." Ituobijd looked up but was momentarily dazed and suffering from diplopia, double vision.

"Do you want to continue in the game?" the referee asked as he lent a helping hand and pulled the boy to his feet.

"Yessir, I'm fine." Ituobijd wiped his elbows and knees. "I think it was just a minor fall." The captain shook his head, spat and held his jaw.

"It's your call." The referee placed his hand into his breast pocket and pulled out a yellow-colored card. "Foul committed by the city team!" he exclaimed, facing the city defender and raising the card above his head. "Yellow card and a penalty kick awarded to the village team."

The villagers rejoiced and were pleased with the verdict. The linesman picked up the ball that was resting at the corner arc of the field and placed it on the white spot in the penalty box, directly in front of the goal. The referee then blew his whistle and all the players except the city goalie vacated the area. Ituobijd and his teammates circled together and said a quick prayer to the heavens. About a minute later, Osaf-Anikrub left the herd and walked towards the ball. The player had meekly volunteered and was sanctioned by his teammates to take the penalty kick as Ituobijd, the lead striker and captain, was still lightheaded. The skinny boy stood in front of the goalpost and touched the ball slightly with his cleats as though gauging its weight. The villagers clapped and stomped their feet; all of a sudden, a strong wind of jitteriness and anxiety blew his way and the boy began to shiver. Standing by the sideline, the linesman raised his handkerchief and the other official blew the whistle. Osaf-Anikrub looked at the metal goalposts and then at the goalie who was wearing a red long-sleeve jersey and black shorts. The tall, stoic goalkeeper rocked back and forth on his feet and looked straight at his rival with both arms spread out. Osaf-Anikrub blinked and kicked the sphere, firing a fast ground-ball towards the left corner of the goal. The goalie reacted and followed the ball; moments later, there was an instant roar on the hilltop.

"*No, no, no!*" the villagers bawled. "*No!!!*"

"It can't be!" Nadus lamented and placed both hands on his head.

"Why now?" Idnurub uttered with sorrow in his voice. "It's not fair!"

Osaf-Anikrub dropped to his knees, cursing and delivering a number of blows to the parched grass. The ball didn't pass the heavily-built goalie and was crisply smothered in his hands. The city goalie kicked the ball into the field and both teams chased after it. Equally gaining and losing possession of the ball, the two teams ran across the field, back and forth like migrating birds. The city boys continued to play heavily on the offensive and pressure their rivals. The village boys, on the other hand, took the defensive stance and continued to send long passes to their striker. As they raced across the field and the bright fiery sphere watched from above, a rising heat wave churned through the field. In no time, all the boys were drenched and feeling the pinch; they were quickly dissipating their water and energy reserves and the intensity of their struggles for the ball dwindled. It wasn't long before the city boys scored again. A few minutes later, before the village team could regroup, the city team scored another goal and the villagers choked on their words. Devastated yet optimistic, they continued to urge on their team with applause and songs. A few minutes passed, and then the referee blew his whistle, signifying the end of the exciting first half; the city boys were leading by three goals.

10

CHAPTER TEN:

"If you provoke a rattlesnake, you must be prepared to be bitten by it."
African Proverb

As the fatigued players sauntered off the battle ground in opposite directions towards their respective coaches, the school choir trotted onto the center of the field and faced the king. They lined up, standing side-by-side and alternating between soprano and tenor. The twenty young boys and girls were similar in age and somewhat similar in appearance. The boys wore black shorts, brown rubber sandals and short-sleeve shirts made from blue hand-dyed cotton, while the girls wore brown shoes and simple dresses made from the same blue material. Shortly after, a petite lady with rivulets of gray shooting through her neatly braided hairdo walked onto the field and faced the children. She was also wearing a simple dress that was sewn from the same hand-dyed material as the young singers with the exception of subtle aesthetic embroidery added around the hem and collar. Her name was *Iahtaam* and she was the only music teacher at the village school. Influenced by her education in the big city, she was an aficionado of classical music and possessed a deep passion to educate and enlighten young minds.

"Boys and girls, heads and shoulders straight!" the conductor cleared her throat and spoke in a soft voice.

The singers raised their heads and beamed with genuine smiles. Iah-taam nodded, winked and smiled back at her pupils. She began to hum and wave her small hands in the air. The eager choir hummed a retort. Without delay, the girls separated their lips and unleashed their vocals from their voice boxes; the boys followed and they sang together. Their sweet, harmonious and near-angelic voices drifted through the warm air current, hypnotizing the audience. The villagers and city supporters alike lowered their voices and began to relish the soothing effects of the youthful half-time carols. The drenched football players from both teams sat on the grass by the sideline, resting and snacking on ripe bananas.

"Hey, Idnurub!" Nadus prodded his friend with his hip and spoke in a hushed voice. "Hey, do you want to follow me?"

"Huh! Why? Where are you going to?" Idnurub gave his friend a wry look. "What do you mean follow me? I don't get you Nadus."

"I need to urinate!" Nadus replied with impatience. "Come on, Idnurub follow me, come on!" Nadus held his crotch, crossed his legs and began to hop slightly.

"Now? They've just started singing. Wait, can you just wait just a little a bit? We'll go right after they're done."

"No, I can't wait till they finish!" Nadus snapped. "Besides we've heard them sing so many times at school. You wouldn't be missing much. Come on let's go!"

Idnurub looked at his fidgeting friend and offered him a simple smile.

"You know what?" Nadus took the smile and turned it into a frown. "It's okay! You don't have to follow me. I'll just go by myself." The young boy turned around as though ready to leave.

"Come on now!" Idnurub grasped Nadus by the shoulders and smiled again. "Don't be like that! I didn't say I wouldn't go with you."

"Well, I can't wait any longer. I really need to urinate. Are you coming or not?"

"Okay, okay!" Idnurub succumbed. "I'll come with you. Where are you going to urinate?"

"I don't know! Probably over there towards the bushes." Nadus flexed his wrist and pointed with his thumb. "Quick, I really need to go!"

"Okay okay! Slow down. I'm coming."

The boys squeezed their way through the mellowed and mesmerized audience and headed straight for the back. Upon freeing themselves from the ocean of people, they jogged towards the far corner and headed down the steep hill. As they quickly descended, their worn-out rubber sandals scattered several loose pebbles on the ground and picked up dust as they hit the parched clay. Before long they were almost a hundred yards away from the hilltop, walking on a narrow, meandering weed-covered path that lead to the back of the school compound and "the rack." The school farm or "the rack" as known by many of the village students was a sizable cultivation of yams, cassava and tomatoes. It was instituted by *Owolowa*, the prior principal, as a place to "positively punish" disobedient students: discipline them, teach them the importance of agriculture and raise funds for the school with the crop profits. The school farm was a dreadful place to work because the soil was difficult to plow, the vicinity was covered with thorns and there were unusual amounts of large, vicious ants roaming the ground; it was truly a place where happy little souls were quickly saddened.

"Haven't we walked long enough for you to go?" Idnurub exclaimed.

"Yes, yes, alright!" Nadus grunted. "I can't even hold it any longer."

Nadus jumped into the bushes; he walked a little further in, unzipped his shorts hurriedly, squatted and began to ease himself. He smiled in relief, gazed up at the sky and opened his mouth as if drinking in the rain.

"Oh I see why we walked so much. Ugh, yuck, Nadus, gosh Nadus! Oh my goodness!" Idnurub covered his nose with his hand and walked a few feet away. "That stinks! What did you eat today, rotten eggs and rats?"

"What are you talking about? Come smell it," Nadus laughed. "It's soft and smells like flowers. Looks nice too, like yam porridge, yum-yum!"

"Stop that nonsense! It's not funny." Idnurub puckered his forehead as he walked away from Nadus who was enjoying a bowel movement.

"Ha! Come on Idnurub! Don't walk away from me, come smell it."

"La-la-la-bah-blah-blah! No, no, I'm not listening! No, I can't hear you!" Idnurub placed his hands over his ears and looked away.

The gravel pathway was shaded from the sunlight by the large trees that were sporadically reaching above the foliage. As a result, the scenery was dim and the plants along the path were still groggy and wet from the morning dew. Idnurub picked up a slender, broken tree branch from the nearby bushes and began to occupy his time by prodding the dead, slimy leaves that soiled the narrow trail. Out of the blue, his small ears perceived some unusual activity. Idnurub looked up and in the distance he saw a muffled figure standing by the bushes, ruffling the leaves and making unusual sounds. He ducked and looked again and the movements continued. He then began to tiptoe backwards.

"Hey Nadus!" Idnurub whispered and looked at his pal who was wiping his behind with several dead leaves. "Nadus!"

"What's the matter?" The young boy was surprised to see his friend so close by, enduring the stench of his stool. "What's going on?"

"There seems to be something moving by the bushes." He pointed and partially covered his nose with his upper lip.

"Oh really?" Nadus arose, pulled up his knickers and wiped his hands on several strands of wet grass. "What can it be? Do you have any ideas?"

"Yes, I don't know," Idnurub replied as he skulked away from the improvised privy. "Thought it was my imagination," he continued, "and my mind playing tricks on me, but look it's still moving." He pointed.

Nadus walked faster and caught up with his friend. "I think we should check it out, might be a monster!" He whispered, smirking with mischief.

"A monster? Don't say things like that. Remember what just happened to us today, at the festival with the masqueraders?"

"Yes, yes, I know. But you of all people should know! Come on!" Nadus chuckled and wiped his fingers on his khaki shorts. "Do you really believe in monsters? Didn't you read all those books from grammar class?"

"Yeah I read the books. Sure! Just don't say things like that, especially here, in the bushes."

"Are you kidding me? Monsters aren't real, probably just a *Galago*!"

"Huh? A what? What's that?"

"Galago, remember that picture in class? The one with the animal with woolly fur, large eyes and ears?"

"Oh yes, the *Bushbaby*! How can I forget?"

"Yes, Bushbaby!" Nadus picked up a stick from the ground and began to tiptoe forward. "Come, let's go check it out, just a peek."

"Wai…" Idnurub hesitated.

"Come!" Nadus whispered as he turned around and beckoned. "Here!"

Idnurub shook his head, rolled his eyes and joined Nadus.

With adrenaline flowing through their vessels and their hearts pounding against their ribcages, they placed each foot carefully on the path and advanced as though reciting a choreographed dance. With each step they took, the subject became clearer; it was a boy who was squatting, defecating and smacking the surrounding leaves with a stick in his hand. They were relieved of their anxiety but disappointed. It was *Iwalam*, the large-mouthed boy in their school who had recently been flogged for cursing at the mathematics teacher.

Nadus worked on his composure and then shouted. "Iwalam!"

"What are you doing over there?" Idnurub queried.

The boy was startled; he looked up and caught eyes of the interlopers. He frowned and continued his business, groaning and breaking wind.

"What does it look like to you?" Iwalam asked in strained voice. "Can't you see that I'm releasing manure on the plants and food for the beetles?" he added as he cleaned himself with some leaves.

"I see." Nadus replied.

"Why are you two just standing there and watching me?"

"I don't know," Idnurub said.

"Are you both crazy or just enjoying the smell?" Iwalam pulled up his tattered trousers and worked on his zippers.

"No, no!" The intruders waved their hands in denial. "It smells awful!"

"Good, that means my belly is working properly." Iwalam turned his head to the side, snorted and spat on the fecal matter, perturbing the flies that were already having a feast. "So what are you two doing over here, in the bushes?" he asked and his face brightened with naughtiness.

"Well Nadus was takin-" Idnurub paused.

"No, no! We're kind of taking a break," Nadus butted in and sneered at Idnurub, "and we decided to take a walk."

The schoolboy looked at Idnurub with his brows raised; he then faced Nadus. "Alright, you're taking a break." He didn't sound convinced.

"Oh yes! We're taking a break." Idnurub got the drift and concurred.

"Okay!" Iwalam nodded in comprehension and as though listening to a favorite tune. "You really don't need to explain to me. I don't care."

"Didn't you watch the game?" Idnurub asked as the three boys walked further along the path, away from the malodor.

"No, not really, actually watched part of it but after those fools scored a goal, I kind of lost interest and walked away. Besides you both know I'm not very fond of Mister 'Oh-so-the-fool.'"

The boys laughed.

"You missed out! It was a really good half," Nadus added.

"Poor me!" Iwalam picked his nose. "I guess it's over now, right?"

"Yes, no, well just the first half," Idnurub said.

"Good for you! Well you two enjoy, I'll see you later at school."

"Hey, wait now, where're you going?" Nadus inquired.

"Why are you asking?" Iwalam snapped a reply.

"Hey, boy slow your roll!"

"What I do isn't your business!" Iwalam uttered. "You're not my dad!"

"Eh?!" Nadus raised his chest and responded in a combative fashion. "I just wanted to know if we could come along."

"Well okay!" Iwalam spoke in a gentler tone. "I'll probably wander a bit, maybe shoot some birds, that sort of thing, something like that." Iwalam pulled out a slingshot from his pocket.

"That is nice!" Idnurub exclaimed as he eyed the Y-shaped stick with black elastic bands tied between the arms. "Can we come with you?"

"Well sure," Iwalam replied in a protracted manner. "I thought the game wasn't over, it was a good game, right? Don't you two want to watch it?"

"Of course we will, the school choir is singing at the moment and you know how many times we've heard them," Nadus retorted.

"Oh, not that singing bunch again! Those kids get on my nerves, they sound terrible. I don't like their voices. The whole spectacle irritates me."

"Spectacle, eh?" Nadus added.

"Yes, the whole spectacle."

"Now that's a big word."

"Iwalam, don't be so negative!" Idnurub interjected, taking a defensive stance. "They aren't so bad! I personally think they sound good, that's just my opinion." From a young age, Idnurub learned that he could sing and secretly wished to be part of the choir, but he feared being called a 'sissy' by his classmates and allowed his talent to wither away.

"Anyway, they'll probably be singing for another twenty minutes. We can play with you for a bit and then head back," Nadus said. "Don't worry, we won't be following you around all day."

"Okay! I like the sound of that," Iwalam replied.

The three boys walked together along the trail, moving sluggishly and aimlessly like fatigued dogs. Iwalam catapulted a few pebbles into the sky and the two other boys commented on the speed and trajectory. Iwalam then turned his attention to the trees and began to terrorize and taunt innocent squirrels and agama lizards as they basked in the sun. It wasn't long before they lost track of time and were infected with boredom.

"Idnurub! Nadus!" Iwalam slowed his pace and placed his hand on his head. "To be honest with you. To be really honest, I'm tired of these lame games. I'm hungry and I want to do something better."

"So?" Nadus slapped the side of his neck and killed a mosquito. "What do you want to do?"

"Yes, what do you want to do?" Idnurub repeated.

"How about we go into the woods and pluck some fruits, eh?" Iwalam asked.

"I suppose that's an option," Nadus faltered. "Sure! I'm down, let's go!"

"But you know, we've never gone out there or at least I haven't. Besides, we aren't supposed to go into the woods," Idnurub lamented. "We're not even allowed near the fence. We could get punished for this."

Nadus and Iwalam looked at each other and exploded with laugher.

"Look at you, you sound like such a baby!" Nadus teased.

"Don't be a sissy, we wouldn't get caught. Who checks at this time of the day?" Iwalam looked at the boys and raised one of his brows.

Nadus and Idnurub didn't respond.

"That's exactly my point!" Iwalam jittered with excitement and enthusiasm. "Nobody, let's go!"

The boys deviated from the gravel trail. They jumped into the bushes and headed towards the fence, bordering "the rack" and the woods. The barricade was simple in its architecture; it was six feet high and was constructed from bundles of plywood bound together with twine and hammered into the soil. The schoolboys watched their surroundings for onlookers and quickly surveyed the structure for possible points of entry. In no time, they found a gap through the pickets and decided to squeeze through it. Iwalam led the way. The skinny boy stepped on a large irregular rock that was adjacent to the fence and grabbed the stakes with his hands. He sighed, grunted and pried the cylindrical pieces apart, widening the gap and weakening the joints. Then, he placed his leg through the gap, established a grip on the other side and squeezed his way through the portal. Idnurub was the next to proceed, followed by Nadus and as he struggled through the crevice, the twine in the joints gave way and a part of fence collapsed.

"Oh nooo!" The young boy roared, sparring and dodging a few planks that hounded him as he advanced into the new territory.

"Are you okay?" Idnurub and Iwalam asked.

"I'm fine!" Nadus rubbed his stained hands on his shorts and looked at the new opening; it was large enough for an average-sized boy to conveniently walk through. "Aw, it's broken!" Nadus cried out.

"Yes it is," Idnurub agreed. "Don't worry. Things happen for a reason."

"Yes, we better leave before someone spots us," Iwalam said. "I'm sure no one will know it's us. It will be fixed anyway. Trust me! It's okay."

"I guess you're right," Nadus sounded remorseful. "We better leave."

The boys turned around and became aware of the panoramic view of their surroundings. The land stretched out far towards the golden horizon; the grasses, trees and many assorted plants were taller, greener and wilder in appearance. The youngsters gaped with the wonderment of an adventurer who had just discovered an uncharted island. In moments, the boys were greeted by anxiety and insecurity upon realizing that they were out of their comfort zone and away from their refuge. They looked around momentarily and visually explored the new ambience. After they got their bearings and garnered their courage, they began their adventure into the land of the unpredictable, the habitat of many wild beasts. The boys walked close to each other and took meticulous strides through the grassland, watching attentively and jumping at the slightest sounds. Ten minutes later, they arrived at a small grove, consisting of five trees that were dancing and conversing with the wind. Ambling from trunk to trunk, they studied each tree in a casual fashion. Of the five evergreen trees, they identified a promising choice, the third one with brigades of ants crawling up and down its wide and rugged trunk. They circled the plant and inspected it, focusing their attention on the large oranges that dangled from its thorny branches. The boys were out of luck as none of the yellowish-green citrus fruits were worth the effort of plucking. They kept on walking, forging a narrow path through the green plains. As they embarked on their venture, grasshoppers hopped erratically out of their way, colorful birds entertained with soothing melodies and naïve squirrels jigged from tree to tree. Even the few colorful flowers and gangly scrubs along the way smiled in the sunlight and waved in the breeze. The scenery was peaceful and spectacular and their unease had disappeared.

"Idnurub, Iwalam take a look at that!" Nadus shouted and pointed; his eyes flushed with emotion. "Let's race! I'll beat you two." The young boy added as he loped towards a large tree in the distance.

"No way, you won't!" Idnurub blurted and took off on his feet.

"No, I'll beat you too!" Iwalam shouted.

The boys raced towards the red mangoes that dangled from the tree branches; their scrawny legs adjusted to the sudden work load and in no time, they arrived. Without wasting time, Nadus and Idnurub picked up rocks and sticks from the ground and threw them at the tree. Iwalam, in contrast, pulled out his slingshot from his pocket, picked up several pebbles from the ground and fired direct shots at the branches. After several seconds of bombardment, the tree gave in and released five mangoes to the boys. They pounced on the fruits like cheetahs and immediately began to bite into the flesh without washing them. Each boy gobbled down a mango and shared the other two, passing them around in circles and taking turns to nibble on the juicy aromatic pulp.

"Slow down! That's too much," Iwalam teased.

"I didn't! Yours was bigger." Nadus smiled as he passed the fruit to his classmate.

"I don't know, it was a big one." Idnurub took the bleeding mango and had a bite. "It's so good."

The boys continued to share their meal and joke amongst themselves until all that remained of the five mangoes were their yellow, hairy seeds. Still hungry and greedy for more, the schoolboys walked around the tree like hyenas circling and stalking a dying animal.

"Will you look at that?" Iwalam exclaimed as he pointed to a brown, rugged and oval receptacle that drooped from an adjacent tree branch.

"Look at what?" Nadus walked towards his pal and followed his finger with his eye. "Very interesting!"

"What's that? What's interesting?" Idnurub voiced his curiosity.

"Why don't you come see for yourself?" Iwalam replied.

Idnurub dropped the stick in his hand and joined the boys on the other side of the tree. He raised his chin and looked up at the foreign object. "Okay, can you tell what that is?" he shifted his head sideways and stared.

"I don't know," Iwalam replied.

"I haven't seen anything like that before."

"I think I know what it is," Nadus chimed in.

"Tell us, what! What is it?" the boys inquired.

"It's a hive, a bee hive," Nadus answered. "I read about it and I've seen a picture of one before. It's the house bees make for themselves."

"I want to live high up too!" Idnurub whimpered.

"Oh, sorry you don't!" Iwalam mocked his classmate. "You know, you can always pack your things and become a monkey, live in the trees."

"Idnurub, I guess that's also an option," Nadus laughed.

"What do you think?" Idnurub asked.

"About what?" Nadus replied.

"The hive! What should we do?"

"Let's break it down! I once overheard one of the farmer boys say that bees make honey. I'm sure it's in there." Iwalam pointed with the catapult in his hand.

"Honey, really? I love the taste," Idnurub spoke with joy in his voice.

"Say we break it down, have mangoes and honey!" Iwalam reasoned.

"Yes, let's break it down!" Idnurub cheered on.

The three boys picked up more stones and aimed it at the tree branch.

"Wait! I don't think this is a good idea," Nadus said. "I also read once that bees if disturbed can become angry! Perhaps we should just focus on plucking more mangoes instead."

"You sure about that?" Idnurub hesitated and lowered his flexed arm.

"Yes, I think so."

"You're not even sure!" Iwalam yelled in disappointment. "Who cares if they get angry? Insects get angry all the time! Mosquitoes always get angry when we don't let them suck our blood or crush them."

"I don't think it's the same thing," Nadus responded.

"You're talking about bees, right? You mean those little black and yellow flies that suck on flower juices?"

"Yes, those are one type of bees, but just like there are different types of people there are different types of bees. Who knows what's up there."

"What are you talking about then? What harm can they do to us? Bees look like pretty houseflies. They'll probably just whine in our ears and land on our faces. Perhaps disturb us a little as we enjoy their honey!"

"Honestly, I don't know." Nadus scratched his scalp and stared at the hive. "I don't like the idea."

As the boys debated, a few winged hymenopterans crawled out of the crevices and fluttered around the hive as though assessing the vicinity.

"See!" Iwalam pointed to the tree branch. "They don't look so bad."

"Yes, you're right!" Idnurub added. "They look like houseflies."

"Exactly! Harmless little bugs!" Iwalam sounded more upbeat. "Alright brothers, let's do this, get out that honey! I'll use the slingshot."

Right away, Iwalam hunkered down, picked a pebble from the ground and placed it into the pocket of the slingshot. He aimed at the hive, pulled the elastic material backwards and released the stone, firing at the waxy entity that hung from the sturdy branch. Receiving a direct hit, the rock pierced the fragile hive at an angle and ejected out of the other side, gashing it with two large holes.

"That's a great shot!" Idnurub clapped and Nadus nodded.

"Thanks, thanks! Let me break it down so we can get the honey." Iwalam bent down and searched for another pebble.

In a matter of seconds, they heard an ominous, churning hum coming from above. The boys stopped their actions and looked up to see a dark strip surfacing from the wound of the hive; it was a buzzing reverberation of aggravated bees ready to protect their abode and beloved queen.

Before they could react, the boys were surrounded by a dark, noisy cloud. Struck by severe pain, they suddenly found themselves in pandemonium.

"Ah aah, my neck!"

"I can't see!" Idnurub screamed and swung his arms across his face.

"It hurts! It hurts!" Iwalam cried out with bloodshot, tearful eyes.

"Aah it burns!"

"Run! We're going to die!" Nadus ran towards refuge, covering his face and tracing a chaotic path out of the woods.

Screaming as they were chased and stung, the schoolboys rushed towards the fence. Unluckily for them, they had disturbed a hive of "killer bees," the most aggressive and defensive types of bees, notorious for attacking relentlessly in large numbers and pursing their victims for up to a mile. The boys ran as fast as their legs could carry them and their hands brandished in the air like those of uncoordinated puppets. In no time, the boys closed in on the border of "the rack" and although their minds didn't fully register it, they had never been so happy to be near the school farm. They ran faster; one-by-one like a colony of bats flying into a cave, they leaped through the opening in the fence and raced to the top of the hill. Attracted to the banana-like scent of the "alarm pheromone," released by the barb stingers that were stuck to the boys' skin, the infuriated insects didn't concede and continued to pursue their foes. The boys moved close together like stampeding cattle; their wet sandals were losing traction and elevated doses of bee venom seeped through their skin. They struggled with the discomfort and continued to run for their dear lives.

"Please help me!" Iwalam called out. "Don't go, please wait for me!" The terrified boy had slipped in his own prior fecal waste and was quickly becoming a prime target.

Scared, exhausted and in shock, Idnurub didn't stop. Nadus heard the cries and couldn't abandon his classmate. The young boy turned around and darted towards Iwalam. Enduring the stench and a few more stings, he helped Iwalam to his feet. The two boys continued to run for cover after their classmate. Idnurub reached the hilltop first and shortly after, Nadus and Iwalam arrived. The boys ran towards the crowd, crying and shrieking. The intense football game was still in progress. The city team was still leading by two goals; the village team, however, had scored two goals and the city team had only scored one since the second half began. The villagers at the back of the crowd heard the wails and responded with looks of bewilderment. Then, they noticed the injured boys as well as the dwindling swarm that followed them. The crowd scrambled and the scene became a jumble; the aggravated bees began to attack and sting everyone in sight and as expected, the football game was halted. The boys were scooped up by the village coach and two other male volunteers and were taken away to safety. The royal guards quickly lit their torches and chased the bees with the flames and smoke. The boys were taken to the booth and were treated by the oracle's apprentice. They were filthy and smelled awful. Their clothes were soiled with a combination of brown and green stains. Their faces, necks, and limbs were swollen. Their joints were bruised and many stingers and dead bees were embedded on the surface of their skin. Pulsating bumps sprung up on their faces and intensified the pain that they were already suffering. The boys were in bad shape and injured from their misadventure. Barely conscious and coherent, they sobbed and cursed, wishing they had never crossed the fence.

11

CHAPTER ELEVEN:

"Cows are born with ears; later they grow horns."
African Proverb

With smirks and giggles stretching and lifting their animated faces, Nadus and Idnurub continued their daily expedition towards the stream and then to school. The boys chatted, shook their heads and laughed loudly as they recalled subtle details of their dreadful attack. Somewhat oblivious to their surroundings, they didn't notice the chirping birds on the trees and the young shepherds that stood on both sides of the clay pathway, holding long crooked sticks and chewing on long stalks of grass; nor did they notice the herds of scrawny sheep that bleated and stopped grazing on the anguished pasture to stare at them. The schoolmates were deeply engrossed in their vivid and wild recollections.

"Ha! Geez Idnurub!" Nadus exclaimed, grabbing his stomach with both hands as he tried to control his mirth. "You were, honestly you were running away and crying like a crazy dog infested with fleas!" He crossed his eyes and stretched out his tongue, heaving like an exhausted canine. "See you couldn't even wait for him when he fell, that's horrible, simply horrible Idnurub!"

"Huh, are you kidding me?" Idnurub halted his laughter and wiped the tears off his cheeks. "I was in a different zone that day! I didn't even hear him, I swear. I'm not lying! The pain was so unbearable and I just wanted to be as far away as possible. Gosh, it hurt badly!"

"I don't think I've ever felt that much pain in my life."

"Me neither," Idnurub concurred.

"We should have never broken that hive! You know, right?"

"Yes, I have to say that was one of the most foolish things we've ever done!" Idnurub swung the black plastic bag in his hand back and forth.

"We?" Nadus raised his voice and grimaced. "I didn't have anything to do with it, remember? I told you and Iwalam not to break the hive but you wouldn't listen to me! You thought I was just trying to stop you from eating honey, eh! Whatever happened to the 'pretty looking houseflies,' huh?" Nadus laughed and shook his head like a wise old woman disagreeing with her grandchildren.

"Indeed! Nadus you did warn us. I can't deny that," Idnurub lowered his voice, sounding a little regretful and silly. "It was a fun day though!" he blurted out, "I mean, the festival, the masqueraders with the big sticks, the intense game!" He smiled, sighed and looked at the light-blue sky.

"It was a memorable day but now," Nadus paused, "I can't stand the feeling or even the thought of insects crawling on my skin." He slowed his tempo as though reading a foreign language. "Ugh, yuck, yuck!" He wiped his forearms and neck repeatedly. Then, he shuddered as though suddenly suffering from a cold spell and a mild case of hypothermia.

"Really!" Idnurub looked intrigued but confused. "That bad, eh?"

"Oh yes definitely! I can't stand anything crawling on my skin."

"Interesting!" Idnurub pouted his lips and nodded as he looked at the ground and kicked a loose pebble. "Hum, I suppose I'm lucky that I don't have that problem, you know." He smiled, pulled out his notebook from his back pocket and tapped his friend on the shoulders with it.

"I suppose you are!" Nadus looked at Idnurub and exchanged a feeble smile, joining his friend and kicking a few stones into the side bushes.

"But Nadus," Idnurub hesitated, "you always used to like insects a lot, most especially those large ants and spiders. Did this just start after the attack with the bees or did this start before that day?"

"I guess so," Nadus butted in. "Well, technically spiders aren't insects!" he added. "Insects have only six legs while spiders have eight legs."

"Oh!" Idnurub chuckled. "You're really being technical, my mistake!"

"No worries! I'm just making sure that you know the difference." Nadus winked. "Anyway, let's save the chats for the stream. The sun is out now! Time is against us and we better hurry." He scratched his eye with his palm and increased his strides, walking ahead of his friend.

"Okay, okay you're right." Idnurub walked faster and joined his pal. "We can't afford to get flogged on the last day of school, you know?"

"Exactly my point!" Nadus replied as he fluttered his itchy eyelid.

Driven by haste and the desire to avoid punishments, the schoolboys continued to pace themselves as they marched towards the village's sole source of clean water. A few minutes later, their nostrils were tickled by traces of detergent, diffusing through the light morning breeze; their ears caught the swooshing sounds of wet clothes wrestling in running water along with the sweet voices of women and children, laughing and singing pleasantly. Nadus and Idnurub beamed and scuttled forward. They were deluged with relief as they had arrived at their first destination of the morning in good time. Only a few yards away, situated near the crossroad that led to the big city and the village school, the stream etched its course through the path of least resistance and hydrated the lush surrounding vegetation. As the boys approached the intersection, five women with large clay pots balanced on their heads loomed from around the corner. They were chuckling and chitchatting and their garments, especially the lower edges of their long and colorful tie-dye wrappers, were damp and stained with blotches of clay; they wore pleasant expressions on their young faces and gleamed with sheer content and satisfaction. Nadus and his classmate scooted along, briefly bowing their shaved heads and greeting the cheerful women. They dashed down the boggy and slippery footpath that led straight to the body of water. The stream was full of life and the ambiance as usual was energetic and noisy. Lined along the rocky shores and wallowing in the shallows like sunburned hippos were several children playing, paddling and dancing in the turbid waters. Standing close by and ensuring the safety of the minors, many persevering women and dedicated mothers washed their clothes vigorously and bathed their toddlers and infants.

Upstream from the hubbub, a group of girls and women sang as they fetched drinking water with clay pots and calabashes. Further downstream from where they stood, quite the opposite was occurring; three boys were laughing, spitting and urinating in the runnel. The women despised littering and piddling in the waters and would never do such a thing. However, their complaints and rebukes always fell on the deaf ears of the insolent. They simply learned to ignore "the goats" and boil the water longer before drinking or using it to cook. Nadus and Idnurub walked carefully along the shoreline, dodging other excited nippers that were laundering or running around. They discovered an unoccupied spot on the edge that was big enough for two and quickly claimed it. The boys squatted and took out their books from their pockets and placed them on a fairly dry spot on the ground, securing them with a few rocks. They untied their plastic bags with haste and dumped the contents, a heap of clothes and a bar of soap made from vegetable oil and caustic-soda, onto the ground. Their immature fingers went to work, digging through and sorting the wrinkled pile that reeked of stale sweat. The boys, especially Nadus, were used to the odor that it became rather calming and therapeutic in nature. Wasting no time, they each picked a piece, dipped it in the running waters, lathered it with the acrid detergent and began to scrub. Fists clinched and perspiring, the schoolboys continued to rub the clothes together, whistling and chattering with their neighbors. The clothes took up the cold water quickly, and with a few tight squeezes and strokes the dark blots that soiled their valued but washed-out clothes slowly evanesced. As they proceeded with the cyclical and tedious morning chore, Nadus mused and allowed his mind to drift into the abyss of his imaginations. He thought about his father and his brother, working hard and sweating on their small plot, and how he could be a "real" helping hand if he abandoned school just like Idnurub had suggested, and the few times he tried to convince is father to let him. He recalled the slobbery face of his dog, "little Mister Dahc," his loud and distinct woofs, and his many canny, attention-seeking behaviors diffused and filled his juvenile head. Nadus smiled and squeezed the ocher foam off his father's blue sleeveless shirt and onto the ground. He knelt down, bent over and as he dipped the fabric into the stream to rinse off the soap residue, his attention was diverted. Through the clamors of the young and old attendees at the aquatic haven, he heard his name.

"Nadus! Nadus!"

The young boy raised his ears and looked around like a suspicious fox in the forest. He heard his name again and right away he recognized the soft feminine voice. In a matter of seconds, the caller appeared in his line of sight and approached him; it was *Muotrahk*, the only girl in the village that he liked. As she closed in on him, a warm and cozy feeling erupted inside his stomach as if he had just eaten a tasty bowl of hot pepper soup.

"Hello boys!" The girl stood behind Nadus and his classmate, smiling and staring at them with pretty oval eyes that glistened in the sunlight.

Idnurub was startled. "Oh, you scared me!" he turned around. "Well, hello Muotrahk! How are you today?"

"Sorry to have scared you!" Muotrahk chuckled. "I'm fine! Thanks for asking! I just saw you two from over there." The girl pointed towards a group of women in the distance; they were chatting, laughing and helping one another balance large pots of water on their heads. "And so I decided to say a quick hello," she gently swung the empty pot in her hand.

"That's very nice of you," Idnurub replied. "You're too kind!"

"Aw, thank you!" Muotrahk smiled and revealed her dimples.

"We're just here, washing some clothes before..."

"Hello Nadus!" she interrupted Idnurub, waving and snapping her fingers over the young boy's head as though trying to get his attention.

"Muotrahk! Hello," Nadus looked up and wavered; he then cleared his throat. "How are you?" He acted and sounded as if surprised to see her.

"Are you that busy with those clothes that you can't say hello to me?" She smiled and scolded him. "I'm good Nadus, happy to see you!" she replied with excitement in her voice. "It's been a while since I've seen you and since we've talked. How's your pap' and Tpyge, your brother? I hope they're doing well."

"Oh yes, it's been a while since we've talked, I think. Father and Tpyge are doing well, at the farm, working hard as usual," the young boy replied as he squeezed the garment in his hand until it resembled a convoluted earthworm agitated by brine.

Nadus was outgoing and he didn't consider himself as shy. However, there was something so genial about Muotrahk, something he couldn't decipher, that made him bashful around her. Nadus continued to stare at Muotrahk but couldn't keep eye contact. He was intrigued by a few of her newly acquired features: increased height, enlarged breasts, wider hips and a few pimples on her face. Like a vibrant garden of wild flowers, her outward appearance and beauty was flourishing with each passing day. The two of them were similar in age; they met several years ago at the market while helping their fathers during the yearly "harvest sale," and became friends ever since. Her father, *Rihsabla*, was a fellow farmer and was acquainted with Nadus's father solely by way of occupation. Rihsabla was different from Nineb in his physical appearance and even in his ideologies; for one, unlike Nineb who was tall and lean in stature, Rihsabla was short, bald, and soaked and round like fried dough. An avid traditionalist marked with narrow views of his surroundings and the world, he enjoyed his rudimentary convictions and limited perceptions with little remorse or guilt. As a father to many, he was surprisingly more interested in his gain than in the well-being of his offspring. From an early age, he made his sons work hard on his farm and bestowed his daughters to be married to "older gentlemen" with fat pockets and deplorable appetites for young virgins. Accordingly, all his children were barred from going to school and all his girls had to learn the trade of becoming "good housewives" to their prearranged husbands; they had to learn to cook, clean, wash and satisfy their partners obediently.

"So how are you enjoying school?" The girl widened her eyes. "What books are you reading now? Quick, tell me all about it," she asked with the eagerness of a passionate pedant.

"Let me see," Nadus placed the clean clothes in the plastic bag, "today is the last day of school so as for books," he paused as though thinking of a polite response, "we're not really reading..."

"Nothing I care about!" Idnurub interjected.

"I don't believe you Idnurub!" Muotrahk looked at the schoolboy, waving her index finger and shaking her head in reprimand. "You know I know that you especially, of all people, don't like books."

"That's true." Nadus giggled. "He's definitely a bookworm, indeed!"

"Nadus, why would you say that?" Idnurub looked at his pal. "I'm not a worm! You know that I hate worms!" He frowned as he complained.

"But I didn't call you a worm!" Nadus giggled again.

"Yes you did call me a worm." He looked at Muotrahk. "Didn't you just hear him say that, huh?"

"No, no!" Muotrahk smiled. "He didn't say that, didn't call you a worm. Nadus called you a 'bookworm' and that's a person who spends a lot of time reading books. You don't do that, you don't like books so he was just poking fun at you!" She leaned forward and patted Idnurub on his head with her palm.

"You remembered bookworm?" Nadus looked surprised.

"Of course! I know the definition of a bookworm." She rolled her eyes, smiled and then hissed.

"Exactly, see what I mean?" Nadus winked at Muotrahk and shrugged his shoulders; he was feeling more relaxed in the presence of his "first love" and was acting more like himself. "Definitely doesn't like the books, please pardon him!" Nadus dipped his hand into the stream and splashed his classmate with some water.

Idnurub closed his eyes as the sprinkles hit his face. "Okay you got me there!" He shook his head like a wet dog and gave out a forced laugh.

"Don't mind him Idnurub! He's just being a little goofy." She turned to Nadus, raised her brows and lips and looked directly into his eyes.

Nadus as though under a magical spell stared back. For an instant, he was weak and speechless, arrested and enamored with fondness and affection for the village girl. Besides being blessed with beauty and a voice that soothed aching ears, Muotrahk also possessed an incredible memory, recalling everything she saw and heard; although, there were a few times when she acted like she didn't remember just so that she could learn new facts and stories. A little introverted and very sympathetic towards toddlers, she loved to learn and quixotically hoped to be a teacher someday so that she could educate "little ones." Instead, she scrubbed, cleaned and cooked all day, basically working as a domestic slave. Nadus was infatuated with Muotrahk; he cared deeply for the girl more than his dog, the hare and the goats in his care, and his crude toys and playthings made from sticks and old cans. In fact, he cared for her more than his own father, brother or anyone he had ever known. On many occasions, he confided in her and divulged his few fears and future aspirations. Muotrahk was the only person who knew that Nadus was scared of failing his father, didn't enjoy going to school as many of his friends thought otherwise and dreamed of becoming a famous juggler in the big city. As usual, she would always encourage Nadus and advise him to follow the rhythm of his heart's desires. Unusually mature and reserved for her tender age, the young girl had also developed a similar emotional connection with Nadus, a genuine bond that she often masked from the world. Muotrahk was depleted of optimism and tired of enduring the agony of "false hope." She guarded her heart steadily and seldom talked about any of her problems, feelings or inner sufferings. Notwithstanding, she was human and a few times, when life got so heated, she confided in Nadus and sought his ears, opening up and letting out her troubles like some steam from a covered pot of rice. She despised her father for marrying her off as a toddler to an "evil stranger" and was terrified of her imminent "honor to motherhood" ritual because of the inevitable female circumcision aspect of it.

"Please help me! I don't know what to do and look at me! I'm already married to an old man that I don't even know," Muotrahk exclaimed during her last heartbreaking session with Nadus a few months ago; she was crying and sobbing bitterly. "I really don't know, Nadus, I don't have a life of my own and the ritual, oh I heard it's very painful, many of the girls are scared. They're badly hurt from being cut and some of them even bleed to death. Why?" She grabbed Nadus by his sleeves and painted all over her face was the ghastly expression of a terrified girl.

"I'm sure it will be okay!" Nadus expressed sympathy as he sat down beside her. "I'm sorry Muotrahk."

"Why are you sorry Nadus?"

"Because you're crying," he replied.

"It's not your fault." She raised her head and looked at the young boy as she wiped her snotty nose with the hem of her wrapper. "You don't have to be sorry."

"I know it's not my fault." He bowed his head and doodled in the dirt.

"Seriously, it's okay! I appreciate you Nadus. You're so kind to me and you make me feel so special." She wiped the tip of her sore nose.

Nadus smiled and looked bashfully at her; he nodded as he continued to listen to his girlfriend.

"Thank you for hearing me out."

Even with cracked lips, dark circles around her eyes, puffy cheeks and a runny nose, Nadus threw glances at Muotrahk and thought she looked very beautiful when upset. On many occasions, while in class, the young boy sketched in his notebook and imagined that he would grow up with her. For a long time, he was even secretly saving up all his pocket-change in hopes of repaying her dowry and persuading her father to annul her contract; he was a long way from doing such a thing. With added effort, Nadus blinked his teary eyes and severed the girl's control over him. He switched his gaze from her face and looked down at his friend who was squeezing a pair of trousers. He then fixed his youthful eyes back on the girl, staring at the simple stone necklace that adorned her slender neck. It was the one he bought for her as a souvenir during his first and only visit to the city; the time he escorted his father to apply for a microloan from the banking company.

144

12

CHAPTER TWELVE:

"He who pursues an innocent chicken often stumbles."
African Proverb

Barely irrigated by the dwindling and frail cumulus clouds, the entire land for several months had been under the weather, suffering from a prolonged drought that distressed the dwellers like the withering affection of estranged lovers. Feeling the twinge and wrestling the storm of desiccation, the village farmers worked harder to rescue and nurture the fruits of their labor, but in return reaped forlorn yields; most of their crops failed and those that stayed were stunted and shriveled in appearance, barely germinating and sprouting from the ground. Insolvent and hectored by desperation, many of the farmers tried to supplement their incomes with hunting wild animals. This, however, was a futile endeavor as many of the beasts that roamed their forests had perished from disease, dehydration and the extreme heat; the survivors were taking cover and hiding from the elements as well as their famished predators. Trawling was the last resort for securing nourishment, but the village waters were drying up rapidly and fish catches were becoming meager with each passing day. Many of the villagers were on the verge of depression. Nineb's mindset on the contrary was different; something unique had happened to him during his brief encounter with the leopard and glimpse of impending death. He was always content and seemed to gleam with unquenchable optimism for the future. Although heavily shaken by the dire season, he didn't lose his composure and continued to maintain a positive disposition. As a result, the young widower didn't give in to helplessness and self-pity. Instead, he and his son invested more manpower and spent longer hours tilling the ground and watering their crops.

Their added efforts, alas, were no match to the high temperatures and after many months of constant uphill struggles with little progress, Nineb decided to heed his brother's advice. A few moons back, Nineb found out from Anahg, who was visiting from the city, that a new governmental agency was helping farmers tackle the imminent famine by offering small loans in return for a "sizable share of future profits." Nineb was suspect of the seemingly romantic terms and didn't allow it to sink in. The diligent farmer took pride in the products of his sweat and didn't encourage the idea of becoming indebted to anyone for any reason; he believed debtors were obligated and enslaved by their creditor. Desperate to feed his boys, Nineb grappled with his conscience and principles for many weeks. As he lost his ground, the generous father of two took extreme measures to tough things out, rationing their portions and limiting their food intake from "two times a day" to "mornings only" and then to once every other day. With little success and on the verge of starvation, he swallowed his pride and decided to take the trip to the "city of peace." Although boyishly fascinated by the city culture, Nineb was at ease in the village and hardly visited. In fact, he had only been there once when he decided to pay his beloved brother a visit. During his memorable trip, for once in his life he felt like a lost sheep in the wilderness; there were so many signs that he could neither read nor understand, and everyone he met seemed unfriendly and in a hurry. After that day, Nineb concluded that he would never venture back into the big city unless driven by necessity. One evening, after working many long hours on the farm, Nineb settled down in their hut and called his son.

"Nadus! Come in here now!" he spoke in a stern voice, sounding upset. "Nadus? Nadus, where are you?"

"I'm here. Yes Papa! I'm coming," the young boy who was playing with his dog yelled from outside. "Yes, Papa?" Nadus dashed into the hut with Dahc and a smile on his face.

"Nadus, come over here!" Nineb pointed to the ground a few feet from where he was standing. "Quick, now, I said!"

Nadus was startled by his father's cold response and wiped the smirk off his face; he hid his teeth and then placed his hands behind his back. "Is everything okay, Papa?" He bowed his head and took a few fearful steps forward as he glanced at his father.

"Closer I said!" His father continued to point to the ground. The room was cool and poorly lit and the flickering flames from the kerosene lantern in the corner casted a large quivery shadow of Nineb on the wall.

"Okay, Papa." Nadus spoke in a lower voice and took two steps forward. The young boy recognized the unyielding tone in his father's voice and his heart and breathing paced up.

He doesn't look happy with me.

I didn't do anything wrong, did I?

I don't think so!

I did all my chores.

I didn't fail any class at school.

"Papa? What's the matter? Did I do something wrong?" Nadus asked.

His father walked forward without uttering a word and stood in front of Nadus, towering over him like a large edifice. His father contorted his face, grasped his son by the shoulders and spoke in a deep voice.

"My son!" Nineb nodded and stared at Nadus. "What do you say about this, eh? You have been..."

"Say about what, Papa?" Nadus butted in. "What didn't I do?" he asked and was almost in tears.

"You've been a good son to me!" His father gave out a loud laugh and embraced his son. "You've been a good son!"

"Ah, that's not fair, Papa!" Nadus blinked and immediately felt lighter. "You scared me! I thought I did something bad or missed a chore."

"Scared you? Why were you scared? You didn't do anything wrong. Or did you?" Nineb looked at Nadus, smiling and raising his left eyebrow.

"No, no, Papa!" Nadus shook his head and waved his hands in denial. "I didn't do anything wrong."

"Good! Then, there's no reason for you to be scared. As I've taught you many times before, when you always do what's right and treat others with respect, you have no reason to fear, to think everyone is talking about you or to worry they're out to get you."

"As you always say, 'a clean mind is a free mind.' Yes, you're right!"

"And fear, unrest is the punishment of being guilty," his father added.

"So, Papa you're not upset or angry with me?" Nadus inquired.

"No! No not at all!" Nineb replied in a protracted manner, laughing as he hugged his son again. "You've been a good child to me! In fact, your brother and I met your schoolteacher today on the way home. He told me you had one of the highest scores on your last exam, I'm so proud of you."

"Oh? Thank you, Papa!" Nadus looked at his father; he wore a genuine smile on his oblong face and felt appreciated.

"You're welcome! Hey, you know your birthday is coming up soon."

"Yes, that's true. I'll be a year older," Nadus replied.

"Indeed, you're growing into a fine young man and I think we should do something to celebrate it." Nineb scratched his beard and adjusted his sagging trousers; the farmer and his sons were thinner than usual and all their garments were loose-fitting.

"No, no Papa, no! It's not necessary. You don't need to spend any more during these tough times. I'm fine," Nadus reasoned with his father. "We can use it to buy more food from the market or more seeds for the farm."

Nineb took a deep breath and sighed as he took a seat on a stool. "You truly make me proud, your heart is big." He gestured with his hands as he reached for a small basket on the floor; he picked up a piece of kola-nut and halved it and placed the small piece in his mouth between his teeth.

"Thank you Papa!" Nadus looked at the flames in the lantern and then at his father. "I just don't want you or Tpyge working any harder."

"Don't worry about money." Nineb looked up and smiled at his son. "I know things are tough, but it's your birthday and you deserve something special. Besides, we didn't do anything last year," he said as he nibbled on the bitter brown seed; the pungent taste and the high amounts of caffeine in the nut suppressed the appetite and relieved hunger pangs.

"That's true, Papa," Nadus smiled in agreement, "but I'm okay."

"Actually, you know what?" his father interjected. "I've got the perfect idea for your birthday, Nadus!"

"Really? What is it Papa, what? Please tell me," Nadus replied; his eyes widened and his pupils dilated.

"What do you say, you and I tomorrow, go to the big city for a day?"

"No way!" Nadus exclaimed and leaped in the air, startling Dahc who was standing behind him. "Papa, really, the big city, you mean the real big city?" He stopped jumping and looked at his father as though waiting for his confirmation.

"Yes the big city! I know you've always wanted to go and I figured it's about time I took you there, you know. What do you say, want to go?"

"Yes Papa!" Nadus jumped again and danced. "I want to go, you're the best!"

"Alright, calm down!" Nineb laughed. "Cool it and be sure to get some rest tonight. We'll leave early in the morning, okay?"

"Yes Papa." Nadus bowed and clasped his hands together as if praying. "I'll go put Dahc in the shed and then head straight to bed."

"Good! I'm about to turn in for the night," Nineb stood up from the stool and stretched. He walked towards the edge of his sleeping mat, took off his slippers, dusted his feet and lay down. "I'll see you in the morning. Be sure to turn out the lantern and make sure you tell your brother that I said he shouldn't be out too late talking to his friends. He also needs to get some rest." Nineb yawned as he covered his feet with a cotton blanket and made himself more comfortable; the invigorating effects of the kola-nut were no match for his tiredness.

"Yes Papa, I'll tell him. Goodnight!" Nadus bowed his head again and trotted out of the hut. "Sleep well and I'll see you bright and early in the morning." He held the edge of the door and turned towards his father.

Nineb smiled with the glee of a proud guardian. "Goodnight! You or your brother, be sure to blow out the lantern before you sleep, okay?"

"Okay Papa," Nadus replied and walked into the moonlit night.

Exhausted from spending many laborious hours on the farm, Nineb closed his eyes and allowed his mind to drift. Like an excited boy, he thought about the upcoming trip and felt the butterflies fluttering in his stomach. He was a little anxious and wondered if he would qualify for the loan. Nevertheless, the fatherly side of him was happy and pleased to be taking Nadus to the city for the first time. Another part of him on the other hand was relieved that he wouldn't feel so lost or have to worry about all the difficult signage; his son could read. Nadus also went to bed earlier than normal, and just like his father he was filled with so much excitement that he found it somewhat difficult to venture into the land of dreams; he tossed and turned all night and imagined what life was like in the big city and how the people would act towards him. Barely rested and running on a few hours of sleep, the young boy got out of bed the following morning before his family and turned on the lantern. In haste, he got dressed in his "holiday clothes" without bathing or cleaning his teeth. He just smothered his face and limbs with generous amounts of shea butter before gurgling with water. Then, he rushed through all of his morning chores and joined his family inside the hut for breakfast and a quick prayer to the heavens. They prayed for safe journey to and from the big city, and most importantly they prayed and pleaded for rain. Not too long after, Nadus and his father hit the road and began the three mile hike to the village stop; Tpyge gladly stayed behind to recuperate and rest his fatigued muscles. Nadus and his father walked briskly along the path, talking about light matters and sharing laughs. The two exchanged treasures from their memory banks and paid no attention to their problems as they enjoyed the blissful and gratifying father-son experience. As expected during most pleasant moments, they lost track of time and before they could silence their loud laughs, they arrived at the motor stop.

"Going to the city? Come, I'll take you for cheap," one driver blurted out, beckoning with his hand. "I'll take care of you."

"No don't mind him!" A second driver honked his motorbike and rode towards Nadus and his father. "Sir, you saw me first. I'll take you there faster and cheaper than him," he yelled and waved his hand.

"Excuse me. They're lying." A third driver rode beside Nadus and his father, intercepting the second driver. "Look at their bikes! They're not nice and they're just trying to take your money. I'll take you there."

Before another minute was born, Nadus and Nineb were encircled by five motorbike drivers, arguing and bargaining for the business of the new potential customers.

"Wait quiet, hold on now!" Nineb said in good humor as he looked at the hungry eyes of the motorbike drivers. "Don't you think you're getting too close to us? Just wait a minute, don't frighten my son." The farmer waved his hands up and down to calm the pitchmen; the men lowered their voices, mumbling and eyeing each other.

"So which one of us do you want to take you?" a fourth driver asked impatiently as he turned his keys and killed the engine.

"I'll beat any of their prices." The second driver chimed in.

Nineb chuckled. "Hold up! This is my son's first visit to the big city." He placed his hands around the young boy's shoulders and pulled him closer. "How about I give him the honors to pick the driver, eh?"

Nadus looked up at Nineb with amazement plastered all over his face. "Are you serious, Papa? You want me to pick the motorcycle driver?"

"Of course, son! I want you to pick the driver."

"Thank you, Papa." Nadus smiled and nodded. "I'll do that."

Like scavenging vultures, the men switched their gaze and fixed their eyes on Nadus as they began to plead and bargain. The young boy immediately felt pressured and his palms sweated. He wiped his hands on his shorts and looked at each driver and their respective motorbikes.

I don't think yellow looks good with it.

Wow, these things look so incredible up close.

Oh black and that kind of matches the purple seat.

No, no, that one I think that's kind of ugly with the red.

Blue! Oh, my favorite color and it looks neat and fairly new too.

"Go ahead son." Nineb patted his son on the back. "Pick a driver, you know we don't want to be here all day, do you?"

Nadus looked at his father and swallowed his saliva. "I choose that one Papa." He pointed to the middle-aged man with the blue moped.

"Are you sure that's what you want?"

"Yes, Papa," Nadus replied as he ogled the fairly new motorbike.

"So be it!" Nineb patted Nadus again and then looked at the drivers. "My son has spoken and we'll go with the blue one," he said in an authoritative tone.

"Ah hah! Yes, you did well lad!" the selected driver exclaimed with the ardor of a victor. "A good choice, this one right here, is super!" The man spat the chewed tobacco in his mouth onto the ground and gripped the handlebar of his motorbike, shaking it and showing off the rigidity of the blue moped. The man stepped on the kick-starter twice, ignited the low-powered gasoline engine and twisted the throttle grip, revving up the engine. The other drivers grumbled, started their mopeds and rode off to be on the lookout for other customers.

"Okay sir. Let's go, hop on!" The man squeezed the brake levers as the motorbike vibrated and warmed up for the impending journey. "Your son should climb on first and then you sit after him so he's secure and doesn't fall off on his behind." The middle-aged driver gave out a dry laugh.

"Alright thank you!" Nineb paid little attention to the joke. "Nadus you heard the man, hop on the back seat."

"Okay Papa." Nadus stepped forward, grabbed the back saddle and raised his leg to sit down.

"Little man, watch your step." The driver turned his neck and looked down at the churning motor in the rear. "That engine can get hot so be careful you don't want to get burnt. If you ever feel scared just grab onto me, okay?"

"Thank you sir, I'll do that and watch out for the engine," the young boy replied as he ascended the moped, watching his feet as he adjusted his sitting position and got more comfortable on the cushioned seat.

"No worries, little man. You're welcome, just want you to be careful."

"You okay?" Nineb stroked his son's head and then got on the saddle, securing his feet and sandwiching Nadus in between the driver.

The middle-aged man inspected the seating position of his passengers and nodded in approval. He released his grip on the brake levers and twisted the accelerator on the handlebar, opening the throttle valve and jerking the moped forward. The engine coughed out black smoke, and in no time the three riders were in motion, sailing along the rugged, po-tholed road that lead to the city. Nadus's eyes were watering and saliva was leaking out of the sides his mouth, but he enjoyed the tingle of the cool breeze caressing his greasy face; the young boy had never moved so fast in his life and his thrill revealed itself through the palpitations of his heart. The moped continued along the pathway for several minutes and without warning the clay turned into a black and narrow highway with white stripes painted in the center. Nadus was wowed and even more excited to be riding on a tarred road; he had seen pictures and read about the tarring process and road construction, but he had never seen one up close. The sun was out as usual and the day was fairly typical: hot, dry and harsh on the senses. Nonetheless, the trip was cool and enjoyable as the speed of the motorcycle and evaporation of the warm sweat from their skin nullified the arid conditions. The young boy suddenly felt a pinch in his thighs. He was uncomfortable and his legs were cramping up. Nadus wanted to adjust his feet, but there wasn't any more room to move and he feared the heat from the hot exhaust pipes. The young boy ig-nored the discomfort and continued to admire the scenery, shifting his eyes and head as he absorbed and relished the beauty and vastness of the variegated land. Nadus turned around and briefly looked at his father who wasn't smiling. Nineb was squinting and staring straight ahead with teary eyes as though in deep thought. The young boy wondered what his father was looking at and what was going through his head. Nadus turned his head and also looked forward but couldn't see anything out of the ordinary; they were the only people on the road and in the distance, they seemed to be approaching a large pool of water. Nadus, although mesmerized, wasn't too concerned because he had learned about mirages in his science class. They passed hilly woodlands with tall and majestic trees decorating and enveloping both sides of the road. They scooted across wide grasslands with several impalas, buffalos, giraffes, elephants, zebras and gazelles freely grazing and exploring their terrain. The young boy had never seen so many wild animals all at once, running, playing and tussling with each another. Nadus right away felt his stomach grumble and wished he could take one of the large-horned antelopes home with him.

Why aren't they closer to our village?

That's not fair. All we need is just one of them!

We'll have enough food and meat to eat for months.

Oh yes! Think about it. Just one leg will last us for two weeks, easy!

Before long, the riders passed the open savanna and approached several large plutonic rocks that stood by the roadside like giant warriors guarding the sacred portal to the land of the ancestors. The driver pitched in to educate his passengers with his knowledge of the terrains. The man shouted as he described certain landmarks; his voice, however, was muffled and distorted by the wind that Nadus could hardly hear what he was talking about. They crossed a narrow wooden bridge that tattled with each quarter revolution of the rubber tires. As they moved along, the driver pointed to his right and in the distance, surrounded by flourishing trees and scrubs, a wide, meandering river that resembled a mighty bluish-gray snake crawled through the green vegetation.

"We're close to the big city," the driver shouted, "and that large river over there? You see it?" They were moving slower on the bridge and the driver was more audible.

"Yessir I see it," Nadus replied. "It's pretty large and long."

"Good! That's one powerful river over there! Some people say it takes the spirits of the dead to the other world." He laughed and Nadus received a few showers of the driver's dribble on his face.

154

"Is that so?" Nadus asked as he wiped his face. "Are you sure?"

"Well, I really don't how true that story is, about the river taking spirits, but I know for sure that it's used to power the entire city."

"What do you mean by power the city?" Nadus squinted as he stared at the river in the distance. Several gulls, storks and herons patrolled the skies like colorful kites, nose-diving in and out of the glistening water.

"You know, like electricity!" the driver replied. "You know what that is right?"

"Yessir, I know about electricity, learned about it in class."

"Okay good! You're one of those schoolboys, eh?"

"Yessir, I go to school in the village."

"Good for you!" The driver turned the handlebar, swerving the scooter to the right and dodging a small rock on the bridge. "That was a close one! Those things, as little as they look, can tear up the tires."

"That's not good!" Nadus released his grip around the driver's chest.

"Yes oh, not good! We'll have to stop and patch it and this bridge can be very dangerous, especially at night."

"How so sir?" Nadus inquired. "Why is it dangerous?"

"You really are a schoolboy!" The man laughed. "You ask many questions, but that's a good thing you know! I was like that when I was young. Stubborn and I just didn't believe everything I heard. I had to question it."

"Thank you, sir." Nadus looked up in the light-blue sky and noticed three large birds hovering over them.

"No, not at all! You don't have to keep calling me 'sir!' It makes me feel kind of old, you know."

"I'm sorry, sir." Nadus hesitated and laughed. "I mean, I'm sorry."

"You're funny, eh?" The driver shook his head as he increased the acceleration of the scooter. "Anyway, at night this bridge can get so dark that some people have actually fallen off."

"Oh really!" The young boy widened his eyes and mouth.

"Yes and down there is all swamp! Crocodiles and alligators are many down there, waiting to eat anything that falls! No joke!"

"Oh geez!" Nadus closed his mouth and then looked down through the gaps between the planks of the bridge, unrealistically hoping to spot one of the reptiles through the dense vegetation below. "That sounds scary," the young boy added.

"Oh yes indeed."

"This entire place sounds very dangerous," Nadus continued.

"Exactly! It is and that's why I don't ever want to have a flat tire here!"

"Yes, but it doesn't make sense to me." Nadus drifted from the topic of the conversation. "How do they get down there to power the city then?"

"Oh, oh! Your question about electricity! Yes, sorry I got carried away by that stone." The driver blinked and tears flowed from his eyes; none of them were wearing a helmet or goggles. "So you see, somehow that river is connected to many wires and used to produce electricity to light the city and power all those really big machines."

"Oh wow! That sounds incredible." The young boy was impressed. "Do you exactly know how it is connected to make the electricity?"

"Ah! No! Not at all young lad!" The driver laughed. "To be honest, if I knew how it all worked I wouldn't be driving people back and forth from the city; I'll be working for the electric company."

"Okay, sir."

"I don't know how they do it, wish I could tell you."

"I'd really like to know how it's done." Nadus responded.

"Yes that sounds like a good idea. Maybe you could learn it at school and work for the electric company. I hear their workers make good pay, you know."

"Good pay? Really?" Nadus smiled.

"Oh yes!" the driver exclaimed.

"Papa? Did you hear him?"

"Yes, I've been listening," his father replied.

"Okay Papa, he said the people who work for the company make good pay."

"Yes, I heard that."

"Papa, think I can learn how to connect the wires and make electricity with the river, maybe even work for the company?" Nadus looked at his father.

"Of course son!" Nineb nodded as a smile crept across his face. "You're a smart boy. I know you can learn how if you really wanted to!" He patted his son on the head.

"Thank you, Papa." The young boy smiled. "I'll think about it."

"Okay my son! Let me know when you learn how to do it. I'll like you to teach me how it's done, perhaps you and your brother can make electricity for our hut."

"Oh, yes Papa!" Nadus sucked in air and puffed up his cheeks. "That sounds like a good idea." He laughed and exposed his teeth.

The moped zoomed along the sloped bridge and crossed the rusty metal demarcation that separated the weathered structure from the wide tarred road. Shortly after, Nadus saw a green moped approaching ahead from the gold and wavy horizon. As the driver neared, the man smiled, waved and honked twice. On the rear saddle, a girl and an older woman were seated like Nadus and his father. The two passengers wore similar flowery gowns and keeping them company were two twine sacs that they both embraced as if their lives depended on them. Unlike the jovial driver, the woman and her grandchild didn't smile; they kept a straight face and looked ahead as they didn't want to invite trouble or disrespect the strangers in anyway.

Nadus's driver pressed his horn twice and shouted, "Good day, bossman!" He waved and greeted his colleague who was leaving the city and headed for the village.

"Are we close to the big city?" Nadus adjusted his benumbed legs and vented his excitement and impatience.

"Hold it young lad! Don't shake like that." The driver held the handlebar and then turned his head. "I know you're excited but you don't want us to fall."

"Come on Nadus!" his father scolded. "What's wrong with you?"

"I'm sorry, Papa. I didn't mean to move. I was just a little uncomfortable and I couldn't feel my legs."

"Apologize to the man!" his father added. "Tell him you're sorry."

"No, there's no need for that," the driver interjected. "Happens all the time! We're a few minutes away, young lad, soon as we climb this hill."

"Great!" Nadus exclaimed. "And I'm sorry for shaking!"

"It's okay," the man replied. "I know you mean no harm."

"That's much better Nadus," his father said.

"I hope you're ready," the driver blurted out, "as soon as we climb this hill we'll be there, in the big city." He twisted the handlebar and revved up the low-powered engine to compensate for the increased grade.

The young boy looked at the top of the paved road and became dry-mouthed; his heart began to drum with excitement and his stomach knotted. At that moment, he couldn't remember ever being so excited about anything in his life.

"Yes, yes, the big city! Finally!" Nadus whispered as he tightened his grip around the driver's chest.

"Come on! Come on!" The middle-aged driver chanted. "Come on!"

The three riders leaned forward by impulse and the scooter like an old, exhausted donkey struggled with the overload, coughing soot and grumbling as it clambered to the crest. As they reached the apogee, the driver stepped up the velocity of the moped, yanking them forward and thrusting down the hill.

"That's right!" the driver shouted with the unconfined enthusiasm of an excited voyager. "Yes, we did it!"

"Yes!" Nadus and his father joined the celebration.

The young boy raised his head and turned to his side and for a short time, he caught a glimpse of the entire city; it was uniquely beautiful and colossal. Before long, the two men and the young boy arrived in the bustling city and were immediately welcomed by the smell of burning rubber mixed with engine fumes as well as the noise from loud cars and buses scrapping for dominance over the dilapidated roads; the city was nothing like the young boy's village with many windless days that smelled of burnt firewood and savory stew, and silent nights that were occasionally interrupted by the howls of hungry dogs in the hillsides. They arrived at an intersection, took a quick right turn onto a busy main road and instantly found themselves stuck in gridlock. The driver, as though suddenly possessed by a bad spirit, began to yell and curse at other drivers and squeeze his way through the chaotic and disorderly traffic. In contrast to the driver who became irritated by the smog, dust and extreme heat from the sun and vehicles, Nadus smiled and stared in wonderment; he was speechless and through his naïve eyes the big city was another world onto itself.

13

CHAPTER THIRTEEN:

"A notorious child at home is notorious wherever they go."
African Proverb

After several minutes of intense verbal warfare with other motorists and passengers alike, the middle-aged man steered the moped out of the jam without scratching its metal surface or chipping its blue paint and with no injury inflicted on his two passengers. Like other cyclists, he left the jumbled road and jumped over the curb, riding along the paved sidewalk that lay parallel to open gutters, which flowed with fresh sewage and excrements and served as the home to many houseflies and mosquitoes. An eyesore and offensive to the nostrils, the edges of the reeking drainage had buckled with age and its surface was covered with slimy green algae that resembled the fur of a wet hedgehog.

"Clear! Hey you, are you deaf?" The driver honked and yelled, shoving a few pedestrians out of his way as he darted along the walkway. "Move it! Move! Quick now! I said to move it!"

Accustomed to the forewarnings and behaving like herds of antelopes running from a lioness, many of the city walkers countered and jumped to the side of the curb, clearing a path for the aggressive motorcyclists.

"Shut up! You're an idiot, a big idiot!" an old man lamented as he was displaced and pushed off the sidewalk. "Learn to respect your elders."

"I told you to get out of the way," the driver replied as he moved along the concrete, spewing dust and paper debris into the air. "Go get your old ears checked! Come on, use your sense!"

"You're a fool!" the older man raised his fist and shouted. "Come back here, let me teach you a lesson. I'll beat the living daylight out of you!"

"Okay, wait there! I'll be back soon." The driver laughed and continued to hustle his way through the crowded path. "What a joke! Old fart!"

Nadus held on to the driver as they were jerked around by each sudden stop, turn and acceleration of the moped, making him a little motion sick. He watched the commotion and tried to assimilate. Nevertheless, he couldn't help but wonder why everyone he saw the in city seemed rushed and on-edge. A few yards in front of them, Nadus saw a woman walking along the sidewalk, carrying a large basket of mixed fruits that she balanced on her head with one arm; on her back she carried a baby that was secured by a wrapper and in her other hand she held an infant.

"Move it! Move it! Quick now! Get out of the way," the driver yelled as he accelerated towards the woman and her children. "I will clear you out of the way if you don't move now!"

The woman didn't budge and the driver continued his pursuit towards them; the young boy flinched and his heart sped up again as they got closer to the fruit hawker and her kids.

"Madam, get out of the way!" the middle-aged man shouted again.

"Please! Please don't do it!" Nadus closed his eyes and whispered as he tightened his grip around the driver.

A few inches before they crashed into the woman and her baby, the driver squeezed the levers, slamming the brakes. Nadus gasped; the rubber tires burned and screeched with the increased traction, halting the moped and lifting the back slightly from the ground.

"Look here madam! Are you deaf or something! Didn't you hear me, eh?" the driver yelled as he pulled his ear. The woman didn't respond to his rebukes or even look back; she just kept on walking. "Fat cow!" The driver revved up the engine in intimidation and maneuvered around the curvy woman. "You're deaf, huh?" He looked at her and spat in the dirt.

The fruit hawker turned her fleshy neck and looked at the driver with a straight-face as if unaffected by his harassment. "You're a bastard!" she pulled her son closer and gestured. "Tell your idiot mother that you're a bloody fool and a bastard child!"

"No! It's your grandfather, a bloody bastard and the son of a real retard!" the driver shouted back as they zoomed away.

"Excuse me, mister!" Nineb sighed and swallowed hard; his throat was parched and his voice was husky. "Please watch your language in front of my son. What's the hurry, eh? We're not complaining, are we?"

"That fat..." the driver stuttered as though ready to vent. "Okay boss!" he replied and nodded. "My apologies sir! You're the one paying me."

"Thank you!" Nineb turned his head to the side and sneezed. "Nadus? Are you okay, son?" he asked as he rubbed his nose.

Nadus looked at his father and nodded. "Yes Papa. I'm fine. Are you?"

"Yes, I'm fine, just a little dust."

"Young lad!" the driver lowered his tone. "Hope I didn't scare you! Just the people in the city can run you crazy with their madness. Sorry, eh!"

"It's okay sir," the young boy responded nonchalantly as he continued to survey his surroundings. He was still intrigued and a little tense from the last incident with the woman, but he was relieved that they didn't get into an accident or injure the baby.

"Excuse me sir," Nadus asked seconds later. "Were you really planning to hit them, the woman and her kids?" he asked with genuine concern.

"What?" The skinny man laughed. "I'm no devil. I can't live with such a thing on my mind, all bluff, you know, just to get people out of the way. You thought I was serious?"

"Yessir, just a little." Nadus replied as he was rocked up and down by the rough and bumpy pavement.

"No way!" the driver scoffed. "It's just the way people act in this crazy city, my friend. You have to act tough or these people will think you're a softy and that's not good, you know; they'll ride you like you're a stupid horse!"

"Oh really?"

"Oh yes!" the driver said in a drawn-out way. "Don't act like you're just fresh from the village! Okay?"

"Okay sir! But why?"

The driver lifted his sunken cheeks and revealed a crooked smile. "You seem like a good kid!" He blinked and shook the sweat off his face. "You have a good mind, your head is correct. I don't want anyone messing with you."

Nadus puckered his brows. "Okay, thank you sir."

"Sorry, eh! For before, that fat cow of a woman just wouldn't get out of the way! I mean, I don't even get angry like that, you know."

"I figured you're just a little frustrated," the young boy concurred.

"You're a smart boy!" the driver exclaimed, nodding as he climbed the curb and guided the moped back on the overfilled street.

It was midday and temperatures were uncomfortably high; the tarred roads crackled and torrid heat waves were visible to the eyes. Encircled by many rusty creatures that quivered as they mindlessly polluted the air with black smoke and soot, the sweaty driver directed the motorbike through the heavy traffic, squeezing through and in-between warped and uneven bumpers. After a few twists and turns, the driver got out of the mess, flipped the signal switch on his scooter and drove into a fenced compound that was located on the left side of the road. With broken gates that barely hung from their hinges and ramshackle, graffiti-blemished walls, the entrance of the city bus-stop resembled a large hole in a termite hill with streams of insects freely coming in and out. The man and his two passengers rode down the rugged, dusty, trash-littered lot that swarmed with activity: street peddlers advertising products, roadside hawkers guarding heaps of treasured goods, bus conductors shouting and collecting fares, and taxi drivers harassing potential clients. Like a puppy in a lively circus, Nadus was overwhelmed. The skinny driver leaned forward, cut the fuel supply to the engine by releasing the rubber handle grip and allowed gravity to propel the moped down the slope. They glided for a couple yards and pulled behind a muddled row of fervent motorcyclists who were chatting and waiting turns to snatch up passengers. The driver squeezed the brake levers and they came to a smooth stop. Then, he placed both legs on the ground before quenching the rumbling engine; the moped heaved as it rested.

"Alright!" The man hawked and spat. "We're here! You can get down."

"Yes, we are in the big city!" Nineb exhaled with the sigh of relief as he descended from the hissing machine. "Yes, in one piece."

"I got both of you here safely, eh?" The man searched his breast pocket, pulled a hand-rolled cigarette and placed it between his lips.

"Yes sir." Nadus shook his head and bounced with excitement. "It was such a fun and interesting ride and I enjoyed talking to you, sir."

"Good! That's nice." The driver grinned and the wrinkled cig danced in response. "I enjoyed talking to you too. You're a good kid."

"Thank you very much," the young boy continued. "Especially when-"

"Okay, okay Nadus!" Nineb interrupted. "Enough talk for one day, it's time to get down!" his father grasped the steel frame of the rear saddle, further stabilizing and balancing the blue moped.

"Yes, Papa." Nadus nodded in obedience and climbed down, watching his step and avoiding contact with the hot exhaust pipe.

With both passengers off the moped, the driver pivoted the kickstand with his leg and leaned the scooter to the side. He stood, stretched and yawned with his mouth partially closed, trying to keep the cigarette between his lips.

"Thank you!" Nineb expressed his gratitude. "It was a little bumpy but you did get us here in time."

"I'm glad sir," the driver replied as he lit the cigarette with a match. He closed his eyes and took a long drag; the bony protrusions on his face were more noticeable as he sucked in his cheeks. "Your kid," he paused, raised his head upwards and exhaled, puffing out smoke, "he's a good kid, smart!"

"Thank you and I thank the heavens." Nineb smiled and nodded as he raised his index finger upwards, "I like to think so." He glanced at Nadus who was preoccupied, captivated by the merchants and their advertisements. "So tell me, uh, how much do I owe you today for this ride?" Nineb asked as pulled out a small pouch from his pocket.

"Yes, money!" The driver flicked the cigarette butt and sprinkled ash on the ground. "Let's see." He leaned over and looked at the odometer as he bounced his head. The man stood erect, placed the cigarette between his lips and then put his hand under his armpit; using his other hand, he scribbled in the air as though calculating the cost. "Okay! I'll take-"

"Please, I don't have much," Nineb interjected. "We're actually here in the city because I'm trying to borrow money from the bank," he walked closer and spoke in a lower voice, watching over his shoulder, "and he doesn't know that."

"Oh!" The driver was taken aback. He sucked his teeth, spat and then looked at Nadus who was a few feet away, laughing and wearing a cheerful expression on his face. "You look like a good father, you know and your son..." He paused, turned his head to the side and flicked his fingers.

"Thank you again," Nineb replied.

The driver nodded repeatedly as though in deep thought. "Don't worry about it!" he spoke in an affirmative manner after a minute of silence. "Yes, don't worry about it. You don't have to pay me. Your son is a good child and he's like my new friend, consider it my gift to him."

"Oh really?" Nineb widened his eyes. "No, no, you worked for it. I'll pay you, but I just can't pay much." He offered the driver a few coins.

"No, it's okay!" The driver gestured with his hands and puffed his cigarette. "I don't do this often, honest! You know, I someday hope to have a son like yours. You know, kind and very respectful. Ha, I just need to find a good wife first." He laughed and his chest wheezed. "Use it to buy something nice for him since it's his first time in city."

"Thank you, but I feel bad, you know. Please take it." Nineb insisted.

"I'm serious," the driver chuckled. "Don't make me change my mind."

"Okay!" Nineb conceded; he put the coins back in the black leather pouch, tied it and placed it in his pocket. "Thank you for your kindness.

May you and your children see many days on earth—may the heavens bless you!"

"So be it." The driver accepted the prayers. "So be it!"

Nineb turned to his son and called out, "Nadus, come here!"

"Yes, Papa." The young boy turned and walked towards his father.

"Say thank you to the nice man who just gave us a free ride."

"Oh really?" Nadus looked at his father and then the driver. "Thank you very much sir!" He bowed his head, clasping his hands together as though praying. "I enjoyed talking to you and you've been kind to us."

The driver smiled and nodded with the satisfaction of a munificent donor. "No worries at all, young lad, enjoy your time in the big city, eh! As I said before, be watchful in this place, especially with your belongings, there're so many pickpockets here." The driver threw the butt on the ground and stepped on it with his sneakers.

"Okay sir." Nadus accepted the man's advice. "I'll keep that in mind."

"Thanks again," Nineb chimed in, "but we have to get going before the sun goes down and it gets late." He winked at the driver, grabbed his son by the arm and walked into the throng.

"Bye sir!" Nadus waved and walked backwards with his father holding his hand and leading the way. "Thank you for the free ride!" he shouted as the distance between him and the driver widened.

"No worries lad." The driver waved back. "Just don't forget about me when you start working for the electric company, making all that big pay, okay?" the man shouted and like a zebra in a herd, he blended into the noisy and superficial world of the city.

Nadus and his father scrambled through the large, overcrowded lot, shoving their way towards the narrow street that served as the business district. The clay soil was hard and cracked from the heat and discolored with black patches of engine oil; the ground was rippled with footprints and littered with a colorful assortment: tattered plastic bags, crumbled boxes, mud-covered pieces of paper, rusty bottle caps, cigarette butts and rotting fruit remains. The air smelled of fumes, sweat and urine mixed with fermenting foods, complementing the diverse and filthy scenery.

"Hey, watch where you're going!" a tall boy shouted as he bumped into Nadus.

"I'm so sorry," Nadus looked up at the older boy. "I didn't mean..."

"Nadus!" Nineb interrupted his son, grabbing him by the shoulders and pulling him away. "Don't talk to anyone in this crazy place—people look for trouble here! They'll bump into you just so that they can pick a fight with you or steal from your pocket."

"I didn't know that, Papa," Nadus replied.

"I know son! It's just that this place is very vicious," his father added. "I even heard from your uncle that certain people here with magic powers can bump into you and steal your testes and kidneys. You wouldn't even know it."

"Oh no!" Nadus exclaimed with a petrified expression and immediately touched his groin. "It's still there, Papa." The young boy sighed in relief.

"I'm glad," his father replied. "Just watch your step son!"

"Thank you, Papa."

"Nadus," Nineb stood and glanced at a crumpled piece of paper in his hand and then pointed to a street sign.

"What does that say son?"

The young boy looked in the direction and squinted. "Hmm, it says Sra-Ge-Be-Av—oh, oh, it's *Sraggeb* Avenue. That's what it says."

"Great!" Nineb thanked his son. "That's where we need to be headed!"

"Oh, why Papa?" Nadus turned to his father and asked.

Nineb heard his son's question and his mouth became sour. He looked at Nadus and wanted to fabricate an appealing response, but he just couldn't lie to him; he would be acting like one of those hypocrites that he detested. "That's the way to the banking company," he replied. "I figured since we're here I could borrow money to help us with the farm and with buying food."

"That's a fantastic idea," Nadus blurted out. "You deserve a break! Yes, let's go there."

"Hope you're enjoying yourself," Nineb tried to switch the topic.

"Yes Papa, I am! Thank you for bringing me here. It's really big."

"Perhaps we, you and I, could go in together and get to see the inside of a bank. I heard it's large, clean and cool and 'very fancy' inside."

"Yes, I'll love to Papa!" Nadus rejoiced as he walked beside his father.

Having navigated through the congested lot that served as an offhand market and the city bus stop, and walked for a mile through the grid-locked roads that were lined with street hawkers, crippled beggars, drug peddlers, tarts with their pimps and counterfeiters, the two naïve villagers arrived at the heart of the busy business district. They stopped at the corner of the main intersection and looked around aimlessly until Nineb found the courage to ask one of the peddlers for further directions.

"Okay, turn right here, then go straight down, take the first left." The peddler wiped his face, pointed and spoke quickly in a distinctive accent. "You'll be there and you can't miss it."

"Thank you sir!" Nineb and Nadus bowed and spoke in unison.

The man didn't acknowledge their gratitude; he walked away and began to advertise his goods again as if unexpectedly struck by deafness. Nadus and Nineb didn't understand the basis to the peddler's cold response or why their appreciation was ignored; despite that, they didn't allow his actions to ruin their moods. The two villagers brushed it off and continued their undertaking. As the two sailed upstream through the lagoon of city dwellers, Nadus couldn't help but stare up at the gigantic edifices that surrounded them like ancient and mighty trees in a forest; curious about the architecture and the intricate designs that decorated the surfaces of the buildings and intrigued by the reflective glass panels that sparkled at the corners, the young boy was truly awestruck.

"Nadus, I think that's where we need to go." Nineb tapped his son on his shoulders and pointed to a building ahead of them with two robust men guarding a large door and many impatient patrons lined up in front.

Above the entrance was a large, white rectangular sign with two visible words inscribed in black capital letters. "What does it say son?"

"Oh, that's a beautiful building," Nadus replied as he stared away.

"Is that what it says? Come on, pay attention!" Nineb reprimanded his son in a light-hearted fashion. "What does the sign say?"

"Pardon me, Papa, I got carried away, sorry." Nadus shook his head.

"Don't be, I know you too well. You're like your mother, a free spirit."

Nadus smiled. "It says..." he paused, "hmm, *KANBDLROW* FINANCIAL."

"Excellent!" his father blurted out. "Yes, that's it, that's the place!"

"Oh really? That's great Papa!" Nadus was equally excited; he couldn't wait to see the inside of the tall building and rest his dusty and achy feet.

The villagers, like *tsetse* flies attracted to the soft skin of a newborn, walked with haste towards the lofty concrete building. Shortly after, they found themselves in a horde, standing a few feet away from two burly men who weren't smiling and who were elevated from the ground by a concrete staircase that served as a platform; they both wore black suits, shoes and dark sunglasses that hid their eyes from daylight and clipped to their ears were tiny gadgets attached to black wires that ran into their jackets. It looked like nothing Nadus had ever seen before.

"Quiet down, everybody!" one of the men shouted.

"I said if you're waiting to deposit or withdraw money, please line up to the right. If you're a farmer looking to receive a loan, line up to your left," the other guard uttered and directed the dehydrated customers.

Nineb heard the instructions and was filled with relief as there was only one other person standing on the left side. "Oh yes, I'm a farmer," Nineb shouted, raising his hand as he and his son muscled their way through the agitated mob towards the front of the line. "Yes sir, I'm a farmer!" Nineb chanted as they climbed the stairs.

"Is he a farmer also?" One of the guards stopped Nadus as he followed his father towards the glass doors.

"Oh yes sir, he's my son and we work together," Nineb replied.

"Is he applying for a loan also or are you together?" the guard asked in a stern voice.

"We are..." Nineb hesitated; he wasn't sure if it was some sort of trick question required to gain access into the building. "Yes sir, we're together, but I'm the one who's applying for the loan," he answered.

"Then he can't come inside!" The burly man snapped a response.

"But we're from the village, this is his first time here," Nineb said. "He wouldn't be of any trouble, a good child! I vouch for him," his father bargained.

"It's the bank's official policy!" the guard spoke without any emotion in his voice. "It has nothing to do with him being a good child or not. We only allow customers inside or the person who is applying for the loan, understand?"

"Sir, please look at him, he's just a young boy..."

"Look here! We've a job to do here, either you go inside now and leave your son outside or both of you can go back to your rural life in the village, okay?" the second guard chimed in; his voice was deep and lacked even a trace of emotion.

"He's..." Nineb choked on his words and felt a heat in throat. His blood began to boil as he realized his dilemma. They needed the money and he just couldn't leave empty handed without trying, but he also feared leaving his son outside all by himself in the strange and dangerous city.

"Step aside to make room for others." The first guard pushed Nineb and his son, directing them towards the edge of the staircase.

"What do you think son?" Nineb scratched his head and then wiped the sweat off his forehead. "Do you want us to just head back home? Your thoughts?"

"I'd like to go inside with you Papa, but I understand that they have their rules." Nadus sighed and looked at the entry and then at the guards. "I'll be fine, honest! We could use the money, you know. I don't want to be the reason you didn't try."

"Nadus, are you sure?" Nineb also looked at the entrance to the bank and then looked at his son. "We could just head back home, try to manage with what we have and I could just come back on a later date."

"No, no, Papa. Please don't do that."

"Okay!" Nineb sighed and his voice was groggy; he placed his hands on his son's head and surveyed the surroundings. "Hey, look over there!"

"What's that Papa?" Nadus turned around.

"It's a book stand and I know you like to read. Perhaps you could wait there for me and read a book." Nineb pointed and sounded more upbeat.

"Yes, Papa! I can do that," Nadus agreed. "But you know, Papa, I'm not so young anymore. I'll be a year older soon," he teased. "I'll be fine!"

"I suppose you're right son. Okay, just wait over there for me and I'll see you soon. Remember," Nineb pulled his earlobe, "don't talk to strangers, just mind your business."

"Yes, Papa. I'll see you soon, good luck in there!" The young boy began to walk down the stairs.

"Wait, Nadus," his father called out, "take this, use it to buy yourself a soft drink, heard orange's the best!" He beckoned and offered his son two coins.

"Thank you, Papa!" Nadus ran up the stairs and took the money without question. Then, he watched his father walk hurriedly toward the large revolving glass doors that soon shoved him into the building.

Taking a deep breath and closing his eyes for a split second, the young boy like a hungry African penguin filled his lungs with oxygen and dived into the crowded street. Without delay, he was pulled in and submersed by the whirling current of hasty pedestrians. Struggling to hold his ground, he wobbled his way towards the bookstand that was a few yards away, planted beside a rusty and crooked lamppost. The cubic counter that gleefully displayed a number of used magazines, novels and novellas on improvised racks had seen better days; nailed together from salvaged wood and painted with garish colors, the makeshift bookstore was rustic, dingy in appearance and was a pathetic attempt at attracting the attention of passers-by. Nadus surfed the tides until he reached the corner of the pavement. Then, he broke free from the horde, clamored over a few trash bags and stood beside the bookstand, leaning against the lamppost. Although having to endure the stench from three garbage cans and fight off a few houseflies, the street corner turned out to be a great location for viewing many of the city's happenings without worrying about being bumped or pick-pocketed. Across the street, the young boy saw a group of street musicians playing their instruments with intimacy and singing out their hearts to passers. To their right, as if using magic, a ventriloquist and a puppeteer controlled several colorful dolls and intrigued gullible spectators. Clustered to the left-hand side and competing for the majority of the audience, five energetic performers with two acrobatic monkeys rolled on the ground, on flattened cardboard boxes, and danced to inaudible songs that were pumped out of a portable stereo; mimes with painted faces stood on wooden crates, acting away and conversing with their gestures and facial expressions. A female contortionist awed fans with her many assumed postures and remarkable bending and flexing of her body. Effortlessly juggling and bouncing sticks of fire in and out of his hand, a conjurer played with fire. The city was truly filled with "unrestricted pleasures."

"This is just wonderful!" Nadus whispered as he watched the cinders and fiery motions of the blazing sticks. For a fleeting instant, everything around him, with the exception of the juggler and his sticks, slowed and faded away; the young boy was consumed and carried away by intrigue. "Oh, if only Idnurub was here, he would be going crazy right now!" Nadus thought about his friend and then thought of his father.

Oh, I'm supposed to be over there.

That's why I'm I so thirsty.

The young boy hiccupped and recalled that he was meant to wait for his father at the front of the bookstore. Without delay, he turned, jumped over the trash and walked around the garbage cans. Lined up on one side of the swanky bookstand and peddling edibles, several entrepreneurs risked their savings and hustled to make a living.

"Fried fish, tasty fried fish!" One woman sang to the crowd.

"Ice cold water, buy your ice cold drinks here." A second woman who was standing in front of a plastic bucket and holding a bottle of water chorused.

Their loud cries and advertisements caught his fancy. The young boy watched the women for a bit before proceeding towards them; his stomach was beginning to grumble and his throat was parched. He really wanted to put something cooked in his mouth to lessen the twinges in his belly, but the smell of the fried fish mixed with all the fumes wasn't appealing. Nadus walked up to the lady with the plastic bucket, bargained and paid for a drink with one of the two coins his father had given him.

"It's just because you're young and you look so thirsty that's why I'm giving you this drink at this price," the seller complained as she removed the top of the bucket and untied the twine sac that sat comfortably inside the container; after groping several ice cubes and slender bottles for a few seconds, she pulled out a clear plastic bottle from the stash, removed the cap with her wet fingers and handed it to Nadus.

"Thank you so much." Nadus took the cold, perspiring container and stared at its contents for a while; it was orange soda and he had never tasted one before.

"No, thank you!" The lady smiled and continued her advertisements.

Nadus closed his eyes and poured the sparkling drink between his lips; dazzled by the sugar rush and the millions of air bubbles tingling in his throat, the young boy savored the flavorful explosion in his mouth. Like a famished calf suckling happily, he downed the entire contents of the bottle as fast as he could without gagging.

"Oooh! Wow!" Nadus sighed and burped as he pulled the bottle away from his lips; then, he looked at it as though suddenly infatuated with it.

That was incredible!

I wish I could have more but I don't have enough money!

Thanks Papa for this!

Oh yes, I have to be in front of the stand.

The young boy reluctantly gave the empty bottle back to the seller and walked towards the front of the bookstand. As soon as he got to the facade, the glossy cover from one of the magazines shined and caught his fancy. Acting like a thirsty traveler at the sight of an oasis, Nadus rushed to the rack and began to devour the foreign publication, tasting the pages with his fingers and flipping through as fast as the vibrating wings of a hummingbird. With each breath he took, the young boy perspired and appreciated the colors and texture of the pages. Brows and lips puckered, Nadus admired all the beautiful, stylish and well-fed people on each page who all seemed to be smiling and laughing at him. At that moment, he wished to someday be as nourished and happy as them; however, he didn't realize that looks are often deceiving and that he was in fact happier than many of subjects in the photographs. Eager for more, Nadus put the magazine back and scanned the racks for other appealing covers and titles. After a few seconds, he couldn't help but notice a unique trend; many of the covers bore the pictures of a particular older, plump woman, dressed in different flamboyant outfits and wearing heavy makeup.

Why's her face all over the place?

The young boy thought it was a little vain and obnoxious. He had once overheard one of his teachers say that people lost a part of their soul every time their picture was taken; as a result, he reasoned that the unknown woman on the front of the covers had surely lost a large chunk of her soul. He shrugged his shoulders, grabbed another one and began to flip through it.

Oh well!

"Boy! What are you doing?" the merchant blurted out. "Are you going to buy it or not?" The old woman coughed as she walked towards Nadus who was standing under the large canopy that protected the merchandise from the weather. "You better not be stealing anything from there!"

"No madam!" Nadus placed the book back on the rack and looked up at the storekeeper. "I'm not stealing anything. I was just glancing at it."

"No, no, no!" The old woman coughed again. "Don't touch or glance! This isn't a library! I don't want your dirty fingers on them!" She blew the used magazines and wiped them with a small rag.

"I'm sorry," Nadus apologized, "and I didn't know I wasn't suppo..."

"Go on, move boy!" She shooed Nadus away. "Move along!"

The young boy, although slightly startled by the old woman's tenacity and her coarse voice, took only one step backward.

"Why are you still standing there?" the woman asked. "I thought I just told you to be gone?"

"I can't leave here!" Nadus declared.

"What did you just say?" The storekeeper was confused. "You can't leave my bookstand, uh? Tell me, are your legs tied up, who tied them?"

"No one ma'am, no one tied my legs!" Nadus stuttered.

"So tell me again, why can't you leave then?"

"My father told me to wait here," he answered.

"Your father? Who's your father, where is he?" she asked.

"I don't want to disobey him in any way." Nadus shook his head, faced the ground and kicked the dirt.

"Huh?" The storekeeper was frightened by his response and seemingly erratic behavior, but she didn't show it. The old woman gave Nadus a wary look and took a step backwards, twisting the cloth in her hand and prepping her lungs to scream if needed. "Where's your father?" she asked again.

"He's inside the bank." Nadus pointed to the building. "We're from the village, he's trying to get a loan for our farm and he told me to wait here for him."

"Why here?"

"Those men over there, the security guards wouldn't let me inside the building with him."

"I see!" The storekeeper sounded relieved. "Oh my, for a minute there I thought you were a little disturbed upstairs." She laughed and smacked Nadus lightly with the rag in her hand.

"No madam!" Nadus looked at her and smiled. "I'm not."

"My dear, you can stand here and wait for your father."

"Thank you."

"I didn't mean to be so unfriendly! It's just that every now and then one of those beggars and lazy thugs wonder in here and starts causing me trouble and I'm particularly scared of the ones with *slim*."

"Okay ma'am," Nadus replied. "It seems like the big city has a strange way of making people act different." The young boy smiled as he thought of the driver and his two dissimilar personalities, the friendly one in the village and the aggressive one in the city.

"Yes indeed!" the storekeeper said. "That's very true."

"Ma'am, sorry to bother you, but what's 'slim?'" Nadus raised his hand as he pondered on her statement. "Do you mean like being very thin?"

"Slim disease," she shook her head in remorse, "is a very terrible disease to have! The people with slim become terribly sick and start getting thinner and thinner like skeletons until they eventually pass away, a very awful way to go."

"Yes, it sounds terrible." The young boy grimaced and felt his protruding ribs. "Ma'am, I recently took ill and lost some weight, do you think I have slim?"

"No, you don't have slim! I don't even wish it on my worst enemies. Come," the old woman walked closer to Nadus, "let me show you one of them." She pointed towards some garbage on the other side of the street. "See that one over there, the one that looks like a dead stick."

"Oh, yes ma'am." He saw a lifeless man lying on flattened cardboards, camouflaged by heaps of litter.

"That man was a thug! He used to come over here all the time to bother me and cause trouble, but now he's there wasting away, very sad!" the old woman concluded.

"But why don't people just help him or a least give him something to eat so he's not so thin and dirty?"

"My dear," the storekeeper heaved, "most people are scared of catching the disease, most believe that if they go close to him they'll get it too! I hear there's no cure once you get it." The old woman looked at Nadus and nodded. "To be honest, I've tried to feed him, give him food and water, but he can't hold anything inside for long. It all comes out of his mouth and behind and most of the food gets eaten by those wandering dogs."

"Sad! So how do people get it then?" Nadus asked fearfully.

"Hmm, good question," the old woman replied. "I don't know exactly how, but I think most people get it from sleeping around, especially here in the city."

People become like that from sleeping in the big city?

"Wow!" Nadus exclaimed. "Starting today, I'll be careful and always watch where I sleep so that I don't catch the slim disease!"

The old woman laughed at his innocence. "Oh yes dearie, you should be careful of where sleep and who you sleep with. You never know!"

"Thank you for the tip!" Nadus didn't catch on to her innuendos.

"No worries dear!" the storekeeper replied as she inspected and rearranged the books and magazines on the rack. "So from all your questions, I assume this is your first time in the city or have you been here before?"

"No ma'am." Nadus surveyed his surroundings and paused. "I mean, yes ma'am this is my first time here, in the big city."

"It's an interesting place, right?"

"Yes, very much so!" Nadus nodded with his hands hidden away in the pocket of his shorts. "It's different from my village and I've never seen so many buildings and cars before in my life!"

"I understand how you feel, dearie. I felt that way many years ago when I also left my village and moved to the city. In fact, I still feel like that sometimes."

"You used to live in the village?" Nadus exclaimed.

"Of course dear, I did! I suppose I don't look it anymore." She smiled.

"Why did you leave for the big city?" he inquired.

"Well, dear, the reason," she paused, "hmm, I haven't given it thought for a while now, I don't even know where to start. Are you sure you really want to hear my boring story, do you?"

"Yes madam! Please, please do tell me, I'll like to hear it."

"Okay," the woman agreed. She dropped the rag on the counter and rubbed her palms together as if trying to remove a tough stain on them.

"I'm listening ma'am!" Nadus smiled.

"Patience dear!" The storekeeper waved her index finger and clicked with her tongue. "You haven't been in here for up to a day and you're already acting impatient like city folks!"

"I'm sorry."

"It's okay. I ran away when I was a young girl," she said bluntly.

"You did?" Nadus gaped. "Why? What happened?"

"So many reasons, some you might not understand at your tender age. See, my mother worked very hard and my father," she paused, "let's just say that he wasn't one of the nicest persons I knew." She sighed. "Anyway, after many nights of crying and suffering and well, with a little fate, I packed my things and I went with the wind.

"Oh!"

"Yes, and ended up in the big city, well it wasn't so big back then."

"Really?"

"Yes, really!" The storekeeper laughed and coughed.

"What 'little fate' are you talking about?" Nadus had a good ear.

"You're clever!" The storekeeper chuckled. "I thought you wouldn't ask me. I suppose I could tell you more since you're actually listening."

The old woman walked closer to young boy and spoke in softer voice as she divulged into her ugly past. She told Nadus about her family and her lonely childhood and how her father was a violent drunk who was very abusive to her and her mother; she told him about her arranged marriage and how her older husband forced her to "lay with him" and beat her all the time.

"I just couldn't take it any more so one night I closed my eyes tightly and prayed to the heavens; I prayed for a miracle! Behold, the following night as he walked into the room, something happened!" the storekeeper whispered and her aged eyes widened.

"What happened?" Nadus asked in suspense.

"Fate happened, karma! That night as he opened his mouth and raised his hand to strike me, his heart stopped and he dropped to the ground."

"Just like that?"

"Oh yes, just like that."

"Did he faint?"

"No, no," she shook her head and whispered, "he died on the spot!"

"Geez, what did you do then?"

"I did what any young girl would do. I ran!"

The young boy was further distraught by the details of the storekeeper's story. She told him more about her long and treacherous journey to the city and how she had to "start from scratch with nothing." Like every human that walks the earth, the young boy also had his own unique story that he shared with the woman. On the verge of tears, he told her about his mother and how she had passed when he was born.

"I wish I got to meet her! Sometimes I feel like she would still be alive if I wasn't born," Nadus spoke softly. "It's my fault, I took her away."

"No dear!" The old lady looked at Nadus. "Don't say such a thing. Your mother nurtured you for many months and she gave you life so that you can make your mark in this crazy world. Your mother performed the ultimate sacrifice, gave up her life so that you can have one, okay?"

Nadus nodded reluctantly.

"Anyway, I'm sure she's mighty proud of the way you turned out."

The young boy smiled. He then told the old woman about his desire to become a juggler in the big city and in return, she told him to do whatever made him feel happy, regardless of other people's convictions; he also told her about the secret love of his life and how he dreamed of someday marrying her but couldn't because of her unique yet commonplace arrangement.

"Yes dear, you're right! It's awful, don't let that be a reason for you to stop showing her your love and affection," the storekeeper said. "Let me tell you something I've learned from experience, you can imprison the body for as long as you like, but you can never imprison the heart. Oh yes, you can never encage a woman's heart, never. See, if you truly care for this girl and she feels the same way towards you, no matter what happened in life, she'll always have a warm and special place in her heart for you. She'll always be thinking of you!" The storekeeper touched Nadus on the nose with her finger and smiled.

Nadus squeezed his face and pulled out a smile. "Is that really true?"

"Oh yes, absolutely dear! Absolutely true!"

"So you think she's thinking about me right now?"

"Yes, my dear."

"Aw, gee!" The young boy became full of emotion.

"Hey," the old lady exclaimed, "since you're here in the city, it will be a good idea for you to get her something special to show your affection."

"Really?"

"Oh, yes silly!" The old woman coughed into the hem of her wrapper. "She's a girl and girls always adore gifts." She clapped once.

"Hmm, okay but I don't have much!" Nadus searched his pockets and pulled out a small coin, showing it to the storekeeper. "This is all I have."

"Well," she looked at Nadus and tapped her lips with her fingers, "that wouldn't get you much around here."

"I suppose you're right!" He frowned and sounded a little let down.

"Come on now!" the old woman scolded him. "Don't just give into defeat like that without even trying, huh?"

"It doesn't matter ma'am. I don't have any more money."

"Hush now, I think I have the right thing for you." The storekeeper stretched out her hand and opened her palm. "Pay me! Give me the coin and I'll show you the surprise!" she giggled like an excited schoolgirl.

Although a little wary, the young boy obeyed and placed the coin in her wrinkled palm; like the supple tongue of a forest frog nabbing an unsuspecting cricket, the old woman snapped her hand shut and clenched her fist. She walked behind the counter, bent over and hummed as she rummaged through an old wooden box on the ground.

"Ha-ah!" the storekeeper exclaimed after about a minute of searching through a pile of scrap. "I found it!"

"What ma'am?" Nadus was eager to see the mystery item. "What is it?"

"Here, take a look." She stretched out her arms, holding and dangling a necklace in her hand; it was simple yet elegant and it was crafted from a thin string of dyed leather and a piece of granite. "Isn't she a beauty?"

"Oh," Nadus took the necklace and inspected it, "it's beautiful!" He was wowed, especially by the miniature statue of a woman that served as the pendant. "Is this for me?" Nadus looked up at the old woman in disbelief.

"Well," she beamed, "yes! Of course it's yours, you just paid for it."

"This is worth more than the coin I just gave you."

"Says who?" the woman interjected.

"It just looks expensive." Nadus continued to admire the pendant.

"Well dear, don't always believe what you see!" She winked. "Now, you have something special to give her."

"Yes, I do!" Nadus exclaimed.

"I'm sure she'll like it."

"No, I think she actually love it!" Nadus blurted out.

"Good!" The storekeeper nodded. "Oh, excuse me one second dear!" She walked away to attend to a man who wanted to purchase a pack of cigarettes and an adult magazine.

"Okay, all done! Where were we?" the storekeeper laughed. "You can blame my old memory on that one, fails me sometimes."

"Who's this woman carved on the necklace?" Nadus asked.

"That's the goddess *Rehtom*!" The storekeeper looked at the pendant and then at Nadus. "She represents the strong and virtuous woman," she raised her clenched fist and waved it, "and she's a symbol of femininity."

"She will be very happy!" Nadus shook his head. "Whose was it?"

"Mine!" the retailer replied. "It used to be mine and it kept me through many years, through many tough times."

"It belongs to you. I don't deserve it." Nadus offered the necklace back.

"Dear, it's not for you silly, give it to her! The lady who has stolen your heart. She needs it now more than I do." The storekeeper sighed, placing the necklace back in his hand and clasping his fingers together into a fist.

"Thank you so much." Nadus bowed his head in reverence and pocketed his newest acquisition. "I think there are lots of kind people here!"

"Well," the old woman smiled, "that's very honorable of you. I see you prefer to see the good in people rather than their flaws."

"Oh, yes, sometimes in the mornings before I go to school in the village I have to fetch water from the stream with a plastic keg. It can get very heavy so I just pull it over my shoulders and..." Nadus stopped his ramble and peeped; he was distracted by the developing ruckus on the street. "What's that all about?" he pointed and asked the old lady.

A convoy of approaching vehicles came into view with sirens that blared through the noisy ambience.

"I didn't know they were coming this way." The storekeeper looked at the procession of five vehicles. "Oh, that's *Awig-Eled* and *Awiw-Oras*," she replied with a smile across her face. "Two very intelligent brothers!" She clasped her hands together as though ready to applaud.

"What do they do?" Nadus gazed at the two smartly dressed men who were standing at the back of two separate pickup trucks; they were beaming and showering the boisterous crowd with campaign gifts: caps, pens, tee-shirts and plastic mugs and plates. "All those people seem happy to see them."

"Yes dear, they're good people, they're the hope for the future and this wild city! The two of them are going to change all this," she looked and pointed at the trash littered sidewalks, "the heaps of rubbish! And they're going to take out all those corrupt leaders and help old folks like myself, mostly with our healthcare needs. Oh dear, they have my endorsement."

"Hmm, I already like them!" Nadus smiled and continued to watch the campaigners as they addressed the crowd with bullhorns and waved to the people shouting and gesturing from the surrounding tall and decrepit buildings.

"They're so kind and they're good people," the storekeeper added.

"Yes," the young boy nodded and pulled his brows together, "they do seem like very nice men, like they truly care for the people."

Enveloped by a throng of ardent, star-struck supporters and partially protected by a pair of police officers who were armed with whips, batons and canisters of teargas, the motorcade like a bright-colored caterpillar crawled through the crowded and narrow street; the twin brothers who were the center of attention were both journalists turned politicians, embarking on a whistlestop tour of the city's dense business and slum districts. Nadus admired the charismatic speakers as well as the energy of their overzealous supporters who sent out praises as they received hand-outs; he was intrigued by the giddiness of the crowd as it was somewhat reminiscent of the excitement at the village festivals. Like any growing child, Nadus wanted to fit in to his surroundings and be accepted and more informed; consequently, he grilled the storekeeper and tapped into her invaluable "chest of wisdom," candidly questioning her views of people, the city and the politicians. Although slightly distracted by the wailing sirens and loud shouts and songs of the animated crowd, Nadus listened attentively to the old woman. The storekeeper told him that there was a big difference between an "eager person" who wants to make a difference and a "bored one" who just wants to do the same thing. He learned that "many of us mistreat others because of inner fears of ourselves and insecurities," and that "true character" is revealed from what "most say in passing" and what they "find or think is laughable." As Nadus watched the swarms of supporters disband from the thoroughfare, Nineb returned from the bank and joined his son under the aged canopy. Nadus introduced the storekeeper to his father and thanked her for the insight. Not too long after that, Nadus and his father headed back to the bus stop and departed for their modest village; they were both excited, as Nineb was approved for the microloan and Nadus truly had a blast in the "wild, big city."

14

CHAPTER FOURTEEN:

🐍

"The frog never runs in daylight for nothing."
African Proverb

Happy voices and hearty laughs of playful children nicely blended with the smooth, eager tweets of nearby birds, and the euphony of running waters produced complex melodies that soothed the mind. The languished morning breeze had returned from hiatus and was rippling across the village stream, cooling off the perspiring washers and aquatic patrons. Still in the moment and immured by his fondness for the young girl, Nadus continued to admire the ornament that beautified Muotrahk and endowed her with a hint of class and elegance.

"Okay, I'm coming big sis! I'll be there shortly, one second!" the young girl turned away from the boys and shouted. "Alright, Nadus and Idnurub," she looked at the schoolboys with eyes that sparkled in the sunlight, "they need me over there," she pointed to a group of women in the distance. "I guess it's been enough chitchatting for one day, better get going before they all get emotional." She chuckled and rolled her eyes.

"Okay," Idnurub replied, "you don't want that to happen."

"Yes, yes indeed."

"It was nice to see you today," Idnurub added.

"Uh-huh," she nodded. "It was nice to see you too. I hope you have a great day at school."

"Thanks, I'll do my best," Idnurub grumbled.

"Come on! It's only school!" Muotrahk teased. "You should be happy."

"You always say that. It stinks!"

"At least after today, you'll both be out on break and you won't have to be there for another two months, right?"

"Yes!" Idnurub exclaimed. "Gosh, I can't wait."

"Then, you didn't have to sound so unhappy." She winked. "I'm sure you can endure one more day. Just imagine that you and your classmate are in a far away island, filled with magic and surrounded by great water-falls and pretty gardens of colorful flowers that smile all day." Muotrahk indulged in one of her fantasies.

"Hmm, smiling flowers and waterfalls?" Idnurub laughed. "Okay, I'll do just that."

"Or you could be boring and act like a good student," she interjected, "and appreciate school and learn a new fact today. That's the least you could do for yourself, right?" She smiled.

"Sure, yes, right! Of course!" Idnurub squeezed the damp garment in his hand and placed it inside the plastic bag that was lying in the mud.

"Okay, I'm coming." Muotrahk shouted and gestured as she answered her older sisters' third call. "I really have to go. Nadus?" She faced him.

"Yes." Nadus looked up and locked eyes with her again.

"I have to go now," she said and fidgeted as though expecting a gift.

"Oh," Nadus replied; he didn't seem to have an appropriate answer.

"Nadus, it was nice to see you," she spoke in a softer voice, breaking the silence between them. "I've missed you," she murmured.

"Thanks Muotrahk." He nodded and began to put the rinsed clothes into a wrinkled plastic bag. "Yes, it was nice to you see you too."

"Really?"

"Of course, really!" He looked up as if surprised by her answer.

"I don't know though." She shook her head. "Well, you just seemed a little more interested or will I say happier to see the necklace than you were to see me."

"That's not true." Nadus smiled as he denied the accusation. "I was just admiring yo-" He hesitated and cleared his throat. "I mean, I was just admiring it, the necklace on you and not you exactly. It looks really good on you!"

"Is that so?" she asked.

"Yes, very much so."

"Aw, that's sweet of you." She touched the jewelry and bloomed with affection and youthful emotion. "Thank you, but I have to get going."

"Bye!" Idnurub saluted.

"See you soon!" Nadus added; the young boy didn't like saying the word "bye," especially to Muotrahk because he feared the day when she would be sent off to the "evil stranger" and he would never get to see her again.

"Bye Idnurub!" Muotrahk waved. "Okay, be good in school today. I'll see you soon Nadus!" She smiled, grasped the pot in her hand and turned to leave. "Yes, there's one more thing!" She stopped in her tracks and walked back to the schoolboys. "You forgot to give me a hug."

"Who me?" Nadus gasped and looked at her and then his classmate.

"Who else would it be silly?" Muotrahk smiled.

"Oh, okay, I'm sorry." Nadus was caught off guard by her forwardness and was a little bashful. "I forgot I suppose."

"That's why I had to remind you." Muotrahk dropped the clay pot to the ground, leaned forward and wrapped her arms around Nadus. "I'm so happy to see you today and I still appreciate you, I love you," she whispered in his ear, and right away the young boy felt warm inside.

"That's really great!" He smiled and awkwardly hugged her back.

"Pretty love birds!" Idnurub coughed and cleared his throat forcefully. "Aw, look at the two of you, so sweet and it makes me want to cry."

"Hush now Idnurub!" Muotrahk closed her eyes and rested her head on Nadus's shoulders. "Don't be jealous."

Smothered with genuine adoration and shielded by their affection for each other, the two young lovers tightly embraced and for a fleeting moment were one in mind, body and soul. With a regretful sigh, Nadus unclasped his wet arms from the beautiful girl and released her to the world, hoping that she would someday return to be his wife. Nadus watched Muotrahk as she joined her sisters and in the span of a few seconds that Nadus was incapable of perceiving through the haze of his reverie, she departed from the vicinity, strolling away towards the village with a pot of water carefully balanced on her head. A few minutes later the two schoolboys packed up their damp laundry in their bags and hurried to school. Jogging only for a quarter of a mile, the two boys arrived at their final destination of the morning in time for them to get settled into the assembly before the "strict principal" took the stage. Lined in front of a bungalow and corralled like cattle, the boys and few girls fidgeted as they awaited their instructors. Adjacent to the unfinished building was a large oak tree that served as a shade, especially on days when the classrooms became unbearably hot. Before long, the schoolmaster walked out of the building and stood in front of the noisy pupils.

"Quiet down boys and girls!" the principal yelled as he rang a brass bell in his hand. "Be quiet or I'll have to discipline you all! Understood?"

The youngsters, wanting to avoid needless punishment, lowered their voices. They diverted their attention to the gentleman standing in front of them and listened to his redundant speech and instructions.

"...Education, boys and girls," the principal spoke avidly and waved his fingers in the air like a wand, "is about learning, about immersing yourself in an environment filled with new ideas, facts that you never knew existed and ideas you didn't know that you didn't know! Understood?"

"Yes, principal," the students murmured.

"Good! Now, in honor of this great land," the principal continued, "it is time for us to say the national anthem. Let's go boys and girls!"

As they did every morning without question, the pupils, in unison, placed their arms to their sides and stood at attention; opening their mouths simultaneously and unleashing their vocals, they began to sing the anthem with no passion and without paying any attention to the words they recited. Afterwards, the principal put on his spectacles, pulled out a pen and a ledger from the pocket of his black blazer and began to take roll of the students.

"*Adnawr*!" the principal called out.

"Here!" A boy raised his hands. "Here, sir!" he corrected himself.

"*Lagenes*!"

"Present, sir!" A schoolgirl in the front of the line smiled and bowed her head, kneeling slightly as she held her long skirt with both hands.

"Nadus?" The older gentleman surveyed the herd. "Nadus?"

"Present!" The young boy raised his hand and jumped; he was at the back of the line and he wasn't the tallest of the bunch. "Sir, I'm over here!" Nadus jumped again and waved his hand frantically as he didn't want to be marked as absent and have to face detention on "the rack." The principal noticed Nadus and continued to call out names from the student list, checking off attendees and asterisking truants.

"As you know," the principal said as he put the pen and notepad back into his side pocket, "today is the last day of school for this term." Immediately, some of the boys whistled and applauded. The principal grimaced and shook his head as he stared at them. "It's time for you boys to pay the price for your accountability!" the principal blurted out; as soon as those words came out of his mouth, the entire school compound fell into an almost tangible silence. "I'm so proud of the girls, you all passed!"

Without delay, the few girls in the assembly cheered and applauded. "Mister Ohtosel!" The principal cleared his throat and turned towards the group of instructors sitting on a bench. "Please come up," he paused and beckoned, "with the grades and please don't forget to bring the cane!"

The lanky man heeded the call; right away, he stood from the bench and picked up a frayed notepad along with a long stick from the cement pavement that lined the front of the bungalow. The arithmetic instructor walked up to the principal, handed him the grade book and then began to bend the cane and swing it through the air; it was punishment time. Tension rising and fear enveloping their minds, the boys were focused and anxious. The principal opened the notepad and flipped through the pages. Then, in a stern voice, he began to call out the names of those students who didn't pass the final test; with each name that was announced, there was a string of moans from the other students.

"...*Adnagu*, *Alogna*, *Sellehcyes*!" the principal exclaimed. "Idnurub!"

"I knew it!" Idnurub looked at Nadus; he was upset but not surprised.

"I'm sorry." Nadus patted his pal on the shoulders. "I'm sure it would not be bad, just take deep breaths," he added and watched Idnurub head towards the principal who was still calling the names of other dismayed boys.

"And finally," the principal reached the last page, "Nadus! All losers!"

"What?" The young boy couldn't believe his ears and the assembly of students seemed equally surprised. "I'm one of the best in class!" Nadus boasted. "This must be a mistake!" he chanted as he made his way to the front; his hands turned pale, his breathing intensified and his heart like a caged elephant pounded against his chest. He wasn't following his prior advice to Idnurub.

Like cattle about to be branded, Nadus, Idnurub and the other "losers" were rounded up in the front of the assembly. One by one, they walked forward to receive their "reward for failure." Grasping the edge of a sturdy desk, leaning forward and trembling, the fearful boys were lashed on their backs and buttocks; six hard strokes for each of them.

"Sir, it must be some kind of mistake." Nadus protested as he walked up to the desk. "I studied hard for the final exam."

"I said to hold the desk!" the math teacher demanded as he tapped the young boy's arm with the stick. "Stop the excuses. It's no mistake, you failed mathematics! Now hold it."

"Sir! It has to be a mistake." Teary-eyed and shaking his head in denial, Nadus held the desk tightly and leaned over.

I didn't fail the exam.

It has to be a mistake.

You're so evil and I hate you Mister Ohtosel!

I hope you get to suffer for this!

Eyes closed and muscles tightened, Nadus felt the dry stick land and stamp its signature on his rear, instantly burning and welting his skin. The pain was very sharp and it reminded him of how much his brother disliked the coach and the concept of learning through punishment.

"Tpyge was so right! I hate school!" Nadus murmured as he staggered back towards the herd, rubbing his backside to alleviate the aches.

After the elaborate sentencing ceremony, the principal wrapped up the gathering with another spiel on diligence and the importance of good grades. Then, he ordered the pupils to quietly march to their classrooms before heading indoors with the other teachers. Inside the dull and child-unfriendly schoolroom, Nadus moved around on a crooked bench, but a long wheal across his thighs hurt badly and he couldn't settle down.

"Hello, class!" a smallish man greeted the pupils as he walked inside.

"Hello Mister *Ailamos*!" the pupils chorused.

"How are you doing today?" the teacher asked as he walked towards the blackboard and scribbled down the date.

"We're fine, thank you!" the pupils, with the exception of Nadus, Idnu-rub and a few other losers, chorused again.

"Good, good to hear!" he placed a large textbook onto a desk. "Are you brilliant boys and girls ready to learn some cool science?"

"*Yes!!!*"

"Are you all excited?" The science teacher actuated the youngsters.

"*Yes!!!*"

"Fantastic!" the teacher exclaimed. "I'm excited, today's going to be lots of fun." He walked towards the blackboard and began to draw a figure, "and I'm sorry to watch some of you get flogged today, especially you, Nadus." He turned around and looked at the schoolboys who were frowning. "Just to let you know, everyone in this class passed the science exam." He paused. "In fact, Nadus scored the highest once again!" Ailamos pointed with the chalk in his hand. "Boys and girls, give him a round of applause, okay?"

The pupils looked at Nadus and began to cheer and clap. Their show of approval uplifted him and he didn't feel so humiliated and let down.

"That's better, much better!" He smiled and winked at Nadus. "Now all of you clap for yourselves, you passed and we had a great term together." All the pupils, including the upset losers, cheered loudly and applauded.

Ailamos, although smallish and feeble in stature, had a big personality and a great way of making his pupils feel happy and eager to learn; he never flogged them or chastised them. Time and again, he encouraged Nadus to study science and convinced him that he could learn new ways to help his family obtain better crops like the bountiful ones they saw in the agriculture textbooks. Nadus jumped on the idea in hopes that he would help his father and patch his relationship with his older brother; they used to be best friends and he missed the good, old days when they did things together: hunting crickets in the fields, racing grasshoppers in puddles of water, making toys from scrap that they salvaged from the dumpsite and running down hills with used tires. As Tpyge grew taller and his voice changed and he began to grow pubic hair, he started to act differently and stopped spending time with Nadus. He didn't want to play "childish games" anymore and was always exhausted from farm work.

"Hey class!" the teacher stopped writing on the board and exclaimed. "Do you want to learn something really splendid?"

"*Yes!!!*" the pupils shouted. "Yes, we do!"

"Okay!" He touched his face. "Did you know that your nose and your ears continue to grow throughout your entire life?"

"No!" the class retorted. "Really?"

"Definitely! They never stop growing."

"Excuse, sir." One of the boys raised his hands. "Do you mean that my old grandmother," he hesitated and pulled his right auricle, "her ears are still growing?"

"Oh yes, her ears are still growing." the teacher responded.

"Then why don't old people have large ears like elephants?" another schoolboy asked as he bit his fingernails.

"Good question!" Ailamos smiled and nodded. "It's because our ears don't grow as fast as those of big elephants, ours grow very slowly."

"If our ears continue to grow," a schoolgirl raised her hand, "why does my grandfather find it hard to hear me sometimes, shouldn't it get better with old people?"

"That's another fantastic question." The teacher laughed. "The way we hear things is a little more complex than just the size of our ears and that brings up a good point! Does anyone know where the smallest bone in the body is located?"

"Me, please pick me sir!" A boy sitting beside Nadus waved his hand. "I know the answer, I know it."

"What is it?" The teacher pointed to the boy. "Let's hear it."

"It's the fingernail sir." He raised and waved his pinky.

The teacher smiled and shook his head. "Nice try, but our fingernails aren't made from bone. It's made from a special kind of protein called *keratin*. Anyone have another answer, anyone?" He gazed at the students. "No one?"

The pupils glanced at each other.

"Alright, the smallest bone in the body is inside our ear and it allows us to hear things."

"How small is it?" Nadus asked.

"It's tiny, as small as a tiny ant," the teacher replied, "and because our bones get weaker with age, old people sometimes find it hard to hear us."

"Oh cool!" the pupils echoed and looked impressed.

"Want to hear another interesting fact?"

"*Yes!!!*"

"Okay!" Ailamos raised his palms and showed them to the kids. "Just as we have unique fingerprints, we also have unique tongue prints." He let out his tongue and showed it to the kids. "Let's see your tongues."

The excited students also showed off their unique tongues.

"I see lots of healthy tongues here with different shades!" The teacher knocked on the desks as he wandered around the class. "Talking about different shades, do you kids know why people have different skin colors and shades?"

"Is it from staying too long in the sun?" one of the schoolgirls asked.

"No, it's from drinking lots of coffee!" another boy uttered with confidence.

The teacher laughed again. "No, it's not from drinking too much coffee and yes, spending too much time in the sun can change your shade, but that's not what causes it." The teacher looked at the schoolboy. "The shade of our skin is caused by how much *melanin* we have in our bodies, the more pigment in your body the darker you'll look."

"Excuse, sir," Nadus blinked and raised his hand, "what's a pigment? Is melanin just another name for pigment?"

"That's a great question Nadus, a pigm-" The science teacher's explanation was cut short by a series of thunderous sounds, followed by the humming of heavy engines and approaching tire treads.

"What's that, Mister Ailamos?" a frightened girl asked as the other pupils ducked slightly, mumbling and exchanging looks of confusion.

"I don't know. I'm sure it's nothing serious." The smallish man spoke in a hushed voice, gesturing with his hands as he tried to reassure them. "You kids just be quiet, okay?" The teacher placed the chalk beside a large textbook on a table. "I'll go see what's going on out there." He picked up a wet rag that was hanging on the wall and wiped the whitish dust off his fingers before stepping outside.

At once, the schoolboys and girls got up from their seats, rushed to the window and began to struggle for the best view. Parked a few yards away in front of the brick bungalow were five military vehicles: a sport utility vehicle with dark tinted windows, two midsized vans and two trucks with oversized tires. Dressed in mufti and surrounding the vehicles like gorillas hanging from a large tree, many young men posed and flaunted the assault rifles that were strapped across their shoulders. A boy in his teens jumped out from the back of the large truck that was at the rear of the convoy; looking like a schoolboy on vacation, he wore a ragged tank top, brown khaki shorts and rubber sandals that had seen better days. His head was shaved and shining like the others and he also had an automatic firearm strapped across his shoulder. The boy darted towards the side of the sport utility that was parked in-between the vans and trucks and stood at attention like a cadet. Embracing his weapon and pointing it upwards, the boy raised his head and hollered. "Stand your ground, present your arms! Salute!"

Without ado, all the guerillas stood still, raised their firearms upwards, yelled and opened fire, each discharging several bullets into the sky and spilling casings onto the ground. A few clicks and shots later, the back door of the sport utility vehicle swung open and a tall, muscular man with a scarred and pockmarked mug stepped out. He had a goatee and was decked out in a black shirt and dark-green camouflage trousers; on his head he wore a black beret and on his feet he wore black combat boots that were splotched with mud and ominous maroon stains. He carried a leather whip around his waist that was made from dried cow's tail, and beside the leather whip were a jagged dagger and a semi-automatic pistol tucked into a leather holster.

"Who's in charge here?" The commandant spat chewed tobacco onto the ground. "Somebody answer me!" he yelled as he stared at the group of petrified educators who were standing by the entrance of school building. "Don't let me get upset! I said who is in charge of this place?"

"Yes sir!" The principal raised his hand like one of his students and walked towards the domineering man. "I'm the one in charge."

"Who are you?" the commandant walked closer and asked in a coarse voice, eyeballing the balding man as though he was a piece of trash.

"The principal," the older man stuttered. "I'm the principal sir!"

"You're the principal?" The commandant cracked his neck. "Correct?"

"Yes sir!" The older man nodded and spoke up a little; his voice was full of fear and it didn't sound as loud and authoritative as it was during the morning assembly. "Yes, I'm the principal," he loosened his necktie.

"And you're the man in charge?" The commandant stroked his goatee.

"Yes I am." The principal swallowed his saliva and responded.

"Good one!" The burly man nodded and laughed as he turned around and fixed his eyes on his confederates. "Can you believe this? Here's the man in charge!" The commandant continued to laugh. "He says he's the man in charge and he can't even look me in the eye."

The other guerillas also began to snicker and the principal bowed his head and looked downwards in shame. Without prior warning, the commandant turned swiftly and slapped the principal so hard on his face that he fell to his knees. "I'm in charge, not you bloody cockroach!" the commander yelled as he pulled out his leather whip; many of the pupils in the classrooms gasped. Although a little startled from the gunfire, the real shock for them was to see their venerated principal sobbing and on his knees. The "losers," on the other hand, smiled and chuckled.

"That serves you right! Now you know how it feels!" Nadus whispered as he and the other pupils stared furtively through the window.

"Okay, sir." The principal looked up with a bloody lip.

"Did I give you permission to talk?"

"No, you di..." the older man pled and gestured with his hands.

"Goodness, you're still talking!" The commandant exclaimed, and with that, he exploded in anger and began to kick and whip the principal without mercy until he bled; crying and wailing, the teachers who were still standing by the door expressed their fears and remorse. The commandant snapped his fingers, signaled and then pointed to the lifeless body. "Get this roach out of my sight!" Straight away, four men dashed forward, grabbed the principal by his flaccid appendages and dragged him away, smearing his blood across the mud. Then, the commandant pulled out his pistol and fired two shots in the air. "I want everyone to the yard now!"

15

CHAPTER FIFTEEN:

"It takes an entire village to raise a child."
African Proverb

Bullets spewed out of hot barrels and cut through the humid air, and the vivacious guerillas grinned as they sprayed the top of the building with many rounds from their magazines. Ducking, screaming and scrambling in panic, a number of the pupils and instructors bolted towards the yard and prostrated in the mud; a few of them didn't make it as they were gunned down by stray bullets. Upon ceasing fire, the guerillas dashed into the bungalow like savages with whips, sticks and machetes in their hands, hunting down and thrashing everyone inside.

"Good execution!" The commandant clapped, smiling as he praised his henchmen. "Sort them, women here and men over there!"

"Captain, what about the children?" a soldier asked.

"Pile the cockroaches over there, I'll deal with them later," he replied.

The commandant's men gestured their deference; they grabbed the schoolchildren by their arms and hair and hauled them under the oak tree, hoarding them together like cheap disposables. They separated the school's men from the women and split them into two groups. They ordered the male teachers to stand in front of the school building, beside the comatose body of the principal.

"All of you, put your hands behind your neck!" the general yelled; he was standing a yard away from the quivering line of teachers with his feet apart and both hands in his pockets. The male teachers trembled, sobbing as they raised their hands in obedience. With their arms up and behind their heads, the hefty solider walked up towards the instructors and began to sniff them like a hound. "I smell fear! You disgusting cock-roaches, pigs!" the general lamented as he eyed each of them and spat in their faces. "You should be ashamed, look at yourselves, eh, shaking like cold dogs! Where are your book smarts now, eh?" The general looked at Ailamos who was weeping and then gave him a "bloody slap."

"Boss, we have all the children under the tree," a young man inter-jected. "We're just waiting for your command."

"Correct!" The general nodded to the report. "Okay, I'm ready." The man walked away from the male teachers. "Get my *brown-brown*!" he ordered. One of the boys dashed towards the sport utility and opened the passenger door. Seconds later, the child solider came back with a rusty can that he presented to his commandant in a servile manner. The man snatched the container, opened it with greed and snorted a pinch of the teak-colored powder. "Ah, aah!" The general held the ridge of his nose and shivered. "Alright boys," he coughed with teary, bloodshot eyes; his voice was deep and stoic, "feed them lead! I have no use for these pigs!"

Without delay, all the guerillas cocked their rifles and opened fire on the teachers, cutting down the helpless men like timber and splattering their blood and flesh all over the front of the school.

No, no, not Mister Ailamos!

Nadus watched the carnage and tears flowed from his eyes. After-wards, a few of the soldiers picked up the bullet-ridden bodies, one by one, and dragged them into the building. Ogling, sniffing and patrolling the line of remaining teachers like wolves in heat, the "senior officers" began to violate the women, licking their faces, ripping their tops and groping their bosoms.

"Look at you," one of the men hissed, "fine thing!" The scrawny man stared as he licked his fingers. "Boss, I haven't poured in a while. Do you mind if I taste her a little, maybe give her some yogurt?" The senior officer grinned as he groped one of the terrified teachers.

The general didn't respond; he stared into space, stroking his goatee as though pleasantly intoxicated.

"Boss? Did you hea..."

"I did!" the general snapped.

"I'm sorry boss!" The man stopped necking the recoiled woman.

"I suppose we have time!" The general held his belt buckle. "I should try out one of them while they're still fresh and clean!"

"Oh yes, boss!" The scrawny man gleamed and gave out a sleazy laugh that made all the women sob louder.

"Shut your mouth!" a second officer shouted as he backhanded one of the women on the lips.

"Bring me that one!" The general hawked and spat, "the mature one with the luscious behind!" He pointed and began to unfasten his belt; he handed his weapons to one of his men. "Hold this, take her inside for me!"

A burly man with a burn scar on the left side of his face scooped up the lady from her feet; the music teacher cried and tried to resist, but she was no match for his strength. The man threw her effortlessly over his shoulders like a small sack of rice and galloped towards the entrance.

"I want a clean room!" the general demanded as he tagged behind.

"Yes boss!" the man shouted as he entered the building.

With the general out of sight and inside the edifice, the officers became wild. Like ravenous hyenas, they rushed the other educators and tackled them down to the ground; spanking them, grabbing their hair and ripping off their skirts and blouses. In broad daylight and in front of the pupils and the other guerillas, the officers began to defile the screaming women. Struggling to assert their dominance and gibbering like apes, the unruly men congressed for several minutes, verbally abusing and penetrating their unwilling partners like woodpeckers.

"Are you deaf?" An officer smacked his "juicy prey" repeatedly on the back of her head. "I told you to keep your knees straight and your buttocks up!" the gaunt man moaned as he grasped the woman by her hips and forced himself onto her.

"What has gotten into you?" The general grabbed the belligerent officer by the collar of his shirt, pulling him away from the teacher and shoving him in the dirt; the battered woman cringed in the mud, crying and attempting to hide her nakedness with what remained of her clothes. Standing over the officer, the general pulled out his pistol and sat on the man's bare chest. "That's not how you treat a lady that you're enjoying! We're resistance fighters not cowardly thugs! We don't rough up women, we make them want it! Beg for it and enjoy it!" He grinned and sniffled and then placed the barrel on the officer's temple. "If I ever, ever catch you acting like this in public, especially in front of the others," he cocked his pistol, "you'll have a lot more to worry about. Am I clear?"

"Yes, boss!" The man nodded. "Please forgive me boss!" He blinked, swallowed his saliva and covered his manhood with his dusty hands.

"Be warned!" The general stood up and put his pistol back in the holster. "Now get dressed, cover yourselves! We have tons of work to do!"

"Yes boss!" the guerillas chorused.

"Go gather up the women and get them all in the truck!" The general yelled and signaled as he and a few confederates marched towards the children that were herded and shaded under the tree; as the heavily built men closed in, the squatting pupils scrambled, pushing each other and retreating like poultry in a coop. The general stood at ease and watched the kids scuttle towards the aged trunk. Then, he turned to his colonel and whispered in his ears. The tall man with the scarred face listened and nodded in accordance.

"All of you to your feet!" the colonel shouted as he began to grab the pupils by their arms and pull them up. "Stand up! Stand up!"

"Hey kids! What's the matter?" the general inquired, sounding sincere and apologetic. "Why are you crying?" He hunkered down and looked at one of the girls. "What's the matter, did someone beat you?" He spoke softly and wiped her tears with his fingers. "There's no need to cry, okay? I'll take care of you, none of these big, scary men will hurt you, okay? Do you want some candy?" The young girl looked up reluctantly and nodded. "Ah, that's a good girl!" The general smiled and pulled out a lollipop from his pocket and handed it to the schoolgirl. Then, he stood erect and faced one of his sergeants. "Take all the girls into the van."

"Yes captain!" the man replied.

"Be nice to my little girls, okay?" the general whispered with a sinister smile. "The young shall grow, you know!" he sniggered.

"Yes captain, I'll be nice to them," the sergeant retorted. "Alright girls, let's go," the sergeant kept a stern face and clapped twice, "come with me! Let's walk over there, no one will hurt you." Similar to inexperienced ducklings following a drake, the young girls were led towards the van in the convoy.

"Now for you roaches, get up and follow me!" the general ordered the remaining boys; his voice wasn't harsh, but he didn't sound as gentle as with the schoolgirls. "You're all growing men," he added, "and I was once like you, in your shoes! Terrified! But now there's no need to fear at all." He smiled and waved his finger. "We're family, you know. Come on! Let's go, all of you to the back."

The guerillas and the schoolboys, as though on an exodus, walked around the brick building and marched towards the grassy backyard.

"This is good!" The commander stopped without warning and faced his confederates and the boys, causing them to bump into one another. "As I was saying earlier, we're a special kind of family, you don't have to fear." The general proclaimed. "However, in order to become part of this family you have to make the choice and join willingly, at your own will! See, we don't force anyone to join us!" The hefty man thumped his hands against his chest like a chimp. "So I present you with a golden opportunity to join us or leave." The general spread out his hands as though sowing seeds; he then fiddled with his beret and slanted it to the side. "If you don't want to join us, raise your hands, step forward and you will be free to leave!"

The schoolboys sweated and mumbled, looking at each other with fear in their eyes.

"Quick!" The general contorted his face. "I know you're not all dumb, eh? I told you to raise your hand if you want to leave and step forward, you'll be free to go!"

Without ado, a number of the schoolboys slowly raised their hands and began to make their way to the front.

"Idnurub!" Nadus whispered as he grabbed his friend by the arm and pulled him back. "No! Don't do it!"

"Why? I need to go home, mother is sick!" Idnurub whispered back.

"No, please don't!" Nadus shook his head and spoke without moving his lips. "I don't like the way he's talking, I think it's a trap."

"Anyone else want to go?" the commandant called out.

"Let go!" Idnurub looked at Nadus and heaved and then tried again.

"Trust me, I have a really bad feeling!" He grasped Idnurub tighter.

"Good!" The general commended the boys as they stepped forward, patting them on their heads and shoulders and pulling on their cheeks. "So you all want to go, uh? Is that right?"

"Yessir!" The pupils looked at the hefty man, nodding halfheartedly.

"No problem at all!" He laughed and pointed. "You're all free to go!"

The boys were flabbergasted; they couldn't believe their ears.

"You're all free to go!"

"Thank you sir!" the boys chorused; bowing their heads and clasping their hands together as if worshipping an idol, they each approached the general and paid their homage. Then, they departed towards the hilly plains, smiling and waving to their classmates who were still in the herd.

"Ugh, that's Iwalam over there!" Idnurub frowned. "See what you've caused! Now, he's free and we're both stuck here!"

"I'm sorry Idnurub!" Nadus whispered. "I just had a bad feeling."

"No you're not! I should have gone with them."

As the two boys argued in hushed voices and the disinclined school-boys were a few yards away, the commandant gave out an evil laugh. He whipped out his pistol, aimed it and released three slugs from the chamber. In response, sharp, loud and piercing cries echoed through the woods and two bodies in the distance slumped onto the grass. "Gun them all down, none of those bastard roaches get to live!" he stormed, waving his gun and stomping his boots into the grass.

"Yes captain!" The guerillas concurred, cocking their assault rifles as they stepped forward and dropped to their knees.

"Hold your stance!" a young boy in his teens ordered. "Fire!"

At his command, the henchmen happily squeezed the triggers of their weapons, expelling sparks and smoke and discharging rounds of ammo. Many of the terrified boys tried to run for cover, but their reaction times were no match to the range and rapidity of the *Kalashnikov* rifles; in shock and disbelief, Nadus and company watched as their friends fell in rapid succession.

"Wait, wait! I told you to hold it!" The commander waved his beret, shouting over the deafening gunfire. "Get me one alive, I want one alive!" Putting on his beret and realigning it on his shaved head, he continued his orders as the men stopped shooting.

"Yes boss!" The guerillas immediately ran up the plains, hollering with their guns drawn and ready to engage in combat.

"Make sure they don't get away. Just get me one!" the general added.

A few more shots rang out and moments later, the rebels jogged back, waving their guns in victory and vocalizing their thrill. Suspended by his arms and with his limp feet dragging and swaying in the grass, a boy was lugged by two guerillas that were in their late teens.

"We caught you this, boss!" one of the teenage boys exclaimed as they threw the pupil on the grass.

"Oh, yes boss!" the second boy added as he panted.

"He's a quick one and he tried to run away into the woods, but you know me," he boasted, "I shattered his leg with just one bullet." The first boy laughed as he revealed his index finger. Then, he aimed his weapon and made gunshot sounds.

"Excellent!" The commandant squatted and spat, staring at Iwalam as he gasped for air and cried inaudibly; the boy was shirtless and drenched in sweat, and on his thigh there was a visible gash that was bleeding. "You cockroaches that were smart enough to stay," the general turned to the boys, "let this be a warning to all of you!" He pulled out his dagger and stared at the sharp, jagged edge. "We're now family!" the general shouted. "Do you understand me? Now, we live, eat, sleep and hunt together, and most importantly, we die together!" He hunkered down and planted his knee firmly on Iwalam. Then, he placed his hand over the boy's nose and lips before driving the knife into his abdomen.

Muscles twitching and desperate for air, the boy widened his eyes and struggled for dear life. The general twisted the blade and stabbed the pupil relentlessly. Iwalam bled profusely and watched with increasing enervation as his assailant gutted him like a fish.

"This can't be happening! It's just a dream. It's just a very bad dream!" Nadus sobbed as he watched the butchering of his classmate.

"Not Iwalam!" Idnurub shook his head and tears flowed from his eyes.

"I just need to wake up!" Nadus reassured himself.

"Will you all just shut up?" the general yelled as he stood and wiped the dagger with a rag. "Real men don't cry, man up! Now wipe your tears or you'll all end up like those cockroaches!" The hefty man pointed to the hilly plains.

Nadus and the other boys stopped sobbing and wiped their tears with their hands and sleeves.

"As I have said, let this be a warning to you! Do you understand?"

"Yessir," the pupils mumbled.

"Answer the captain, 'yes boss!'" the colonel demanded. "Louder!"

"Yes boss!" the pupils chorused.

"Good! You're fast learners, a plus in my book." General *Yonk* put the army knife in the sheath around his waist. "Tie all these roaches up and toss them in back of the second truck, okay?"

"Yes boss!" a man with a backpack replied.

"We need to head out." He looked at his wristwatch and headed back to the convoy. "Rendezvous in two hours!"

The schoolboys were ordered to lay flat in the dirt and their hands were bound together behind their backs with twine; they were still in shock and suffering from temporary muteness. Afterwards, the guerillas put their "new recruits" in the trucks, started the engines and headed out.

16

CHAPTER SIXTEEN:

✳

"When the music changes, so does the dance."
African Proverb

Restrained in the back of the moving truck and unable to vocalize their apparent agony, the schoolboys squatted uncomfortably and moped in silence as they were transported across town. The procession of vehicles traveled together along a muddy road and the passengers were rocked and swayed from side to side as the tires wrestled with the rugged terrain. Smoking *ganja* with clay pipes and reluctantly sharing the crude drug paraphernalia, the gregarious rebels laughed to lewd jokes, caressed their rusty armaments and taunted their "new recruits" with the barrel of their guns.

"Hey bros!" one of the rebels yelled as he scratched his cheeks. "Pass it to me, let me take another quick hit." The teenage boy signaled with his hand and wiped the sweat off his face. "Why are you trying to smoke it all, eh?" He scratched his face again.

"Wait your turn boy!" a second guerilla barked as he planted the pipe on his lips and sucked it with force. "Look, look, it's floating!" the older boy blurted out after taking a long and deep drag.

"What is?" a third guerilla asked as he fidgeted. "Pass it along!"

"My gun!" The second guerilla coughed out an answer. "Look at it and feel it!" The older boy grabbed his rifle, shook it and pointed it at one the pupils who was squatting beside a forest-green metallic crate. "It's so light! It's like a feather, sergeant! Hey, you bloody idiot," he bent over and placed the cold barrel on the terrified pupil's sweaty forehead, "I can just scatter your big head now, you know, right?" The pupil indicated his assent by nodding fearfully. "Good one!" The rebel suspired spasmodically as he stood straight and released his grip on his weapon. He then stared intensely at his fingers as though in awe.

"Yes indeed!" The first guerilla laughed scornfully as he grabbed the pipe from the third rebel and sucked on it again.

Irritated by the pungent smell of burning hemp, Nadus slowly raised his head and with a bleak expression he glanced at the teenage boys who were standing close together, shouldering one another and coughing as they puffed out whitish smoke from their nostrils and mouths. Nadus was parched and the sensation in his arms was dwindling by the minute. The young boy looked at Idnurub who was squatting to his left with his head slumped downwards. Then he glanced at his other dejected mates who were also sobbing with their heads bowed. Their uniforms were stained with mud and their oily faces were dotted with beads of sweat. Nervous and uncertain of their final destination, Nadus peeped furtively through the gaps in the threadbare tarp that covered the rear of the truck. Squinting and straining his eyes, he recognized the ambience; they were driving through the marketplace. The young boy was surprised to see that the usually bustling village outlet was deserted and devoid of marketers.

"Where's everyone?" Nadus mumbled as he continued to stare, hoping to spot one or two people through the peephole. "Idnurub! Hey Idnurub," he whispered, turning to his friend and nudging him with his shoulders.

Idnurub looked at his pal; his face was devoid of its familiar, boyish zest. "Nadus. What's the matter?" he asked in a low, monotonous voice.

"We just passed the marketplace," Nadus replied. "I think we're headed to the village square."

"So?" Idnurub asked. "What's the point?

"Well," Nadus paused, "at least we know where we're headed."

"It doesn't matter, my mother is ill." Idnurub dropped his head again and began to weep. "She's all alone, she's very sick and needs her tea."

"Idnurub," Nadus said, "I don't know what's going on, I'm sure she'll be fine." The young boy furtively jolted his comrade with his knees in an effort to raise his morale.

"But Nadus, you really don't know! You have no idea how sick she is!" Idnurub snuffled. "She's dying! I know you're just being a good friend and I truly appreciate, goodness," he hesitated, "you just saw what happened to Iwalam!" He turned to Nadus with tearful eyes and a snotty nose. "Our friend was killed today, like a goat! How do you know we're not next, that we're not going to be killed at the village square, uh? Tell me!"

The direct question stabbed Nadus in his heart and a smoldering fire enveloped his throat; he had flashbacks of Iwalam rebelling in the classroom with mischief painted all over his face, laughing as they plucked mangoes in the woods, yelling as they ran from vicious bees and his expression of pure horror as he was bled out like one of those "helpless farm animals."

The young boy closed his eyes tightly and tried to shake off the gory images in his head. He wiggled his bound hands to ease the discomfort and then looked at Idnurub. "I really don't know what to say," Nadus spoke with a dry voice and tears filled his eyes once more. "You're right. Doesn't matter where we're headed." At that moment, he thought of his family and Muotrahk and suddenly felt cold and abandoned.

"Nadus!" Idnurub coughed; the haze from the drugs was bothering his sensitive lungs.

"Yes?" Nadus closed his eyes and tears flowed down his cheeks.

"Thank you!" Idnurub whispered.

"For what?" Nadus opened his eyes and gave his friend a baffled look.

"Thanks for being kind to me," Idnurub added, "and also for saving my life earlier. You know I could have been killed like Iwalam if you hadn't stopped me, so thank you!"

"You're welcome." Nadus gave a halfhearted nod. "Don't mention it! You're a good friend. Thanks for being kind to me too." The young boy could taste the clear saline solution seeping out of his irritated eyes and dripping into his mouth as he spoke softly.

"Ugh, shut it! Ah!" One of the inebriated rebels stormed towards the two schoolboys. "Shut your dirty mouth!" He slapped Nadus across the face and then punched him in the gut. "Who told you to talk, eh? Answer me! Show respect!" The teenage boy pointed to the other insurgents who were still laughing and smoking. "If I hear another word from you, I'll put a bullet, personally put one through your mouth!" He grabbed Nadus by the cheeks, squeezed it and then slapped him once more. Nadus winced in pain and felt his stomach curling up.

Expressing his mirth and staggering as the vehicle shifted sideways to a slight angle, the belligerent teenage boy joined the other orderlies and continued to intoxicate himself with the euphoriant in the clay pipes. Before long, the truck came to a stop and one of the rebels unlatched the wooden tailgate. Like enraged dogs, the other insurgents pounced on the pupils; they punched them, pulled their uniforms and shoved them out of the vehicle and onto the ground before jumping out with their rifles drawn. Landing on their sides with their hands tied behind their backs, the schoolboys scrambled to their feet and found themselves in the famous village square, frightened and immersed in utter chaos. Covered in dust and with his right elbow slightly scraped, Nadus rose to his feet with good bearing and spewed out the muck in his mouth. The young boy surveyed his surroundings and was shocked and bothered by the gloom. Many of the villagers were separated into groups based on their age and sex, and they were crying and huddled together like schools of fish. The ground was littered with trash, liquid waste and bodies, and the air possessed the acrid aroma of fresh excreta mixed with burning flesh.

"Bring those cockroaches!" General Yonk called out in the distance. "I said, pile them over here." The burly man beckoned and scolded his officers as he waved his pistol in the air.

"Yes boss!" One of the insurgents stomped his foot on the ground and saluted. "Straight line, move them there quick!" the man shouted and the other rebels began to flog and direct the pupils towards a group of boys who were herded and tied together in the dirt.

As Nadus and company were ushered along and neared the commander, they were further aghast by what they saw on the ground: battered, half-naked women screaming, sobbing and bleeding from their lips and labia, roasting stiffs, hacked and fly-infested remains of a few rebels, and bullet-ridden bodies of the hefty Snoitandetinu. The royal guards had stormed into the square with their weapons in hopes of defending the king and their village from the invasion. Alas, the speed and accuracy of their swords, bows and arrows couldn't compare to the rebel's automatic firearms; they were all gunned down before they could deter but a tiny fraction of the insurgents. Kneeling in the gravel with their mouths gagged and their hands tied up and surrounded by heaps of jewelries and treasures that were looted from the palace, the king, his chiefs and the oracle watched helplessly as the aggressive invaders pillaged their community. A few yards from the ensnared dignitaries, a woman crawled in the mud; mascara was streaking down her cheeks, and the newly widowed villager clung onto a young boy's arm as he was pulled away by one of the rebels.

"Please, oh please officer! I beg of you!" the woman screamed. "Please don't take my baby away from me!" she wailed and continued to grasp her son with both hands. "Oh, he hasn't done anything wrong! He's just a little boy!"

"Let go!" the teenage rebel demanded as he kicked the woman and began to bite her fingers. "I said let him go, he's now part of our family!"

"Have mercy sir," the widow begged and didn't surrender, "don't take away my son. He's all I have left!"

"I said let go of him or I will gun you down!" The infuriated guerilla stepped backward and aimed his weapon at the woman. "I'll blow you to pieces if you don't let go now!" the boy yelled as he cocked his oversized rifle.

"Please, please, don't do it, you don't have to do it!" The woman closed her eyes, crying as she clinched her child by his leg.

"You're not my mother, don't you ever in your life tell me what I can or can't do!" the teenage boy shouted.

"Please my son," the woman pled again. "You don't have to do this!"

"What, woman? You're really testing me!" The rebel smacked the side of his head with his fist. "Just watch, see what I'll do to you." The good-looking teenage boy spat chewed *khat* and then placed his slender finger on the trigger.

"Officer, hold your stance!" the colonel with the scarred face ordered.

The orderly glanced at his superior and slavishly lowered his weapon.

"What's going on here, uh?" Colonel *Ameduba* approached the vehement teenager. "Is this rat giving you any trouble, eh?" The tall man stood in front of the teenage rebel. "Is she giving you any trouble, huh? Look at me when I speak to you!" he demanded as he stroked the boy's cheeks.

The boy looked up timidly and mumbled. "Just a little, daddy!"

"Ah, don't worry! I'll take care of it, just for you! Okay?" He grinned and ran his fingers through the boy's hair. "Yes!" he nodded as he caressed the boy's ear. Then, he grabbed the boy by his neck and pulled him closer. "I'll take care of this, just like you'll take care of me, later tonight, okay?" the haughty man spoke softly. "Okay?" He raised his voice and tromped his heavy boot on the ground without notice.

The juvenile was startled. "Yes daddy!" he stuttered; his petrified visage revealed his thrall and the recurring exploitation.

"You really are something!" the colonel expressed his anticipation; he licked his lips and then winked at the boy. "Alright you rat!" The man turned his back and glared at the widow in the mud. "You're being a stinking rat!" he yelled as he pulled out his whip and released the flexible, beaded lash.

"Please, no sir, I'm not!" The widow looked up; her face and tender eyes were puffy and filled with emotion.

"Let go of that boy," the colonel demanded. "He's mine now!"

"Please officer!" The woman refused and didn't let go of her son. "He's just a little boy!"

"Release him!" the colonel yelled and began to lash the woman without pity. "You're a worthless rat!"

"Officer, please!" the widow cried louder as the leather whip welted her supple skin. "Please, daddy!"

"Are you crazy?" The colonel was berserk with fury. "Daddy, you're calling me daddy!" He gave out a sour snicker. "I don't allow women and especially dirty rats like you to call me that!" he yelled as he whipped the widow with added effort; in response, the woman bawled and screamed at the top of her lungs.

"Please officer, stop flogging mama!" the boy in question grabbed the lash in midair and held it; then, he knelt in the dirt and looked up at the colonel and sobbed. "I'll do anything sir, just don't hurt her anymore!"

"Serious? You're a bastard!" The officer looked at the boy with rage in his eyes; he pulled on the handle of the whip to initiate another powerful stroke, but he was unable to because the boy grabbed the lash with both hands.

"Oh yessir!" the boy pled. "Please don't hurt mama!"

"So you're struggling with me, huh?" The colonel looked at the village boy and spat on the ground. "You think you're strong, huh? So you want to fight me?" He released his grip on the whip.

"Oh, sir, no sir!" The boy shook his head and squeezed the whip and kept it at arm's length as though it were a poisonous cobra. "I don't ever want to fight you sir!"

"Can you believe this? This rat wants to fight me, right?" The colonel looked at the rebels in the vicinity and laughed. "Imagine this rubbish!"

"Yes lieut!" The teenage rebels nodded in response and revealed their stained teeth. "Yes lieut, he does!"

"No, no sir!" the village boy continued to plead. "Honest officer! I don't ever, ever want to fight you! I respect you sir!"

"Yes, you do!" The colonel slapped the boy so hard on his face that he fell to the ground like an aged tree. "Corporals!" the burly man barked as the boy cried and his mother tried to comfort him. "Come here now!" He pointed to four teenagers who were standing a few feet away and then pointed towards his boots.

The rebels heeded the call and dashed in the direction of their superordinate.

"Yessir!" they chorused like happy birds, flashing their rusty arms as they hurtled forward.

"Get him to his feet!" the colonel ordered.

"Yessir!" The rebels walked towards the boy who was still cringing in pain, holding his face and rolling in the dirt. "Get up!" the teenagers yelled in unison as they pulled him to his feet.

"So you want to fight me, eh?" The colonel inspected the village boy like merchandise, hovering around him like a predator.

"No sir!" The boy shook his head and bawled.

"You think you're a big man now, uh? Answer me!"

"No sir!" the smallish boy replied and his legs began to shake.

"You think you're a man, you think you're a big man, huh?" the burly man bellowed. "You have no idea!" he pulled out his handgun from his holster and cocked it. "Take it!" He handed the firearm to the village boy.

"I'm not a big man, sir!" the boy insisted. "I'm not trying to fight you!"

"Take it!" the burly man shouted again. "I said now, wipe those tears!"

Sniffling and trembling, the village boy stretched out his frail hand and took the pistol from the man. Unaccustomed to the weight of the gun, the boy struggled to hold the firearm up and keep it at bay.

"Respect it, you fool! Hold it tight and raise it up!" The colonel smacked the boy at the back of his head. "Now," the scarred rebel cleared his throat, "you see that rat on the ground?" He pointed to the fatigued widow. "I want you to kill her right now!" he ordered and took a few steps backwards. "Pull the trigger and finish her, shoot her now!"

"Sir, I can't!" The village boy looked at the colonel in disbelief. "I can't kill my own mother!" he stuttered in panic. "I can't!"

"You're disrespecting me, boy!" the colonel yelled. "It's simple, I told you to point and pull the trigger, now!"

"I can't do it, sir!"

"Please officer!" the widow begged and crawled towards the colonel.

"You can't do it?" The officer lowered his tone and nodded as though in agreement. "So you can't do it, right?"

"I can't do it! I'm not a man, I don't want to fight!" the boy dropped the gun on the soil, shaking his head and chanting his thoughts like a mantra.

"Corporals," the colonel shouted, "enter formation with the enemy!"

"Yessir!" the rebels responded and encircled the boy and his mother.

"This rat doesn't want to follow my orders!" the burly man spoke with his hands behind back. "Is this acceptable?"

"No sir!" the rebels shouted. "It's unacceptable!"

"Officer, I beg you with my heart!" The widow embraced her son.

"What do we do with unacceptable behaviors?" He ignored her pleas.

"Correct it on the spot!" the teenage rebels replied.

"Exactly!" the colonel nodded. "We correct it on the spot!" He hawked and spat and scratched his brows. "Okay, correct it now!" he exclaimed as he pointed to the two villagers. "Execute!"

"Yessir!" they hollered.

Without ado, the rebels, with blank and callous expressions, unlocked their rifles and opened fire on the widow and her child, splashing their blood in every direction. After discharging several rounds apiece, the rebels halted their gunfire; undisturbed and standing at attention, they all replaced their magazines and cocked their rifles. The nearby villagers, including Nadus and his classmates, began to moan and cry at the sight of the horrendous bloodbath.

Acknowledging the shots and the whimpers of their hostages, the general and a few of his posse walked towards the tall, burly man with the burn scar. "Colonel!" Yonk called out. "Can you tell me what's going on over here?" the malevolent general asked casually as he glanced at the two disfigured villagers. "What happened to these cockroaches?" Yonk inquired as he squatted. Using his fingers like a curious and playful child, he touched a trail of blood that flowed his way from the bodies.

"Disobedience, boss!" the colonel replied. "I told the foolish boy to execute his mother because she was useless to us; he refused to follow my orders and disobeyed me! He even dropped the weapon on the ground. So I told the boys to finish them."

"I see." The general stood to his feet and nodded as he tasted the smear of reddish-brown fluid on his fingers. "Fresh indeed!" he continued to nod with his eyes closed as though savoring a complex flavor. "Disobedience, you say?" He sighed and looked at the colonel.

"Yes boss! Those stinking rats disrespected me! You know we can't afford any weak boys on our force, can't afford any weak links."

"You don't have to explain yourself to me," the general replied. "You did the right thing, you did good officer!" he commended the colonel.

"Thank you, boss!"

"Let this be another valuable lesson to all of you," the general said while patting his colonel on his shoulders, "that you have to be proactive with your insight." The commander turned towards his armed disciples, staring at them and waving his fingers in the air like a well-read philosopher. "Ameduba was quick to think and execute his actions, he saw an unacceptable behavior that could damage our unit and took an immediate and appropriate step to correct it."

"Thank you boss, you're a brilliant leader." The colonel grinned.

"As Ameduba said earlier," the general continued, "we can't afford and we don't have room for weakness in our unit, such a simple mistake costs lives! Do you understand me?"

"Yes boss!" the rebels responded in unison.

"In the event that we notice any such nonsense, we nip it at the source before it becomes a problem." The general made a fist and drove it into his other palm as though delivering a powerful blow. "That means eliminating any and all culprits on site. Do you understand me?"

"Yes boss!" the rebels agreed.

"Good!" the general hunkered down and picked a nearby twig from the ground. "Now, back to the business at hand, we've already secured this village and the four surrounding ones." He dipped the tip of the desiccated stick into the pool of dark, coagulating blood and with his crude pencil, he began to sketch in the mud, "and we've gathered enough food to last us for several days."

"Yes boss!" the guerillas concurred.

"What's the status on the foodstuffs, where are they?" one of the officers asked.

"They're in the back of the large truck," one of the rebels replied.

"Nice one, good!" the senior officer exclaimed as he rested his elbows on the automatic rifle slung across his neck.

"We have new goodies that we can trade for more weapons," the general pointed to the king and his chiefs and the looted treasures. "We're getting low on ammo! Next we'll head to the city with our new recruits, drop some off at the post to guard and secure our presence over there." The commandant drew four squares in the dirt and pointed to one of them. "Then, we head back to the barracks, regroup and refocus our efforts. Am I clear?"

"Yes boss," the rebels chorused. "Loud and clear!"

"Good to hear!" The commandant stood up. "Alright officers, let's get to work!" He looked at his watch. "Rendezvous in the city in approximately eighty minutes, round up all the girls and women and get them in the truck. Come on boys, get to work!" The general whistled and clapped his hands.

"Yes boss!" the guerillas yelled and dispersed.

As Nadus and the other "village recruits" cowered together in the mud and watched as the "senior officers" packed up the royal booty and the corporals shoved the unwilling women into the truck, the young boy felt a slight nip from a small pebble that struck him on the side of his head.

"Nadus! Nadus!" the young boy heard his name as whispers through the tumult. "It's me!" the voice became louder. "Nadus! It's me!"

The young boy recognized the voice and was overwhelmed with joy and relief; he turned around, and a few feet away he saw his older brother crawling towards him through the horde of petrified village boys.

"Tpyge!" Nadus exclaimed with tears of joy. "I'm happy to see you!" He wanted to embrace his brother but he couldn't.

"I'm happy to see you, too!" his brother whispered; his hands were also tied behind his back and he wore a tired expression; his clothes were disheveled and soiled with mud.

"Tpyge, how are you?" Idnurub looked up and noticed the older boy.

"Could be better!" Tpyge blinked with effort and then shook the sweat off his face; his left eye was swollen and bruised. "You, how are you Idnurub?"

"I'm scared, very scared!" the schoolboy replied.

"Your eye is puffy! What happened to you?" Nadus interjected. "Are you okay? Where's Papa? Do you know what's going on?" The young boy bombarded his brother with several questions before he could answer one of the inquiries.

"No, I don't know what's happening!" Tpyge's swollen eye flickered.

"Where's Papa?" Nadus asked his brother.

"It happened all of a sudden, without warning!"

"What happened?" Nadus crawled towards his brother and nudged him. "Where's Papa?" The young boy's heart rate paced up in its rhythm.

Tpyge didn't respond; he simply shook his head in silence.

"Answer!" Nadus shouldered his brother once more and tears formed in his eyes; he sensed that something was amiss. "Tpyge! Please, I beg you! Please answer me, where's Papa? Is he okay?"

"Papa is dead, he's dead!" Tpyge finally broke down and his machismo front came crumbling down. "He's dead, they killed him on the farm!" He bowed his head and cried out like a baby. "Papa was just trying to protect me! Why?"

"What? What? Papa is dead!" Nadus closed his eyes and tried to clasp his trembling lips together. "It can't be!" He tried to reason with reality. "Papa can't be dead!"

"He's dead!" Tpyge wailed out. "I saw him die with my own eyes!"

"Nadus, I'm so sorry!" Idnurub consoled his friend and also became teary-eyed.

"Tpyge, it really can't be!" Nadus protested as he sobbed; the young boy was sick to his stomach and felt as though he had just consumed a large amount of rotten fish. He felt so sick that he wanted to vomit, but his belly was too empty.

"It's true, Nadus! It's true. Papa is no more!"

"No, no, don't say that!" Nadus shook his head in disagreement. All he could think about was smiling and laughing and feasting with his father a few hours earlier during breakfast. "This isn't fair!" Nadus was getting lightheaded; his throat burned and he was running out of tears to shed. "Why? Why Papa? Why?" Nadus looked up towards the clear, blue sky that was dotted with a few gliding vultures and cried out. "Why now?"

"Corporals, gather those bastards, get them up!" A muscular man that was standing a few feet from the procession of vehicles gestured and shouted in the distance. "We're running out of time!" He tapped his wrist.

"Yes sir!" One of the teenagers raised his hand and saluted the short man. He then signaled to four other boys in the vicinity. At once, they all darted towards the villagers like wild beasts, shouting and pointing their rifles. "Get up! Get up now!"

Like a herd of gazelles under attack, the village boys scrambled to their feet and stampeded. "Straight line! Bloody fools, form a straight line!" the power-drunk teenagers punched, slapped and even kicked the recruits as they struggled to form a suitable line.

"Yes, I'm sure!" the commander talked to a few of his posse as he walked towards the village boys who were in a straight file. "They're of no use! Yes, very useless to me, they're harder to mold!"

"You're right, boss!" One of the rebels nodded in agreement.

"What should we do with them then?" a second man asked; there was a slight twinkle of excitement in his eyes.

In response, General Yonk stopped in his steps and glanced at the men who were a few yards away, lying on their abdomens with their hands and legs bound together with ropes. "What should we do with them?" He scratched his chin for a bit. "Good question!" He paused for a few seconds. "Execute them all and then torch them!" he ordered without any form of remorse.

"Boss, are you sure?" A third rebel hesitated as he spoke. "Are you sure that's what you really want? We could put them to work!"

The general didn't respond; he walked towards the man and without warning, he pulled out his knife, grabbed the man by his neck and placed the sharp, jagged blade on his temple. "Look here," the general said calmly, "if you ever question my authority again," he tightened his grip around the man's neck and whispered in a calculated manner, "that will be your very last day on earth! Do I make myself clear, officer?"

The man nodded as he stared at the lustrous piece of steel.

"Good!" The general put the knife back in his sheath and patted the man on his cheeks and then on his shoulders. "In fact," the hefty man spat, "why don't we torch them first before execution, spice things up!" He gave out a loud and sadistic laugh. "Get the container from the truck!" the general ordered.

In no time, one of the teenage rebels darted towards the commandant with a rusty canister in his hand.

"You're a smart boy, sharp and quick!" Yonk commended the rebel as he took the brownish-green can from him. "You'll make a fine officer someday, boy."

"Thank you, sir! I appreciate it, sir!" The teenage boy bowed his head in reverence and stepped backwards.

The general sauntered towards the village men with the container in his hands and began to douse them with gasoline. Crying and writhing like freshly caught fish, the scared men begged their assailants for mercy. Intoxicated and driven by malice, the general and his party laughed and relished the pleas of the helpless men.

"Look at them crying like filthy maggots!" one of the officers commented as he stepped backwards from the wet and restrained men.

"Yes, indeed!" The general laughed again as he placed the canister on the ground. He wiped his hands on his trousers and then whipped out a used, halved cigar and a silver lighter from his pocket. "We have no use for you, cockroaches." The commander mumbled as he positioned the roll on his lips and lit it. "This is some good tobacco!" he exclaimed after taking a few puffs, nodding and staring at the cigar.

"Yes boss! It smells like quality smoke," one of the insurgents replied in adulation.

"Shut it!" the colonel yelled as the village prisoners cried louder. "You are right, boss! We don't need these stinking rats. Let's them burn!"

"Ah, well said, Ameduba!" The general smiled and took another puff.

"Oh look, look at that one," a lanky rebel ridiculed. "He's shaking like a worm."

"It's too bad that I don't have time to enjoy this fine roll of tobacco." The general looked at the cigar once more. "Oh well," he sighed, "good things always come to an end!" He smirked and tossed the burning cigar towards the captives.

The village men were instantly engulfed in a tall orange flame, and the panicked motions of their bodies were mimed in the blue heat. The general and his confederates, who were standing several feet away from the human bonfire, watched with blank expressions. Disoriented from the excruciating pain and witnessing the scalding of their skin, the men screamed with terror in their voices as they struggled to lift themselves up from the ground and escape the inferno.

"Our job here is done!" The general unwrapped a lollipop and put it in his mouth. "Do those cockroaches a favor, take them down!" he ordered as he sucked on the candy. He turned and headed towards the convoy. "Get those so-called royal fools," he said as he pointed to the village dignitaries. "They could be useful bargaining tools! Throw the recruits also in the truck! Time is our enemy!"

"Yes boss!" the nearby rebels chorused with glee, and like automatons they cocked their rifles and began to spray the men with gunfire, ending their apparent misery.

17

CHAPTER SEVENTEEN:

"The evil spirit of a man is a man."
African Proverb

Peeping through the frayed, army-green tarps that covered the back of the trucks and expressing their apparent agony, many of the detained women watched as their fathers, husbands and sons were put to death. Like an army of ants filing through a crowded forest basin, Nadus, Tpyge, Idnurub and the other village boys careened towards the last vehicle in the convoy. One by one like worthless cargo boxes, they were each lifted by older guerillas and tossed into the back of the cramped truck. As Nadus was grabbed by one of the rough hands and held up in the air, he heard his name again through the loud cries of mothers, grieving and watching as their sons' were snatched and taken away.

"Oh, Muotrahk? Is that you?" Nadus whispered as he was slammed against the moist, metallic surface of the truck's interior. "Is that really you?" he asked as warm tears filled his eyes; similar to a lemur on the lookout for predators, Nadus raised his head and his body and scrambled on his knees to the corner in hopes of spotting his "first love" amidst all the chaos. "Where are you?" he mumbled as he peeked through the weathered, waterproof sheeting. The bright sunlight beamed through the small opening, and the intense glare obscured his vision.

Like a penguin in a bevy heeding the calls of her offspring, Nadus continued to hear Muotrahk's voice, echoing and resonating through his head.

Oh, she's in that truck with the other women!

I pray you're alright.

I hope she's okay!

"I hear you too!" Nadus shouted as he caught glimpses of the other truck yards away and fought to hold his own amongst the herd of horrified boys. "I'll come for you, I promise!" He retreated from the peephole, sat on his thighs and sobbed. "I'll be back for you. I promise you!"

Shortly after, two armed boys jumped onto the back of the truck, pulled up the tailgate and latched it. Then, they turned around, whistled and pointed their rifles at the young villagers who were heaped together. Outside the large vessel, one of the "higher-ranking officers" inspected the appearance of the vehicle in the convoy and nodded his approval.

"We're good to go, boys!" the stocky man shouted as he thumped the side of the vehicle with his fist. "Fire up the engine!"

Upon hearing the statement, the corporals hollered their excitement. They began to climb and ascend the steel frame of the trucks, hanging from the sides like chimpanzees and raising their weapons up towards the sky. The lukewarm diesel engines sprung to life and rumbled in unison, preparing to conquer the rugged terrain; moments later, the seven metallic beasts, five that came from the school and two that were already stationed at the square during the initial raid, were in motion, traveling along the muddy road that led to the big city. In a short while, the procession of vehicles was on the trail along the village stream. Staring through the gaps in the canvas and still dazed from the news of his father, Nadus watched in dismay and was appalled by the sight of decedents floating in the shallow, still areas of the water. He couldn't believe his eyes, because a few hours earlier the waters were filled with cheer and bustling with life. Nadus squinted again, but he couldn't make out the identities of the persons that drifted along in the languid current.

This is just so horrible!

This is really a horrible nightmare!

Nadus blinked and switched his gaze from the eyehole towards his brother and classmates who were straight-faced and outwardly deep in thought. The young boy had an itch that was bothering him; he wanted to talk to his brother about the incident at the farm and learn more about their father's final brave moments. But Nadus had received enough beatings for one day and didn't want to draw any more attention; he endured the discomfort and kept his mouth shut. Five miles past the body of water, the convoy slowed and parked along the side of the road. Nadus, like many of the other boys, was curious of the sudden halt. He leaned forward and peeped through the tarp. A few of the rebels that were hanging from the side of the trucks jumped down, gathered along the side of the road and talked amongst themselves. Before long, the truck that was transporting the women, along with the two vans, steered off the road and climbed onto the bushy plains that bordered the road. The forgathered rebels picked their arms and walked beside and behind the vehicles towards a narrow opening in the edge of the forest that was a few yards away.

Nadus was overwhelmed by panic and his heart throbbed; he was gripped with emotions as he watched his "true love" slowly fade out of his sight without assurance that he would ever see her again. "Muotrahk," he whispered as he clenched his bound hands, "I'll come back to you, and I promise you this!" He licked his parched lips. "I promise!" he repeated as he pulled away from the hole. Then, he rested his head against the rusty, metal frame of the truck. "I promise!" He closed his eyes and allowed his mind to drift into his blissful past. "Papa, I'm going to miss you!"

The vehicles continued to sail along the rugged path that led to the big city; the cramped boys in the back of the trucks sweated and coughed rhythmically as they were transported and their dry lungs pled for fresh air. A few minutes later that felt like an eternity to Nadus, the convoy slowed almost to a stop as they arrived at the entrance to the city. Feeling the change in velocity, he opened his eyes and surveyed his environment. He was anxious of the unknown, yet fascinated by the expressions that his peers wore on their faces.

I know we're all sad, at least some of us.

Those evil boys are smiling, especially the one who punched me!

Why do some look sadder than the others?

As the vehicles neared the main intersection, the rebels jumped down from the side of the trucks and began to walk stealthily alongside the convoy like a pack of lions cornering a group of bison; looking vigilantly at the surrounding buildings with their rusty rifles drawn and ready to engage, the rebels guarded their cargos and watched for intruders. Inquisitive of the happenings outside, Nadus peeped through the canvas and was besieged by the unique visuals of the streets; the big city looked nothing like what he saw during his last visit. Littered with garbage and rotting stiffs and seemingly devoid of life, the streets resembled those of a long-deserted town. The few cars that remained were flipped over, badly dented and burned. The buildings had been mistreated: windows shattered, doors torn down, paint coats chipped and concrete walls blemished with bullet holes; the colorful billboards that once beautified the city and displayed enticing advertisements to the dwellers were destroyed. Vultures paraded the streets like noisy and nosy tourists, quarreling and scavenging for carrion; cackling amongst themselves in a morbid cacophony, pied crows croaked loudly and several gunshots from distant engagements echoed through alleys that were once full of people engaged in their peaceful daily business. The "ground troops" were alert, flinching at the foreign sounds and the barks and excited motions of the feral dogs that roamed the streets. The vehicles huddled close together and slowly navigated through the streets as though maneuvering through a labyrinth. In a short time and without exchanging gunfire, the convoy arrived at a barricaded street that was guarded by several armed rebels.

"Boys, open the road!" The driver of the large truck that was in the front of the procession looked out of the window, yelling and banging his fist against the door. "Open up!" The older man honked twice.

Three of the five insurgents that were manning the entrance left their post and walked towards the van and the ground troops.

"Where's the boss?" one the insurgents asked as he neared the driver of the truck. "Where's the general?" The boy looked up at the driver and then spat to his side.

"Open up the way, sergeant!" the driver in the truck relayed his impatience. "Can't you see my red hand band—we're all part of this platoon?"

"Yes, I see it. We still can't let you in, not until we see the general!" the second rebel retorted. "It's the official rule, the major's orders! We can't let anyone inside without his permission!"

"That's the rule, sir!" the first guerilla chimed in a louder tone. "We can't let you in without the general or the major's approval." The tall teenager nodded as he embraced his automatic rifle and prepared himself for an imminent altercation.

"Okay! Enough!" The driver grabbed the steering wheel and squeezed it tightly as though enraged. He scuffed and cursed under his breath. "General is at the back, in the SUV as usual!" he gestured with his hands. "Look, we don't have time," he pointed to an old mechanical clock that was plastered to the dashboard with duct tape.

"Please, wait here." The gatekeeper nodded and jogged towards the sport utility vehicle that was behind the truck, leaving behind his two allies with the ground troops and the truck driver. The juvenile rebel reached the vehicle and tapped the windows with his knuckles. "General? Sir, are you there?"

Seconds later, the tinted window on the passenger's side dropped and a cloud of white smoke effused out and enveloped the child soldier's face.

"Sergeant!" the general exclaimed as he tossed his exhausted cigar on the ground. "What's the problem?"

"Yes, boss!" The boy stomped his sandals on the ground and saluted. "I was just following orders, sir!" he stuttered and stood with his hands at his side. "I was told not to let anyone inside without your permission."

"You did good, boy!" the general wiped the side of his lips. "Go ahead, open it!" He snapped his fingers and patted the side of the door, revealing his edginess.

"Yes, right away, sir!" The boy nodded in obedience; he darted back towards the wooden barriers and began to discuss with the other guards, gesturing as he relayed the information.

"We're all clear! Open up the road!" a large man that was conversing with the sergeant shouted as he waved a white rag in the air.

Recognizing the signal, the insurgents who were standing a few yards away along the roadsides lowered their arms, whistling as they waved white flags in the air; the sharpshooters with binoculars and long-range automatic rifles that were stationed on the top stories of nearby buildings also whistled and waved white flags. Wasting no time, the gatekeepers picked the planks, logs and metal rods that blocked the entry and dragged them aside to make room for the motorcade to proceed towards the improvised safe house. The truck drivers ignited the engines and the automobiles arose from their brief slumber like exhausted camels. The rebels cruised along a heavily buckled and pockmarked road for a quarter mile and arrived at their place of refuge, located in the heart of the city. As soon as the convoy halted, the passenger side of the high-performance vehicle flung open and the general stepped out with a dignified demeanor and a frown smeared across his face. The rebels exited the trucks and joined the troops on the ground. Under the supervision of the colonel and two senior officers, they began to offload the village boys along with a portion the looted goods and foodstuffs.

"What's the current status, any progress?" the general stood in front of the vehicle and barked at a pack of corporals that stormed forward to greet him. "I said, have we made any progress?"

"Welcome boss! Hello boss, general!" Sounding like a flock of excited sheep, the child soldiers extolled "their leader" as he swaggered toward an old canopy that was erected beside a run-down bungalow.

"Answers! I want answers!" Yonk demanded as he marched forward. "Where's the major in charge of this district?"

"Sir, general," one of the rebels responded, "I believe he just walked inside a few minutes ago to relieve himself."

"Relieve himself?" The general sounded bewildered and confused.

"Yessir!" the orderlies replied. "He went inside to ease his bowel, sir!"

"Nonsense," the general yelled, "this is disrespectful! One of you, run inside now and tell him that I'm giving him ten seconds to get his behind outside or I'll castrate him and feed his rotten testicles to the pigs!" the hefty man exclaimed.

"Yes boss!" the rebels scrambled towards the bungalow.

The general took the weight off his feet and sank into a large, washed-out office chair that was placed under the canopy. He pulled out his dagger and began to fiddle with it. Seconds later, a tall, lanky man burst out of the building and jogged towards the tent with his trousers barely sitting around his waist.

"I'm sorry, boss!" The man stood close to the general who was resting his crossed legs on a table. "I swear to you!" He bowed repeatedly as he tucked in his shirttail and fastened his belt buckle. "I just went inside a few minutes ago to use the toilet. We've been hard at work!"

"Enough with the gibberish!" Yonk interjected. "What's the status of our men on the battle ground? Quick, get me up to speed."

"Yes, boss!" The major walked towards the wooden table and began to sort through a pile of papers and blueprints. "Since our last briefing," the lanky man cleared his throat and spread out a map, "we've conquered much of the downtown area of the city," he pointed to various points on the large, colorful piece of paper. "Here, here, here and here! All belong to us now!" He drew several circles with a crooked pencil. "It wasn't an easy acquisition." The major grinned and coughed and glanced at the general who was tapping his fingers on his lips.

"What about that?" The general used his dagger to point to an area on the map. "The business district, have we conquered that area? Is it ours now?"

"Well, yes, no, no sir!"

"Which is it, yes or no?"

"That would be a no, sir!" The man shook his head and swallowed his saliva before looking fearfully at the general.

"Why haven't we conquered that area?" the general rammed the tip of the dagger into the wooden table. "Tell me, why haven't we conquered the business district?" He slammed his fist on the table, perturbing the pieces of paper in the pile. "Answer me!"

The major drew back. "Resistance! Governmental forces are guarding that region with serious firepower! We've tried several approaches, but we're unable to breach their security or weaken their stronghold."

"Really? Is that so?" the general inquired.

"Yes, boss!"

"Did you try using a 'wave attack' with the boys?"

"Yes, boss! We tried the wave attack!"

"And, how did you implement it?"

"Sir, sixty boys were deployed to the corner of Fifth and Sraggeb Avenue," the major nodded as he drew an asterisk on the wrinkled map, "and then they separated and hid at nearby buildings, on both sides," he drew five boxes close to the asterisk, "and at my signal they rushed towards the stronghold right over there," the major tapped the end of the pencil on the map, "shouting and firing their weapons." He scratched his eye and then looked up at the general.

"I'm listening! And?" The general hawked and spat on the clay ground.

"They were taken down, sir! Gunned down! They didn't make it past the first set of buildings."

"Is that so?" the general scuffed.

"Yes sir!"

"Any backup plans in place?" The general picked up a pack of cigarettes that was resting on the table and belonged to the major; he helped himself to stick of tobacco and lit it with a match. "Smoke?" He grabbed the packet and offered it to the lanky man as he puffed out.

"I'm fine!" the major replied. "Thank you, sir."

"Okay," the general pocketed the cigarette and took a long drag. "So you're telling me, that's it! That's all you did today?"

"No!" the lanky man shook his head and hands in denial. "Oh, no, boss! We even tried to 'shock and awe' them! We hid at the corner of the street, firing several grenades and sending several rounds of ammo their way, but with little luck, their defense system is solid and they have aerial advantage over us!"

"What's the casualty count?" The general puffed smoke out his nose.

"I don't have an exact count, in the hundreds, sir! We lost a large chunk of our ground attackers today, out on the field." The major tapped the map with the pencil. "Things aren't looking too hot for us. We're running low on supplies and ammo, especially manpower, that's the reason we had to retreat, regroup and refocus our efforts for another possible strike."

"Is that so!" the general grimaced.

"But we still have many of our guys in the field!" the major quickly added. "They're seizing the other parts of the city and fighting off the local resistance."

"I see!" the general took another long drag, scratched his cheeks and spat; he glanced to his left towards the corporals in the distance who were chattering as they offloaded and sorted the recruits and the cargo into separate piles.

"Boss, to be honest," the major placed both of his hands on the table and sighed, "the guys are exhausted and they don't feel that they can win over that region of the city without additional supplies and manpower."

"Failure isn't a chapter in my playbook!" the general fired back. "Do you understand me?" He pointed at the major.

"Yes, general!" the major stuttered as he leaned away from the counter and glanced at the surrounding senior officers who were mumbling and nodding in agreement.

"Failure isn't an option!" The general raised and waved his finger in the air as he gave his confederates a stern look.

"Yes, boss!" they concurred.

"Do I make myself clear?"

"Yes, boss!" the men spoke in a louder tone.

"We're participating in an active war," the general shuffled the war documents on the table, "and as a result, we should expect bloodshed and sacrifice, but as I said before, failure isn't an option! This isn't a child's game, this is war and we fight to the end!" Yonk pulled his dagger out of the wood and slid it back into the leather sheath around his waist. "This isn't a negotiation! We need to acquire the financial district to take things to the next level, get the upper hand in this conflict. Do I make myself clear?"

"Yessir!" the rebels chorused.

"Rising casualties are inevitable in any type of warfare!" the general picked up the crooked pencil and began to sketch on a blank piece of paper. "Major!" The general paused and looked up at the lanky man. "I commend your good work!" He nodded and scratched the tip of his nose. "You've proven to me and your peers that you are a soldier! You're brave and dependable, your knowledge of the city is invaluable to this mission."

"Thank you, general."

"Be resilient! Don't lose hope, we'll be triumphant soon!" The general looked downwards and continued to sketch on the rumpled piece of paper. "We'll have to rethink our strategy and rely heavily on our small unit," the general said, "and employ a stealth attack like a pack of cobras! Understood?"

"Yes, boss!"

"Listen up! Gather the men to the neighboring street, over here!" He drew a line and pointed to it. "Have five groups of ten soldiers crawl through the city gutters with their guns and ammunition wrapped up in plastic bags, I believe the trenches will be hidden from their gunfire and the blasts. Are you listening?"

"Yes, boss!" the rebels chorused.

"Excellent!" the general furnished a smile. "Are you paying attention?"

"Yes, boss!"

"War has its unique sacrifices, plant them here and over here." He marked five asterisks on the paper. "I'm sure a couple of them will get gunned down at first sight," the general looked up as though fishing for signs of approval, "but it'll be worth it! They'll stay put over there and pound at them! They'll open fire at them from these critical angles and weaken their hold. After bombarding them for fifteen to twenty minutes, have the ground unit zone-in with a series of swift, but powerful surprise attacks! Listen up! This part is critical to the success of this strategy, as the governmental forces begin to respond to our attacks, fire a couple cans of teargas their way and as soon as the smoke clouds blind their view of our troops, we'll launch several grenade attacks and supplement the blasts with several rounds of gunfire! Understood?"

"Yes sir!" the rebel's deep voices were oiled with excitement.

"As the smoke begins to clear, say about ten minutes, have the rest of the platoon cover their mouths and noses with wet rags before storming in with their machetes, ready to hack down everything in sight. Do I make myself clear?"

"Yes, boss!" the rebel bellowed and raised their guns.

"Any question?" General Yonk asked.

"I have a question, boss."

"What is it, lieutenant?"

"Why do the troops have to cover their noses with wet rags?"

The general looked at the man with no emotion. "Can any of you answer his question?" He glanced at the other officers that were standing around the table.

"It makes us look vicious like ninjas!" one of the rebels blurted out.

"Close, but incorrect!" Yonk didn't smile. "The rags lessen the burning effects of the teargas!"

"Yea, boss! Good call!" One of the officers bobbed his head as he held his chin.

"Any other questions about this attack?"

"No! No, boss! No, sir!" the rebels echoed.

"Great! Get to work, all of you!" the commandant stood erect with his shoulders broadened and turned towards the piled foodstuff and loot. "I want control of the entire financial district!" He faced his senior officers, "*Obmaihdo, Ayiwkul* and *Newgno!*"

"Yes, general!" they replied.

"I want you three to stay and assist Major *Iyhalb* to victory! Okay?"

"Yes, boss!" The officers grasped their rifles and saluted.

"Obmaihdo and Ayiwkul, I want you in charge of ensuring attacks go as planned. Understood?"

"Yes, boss!"

"Newgno, you're in charge of trading the jewelries with the foreigners for weapons as well as distributing the foodstuff amongst the troops."

"I'm honored!" The cheeky rebel placed his hand over his heart and nodded.

"Good!" Yonk exclaimed as he walked away from the tent. "Ameduba," the general turned and pointed to the burly man with the burn scar, "come with me!" he beckoned as he strode towards the recruits who were assembled on the concrete pavement with long, weary faces.

"General!" Ameduba jogged towards Yonk and caught up midway to the recruits. "Boss! What do you need, boss?"

"They need more troops here!" the general stopped in his tracks and looked at his confederate. "Gather the recruits and select the ones strong enough to join the ground troops, leave the young ones!" He cracked his knuckles. "We'll take them to the hideout for some serious molding!"

"Yes, General!" Ameduba darted towards the boys and began to yell. "All of you, get up now! Stand straight!"

Nadus and the recruits, like terrified cattle, staggered to their feet in a desperate attempt to "stand straight" with the pain of having their hands bound.

"You stinking rats, straight line!" Ameduba yelled, knocking the boys on their heads as they struggled to balance on their feet.

General Yonk stood a few feet away from the boys with both hands in his pocket, watching as the colonel handpicked the "new ground troops."

"You and you, step aside!" the colonel yelled as he yanked two boys out of line. "Stand there, stand over there, you fool!" Ameduba walked along the bank of recruits, inspecting them and selecting the "ripe ones." The man stood in front of Nadus. "You, move over there!" he yelled.

Nadus flinched and elicited classic signs of distress: amplified brain waves, parched throat, accelerated heartbeat and increased perspiration. He didn't know why the guerilla was singling out his peers, but he knew the colonel's motives were baleful in nature.

Please!

Please!

Please, don't pick me!

"Boy, are you deaf?" Ameduba stretched out his muscular arm and grabbed the collar of a boy who was standing in between Nadus and Tpyge. "Stand over there!" He pulled the boy closer and slapped him.

Ameduba sneezed, walked over to the next boy in line, and hovered over him like a dark cloud. Relieved that he was selected, the young boy released his breath and exhaled.

"Iyhalb!" Yonk turned to his side and called out. "Over here, come take a look at the selection!"

The major, who was still standing by the wooden counter, looked in the direction of the general. "Yes, boss!" He nodded and plunked the pile of papers in his hand before heading towards the assembly.

"And you also," Ameduba resumed the selection process, "go over there, now!"

"Me?" the village boy looked at his chest. "Sir?"

"Yes," the colonel chuckled as he pulled the boy by his ears, "you fool!"

Like a bull immobilized by a force applied to its horns, Tpyge cringed as he was pulled towards the other selected "ground attackers."

"No, please! Don't take him!" Nadus tightened his muscles and ground his teeth together. "He's all I have left!" the young boy spoke inaudibly and watched as his only sibling was pulled away. "Please!" He didn't want to be away from his brother and wished that he had been selected.

"Iyhalb, what do you think of these rats?" The taller colonel placed his hand on the major's shoulder. "Think they'll get the job done, get us that district?"

"Yes, colonel!" the major walked towards the boys. He stared at them and inspected their shoulders, arms and biceps. "Quick crash course is all they need to be ready for battle, I'm sure they'll get the job done."

"They had better!" Yonk interjected. "We don't have time to waste!"

"Yes, boss!" Iyhalb replied.

"What about these?" the colonel pointed in the direction of Nadus and a number of his mates. "Did I miss any with potential?"

The major looked at the boys and shook his head. "No, no, they're not ripe enough for this task!" He walked towards the young boy; acting like a practiced appraiser with a knack for finding good deals, the major inspected Nadus's arm and neck. "Yes, they're not ripe!" Iyhalb shook his head as he let go of Nadus.

I've seen his face somewhere!

His face looks familiar.

Nadus stared at the man as he signaled to the nearby corporals.

Where have I seen this face?

I know this man!

Nadus rummaged through his distracting thoughts and in a flash the answer came back to him; the major was the driver who took him to the big city during his first "real outing." Although gifted with a photographic memory, the young boy had experienced a fleeting case of amnesia from the trauma he had just experienced. Iyhalb didn't look or act much like the "jovial, foul-mouthed man" that he remembered: unkempt stubbles sprouted from his sunken cheeks, rage filled his stoic, bloodshot eyes, and his face was hardened from insomnia and the surrounding decay.

"Drop it over here!" Iyhalb pointed.

"Yes, sir!" two boys with strained expressions bobbed their heads and placed a rectangular, army-green box in the dirt, close to the major's feet.

"Open it and hand one to them!" Iyhalb ordered as the two teenagers unlatched the metal box. "Quick, the general doesn't have time to waste. You," he turned to one of the rebels, "get me that cloth." He pointed to a red flag that drooped from a nearby pole.

"Yes, major!" the teenage rebels pried the footlocker open while the others untied the villagers. They began to hand out machetes and rusty rifles to the new ground attackers.

Sweat exuding through their pores and tears rolling down their eyes, a few of the village boys sobbed as they took the "killing tools" from the corporals. Tpyge, however, didn't shed a tear. The brutal slaying of Nineb had cauterized his emotions; revenge clouded his mind and he was ready to take a life.

"Man the hell up, grow some balls!" the colonel shouted at the village boys. "If I hear another sound from you rats, I'll flog you so hard that you'll wish you were never born." Ameduba yelled as he pulled out his cowhide whip. "Do you understand me?"

"Yes sir!" The village boys obeyed and silenced their cries.

Holding a piece of red cloth in his hand, the major walked towards the trunk, picked one of the machetes from the pile and inspected the edges. Then, he started ripping the cloth into thin strips before handing them to the orderlies. "Tie it around their left arms!" he said. "Listen up soldiers," the major yelled at the village boys, "it's important, very important that you keep these red bands on your arms, if you want to survive! We'll consider anyone without one an outsider, an enemy and you'll be taken down like the enemy."

"Well said!" The general clapped and stood beside the major. "Yes, the boys seem ready for the mission!" He looked at the armed boys and smiled.

"Yes, boss!" Iyhalb replied.

"Keep up the good work!" The general lit another cigarette and took several puffs. "I'm heading to the center with Ameduba."

"Okay, boss!" the major concurred.

"Next time, I want to hear good news, get me that financial district!"

"Yes, general. I'll make sure we capture that region of the city."

"Very good, soldier! Very good!" Yonk tossed the burning cigarette butt on the ground and crushed it with his combat boot. "Ameduba," he turned to the colonel, "get those roaches in there!" he pointed to the younger boys and then to a truck that was parked a few yards away. "Iy-halb, make sure the vehicles have been refueled and ready to go. We're heading out now!"

"Yes, boss!" the major replied.

"Follow me, you rats!" the colonel shouted and the corporal began to push the younger boys towards the truck. "Move it girls! Move it!"

Dragging their feet together, Nadus and Idnurub moved with the herd and trailed behind the hefty colonel. In a minute, the distance between Nadus and his brother along with the star players, Ituobijd, Osaf-Anikrub and Enoel-Arreis, and the older village boys had widened to several feet. Nadus glanced at Tpyge who was standing at attention and staring into space as one of the officers lectured them on their "deadly assignment."

"Dear brother," the young boy prayed in whispers, "wish I had more time to know you." He blinked as tears yet again began to form. "May the heavens and the spirit of our father keep you safe, till we meet again!"

Nadus tried to keep an air of optimism, but an ominous feeling choked him. Bushed and torn apart by the sudden loss of the things he loved, the young boy wobbled towards the grumbling mechanical beast. Acting like a defeated fighter, Nadus walked up the ramp of the truck and entered the cell without putting up a fight. He sat in the corner and again allowed his mind to drift back to his past life. "Wonder if my dog and goats are alive and well!" he whispered.

18

CHAPTER EIGHTEEN:

⬛

"When two brothers fight, strangers always reap the harvest."
African Proverb

Dejected and helpless like usurped crickets in the mouth of a toad, Nadus and the "young roaches" were pinned in the back of the truck, watching as one of the corporals latched the tailgate and shrouded them from daylight with a army-green tarp. Joining the truck in noisemaking, the engine of the sport utility came to life and also began to grumble and expel soot from its exhaust. The colonel hollered a set of commands and a handful of rebel cadets who were in formation cocked their rifles before dispersing and jumping onto the side of the truck. In no time, the two automobiles along with the "foot warriors" were on the move, slowly navigating through the desolate streets and avoiding the "hot zones" that were prone to hostile engagements. A couple of miles through the mess and with no shells discharged, Yonk and his squad reached the border and exited the collapsed metropolis; successfully guarding the cargo and deterring an ambush, the ground troops got onboard the truck and joined the other rebels as they drove towards the skyline.

The midday sun blazed from above and pursued the vehicles as they sped along a meandering pathway; sunbeams bounced off the cracked windscreens and dust spiraled from the ground as the tires made their mark and caressed the hot, dried clay. Jerking and rocking from side to side, the convoy continued to wrestle with the rugged terrain and the passengers, like a pot of water balanced on a child's head, swayed with the quick jolts. Before another hour passed, the procession of vehicles arrived at a shaded swamp with wet spongy soil covered in decomposing foliage and trees that towered from both sides of the road, revealing their sacred roots above the shallow bodies of water; in response to the reduced luminance and the perilous terrain, the drivers flicked on their headlights, slowed their velocity and began to drive with caution. A little further into the woodland, the procession slowed and halted near one of the many hammocks. Without ado, Ameduba opened the passenger door of the truck and jumped to the ground; the rebels who were hanging on the top and from the sides of the truck followed and forgathered around the colonel for directions.

"Alright boys," Ameduba stretched and cracked his neck, "get those rats off the truck now and bring them here!"

"Yessir!" The rebels dispersed and flocked at the back of the truck.

"Line them up here!" Ameduba fought off some mosquitoes that were already buzzing in his ears and declaring their scrounging intentions.

"Yessir!" the guerillas replied.

Similar to woodpeckers boring for insects, the rebels unlatched the tailgate and began to drag the recruits onto the ground.

"All of you, move over there, move!" the rebels exclaimed as they pulled, pushed and butted the village boys with their rifles.

With their hands still tied, the recruits floundered along in the marshy ground and filed towards the colonel like chicks fleeing towards a fowler.

"Alright, untie them!" Ameduba ordered. "We need to get going!"

"Yes, colonel!" the teenagers retorted and began to loosen the twine around the recruits' wrists.

As the rebels untied the villagers and removed the tourniquets that restricted the flow of vim into their digits, Ameduba walked around the truck and headed towards the utility vehicle. "General!" he tapped on the passenger window. "General, we have the boys ready to go!"

"Excellent work, major!" the general lowered the window halfway and offered a nod. "Offload the foodstuffs. I'll be out in a second."

"Yes, boss!" Ameduba saluted and walked back to the recruits. "You and you," he pointed to two of the cadets, "put the recruits to work and gather all the supplies! We're heading out any minute from now."

"Yessir! Yes, colonel!" The teenagers bobbed their heads and began to bark. "Come here! Move over there! Pick that up!" they shouted.

Following the orders, the other rebels jumped into the back of the trucks and began to channel the bags and cases from the vehicle and towards the line of weary recruits. "Take it and put that on your heads!" a cadet walked around the village boys, yelling and clapping his hands. "Quick, quick, move it!"

Sweating and trembling from the added weight, Nadus, Idnurub and the other recruits each took an article from the rebels and placed it on their heads.

"Ameduba!" the general called out as he approached the squad. "How are we looking on getting things together?"

"Boss!" the colonel turned and faced the general with both hands to his side. "Aah, yes!" he exclaimed. "We're just about done, ready to go!"

"What's left to do?" the general asked in a stern voice.

"Nothing else, boss!" the colonel retorted. "We're good to go!"

"Good!" Yonk chuckled. "That's more like it! Line them up, let's get going," the general cleared his throat, "my stomach is beginning to rumble, need food!"

"Yes, boss!" Ameduba replied. "Alright boys, let's go!" The colonel started to thump on the side of the truck with his fist. "Let's go, boys! Let's go, make sure nothing's left behind!"

"Yes, colonel!" the guerillas hollered as they gathered together by the side of the truck, in front of the general. "We're clear, sir!" they chorused. "We're all ready, sir!"

"Excellent!" Yonk responded, and like a proud father he patted the rebels on their heads and shoulders. "You did good today, very good!"

"Boss, we're good to go!" Ameduba shouted from a distance and signaled with his hand. "We're just waiting on your command."

"Excellent!" The general faced the colonel. "Ameduba, have the drivers and three of the ground warriors head back to the city base!"

"Okay, boss!"

"And tell them to use their sense out there and be watchful!"

"Yes, boss!" Ameduba replied. "Alright, you, you and you, come with me!" He pointed to three of the rebels. "You," he pointed to a tall, teenage boy, "go inside the SUV and guard the driver and vehicle at all times!"

"Yes, sir!" the teenager exclaimed and a smile crept up his face. "Yes, colonel!" the boy repeated in a higher tone of voice; he was excited by the notion of riding in a sport utility vehicle for the first time.

"You and you," the colonel signaled to the other rebels, "I want you two in the truck."

"Yes, colonel!" They both saluted.

"All three of you are to guard the vehicles with your lives and get them safely to the city base. You're not to leave the vehicles unattended and unoccupied for any reason until you're in the base! Understood?"

"Yes, colonel!" they interjected.

"Guard it with your lives and your firearms!" the colonel grabbed the rifle of one of the rebels and shook it. "You only leave when your spirits leave your rotten bodies, that is, leave only when you're dead! Get it?"

"Yes, colonel!" the cadets exclaimed.

"Okay, now move it, get going!"

"Yessir!" the rebels chorused as they darted to their new assignments.

Ameduba walked up to the driver's side of the truck and stepped on the muddy, rusting running board. He climbed up to the window and exchanged a few words with the driver before jumping down. Seconds later, the open doors slammed shut and the hatchback was fastened; the engine of the truck wheezed thrice and started grumbling again. Almost instantly, the sport utility vehicle awoke and began to rev up like a fuming Cape buffalo.

"Let's get moving, boys!" The colonel thumped the side of the truck. "Move it!"

Starting with the sport utility that was in the lead, the vehicles moved forward for a few feet before turning around on the grassy pathway and heading for the big city. As soon as the automobiles were out of sight, the guerillas along with the recruits who were carrying most of the food and looted goods began to march further into the swamp through the interposing thicket. The condition of the marshland was uncomfortable: hot, humid and clammy. Nadus, Idnurub and the other villagers had lost their sandals during the raid and were trekking barefooted along the coarse and murky trails like roving vagabonds. Although he was struggling with the load on his head and aching all over, Nadus still took the time to appreciate his surroundings. Copses and groves of trees whose boughs were covered with delicate moss gossiped and kept to themselves. The aromas of dead frogs, rotting crawfish, sulfur, methane and waste filled the damp, musky air. Wet and slimy with dew, many of the weed clusters that shrouded the pathway trembled and bowed in the presence of the rebels' heavy strides. A few yards away, a turtle nestled on a moldered log and swarms of fireflies glowed and danced around effortlessly; twinning dragonflies tickled and poked one another as they glided and crisscrossed in the air. Bashful crickets chirped in hiding and jumpy toads croaked at liberty. Water striders raced across leaf- and debris-covered puddles and the sporadic groans of nearby alligators echoed and stirred the slow-moving waters; nature gleefully engaged in her daily routine, full of bliss and undisturbed by the madness of man. Nadus on the other hand was troubled, yet intrigued by the mysterious ambience that seemed to envelop him from all directions and for many miles.

"Face forward and lift your chicken legs!" One of the rebel officers who was trailing behind flogged Nadus and a few other recruits on their necks and backs with a long and fairly flexible stick. "This isn't some kind of parade, you bastards! Carry on, move it quick, quick!"

Feeling the twinge as the freshly cut cane nipped a patch of his skin, Nadus grimaced, staggered on his feet and succeeded in keeping his balance. One of the five boys that were flogged wasn't as agile or fortunate as Nadus; he slipped to the ground and dropped the large sack of food on his head. Similar to a rodent accidently falling into piranha-infested waters, the unlucky boy was attacked by a number of the teenage rebels and trashed without pity.

"Idiot!" one of the rebels yelled as he rammed his fist into the boy's stomach.

"You!" A second boy tried to breathe and control his thrill. "You, son of a bastard!" he exhaled as he slapped the recruit on his oily and fluffy cheeks.

"Please! Please!" The village boy covered his face and tried to duck for cover.

"How dare you?" a third rebel scolded the younger boy; he grabbed the recruit by his legs and began to drag him in the mud. "Foolish pig, threw down the food!"

The cadets continued to beat the recruit for several seconds and the village boys that were close by simply watched as their own was brushed and abused.

"Enough!" Yonk shouted and fired a shot in the air, startling the boys and scaring a few birds out of their nests. "Are you boys going mad!" The general who was standing in front of the herd marched towards the cadets. "Did I give you rats the permission to punish anyone?" The general pointed to the village boy as he wallowed in the mud. "Did I?" He backhanded the testosterone-driven teenagers. "Answer me!"

"No, sir!" they chorused as they squeezed their sore faces.

"I can't hear you!" he shouted again. "Give me an answer!"

"No, boss!" the boys shook their head. "You didn't give us permission."

"Exactly!" he grunted as he leaned forward and slapped two of the boys again with both hands. "Don't let power get to your heads!" Yonk chastised the boys in a hypocritical manner. "Do I make myself clear?"

"Yessir!" the teenage rebels replied.

"Now, let's get going!" Yonk turned around, headed back to the front of the line and ordered the troops to "keep moving."

Comparable to zombies, Nadus and the others proceeded further into the treacherous forest, staggering as they lurked behind the general. After several confusing twists and turns through the thicket, the insurgents arrived at a fairly wide and roughly-blazed trail; the plants along the path were trimmed and the sides were demarcated with gravel and a few large rocks. Without warning, the general halted and raised his hands up towards his side like a large bird spreading its wings, interrupting the flow and causing the inattentive followers to wallop into each other.

"Hold!" Yonk ordered. "Quiet down!" he hushed the mumbling group. "Ameduba!" he turned and beckoned to the colonel. "Make the call!"

"Yes, boss!" Ameduba responded. "Right away, boss!" He walked past Nadus and met up with the general.

"Make the call!" the general raised his hands and grasped the colonel's right shoulder. "Make the call!"

"Yes, boss!" Ameduba cleared his throat and placed his hands around his mouth as though ready to blow a hornpipe.

Then, he began to crow at intervals and produce high-pitched chattering that resembled troops of monkeys. From the distance, a series of similar animal-like responses echoed through the swampland and in return, the colonel crowed again. Seconds later, a handful of men crawled out from both sides of the dense growth of bushes. Inconspicuous in the jungle to untrained eyes, they wore camouflage uniforms, slung assault rifles around their necks and masked their cold faces with green paint.

"General Yonk! Colonel Ameduba!" One of the guerillas saluted the two men. "Welcome back, boss!"

"Brigadier *Itto*!" the general exclaimed. "Good to see you and the boys!" he added as he walked towards the band of commandos.

"Good to see you, sir!" The brigadier shook hands with the general. "I see you've brought us some recruits." Itto steered to his side and peeked at the boys.

"Yes, indeed!" the general replied. "How's the base? Everything good?"

"Everything is just as you left it, sir!" Itto scratched his cheeks and adjusted his firearm around his shoulder. "We've all been keeping an eye out."

"Good! Good!" The general pulled out the box of cigarettes from his pocket and handed a stick to the brigadier and placed another one on his lips. "Detect any suspicious activity out here?" Yonk inquired as he lit the cig hurriedly.

"Nothing!" Itto took the lighter from his superior. "It was as peaceful and calm as dead, nagging wives!" The brigadier gave out a dry laugh as he puffed on the addictive substance.

"I like that!" Yonk moved his hand as he spoke, swirling the burning cigarette like a pyromaniac. "Yes, I like the sound of that!" He nodded again. "Are you sure?" Yonk glanced at the officer as they strode along the pathway.

"Absolutely, boss!" Itto sucked the cig. "Just the occasional critters! Rabbits, bats, monkeys, birds, you know, the usual! Nothing out of the ordinary, sir!" He turned to the members of his team. "Boys, do I lie?"

"No, sir!" The cadets nodded and mumbled their responses.

"Good!" the general said in a protracted manner. "And my sweeties?"

"They're also good!" Itto replied as he tossed the butt and rubbed his hands together. "I believe they're awaiting your return, sir!"

"That's very good to hear!" Yonk smiled. "I'm hungry, let's go!"

Yonk and the rebels along with the barefooted recruits continued to trek along the crooked trail. In a short time, they reached the end of the trail and arrived in front of a tall, makeshift fence with an imposing gate.

"Itto here!" the brigadier picked up a smooth stone from the ground and knocked on the wooden structure. "Open up for the general!"

"Brigadier, yes sir!" A muffled male voice reverberated through the gaps of the gate. "Yes, sir, opening!" the cadet continued as he jingled a bunch of keys and unlocked a large padlock.

Unclasping like a snake crawling down a tree branch, the rust-brown chain that grasped the arms of the gate and restricted access into the compound was pulled and removed. Shortly after, the wooden structure began to creak as it opened inward. Driven by haste, the general barged into the "command center" and the band of men and boys marched inside in pursuit. As soon as Nadus entered the complex with the baggage still planted on his head, he was taken aback by the appearance of the hideout; it resembled a small village with rows of mud huts and army tents that sheltered several equipment and ammunition boxes. Dressed in mufti and patrolling the periphery with their firearms strapped over their shoulders, a number of men guarded the safe haven with their lives. Sitting in silence around firewood stoves and perspiring heavily, in the left corner a few women and girls cleaned foodstuffs for the rebels; their bland faces barely concealed their agony. Scooting towards the group of arrivers and assuming a military formation, the nearby men raised their hands up to their foreheads and saluted the hefty man.

"Welcome, general!" they retorted. "Welcome, boss!"

"Thanks!" Yonk nodded and shook hands with his followers. "Thank you! Thanks! How have you boys been keeping up?" he asked in a deep, detached tone of voice as he marched further into the complex.

"Great, sir! Fantastic, sir! Couldn't be better, sir!" the rebels replied.

"Any mishaps?" Yonk asked. "Any mishaps that I should know about and be aware of?" he looked up and glanced at the faces of the young men and teenage boys. "Huh, anything?"

"No, sir!" a few of the rebels responded in unison.

"It was a good day, boss!" a sergeant added. "There was no trouble at all and we trained a few of the kids and taught them effective combat and firing tactics!"

"Is that so?"

"Yessir!" The guerilla replied.

"Good!" The general hawked and spat. "See any improvements in them?" Yonk smacked his lips and wiped saliva off the corner of his mouth with the back of his hand.

"Absolutely, boss!" the sergeant replied. "Boss, you should've seen them out there in action! They're so steady with very good range!" The teenage boy smiled. "I swear to you, general! They'll easily, no problem at all, take down anyone from many yards away!" the young marksman said with pride in his voice.

"Impressive work!" The general stopped walking and tapped the boy on his cheeks. "Keep up the good work, son!" He patted his head. "Keep it up!" he added.

"Thank you, boss!" The teenager bowed as he stalked the general. "I thank you General, you're such a great father figure and I want to..."

"That's enough Sergeant!" Yonk interrupted. "Leave compliments for after we win this bloody war!"

"Yes, boss!" the boy hesitated, choking on his words and slowing his pace. "I thank you, boss, my apologies!"

"Ameduba," Yonk paused and then turned to his confederate. "I want it over there!" he said, signaling to the colonel and pointing to the ground.

"Yes, boss!" Ameduba replied. "Alright!" he raised his tone and began to clap, "all of you, drop it over there! Carefully, don't throw it on the ground! You will get opened up if you do, trust me!" He pulled out his whip and uncoiled it.

Elated by the announcement, the sweat-covered, fatigued recruits sighed and began to struggle, fighting to keep their poise as they "carefully" unloaded the cargo they had been carrying on their heads.

"Quick, quick!" the colonel swung the whip and swished it through the air. "Move, you fools, move it! You're not all pregnant goats. We don't have all day, move it!" he shouted.

As Ameduba continued to threaten and bully the recruits, the general vacated the commotion of confused boys and marched towards his left.

"My sweeties!" Yonk called out as he approached the girls.

"Pappy!" the girls wore exaggerated smiles and ran towards the tall man, voicing after each other as if singing a cappella. "We've missed you!"

"My sweetie pies!" the general grinned. "Have you really?"

"Yes, pappy!" they chorused as they each hugged the general.

"I've missed all of you!" Yonk grabbed one of the girls by the waist and then pulled her closer; he squeezed her backside and kissed her cheeks and gave her a deep, openmouthed kiss. "Yes, just as I like it!" The general unclasped his lips from the girl, smiling as he pushed her away. "You!" the man exclaimed as he grasped a second girl by her hand and began to neck and kiss her.

Surrounding Yonk like flies on a carcass and giggling as he kissed, fiddled and molested each of them, the brainwashed girls freely shared their undeveloped bodies; they were all barefooted and their nakedness was concealed by tie-dye garments wrapped around their bosoms and down to their knees.

"Pappy!" One of the girls tapped Yonk on his shoulders and chuckled.

"Yes, sweetie!" Yonk paused his smutting and turned to the schoolgirl. "What's the matter?" he asked. "Do you want some too?" He laughed like an excited boy.

"You must be hungry!" she responded. "I washed these especially for you." She bowed and offered Yonk a basket of fresh mangoes, guavas and oranges.

"That's why you're one of my favorites!" The general picked a fruit and bit into it. "You're always thinking about my heart," he said with the pulp bouncing in his mouth. "This is very good!" He bit and held the fruit in his mouth. He then ran his fingers along the young girl's cheeks.

"Thank you, pappy!" she blushed.

"You're a good girl, one of my favorites!" the general added.

"But I helped her wash it too!" one of the girls interjected, exposing her eminent envy. "She always tries to take all the credit, all the time!"

"No I don't!" the first girl fired back as she eyed her peer. "You're just jealous that you're not as pretty as me and pappy likes me better!" she hissed.

"You're not that fine!" the second girl replied. "You think you're so pretty, but you are the ugliest of all!"

"Shut up!" the first girl replied. "You're just jealous!"

"I'm not jealous!" the second girl exclaimed. "You're the one who is!"

"That's enough!" Yonk reprimanded the girls; although he had a perverted fondness for watching girls bicker and "catfight," he didn't want to look weak in front of his men. "You're all my sweeties, be nice!"

"It's her fault!" The first girl shook her head and waved her finger.

"No, it's not, it's you!" the second girl uttered.

"That's enough!" the general added. "There's enough of me to go around!" he laughed and groped a third girl who was standing close by. "What've you been eating, girl?" The general showed his teeth and licked his lips with the arrogance of a philanderer. "Your body is getting soft and succulent, so soft!" he said with a grin.

"General!" Itto cleared his throat to garner his superordinate's attention. "General Yonk!" he called out again.

"What's the matter?" Yonk turned around sluggishly and responded with an irritated spasm in his voice. "Officers, what's the matter, eh?"

"We've gathered the food and placed the supplies in storage." Itto replied.

"We'll just like to know how you want us to split the bags of food." Ameduba added.

"Okay!" Yonk replied. "Excellent work, colonel! Let me see what we have over here." Yonk strolled over with the officers towards the boys and the piles of mud-stained twine bags, floundering with his large arms resting over the shoulder's of two of his "sweeties."

"Stand straight in his presence!" A rebel reproved the recruits. "Show your respect." He smacked Idnurub on the back of his head.

"Everything looks good, real good!" the general nodded and agreed.

"Boss, what would you like us to do with them?" the brigadier asked.

"Move it, wait!" Yonk stared at the brown bags. "Yes, move it all to that tent. We'll deal with it tomorrow! You boys have worked hard and deserve a break. Beside I want to spend some time with my sweeties," he looked downwards and peeked at the young girl's bosom, "so that I can get a real nice massage from you, right?" He grinned.

"Yes, pappy!" The girls looked up with flirtatious eyes and chuckled.

"That's right!" the general retorted.

"Boss, what do you want us to do with them?" the colonel grabbed the head of one of the recruits, shaking it around as he pointed to the others.

"Boy, what are you looking at, huh?" Yonk asked with contempt. "Are you eyeing my girls? I'm talking to you bloody roach!" He pointed to one of the boys. "Are you eyeballing my girls? You want to taste them, eh? Answer me!"

"No, sir!" Alogna shook his head; he looked up briefly and continued to stare at the ground. "No, no, sir! I wasn't eyeing them, sir!"

"You must be mad!" Yonk walked up to the boy and punched him in the face. "You must be mad, you roach! You look at those girls, you're looking at me. Understood?" Yonk surveyed the flock of recruits. "Answer me!" he yelled.

"Yessir!" the boys replied.

"These are my sweeties!" Yonk twitched like a maniac.

Nadus glanced at his schoolmate who was weeping in silence from the "dirty slap" and then looked furtively at "the sweeties" in question. The young boy was astonished and disturbed by the age of the girls; they were only a few years older than him and the idea drew his mind back to the love of his life.

Muotrahk, I'll come for you!

I wouldn't let you become this horrible man's slave!

"These are my sweeties!" Yonk repeated. "You don't look at them!"

"Hey, boss!" the brigadier interjected with an exasperated look. "What do you want us to do with these boys?"

The general looked at the recruits and then wiped the sweat off his face with a handkerchief. "Just throw them in 'the hole' for now. I'll deal with them later!" the general expressed his impatience.

"Yes, boss!" the brigadier raised his head and clutched his rifle.

"Corporals!" the colonel beckoned to five cadets. "Come here!"

"Yes, sir!" the boys sang out and dashed forward.

"Take them to the holding cell, now!"

"Yes, colonel!" they saluted. The cadets walked towards the school-boys, shouting as they pointed their rifles and jabbed them with the rounded muzzles. "Come on! Come on! Let's go! Let's go!"

Nadus and his peers, although fatigued from the long day, followed the older boys as they were ushered towards the back of the compound. After marching for a few yards, they reached a rectangular structure that was made of cement blocks and raised three feet above the soil. Covering the top were multiple thin, rusted aluminum sheets that were nailed to vertical slabs of wood. One of the corporals walked forward and picked up a concrete block that was resting on the right corner and placed it on the floor; he then slid part of the sheeting off the top and uncovered the shaft. Right away, a draft oozed out from inside and engulfed the boys with malodorous gases, temporarily choking and strangling them.

"Get inside now!" the cadets ordered the boys to enter the abandoned cesspit. "Get inside!" they shouted in unison. "Or we'll shoot you all!"

19

CHAPTER NINETEEN:

Ç

"When the elephants fight it is the grass that suffers."
African Proverb

Coerced at gunpoint, the recruits didn't utter a word of protest as they were shoved into the hole, one after the other; the awful smell of dried feces, urine, vomit and sweat welcomed each of them as they landed inside. Crouching in the corners like nocturnal bats in a cave and recoiling from sunlight, a few young boys were already serving time in the grungy prison. The basin of the ditch was hard, rough, warm and moist, and it swarmed with wiggly maggots. Utilizing the sunbeams that shined from above, through the opening, Nadus caught glimpses of his new inmates; they were frail and their gaunt faces were splotched with grime. With the boys jam-packed inside the derelict reservoir, the cadets slid the slab to its original position and covered the opening. Then, before exiting to join the others for "merriment and celebrations," they placed the cement block over the wooden slab to prevent the prisoners from escaping. The interior of the cesspit lost light and the schoolboys found themselves in a dank, scary and miasmatic setting. Unaccustomed to the sadistic conditions and the elevated levels of ammonia gas in the pit, the new recruits gagged, coughed and a number of them began to empty the contents of their stomachs. Squatting in the center of the dungeon and enduring the stench as he tried to a get feel for his surroundings, Nadus scurried to the corner in hopes of dodging the cascade of vomit that was ensuing; he was certain that the "seasoned boys" who had claimed the corners of the cell were used to the odors and unlikely to throw up.

"Watch it! You're stepping on my toe!" one of the prisoners voiced his anger as Nadus bumped into him. "Get away!" he yelled in a weak voice.

"I'm sorry!" Nadus apologized. "I didn't mean to hit you! I was just…"

"I don't care!" the boy interrupted. "Just leave me alone, get lost!"

"I didn't know, what's your problem?" Nadus replied. "I said, sorry!"

"Stop talking to me!" The prisoner hawked and spat. "Get lost!"

Nadus grimaced as thick phlegm landed on his face. "Hey! Seriously! What's with you?" He wiped his face and raised his voice. "What's your problem? I apologized to you, didn't I? What's your problem?"

"Shut up!" the boy replied with added effort. "You want to fight with me, uh? I'll finish you, today, break you to pieces!"

"No!" Nadus replied. "I don't and I don't need to fight with you either!"

"Say one more word!" The boy hyperventilated. "I'll mess you up!"

"I said, no!" Nadus yelled; his body began to gear up for a brawl. "No!"

"You're still talking!" The emaciated boy pushed Nadus. "I'll mess you up!"

"What's your problem?"

"You're so dumb!" The boy grabbed Nadus by his collar. "I told you to shut it!"

"Take your hands off me!" Nadus squeezed the boy's fingers.

"Shut up! Shut up!" The prisoner pushed Nadus with both hands. "I told you to shut your basket mouth!"

"I don't want any trouble!" Nadus waved both hands. "I don't!"

"I told you to shut it!" The inmate gave the young boy a quick, surprise slap. "I'll smash you to pieces!" The boy raised his hand again. "Idiot!"

Infuriated and trying to avoid another blow to the face, Nadus ducked and in retaliation, he ran his fist into his opponent's stomach. In the blink of an eye, the two boys were scuffling, rolling in the filth and exchanging a number of facial and body shots.

"*Fight! Fight! Fight!*"

A large number of the inmates gathered around the fighters, clapping and chanting loudly like ravenous savages.

"Give him a headlock!" a thin boy cried out.

"Punch him!" a second inmate exclaimed. "Give him an uppercut!"

"In the ribs, hit him in the ribs!" A third boy pointed as he offered his advice. "It'll take him out."

"Oh, yes! Nice one!" the inmates commended as one of Nadus's blows landed on his rival's left cheek. "Great shot, boy!"

"That's nice!" Another boy couldn't control his excitement.

"Give him another one!"

"Quick, he's still open!" the first boy shouted. "Right, right hook!"

"Break his neck!"

"Pluck out his eyes!" another boy yelled.

"Nadus!" Idnurub called out. "Please, no! Don't listen to them!" he added as he struggled towards his friend.

"Finish him, he's pinned!"

"Teach him a lesson. A permanent lesson!" The third boy clapped rapidly like a chimp. "Leave him for the maggots to eat."

"Nadus!" Idnurub grabbed his friend's fist in midair and held onto it. "Stop it, Nadus! Stop it, please, don't do it!" Idnurub reasoned with his friend. "It's not worth it! That's what he wants you to do! Look, he's near death!"

"Aaah!" Nadus yelled; he was still sitting on his rival's abdomen with his fist elevated to deliver a punch. "I told him to let go!" He looked at Idnurub and then fixed his gaze on the inmate who was gasping. "I begged you and you just had to spit on my face! You bloody toad!"

"It's not worth it!" Idnurub chimed in. "Just let go! You punished him enough! Let go, Nadus!"

"Thanks Idnurub!" Nadus sighed and blinked. "I'm so sorry, he just made me very upset!" He lowered his arm and looked up at his friend; his right eye was swollen and the side of his lip was bleeding. "I'm sorry!" he tried to catch his breath.

"Aw! No! Ugh!" the spectators exclaimed. "Why are you stopping the fight?"

"Are you crazy or something?" one of the prisoners asked. "Don't stop them!"

"He's my friend!" Idnurub turned around in defense and faced the inquirers.

"Who cares?" a second boy replied. "Nobody gives a hoot!"

"Yes, no one cares!" the first boy agreed. "Fight!"

"*Fight!!!*" the spectators shouted. "*Fight! Fight! Fight!*" they began the chant again.

"Let them fight!" A third boy pulled on Idnurub's shirttail. "Let them fight!"

"Let go, don't touch me!" Idnurub faced the inmate. "He's my friend!"

"Get out of the way!" the boy barked like a rabid dog. "Let them keep fighting!"

"No!" Idnurub replied. "He's my friend, I wouldn't let that happen!"

"Are you trying to start something also?" The boy clenched his fists. "You?"

"No! I'm not and don't want any trouble either. I just won't let you use my friend for your sick entertainment. Look, look at them!" He pointed to the two drained wrestlers. "They're injured and bleeding."

"You're really trying to start a fight with me!"

"No, I'm not!" Idnurub replied.

"Then, you better get out of the way. Let them keep fighting!" He spat on the floor and showed off his bony fists.

"No!" Idnurub shook his head. "He's my friend!"

"You're about to get it!" the inmate spat again; he raised his fist in the air and slung it backwards to deliver a heavy blow.

"Don't do it!" Idnurub stood his ground, closing his eyes and tightening his muscles in preparation for a shot.

"Leave them alone!" a voice echoed from the dark corner. "That's enough! Let them go!" The husky tone grew louder as the speaker approached. "Let them go and don't you touch him!"

"Or else?" The boy lowered his arm and faced the taller boy. "What?"

"Let them go!" the taller boy reaffirmed as he neared Idnurub. "Don't try to be smart, nothing foolish!" He grasped Idnurub by his shoulder and pulled him closer. "Easy! Easy, boys, don't try anything stupid!"

In response, Idnurub bent over and grabbed Nadus by his arms, grunting as he lifted his pal to his feet. "There you go!"

"Thank you!" Nadus sniffed as he slouched forward. "Thank you, Idnurub."

"What are you going to do?" the inmate spoke louder. "What, huh?"

"Don't try anything stupid," the taller boy responded.

"What are you going to do, eh?" The belligerent boy and a number of his posse stepped forward with clenched fists and strained mugs. "Uh? Talk!" He swung his arms in the air and prepped them to box; the other inmates also began to dangle their mitts.

"Come any closer and I'll slice you all up to tiny bits!" The taller boy revealed an improvised stabbing weapon that was made from wood, twine and scrap metal.

"That's all you have, huh?" The prisoner lowered his voice and took a few steps backwards. "That's all you have, eh! You're lucky you have that thing in your hand!"

"That's right!" The taller boy nodded. "Go back to your side!" He turned towards Nadus and Idnurub. "Come with me!"

"Thank you!" Idnurub said.

"Yes, we appreciate it." Nadus concurred.

"Don't mention it!" the taller boy replied. "You two, just come with me before I change my mind!" he beckoned and continued to display and wield his weapon towards the angry spectators.

Nadus, Idnurub and their new acquaintance retreated out of the dim light and into the dark corner like phantoms; they sat on the ground and watched as their adversaries dispersed to their respective niches. Using the tip of his fingers, Nadus felt his face for bumps and examined his chin and jaw for signs of injury. He noticed a bulge around his eye, a cut on the side of his lip and a few shaky teeth that bled. Nauseated by the viscous, metallic-tasting fluid in his mouth, Nadus spat a few times and blew his nose repeatedly in an attempt to get comfortable. Adjusted to his vicinity, the young boy was oblivious of the stench and although initially wanting to avoid being soiled, he realized that his once-prized white shirt and green khaki shorts were covered with the filth that he tried to dodge; he was disappointed in himself for allowing his anger to take the best of him and wished he didn't fight back.

"Papa wouldn't be proud of you!" he whispered. "Yes, I know that!"

Papa! I'm sorry for letting you down!

You taught me better to avoid unnecessary fights!

"But, it was necessary, the boy attacked me first!" Nadus tried to hide his guilt and rationalize his actions. "Honest!"

No! No! That's not entirely true!

You could have walked away when he told you to get lost!

"Yes, that's true but he made me so mad and got on my last nerve!" the young boy continued to discuss with himself in whispers. "You're just as guilty!"

Yes! You are right!

"I'm sorry!" Nadus shook his head. "Don't apologize to me—apologize to the boy you nearly killed!" the young boy replied to himself.

No, no, that's not true!

I didn't nearly kill him!

"How are you feeling guy?" The taller teenager nudged Nadus as they squatted in the corner of the dungeon. "How's your eye treating you?"

"S'okay," Nadus mumbled as he flicked his eyelid. "I'm fine. I shouldn't have fought with that…" the young boy expectorated a red, foamy mix of blood and saliva; his head throbbed and the veins on the side of his head pulsated.

"It hurts, uh?" the taller boy asked.

"Ugh, it hurts badly!" Nadus placed his dirty fingers in his mouth and grabbed onto one of his rickety molars; groaning from the sharp pain, he began to shake and pull on the tooth.

"Nadus, are you okay over there?" Idnurub leaned forward and held onto the young boy's knee. "Leave it alone and let it fall out by itself." He puckered his brows as though experiencing his friend's agony. "Just leave it alone!" He patted Nadus.

"No, I can't wait!" the young boy mumbled in response. "It hurts a lot."

"I can see!" the taller boy responded. "Take it easy on yourself!"

"Listen! Stop pulling on it!" Idnurub added. "You're hurting yourself."

"I think I have it!" Nadus shrieked and jerked his head backward. "I got it!"

"What?" Idnurub asked. "What?"

"The tooth!" the young boy spat and revealed his bloodstained fingers and one of his right molars. "It burns!" he spat again.

"Some fight you got yourself into!" The taller boy chuckled.

"Ugh, burns bad!" Nadus wiped the tooth on his shirt and pocketed it.

"Nadus! Geez, I didn't know you had that in you!" Idnurub smiled. "You were vicious out there!" Slowly acclimated to the horrendous conditions, Idnurub was less uptight and revealed a bit of his jovial character.

"So, tell me!" The taller boy stopped picking his nose. "What part of the city are you from?" He swiped his finger on his dirty shirt and glanced at Idnurub and then at Nadus, rubbing his hands together as though trying to keep warm in the cold. "Eh?"

"We're not from the city!" Idnurub replied.

"Really?" The taller boy sounded surprised.

"Yes," Idnurub said. "I had never been to the big city until today!"

"Yes, he's right," Nadus added. "We're not from there."

"Interesting!" the taller boy bobbed his head. "So where did they capture you boys from?"

"We're from the village, they took us from our village."

"Yes, we're from the village," Nadus concurred. "And you, where are you from?"

"I see! Village boys, huh! So they're going to the villages now?" the taller boy asked with intrigue in his voice. "Well, me?" he snapped out of his reverie and pointed to his chest. "I was born and raised in the city. Yes, the big city, for all my life!" he protracted his speech. "Midtown area to be precise!" he said in a jovial manner.

"How was it, living in the city?" Idnurub asked.

"I loved it, loved living there! That was until the war broke out and hell was let loose!" The taller boy slapped his thigh and scratched it. "It's quite different now because of the huge riot."

"Yes!" Idnurub agreed. "It does look like hell but it's a lot better than in here!"

"I wish you had seen it before the war!" the city boy spoke with passion. "It was a truly magnificent place!"

"Oh, yes! I visited the big city once with my father," Nadus interjected. "Idnurub is right, you know! It looks different now." The young boy continued to massage his cheek. "Nothing like what I remember!"

"I assume your name is Idnurub." The taller boy turned to the schoolboy.

"Yes, that's my name," Idnurub replied. "My friend's name is Nadus."

"*Nanna-Ifok*," the taller boy said as he shook hands with Idnurub.

"Nadus!" The young boy shook hands as he introduced himself to the taller boy. "Nice to meet you, I guess!"

"Sure! Nice to meet you, Nadus!" the city boy smiled. "Friends call me Nanna for short!" he added. "I guess you could call me that since we're all in this dump together!"

"Okay!" Nadus replied with a strained expression. "Okay, Nanna."

"Yes, talking about introductions!" Nanna paused and sighed. "Meet a good friend of mine!" he turned to his left and pointed to a boy who was sitting a few feet away in silence. "He's a little reserved but he's strong!" he added. "Come!" Nanna beckoned. "Come say hello to our new friends."

The older boy raised his slumped head and looked in the direction of Nanna. "Hello!" he waved halfheartedly and spoke with a raspy voice. He then began to crawl towards the three youngsters. "Hello, hello friends!" the older boy said as he reached the lads; he wiped the grime off his palms and knees before extending out his hand in acknowledgement. "*Olipm-Utut* is my name, Utut for short."

The village boys revealed their names and nodded their heads as they exchanged handshakes.

"Are you from the city too?" Idnurub asked their new acquaintance.

"Yes, I'm from the city and I lived downtown, close to the financial district. Are you familiar with that area?" the older boy asked.

"No! I'm not," Idnurub replied. "We're from the village!"

"I've been there before," Nadus interjected. "It was so busy and filled with lots of people who seemed very angry and in a rush!"

The older boy chuckled. "Yes, that's sounds like downtown to me!"

"It's just a front though," Nanna butted in. "Most of them are nicer than they appear, you just need to get to know them first. That's all."

"That's so true," Utut concurred. "Once we know a person, we'll treat you like family."

"Indeed!" Nanna said. "Indeed!"

"I suppose you're both right," Nadus said; the city boys' comments reminded him of his encounter with the bookkeeper. "Actually, during my visit to the city I met this nice old lady and she even gave me a gift."

"Really? Is that so?" Idnurub gave his friend a surprised look. "You didn't tell me about that."

"See, what I was talking about!" Nanna looked at Idnurub. "It's just a front to look very tough!"

"Where did you meet her?" Utut asked with a hint of skepticism.

"In downtown!" Nadus sneezed and offered a defensive response. "In front of the large, glass building! What's the name again?" He fiddled with a leather bracelet that was around his wrist as he tried to remember the signs he read. "Kan, Kanb, Kanbdl Financial!" he blurted out.

"You mean, Kanbdlrow Financial?" Utut inquired.

"Yes, that's it! Kandblrow Financial! Yes, the older lady is the owner of a colorful bookstand with many magazines and books."

"I know where that is!" Nanna uttered aloud. "It's right by the corner!"

"Yes!" Utut exclaimed. "It's close to where those magicians perform!"

"I don't know what you're all talking about!" Idnurub felt left out.

"I even know the bookkeeper by her full name," Utut bragged.

"What is it?" Nadus was curious; a part of him had always felt bad that he didn't ask the bookkeeper for her full name before departing for their village.

"Her name is Ms. *Enidan Remidrog*!" the teenager spoke in a forced, nasal voice as he attempted to imitate the bookkeeper's eloquent accent.

So that's her name? Enidan Remidrog!

"Yes, sounds like her!" Nadus revealed a crooked grin; it was his first since he last saw Muotrahk at the stream earlier in the morning. "Sounds a little like her."

Nadus flexed and rubbed his sprained wrist joint and fixed his eyes on the leather wristband that once belonged to his father. Nineb had given it to him after their treasured trip to the city as a gift for his birthday.

"Well spoken lady!" Utut commented. "She is liked by so many people, especially the street beggars. She's very kind to them so I hear!"

"I've seen her in passing," Nanna contributed to the conversation, "but I have never been inside her bookstand."

"Do you know where she is?" Nadus asked. "Do you know if she's still alive?"

"What a question!" Utut looked at the village boys. "I don't know and I wish I knew where my family is!" The older boy kept his cool, but there was a daub of frustration in his voice.

"I don't know if my sick mother is okay!" Idnurub was remorseful.

"After the riots started," Nanna coughed twice and spat, "the entire city was destroyed and many people have been killed and have died. There's no telling if that old woman is still alive, Nadus."

"What caused the riots, do you know?" Idnurub asked as he rubbed his eyes.

"I believe it's because of the rigged elections," Utut answered.

"What rigged elections?" Idnurub inquired.

"You know, the elections for the president's seat!" Nanna retorted.

"I don't get you!" Nadus admitted.

"Nanna, the village boys don't understand you!" Utut teased.

"Okay!" Nanna smiled. Nadus and Idnurub were perplexed by the city boys' pleasant demeanor despite the dreadful surroundings and their bony appearances. "So, there was an election for the new president and the older people in the city all voted on one day. Does that make sense?"

"Yes," the village boys chorused; they had learned about voting and elections at school.

"After the election day, apparently, the winners were two men..."

"Two brothers!" Utut chimed in. "Awig-Eled and Awiw-Oras!"

"Yes, two brothers!" Nanna nodded in concurrence. "They were the winners of the election, but then the army took over the city, right Utut?"

"Exactly, they claimed the brothers didn't win!" Utut said. "The brutal soldiers declared that they weren't going to leave, they wanted to keep ruling the city and that's what caused the riots!"

"That's it! That's why my village was destroyed?" Nadus was bitter. "Because two men, brothers," he corrected himself, "weren't allowed to win an election!"

"Well," Nanna paused and picked a larva off the floor, "the brothers and many of their supporters were arrested and then executed on national television!" He bit his lips as he squeezed and crushed the maggot with his fingers. "That's what really started the deadly riots!"

"People took to the streets and began to burn down buildings!"

"Soldiers and rebel forces blocked off and controlled parts of the city and the bodies began to pile up like dead pigeons!" Nanna spoke with little emotion.

"That's just how those evil men left our village!" Idnurub exclaimed.

"Yes!" Nadus spat; the bleeding and the pain in his mouth had subsided. "And those bastards killed my father, took away my life!" he cursed under his breath.

"I'm so hungry!" Idnurub groped his growling stomach and whined. "Why?"

"Why, what?" Nanna asked. "Why you are hungry?" He chuckled.

"I'm so hungry and it hurts!" Idnurub responded. "It's not fair! Why are we in here? We didn't do anything wrong!"

"I'm hungry too!" Nadus could smell the rising levels of acetone in his breath; an indication that he was metabolizing his fat reserves. "Have you two eaten recently?" he asked the city boys.

"No!" they shook their heads in unison.

"How long have you been in here then?" Nadus was curious.

"Two days, maybe three days!" Nanna and Utut spoke over each other. "Not sure!"

"And nothing to eat at all?" Idnurub shook his head in dismay.

"Yes!" Utut replied. "Nothing!"

"After the second day, your body gets used to it and you feel less hungry."

"That's so evil!" Nadus exclaimed. "The heavens have deserted us!"

"Yes!" Idnurub agreed. "How did they catch you, were you together?"

"We were both on the run when we were caught!" Utut replied.

"When the riot broke out the army and the rebels began to gather all the young men and boys to fight, either you joined the governmental forces or you joined the rebels! It's one or the other, no way around it!" Nanna added. "Utut and I and a few others, men, women, boys and girls, were hiding in an old, abandoned factory until the rebels took over that part of town and found us inside!"

"They beat us without mercy and killed all the men!" Utut closed his eyes and his head drooped downward. "The rebels claimed they were all 'cowards' for hiding and 'deserved to die' for that!"

"Just like our village!" Idnurub boiled with anger as he thought of the village men who were scorched and shot. "That's just like our village."

"What happened to the women and the girls?" Nadus asked.

"Separated us from them and taken away," Nanna answered.

"Where exactly did they take them to?" Nadus raised his voice slightly.

"Why do you care so much?" Utut inquired.

"I'll like to know, they took away my girlfriend! I'm going to find her!" the young boy proclaimed in a romantic fashion.

"Muotrahk?" Idnurub looked at his classmate.

"Yes, Muotrahk!"

"But, how do you know they took her and she's even alive?"

"Idnurub, don't say that!" Nadus snapped at his friend. "She's still alive and I heard her voice calling me from inside the other truck."

"Okay, Nadus!" Idnurub didn't sound convinced.

"So where exactly are they?" Nadus glanced at Nanna and Utut.

"The girls should be the last of your problems!" Utut replied. "If I were you, I'll worry about getting out of here first."

"I'm so worried!" Nadus gave a sarcastic answer. "If you know where they are please tell me!" He was getting a little edgy and it showed all over his face.

"Slow down!" Utut smiled. "You look like you're about to blow up."

"Okay!" Nadus sighed with a straight-faced. "Please tell me."

"I don't know exactly where they are! Do you know, Nanna?"

"Overheard one of the officers say they are kept in a camp that's about a mile away from here." Nanna retorted. "Is that good enough for you, Nadus?"

"Yes! Okay, thank you!" Nadus sounded relieved. "Thank you!"

Muotrahk!

I'll come for you!

I promised you!

"Glad to have helped!" Nanna grinned as he nudged his "new buddy."

In the swirling moments, as the inmates acquainted themselves and learned more about their seemingly hopeless situation, a rattle from above startled them and pilfered their focus; in an instant, they were blinded by a bright light that beamed on their dirty faces. Shrieking like startled moles, many of the recruits shielded their eyes from the piercing sunrays and scuttled to the darker corners of "the hole."

"General wants to see you useless crickets!" A cadet poked his head through the opening, yelling as he fished out the boys with a flashlight. "I see you there! I see you over there!" he yelled as he flashed the bright torchlight on their faces. "Get up, you! Get up!" he shouted repeatedly.

Nadus and the other recruits, as though terrified by the light, stood to their feet and crawled out of the crevices towards the corporals above. Adjusting to the added luminescence, the boys squinted and rubbed their eyes in an attempt to alleviate the discomfort and refocus their blurred vision.

"Come closer, all of you!" the cadet barked as he continued to flash the boys with the torchlight beams. "Closer!"

A second teenage boy lowered a shabby rope ladder into the eight-foot shaft and fastened the end to a metal pole. "Quick! Quick, climb on!" he looked through the opening, pointing and shouting at the boys. "You deaf or something? I told you to climb on!" he yelled and began to shower the boys with saliva. "Boss is waiting for you rats!" he spat again. "We don't have time for rubbish! You better get moving or we'll shoot you all out of there!" Five cadets cocked their weapons and each discharged a shot into the air before pointing the smoking barrels into the shaft. "Move it or we'll gun you down!"

Grunting, squealing and struggling like a litter of blind piglets suckling, the boys rushed to the ladder and began to curse and elbow each other; one by one, the recruits grabbed onto the unsteady rungs, held on tightly, and began to climb out of the deplorable holding cell. Pulling them by their arms and hair, the teenage orderlies dragged and jostled the recruits into the mud.

"Get up!" The cadets clapped their hands. "Get up rats, form a straight line! Get up!" They smacked the boys as they staggered to their feet.

The recruits obeyed the cadets without question and headed for the center of the secluded compound; facing forward and lurching along in a crooked line, the famished boys filed through a cluster of banana trees and marched past the huts and army tents that housed the rebels. A few yards and lashes later, Nadus and company were staggering in front of the general, surrounded on all sides by a row of inebriated rebels; the men and boys were dancing around a bonfire, splurging on pints of palm-wine and singing loud, incongruous songs.

"Boss! Boss!" One of the orderlies faced the general. "The recruits are here!" He turned and pointed to the boys who were herded together. "What should we do with them?" The teenager bowed his head. "Boss?"

"I hear you, young blood!" Yonk answered; he was sitting on a cast iron chair and grinning. Rubbing his nose with his fingers, the general leaned forward and dipped his thumb into a mountain of powder that was heaped on a table in front of him. "It's time for molding!" He snorted the cocaine with the zeal of an addict. "Yes, some real molding!" He sniffed as he wiped his nostrils with the back of his hand. "Right, girls?"

Yonk glanced at his concubines who were hovering around him, smiling maliciously as he relished the energizing effects of the drug. "Right, sweeties?"

"Yes, pappy!" the young girls giggled as they massaged and caressed his head and neck. "It's time to mold the silly boys!" they sang with uncanny arrogance.

"Indeed!" Yonk nodded. "Indeed!" He leaned over and took one more "manly hit." "Ameduba!" the general raised his head and beckoned; his bloodshot eyes were traced with rage and his upper lip and nose were daubed with white dust.

"Yes, boss!" Ameduba who was a few yards away darted towards the general; he handed his gourd to one of the corporals and wiped the palm-wine residue off his lips before clearing his throat a few times. "Yes, boss! What can I do for you?" He revealed his chipped, browned teeth.

"You know what to do!" Yonk stood to his feet; he stretched, wiped his nose and shook his head as though trying to chase away sleep. "Show all the roaches what it means to be a real man, to be a resistance fighter!"

"Absolutely!" Ameduba spilled out a sour laugh. He continued to stare at Yonk, bobbing his head as though engaging in a telepathic dialogue with his superior. "Okay, alright!" the colonel uttered aloud after a few seconds' delay. "I'll show them what it means to be a real man!" He turned around and approached the recruits; his charred countenance and heavy build were made more terrifying by the setting sun behind him that brought out his features in murderous, sharp relief.

As the space between Ameduba and the recruits shortened, Nadus recoiled inwardly; his stomach knotted up and he began to suffer from anxieties. Like an abused puppy, the young boy had witnessed the colonel's wrath firsthand and was terrified of what the large man had in stock for them.

"You stinking rats!" the colonel stood in front of Nadus and shouted and then cuffed the young boy on his cheeks.

Nadus trembled from the slap and expelled intestinal gas on reflex.

"You stink!" Ameduba frowned as he smelled his palm. "Did you just gas?"

"Yessir," Nadus hesitated and mumbled; he was embarrassed and his gums were beginning to sting from the heavy blow.

"I said," the colonel paused and took a step backwards, "did you just reap gas out from your tight anus?"

Nadus hesitated. "Sir."

The colonel leaned forward and barked. "Answer me!"

"Yes sir!" the young boy replied.

"I can't hear you!" Ameduba walked forward and raised his fist again.

"Yes, sir!" Nadus coughed up a loud, exhausted response. "Yessir!"

Ameduba laughed as he turned towards the insurgents. "Soldiers, can you all imagine, this bloody rat just let one powerful shot out of his tight anus!" The colonel squeezed his face and fanned his nose with his hand.

In response, the wild, drugged and unrestrained insurgents expressed their glee, laughing at the top of their lungs.

"You're a stinking rat!" Itto smirked as he headed towards the colonel and Nadus. "Is that how real men act, eh?"

"That's too funny!" One of the guerillas stooped over as he laughed.

"Yes! Yes!" A second man with tearful eyes pointed at Nadus. "I can't breathe, this is too funny!"

"Gaseous pig! We don't even need weapons to fight our enemies, all you have to do is just release some of your chemical weapons on them!" the sergeant laughed as though in pain.

"Gas! Gassy!" A teenager laughed and made explosion sounds with his mouth and moved his hands as though firing an automatic firearm.

"Enough!" the brigadier raised his hand like an umpire and shouted; almost immediately, the rebels lowered their voices and laughter.

"All of you rats listen up now!" Ameduba spoke in a loud and stern voice. "You think you know what it takes to be a real man? Do you? Answer me!"

"No, Yes, No, sir!" the recruits faltered.

"No, you don't!" Itto admonished the boys. "You have no idea! All of you," the brigadier yelled and began to clap, "take off your shirts now!"

Scared and unsure of the officers' motives, the terrified recruits obeyed and quickly began to unbutton their ragged shirts.

"On the ground, drop them on the ground!" the brigadier yelled as he sailed and weaved through the herd.

"Good, very good!" the colonel applauded. "You're obedient, real men listen! Real men always follow orders! Understood?"

"Yessir!" the boys chorused.

"Say it, real men always follow orders!" Itto shouted.

"Real men always follow orders!"

"One more time!" the colonel shouted again.

"Real men always follow orders!"

"To your knees, all of you! Drop down on your knees and plant your dirty, ugly faces in the mud, now, now!" the colonel screamed. "Now, follow orders!"

All at once, like a collapsing tower, the recruits dropped down to their knees and planted their faces in the earth.

"Real men suffer! Real men sacrifice! Say it louder!" the brigadier sang out.

"Real men suffer! Real men sacrifice!"

"Louder! I can't hear you!" the colonel added.

"Real men suffer! Real men sacrifice!"

"Yes, indeed!" Ameduba laughed as he pulled out his whip. "Real men suffer!" the colonel proclaimed as he began to lash the schoolboys on their bare backs. "And, real men endure pain!" he yelled with each vehement welt he produced.

Twisting and gyrating like injured snakes, the new recruits rolled in the soil and loudly vocalized their anguish.

"Not a sound from you rats!" the colonel barked and sweated profusely as he flogged the boys. "Not a word from you! Real men suffer, real men endure pain! Say it, now!"

"Real men suffer! Real men endure pain!" the boys wept and barely completed the sentence in its entirety.

"That's right, real men endure pain!" the colonel paused to breathe.

"Great work, Ameduba! Excellent work, Itto!" The general walked towards the welted boys, watching as they swayed in distress. "You're definitely good at molding the next generation of soldiers." Yonk clapped in admiration.

"Thank you, boss!" the brigadier saluted.

"I'm just following orders!" Ameduba replied.

"Say no more, officers!" Yonk replied. "Say no more! Let me leave you to your fine, commendable jobs." The general saluted and headed back to his "throne" that was a few yards away.

"Thank you, boss!" Ameduba wiped the sweat off his face. "Cadets!" he yelled as he signaled to a few teenagers. "Bring the pots of 'cold water' right now! They must be thirsty for some!" he grinned. "I want one regular and three cold! Okay?"

"Yessir, right away!" the teenagers jogged off towards one of the tents.

The boys, although bothered and hurting from the lacerations on their skins, were relieved to hear the word "water" from the bitter mouth of their nemesis. Through the course of the day, they had shed large amounts of water and were dehydrated; for many of them, including Nadus and his friends, securing a drink and a bite was the most urgent issue on their minds, with the exception of safely returning home to normalcy.

"Put the regular one here!" the brigadier ordered. "Over there!" Itto marked the ground with his boot and pointed to the line. "Put the others over there!"

"Yessir!" the corporal picked up the clay pot by its handles and wobbled towards the brigadier. "Yessir!" he reiterated.

"Bring it closer!" Itto demanded. "That's right, closer!" He signaled his request.

Ameduba, who was standing nearby, walked in an ostentatious fashion towards the cadet. "Clear out of the way!" he yelled and pushed the boy as he attempted to balance the vessel in the mud. The colonel then bent over and using a gourd that was floating on the cool fluid, he claimed a scoop of water and downed it.

"Good, eh?" the brigadier laughed.

Ameduba sighed and wiped his lips; he glanced at the small calabash in his hand and then at the boys. "This is the best water I've ever had!" he exaggerated with several nods of approval. "Any of you rats want a drink?" the colonel smiled and asked the recruits as they lay in the dirt. "No answer?" he dropped the gourd back into the vessel. "To your feet, all of you!" he spoke in an angry tone.

Once again, like automatons, the battered boys scrambled to their feet and stood still and erect out of fear of repercussions; the recruits were terrified by the large man and his seemingly erratic personality.

"When I ask you a question, you answer!" Ameduba barked. "Any of you rats want a drink?"

"Answer your superior!" the brigadier shouted. "Answer!"

The recruits jumped at his angry tone. "Yessir!" they shouted.

"Louder!" the colonel added. "Yes, what?"

"Yes sir! We want a drink!"

"Real men answer orders, say it!" Itto shouted again.

"Real men answer orders!"

"Louder, I can't hear you!" the brigadier paraded the recruits.

"Real men answer orders!"

"Good!" Itto smirked; he blew his nose, flung the thick, slimy discharge in the dirt and wiped his fingers on one of the recruit's head. He walked towards the colonel and whispered in his ears.

Ameduba kept a straight face and nodded repeatedly. "Hey, you!" the colonel signaled to a few cadets who were standing close by. "All of you," he yelled as he offered up the gourd and pointed to the pot of water, "give those rats a drink!"

"Yes sir!" The cadets dashed towards the colonel; two of them carried the clay pot and a third teenager took the gourd and began to offer the recruits a sip.

Thirsty and dirty faced, the schoolboys moved hurriedly towards the cadets; one after the other, they placed their parched lips on the gourd for a few trickles of water. In a few agonized moments, the volume of water in the clay vessel was reduced to a few pitiful drops. In response, the corporals pulled back and pushed away the encroaching swarm of unsatisfied youngsters.

"Get back!" one of the cadets yelled as he pushed the boys. "There's no more water for you!" The older boy was saddened by their pleas, but he continued to display a macho front. "Get back!"

"It's finished!" the second cadet unclasped the hands of the recruits as they held onto the pot and begged for "more water."

"Soldiers, assume your positions!" shouted a lieutenant standing in front of the recruits.

Driven to borderline insanity by their thirst, Nadus, Idnurub and the others continued to plead and beg for more water.

"Assume the military stance!" A second officer commanded. "Straight line!"

"It works all the time!" Ameduba looked at Itto and shook his head. "It's mad!"

"It's almost like magic!" the brigadier chuckled. "Alright officers," he hawked and spat, "shower them with some ice-cold!" He pointed to the other pots.

"Yessir!" two officers and a few of the cadets manned the vessels and utilizing the gourds that were floating on the liquid, they began to shower the recruits with "cold water."

"Water! Water! Thank you! Heavens bless you!" The famished boys revealed their gratitude by chanting aloud; they opened their mouths and waved their hands in the air as the rebels splashed them with the cool, colorless liquid. "Thank you, sir! Thank you!" they continued to chant.

All of a sudden, as though afflicted by acute tetanus, Nadus, Idnurub and the other boys grabbed their faces and fell to their knees. Shrieking at the top of their voices and rolling on the ground in an erratic manner, the recruits began to sob and cry and shake involuntarily. In reply, the rebels laughed incongruously, clapping and pointing and weeping as a result of their unrestricted joy.

"Mama! My eyes! Help me! Fire!" the children wailed out. "It burns!"

Unknowing to the recruits, the phrase "cold water" was a misnomer that was coined by the general solely for his cruel intentions; the water in the three other clay pots that the corporals were freely dishing out to the parched schoolboys was "fired up." It had been used to soak and wash fiery hot chili peppers that the women used to cook and prepare spicy meals for the rebels. As a result, the recruits were in pain, temporarily blinded and incapacitated by the improvised chemical weapon; their bruised and tender skins along with their parched lips and nares were inflamed and stinging.

"Look!" Ameduba laughed as he pointed at Nadus who was crying and swaying on the ground. "Look!" He laughed louder. "This one is dancing like an excited pig! Oh, look at that one over there!" he pointed to another boy. "That's one drunken monkey of a boy!"

"Yes!" Itto was also laughing loudly; he grabbed Ameduba by his shoulders and leaned forward against him. "Oh, yes! Yes!" the brigadier sounded as though he was suffocating. "It happens all the time, they're like rats!" he laughed again. "Right, boys?" He turned and glanced at the besieging cadets.

"Yessir!" the rebels chorused through their hysterical laughter.

Still sitting a few yards away on the large chair that he called the "real throne," Yonk was pleased and also amused by the "molding process." The general, however, didn't laugh as hard or as loud as the others; he just showed off a smirk on his hardened face, nodding as he sucked and puffed on a pipe. Like a deranged and yet caring guardian, he enjoyed watching the recruits get tortured and always derived a sick sense of satisfaction and pride as he witnessed their drastic transformation from "naïve little boys" to "heartless killers."

"Okay, that's enough!" Yonk stood up from his throne and snapped his fingers. "I said, 'enough!'" he rumbled in a deep, authoritative tone.

Without ado, the rebels lowered their voices and stopped their buffoonery.

"All of you, to your feet!" Yonk ordered as he marched towards the recruits. "Stand up now, at attention like the soldiers, the warriors that you are!" he barked.

The recruits, who were still suffering from the stinging and irritating effects of dissolved *capsaicin*, barely responded; rubbing their tearful eyes, Nadus and a few of the boys staggered to their feet and attempted to stand erect.

"I'm giving you all ten seconds to be on your feet and stand at attention!" the general shouted.

"For those of you standing," Itto interjected, waving his hands around as he spoke as though performing in a public recital, "pull all the weak fools up or else!"

"You'll all be flogged and sprayed again!" the colonel joined the ensemble.

"Get up, get up, now!" Yonk yelled and began to extend his fingers as he counted. "One, two, three…"

Fearing the repercussions, the boys were consumed by panic and they began to attack the "weak ones" and force them to their feet.

"Get up! Stand up! What's wrong with you! Idiot! Bastard!" the boys yelled at each other as they fought to stand at attention in the herd.

Yonk hissed loudly. "Boy, yes, you boy!" he signaled to one of the cadets. "Go get the milk for the recruits!"

"Yes, boss!" the cadet bowed his bald and flaky head before dashing towards the tent where the "coldwater" was initially stored.

Moments later, the lanky teenager wobbled towards Yonk with a large clay pot half-filled with a white, coagulating liquid that possessed a pungent and fairly acidic odor.

"Good!" The general looked in the pot; he dipped the tip of his ring finger into the chunky liquid, swirled it a little and then took a whiff of the gelatinous blob resting on the tip. "Good!" he frowned and spoke in a strained voice. "It smells just right!" he said to Itto.

"Looks like it!" The brigadier spat on the ground and wiped his lips with his sleeve. Then, he kicked up some dirt with his boots and covered up his saliva.

"Put it on their faces, stop them from jumping around like mice!" Yonk ordered.

"Cadets!" The colonel beckoned to three of the rebels who initially bathed the recruits with the "pepper water." "Give it to those rats," he pointed to the pot. "Rub it on their faces and give them a little for their hands and legs."

"Yes colonel!" the boys shouted; once again, they walked towards the pots and stood in front of the vessels. Using the previous gourds, they began to serve out the fermenting milk to the jumpy recruits. "Rub it on your face, it'll stop the burning!" the boys chanted as though advertising an elixir.

"Open your chicken hands!" one of cadets stood in front of Nadus and yelled.

Nadus looked up at the tall boy and he could barely keep his watery eyes open. "Yessir!" he stretched out his hands towards the corporal; he then clasped them together as he received a drop of the antidote.

"Rub it on your face and hands!" the cadet yelled again. "Now!"

"Yessir!" The young boy splashed his face with the milky substance; he then rubbed some of it on his arm and around his neck. To his surprise, the peppering effects lessened almost instantly and he was able to keep his eyes open.

"Your hands, open up your hands!" the corporal walked towards Nanna who was standing beside Nadus and yelled. "Open up before I slap you across the face!" the power-drunken boy shouted again.

"Spoiled, it smells! This is rotten milk!" Nadus whispered to himself, staring at his hands as he sniffed it. Relieved by the counterpoison and experiencing less pain and discomfort, the young boy was regaining part of his reasoning.

This is just so awful and it smells so terrible!

School gone! Tpgye gone! Papa gone!

Today's the last day before holidays.

These men are so wicked and evil!

Why is this happening to me?

I'm tired and my neck burns.

It's not fair!

Muotrahk!

"Weak links!" Yonk shouted and abruptly interrupted the young boy's musing; he was standing a few feet away with his chest elevated and his muscular arms flexed behind his back and his feet spread apart. "That's a no-no in our team. There's absolutely no room for the weak of heart! Do I make myself clear?"

"Yes, sir!" the less agitated recruits responded.

"To become a solider that fights for a cause, you need discipline and need to learn to battle, kill enemies and lay down your life if needed! Understood?"

"Yes sir!" Nadus and the boys hollered, paying little attention to the gravity of their response.

"Louder, I can't hear you!" Ameduba chimed in. "Louder!"

"Yes sir!" the recruits shouted.

"To be a warrior, you must adapt and be willing to lay down your lives! You must be willing to destroy and kill all that belongs to our enemies! Do I make myself clear, be willing to kill!"

"Yessir!" the boys chanted.

"Say it, be willing to kill!"

Be willing to kill!

"Louder! I can't hear you!" the colonel shouted. "Be willing to kill!"

"Be willing to kill!" the recruited reiterated in a louder voice.

"Excellent!" Yonk exclaimed.

Yonk turned to Itto who was standing to his left and whispered in his ear; the brigadier nodded in accordance and then signaled to Ameduba. The colonel cleared his throat and a malevolent expression sprouted on his face.

"Officers and corporals!" the colonel barked. "Circle around and assume your positions! We're about to separate the weak recruits from the strong!"

Upon hearing the announcement, the teenagers and the young men that were in the vicinity hoorayed and began to scuttle around and enclose the schoolboys like an encroaching, impenetrable wall. Nadus looked around and he didn't like the fact that all the guerillas appeared to be thrilled and filled with anticipation. As a result, his stomach tightened and his palms turned pale and the inner lining of his oral cavity dried out even more.

"Get me two!" The general pointed to the recruits.

"Yes, boss!" Itto replied as he stomped towards the recruits. The tall and thin man stood in front of the boys and scanned their faces as though searching for a familiar face in a crowded room. "You!" he grabbed one of the schoolboys by his ears and pulled him out of the herd. "And you! Yes, you!" he pointed. "Towards me now! Let's go, move it!"

Right away, Nadus's heart began to flutter, moping as his best friend was dragged towards Yonk and his concubines. "Idnurub!" he whispered.

"Stand straight, you roaches!" The general who was back on his makeshift throne spoke as he peeled the sheath of a ripe banana. "To be a true warrior," he took a bite of the banana, "you need to be quick!" he spoke with a mouth full of the pulpy fruit. "I can't, absolutely cannot afford any weak links in our force! Ameduba, right?"

"Yes, boss!" the colonel retorted.

"Only the strong survive, you two," Yonk pointed at Idnurub and the other boy, "will show who is stronger!" He handed the banana peel to one of the girls and took another banana from one of his sweeties. "Ameduba, Itto," the general glanced at the senior officials, "set it up!" he added as he pulled out his jagged dagger and handed it to the colonel.

"Yes, boss!" the officers replied.

"Cadets, assume your positions!" Ameduba snapped his fingers and signaled to a number of the teenage boys.

"Yes, colonel!" The cadets stepped forward and cocked their rifles. "Yessir!"

Ameduba began to walk away from the general's throne, counting each stride he took. "...Twenty-four! Twenty-five!" the colonel exclaimed as he turned and faced his superiors. "All ready, boss!" He waved his hands in the air and then dropped the knife on the ground.

"Every battle begins with a set of rules, they are called rules of engagement! Are you listening?" Itto smacked the boys on their heads.

"Yessir!" the boys replied.

"Two of you are about to engage one another, rules are simple! At his call," Itto pointed to the colonel, "you are to run towards him and pick up the dagger!" the brigadier scratched his eyebrow. "The fighter who gets there first is to finish the loser with the knife! It's that simple, the last person alive wins!" he declared with a menacing chuckle.

Idnurub and "his enemy" were in disbelief and their pale faces revealed their fears. The schoolboys thought they had seen, heard and experienced the worst that could happen to them, but this undisputable task to "engage and finish one another" was by far the most horrible.

"It can't be!" Nadus couldn't believe his ears. "This can't be happening, this is just one bad nightmare!" the young boy repeated in a hushed voice as he tried to internalize the solemnity of the current undertaking. "I just need to wake up!"

"Ready, set, go!" the colonel shouted.

"Alright, move it!" Itto yelled as he slapped the boys on their necks.

The boys hardly moved forward; they were still in disbelief and weren't sure if it was some sort of trick that the guerrillas used to test the loyalty of their captives.

"Move! Run now! Move it, you rats!" the cadets that were lined along the artificial pathway yelled and began to flash and wave their machetes.

"Move it now!" The tall brigadier cocked his pistol and fired a shot in the air. "Real men, listen! Move it now or I'll personally place a hot bullet through both of your thick heads." He fired a second shot close to their bare feet.

The two villagers jumped at the sound of the shots; they were pricked by a few rock fragments that were dispersed upwards as the slug grazed along the dirt.

"I'll destroy you!" Itto pointed his pistol at the boys. "Move it!"

Slipping and falling a few times, the boys dashed towards the dagger that was resting on the ground. Before long, the rebels began to cheer and clap and a few drummers doled out rapid beats as Idnurub and his classmate engaged in a true life-or-death struggle; tussling in the mud and trading blows of desperation, the terrified villagers fought to display their "inner strength" and be the first to acquire the sharp "killing tool." The sun, as though appalled by the wrestling match and mortified by the actions of the guerillas, dipped gradually into the apparent horizon, bathing the arena in grim shadows. Grappling with the thoughts that they were next in line, the other recruits watched fearfully as their colleagues moved violently across the rugged terrain. Nadus was rooting for his pal and although voiceless, he contorted his face with every punch Idnurub received. At the same time, a part of the young boy was consumed by guilt as he was acquainted with Idnurub's contender who was his fellow classmate. Adnawr was his name and he was one of the most popular and well-liked boys at the village school. All of a sudden, one of the fighters yelled with so much agony that it horrified Nadus and the other recruits and sent chills through their bones. Without delay, Adnawr staggered to his feet while Idnurub remained motionless, face down in the mud. Grasping his stomach with both hands, Adnawr turned towards his peers and took a few steps forward before slumping to his knees. With tears flowing from the corners of his reddened eyes, Adnawr gave out a weak, inaudible cry as he struggled to his feet. He wobbled forward and dropped back on his knees like a newborn calf. Wearing an expression of despair and defeat, he unclasped his fingers from around his navel and revealed a deep gash to the spectators. The terrified recruits moaned at the amount of blood that oozed out of their peer while the rebels cheered and applauded; he had been stabbed in the gut and was shedding heavily.

"So it wasn't him, not Idnurub?" Nadus whispered with parched lips and tearful eyes. "It sounded like him! Is he alright?" The young boy continued to watch as his injured and dying classmate fell on the ground, coiling up in the mud as he slowly passed. "Idnurub, Idnurub! Why are you just sitting there?" Nadus bite his lips anxiously as he gawked. "Stand up! Please, let me know you're alive!"

"Get up you rat, move over there!" Ameduba kicked Idnurub as he sat on the ground and stared at his bloodstained hands; the schoolboy was still in shock and immobilized by guilt. "Move over there, I said move!" Ameduba bent over and knocked Idnurub on his dusty scalp. "Get up and move there!" He pointed.

Idnurub didn't utter a sound despite the number of blows the colonel offered him; he just crawled towards the corner of the wrestling ring.

"And you two get that bleeding dog off the ground, toss him into the bushes!" Ameduba yelled. Two cadets responded right away and dashed towards the dying boy, each grabbing him by his arms and legs and lifting him off the ground.

"Halt!" Itto raised his hand and snapped his fingers as he shouted from the distance. "Halt cadets! Hold it right there!"

The cadets paused as they suspended Adnawr inches from the soil.

"Boss!" The brigadier turned and strode towards Yonk. "Do you have any plans to use the organs this time, maybe to sell or to make more bulletproof?" he asked in a lower tone of voice as if trying to be discrete.

"Good call!" Yonk uttered, nodding as he stared at his dirty fingers. "Yes, have *Agubak* take out the organs from those weak rats," he looked up at the brigadier, "and have him grind the other parts to make more of his special 'bulletproof potion.' Then, have him package the eyes and kidneys and hearts into clean plastic bags!"

"Yes, boss!" the brigadier responded.

"And place the bags in the ice coolers, don't want the organs to go bad. We might be able to sell them tomorrow to those foreign doctors for some big money when we head back to the city base!" The general spoke with little remorse and with the directness of a mercenary. "Is that clear, officer?"

"Yes, boss!" Itto raised his hands towards his forehead and saluted. "Excellent!" The brigadier dropped his hand and grinned, accentuating the remnants of the green dyes that previously covered and camouflaged his stoic face. "Okay boys! Take that rat there!" Itto faced the cadets and pointed to a large tent.

"Yes, sir!" the cadets mumbled a reply as they carried the boy to the canopy.

"And you, sergeant!" Itto beckoned to the tall teenager. "Go inside and inform Papa Agubak that the boss wants him to harvest organs and make more potions!"

"Yessir!" The sergeant grasped his rifle and headed towards one of the huts.

"Harvest organs. Potions?" Nadus whispered. "What does he mean by that?"

"And be sure to show some respect!" Ameduba smacked the teenager on the back of his head as he scuttled by. "Do you understand me, boy? Speak to the old man with utmost respect!"

"Yes, colonel!" the sergeant stopped to reply and then continued walking.

"Okay! Back to business!" the general clapped his hands, hollering with a hint of impatience. "Weed out the weak links!"

"Yes!" Itto uttered a sigh. "Alright, you!" The thin officer pointed to one of the recruits. "Come forward, quick! You're next!"

"Me? Me? Me?" A few of the boys asked as none of them wanted to be "next."

"Yes, you, with the large elephant ears!" Itto yelled as he pointed at one of the boys. "Move it before I teach you a lesson or two in obedience!"

Identifying with the degrading depiction, one of the recruits with pro-truding auricles stepped out of the group and walked timidly towards the tall officer.

"And you! Yes, you with that frog eye," Itto pointed to Nadus's swollen eyelid and beckoned, "step up! Step out, come over here! Show me who's stronger!"

No! No! No!

Why me?

Nadus cried in his mind, shaking his head in dismay as he neared Itto.

I can't do it.

I can't kill him!

But if I don't kill him.

He will stab and kill me.

I have to protect myself.

I need to save Muotrahk.

I have to get the knife first!

Nadus was torn apart and he was experiencing a conflict within his conscience. The young boy looked over at Idnurub and noticed that his friend didn't look the same; he wore an appalled expression on his mud-dy face, trembling as if suffering from the paroxysm chills of malaria.

No! No!

I can't do it.

I just can't kill Adnagu.

I know him too well!

Adnagu happened to be one of "the losers" at school who was flogged earlier in the morning for flunking the final exam, and Nadus just couldn't see himself murdering a classmate; he was faced with a mental quandary: kill or be killed.

"Okay!" Itto cleared his throat aloud. "Alright, you heard the rules before and saw how it went down! At the colonel's call, you are to run over, pick up the knife and finish the weaker one! It's that simple!"

"On your marks," Ameduba raised up his hands, "get ready, go!" he shouted as he dropped his hands down to the ground.

Without delay, the two recruits dashed towards the colonel, running side by side and nudging each other like panicked antelopes. Frantic and terrified of the thoughts of being stabbed and bleeding to death, Nadus took a deep breath and filled his lungs with air; he then increased the length and speed of his strides and was jostled a few inches ahead of his contender. Halfway to the mark, Nadus stopped abruptly and watched as Adnagu took the lead. Nadus changed his direction and headed towards the large bonfire that illuminated the yard.

"No! No! Run to the colonel! What's wrong with you boy? Run to the colonel!" A number of the cadets expressed their excitement as they hollered and clapped and whistled. "Quick! You're headed in the wrong direction! Get the knife. Kill him!"

"Alright! You know what to do, finish him off!" the colonel yelled as Adnagu grabbed onto the dagger and picked it up in victory. "Finish him off, move it!"

The recruit stood up and whirled around with the "butchering instrument" in his hand, wielding it as he walked warily towards Nadus. The young boy saw his opponent in the distance and the glint from the jagged blade opened his pores and he began to sweat; his breathing quickened and his heart rate and the hairs on the back of his neck rose. Doubt quickly crept in and Nadus began to question his decision to forgo the razor-sharp weapon.

Maybe I should have gone for the knife!

This might be your only chance!

Muotrahk is depending for you!

I just can't kill another person!

But I just can't do it.

Save yourself!

Go for it.

"Focus, young lad!" Nadus recalled the advice of the old man from the marketplace. "Believe in yourself!" The young boy recited the words of wisdom in whispers. "Be confident, and once you believe you're a product of success, everything about you...becomes a form of success!"

Go for it—this might be your only chance!

Cautious of the radiating heat and crackling fires, Nadus hunkered down and began to feel the ends of the blazing logs with his palms. The rebels were perplexed by the young boy's actions and a handful of them thought he had lost it and was possessed by lunacy. Using both hands, Nadus picked five sticks of firewood, rose to his feet and faced his rival who was quickly closing in.

"Run to the colonel! Boy, he's getting closer! Drop the sticks and fight like a man! Quit playing or you'll get cut!" Nadus's supporters screamed at the top of their lungs. "Give him a surprise attack! Quick! Move!"

"Kill him! Stab him in the stomach! Cut his face! Slice his throat! You have the knife in your hand!" a few other rebels yelled in favor of Adnagu.

"Finish him!" the colonel shouted. "We don't have all day!"

"Yes, you have the dagger, gut him up!" the brigadier ordered.

"Once you believe you're a product of success," Nadus iterated as he tuned out the noisy background, "everything about you...becomes a form of success!"

Go for it—this might be your only chance!

Nadus blinked and for a split second the chaos around him dampened, slowed almost to a standstill. "Focus, lad! Focus!" Nadus reiterated as he propelled the sticks out of his hands and upwards into the damp air. "Focus, lad!"

This might be your only chance!

"In an arc, young lad, keep them all in an arc!" Nadus heard the calm and shaky voice of the old beggar in his head. "Focus, lad!"

"Always follow your dreams, my dearie!" the warm voice of the book-keeper echoed in his head. "Believe in yourself, you can do it!"

"Yessir, I'll keep it in an arc!" The young boy uttered as he took a deep breath and watched the fiery logs sway and whirl and elicit a dazzling array of bright colors and cascades of sparks.

I'm doing it!

I'm juggling!

"I'm juggling!" Nadus smiled as he caught the torches and at the same time threw them back up towards the sky. "Yes, I'm doing it!"

"Move it, go for the kill!" Ameduba uttered with edginess.

"Yes, solider! What are you waiting for? Finish him! Finish him off, now!" Itto clapped both of his hands noisily as he took a step forward, yanking Nadus out of his psychedelic trance and refocusing his mind on the imminent encounter. "We don't have all day!" the brigadier shouted again from a few feet away.

Straightaway, the young boy's world returned to its preceding state: swift, vicious, noisy yet full of desolation and flourishing with the wrath of man. The cadence of the drums also increased and the cheers and roars of the guerillas rose in accordance. Battling his many distractions as he juggled the five sticks, Nadus switched his gaze from the flames and fixed his eyes on his rival who was already dangerously close and prepared to save his own skin at all costs.

"Kill him! Kill him!" The rebels clapped and stomped their feet.

Responding to the chants and the officers' orders, Adnagu raised the dagger to his shoulder level and continued to press on, despite his fears for the flames in the hands of his "enemy." The sweaty pupil then began to swing the "killing tool" up and down at a diagonal angle in a swift and uncoordinated manner. Nadus didn't falter. The young juggler jumped sideways and away from each sweeping stroke that Adnagu offered; he kept on rearranging the torches in the air and mesmerizing the audience with his acrobatics. The inexperienced Adnagu chased Nadus around the ring as he performed and with utmost desperation to "finish him off."

"Closer! Move in! Stab him!" The animated guerillas booed and hailed each time Adnagu fumbled with the blade or tripped on the ground. "Get up! Knife him!"

"Solider! Solider!" a loud voice resonated through the arena.

Adnagu stopped in his track and faced Ameduba.

"I told you to execute him!" the colonel shouted again. "Execute him or else!" The bulky officer cocked and pointed his pistol. "I will put one between your eyes."

Adnagu turned towards his mate with an anguished expression on his face. Then, as if suddenly energized and acting on impulse, he darted towards Nadus, yelling and brandishing the army knife in a final attempt to claim victory.

"I just can't do it! I just can't!" Nadus shook his head as he continued to juggle, standing his ground and watching as his attacker proceeded. "I can't kill another person! I can't!"

Yes, you can!

Protect yourself!

"No, I can't! I can't do it!"

Yes, you can!

The deep, domineering voice in the young boy's head grew louder.

Look, look!

He's getting closer.

Protect yourself!

Protect yourself now!

Save Muotrahk!

"Okay, okay! I'll do it!" Nadus exclaimed as he propelled the fiery logs out of his hands and towards Adnagu who was stationed a few feet away with the dagger raised to deliver a succession of deadly jabs. "Yes, I'll do it!" he yelled again.

Adnagu dropped the knife on reflex and tried to cover his face and dodge the flares, but he wasn't fast enough. The ashes got into his eyes and the flames burnt a part of his face and his forearms. "Oh! Mummy! My cheeks! Eyes! Hands! Fire! I can't see!" the schoolboy began to wail.

Wasting little time and seizing the window of opportunity, Nadus capitalized on the swift disarmament; he slid in the dirt and kicked Adnagu on his ankle and then on his knee, sweeping the pupil off his feet and onto the ground. Before his opponent could recover from the fall, Nadus dove towards the loose dagger and grabbed onto it. Then, like a wildcat attacking a pigeon, Nadus turned to his side and pounced on Adnagu, immobilizing the boy as he placed the sharp, jagged blade on his throat.

I can't do it!

Nadus screamed in his mind as he stared into the feeble eyes of his opponent. "I just can't!" he whispered. "I can't do this to you, Adnagu," he said, almost in tears.

"Bravo, solider!" The general stood up from his throne and spat. "Fantastic!" Yonk clapped as he strode towards the boys. "Excellent! Excellent execution!"

"Well played out!" the colonel chimed in as he neared the general.

"Boys," Yonk glanced at the faces of the surrounding rebels, "now this is how you take down your enemies!" The general gave out a short-lived laugh. "Always use the element of surprise to your advantage, cut down the devils that stand in your way!" Yonk stood close to the exhausted fighters, glanced at them and continued his sermon. "Let this be a lesson to all of you! Always be prepared and ready for the unexpected, look at this boy over here!" He pointed to Nadus who was still sitting on his classmate. It was the first time Yonk had called any of the recruits by the term "boy" rather than the usual "rat" or "cockroach." "He was calculated and very meticulous!" Yonk continued to preach. "He took his enemy's strength and turned it around," Yonk ran his fist into his other palm and clasped both hands together, "and used it against him! He used it against him! Do you hear me, do you understand me?"

"Yes sir!" the rebels shouted.

"Yes, he used his enemy's strength, turned it into a weakness!" Yonk turned towards the bonfire with his hands spread apart. "And what did he get in return?" Yonk nodded as he stared into flames; the burly man was getting more in sync with his speech and his stoic face looked colder than ever. "Answer me?" he barked. "What did he get in return?"

The rebels looked at each other with confused expressions.

"Are you all deaf?" the brigadier admonished the pack. "Speak up!"

"Victory!" One of the young rebels in the front cleared his throat and coughed out a response. "Victory, sir!"

"What did you say?" Yonk faced the teenager. "What did you just say?"

"Victory!" the teenage rebel stuttered. "He got victory, sir!" He swallowed his saliva as he pointed at Nadus.

"Yes, exactly!" Yonk swung his fist forward as though delivering a low punch. "Yes, he got victory! Say it again! What did he get in return?"

"Say it!" the colonel interjected, raising his pistol as he hollered.

"Victory!!!" the rebels yelled and many of them raised their weapons.

"Victory, indeed!" Yonk exclaimed. "Be ruthless, show no mercy to the enemy and in the end," the general raised his index finger up towards the darkening sky, "victory will be ours!" He waved his digit as though in rebuke. "Do you hear me?" He pulled his ear.

"Sir, yessir!" the platoon howled.

"Do you hear me?" Yonk repeated in a deeper, more imposing tone.

Yessir!!!

"Good, very good!" The general wiped his nose with the back of his hand as he snickered. "Now, solider," Yonk turned towards the young boy and spoke in a calmer voice. "Execute this bloody rat, he had his chance and he blew it!"

No, I can't do it!

"Finish him off!" He patted Nadus on his bald head. "Make him bleed!"

The young boy looked at his colleague as he sweated and gasped for air. "I can't kill another person!" Nadus blurted out. "Sir, I just can't do it!" He raised his head and looked up at the general.

"What?" Yonk was taken aback by the response. "What did you say?"

"Papa wouldn't be proud!" Nadus confessed.

"What did you just say?" the general asked again.

"I'm sorry, sir!" Nadus dropped the knife on the ground. "I can't do it! I cannot kill him!"

"Have you lost your mind?" Ameduba shouted at Nadus. "Pick it up now!"

"Are you mad?" Itto interjected. "How dare you disobey the general?"

"What did you just say?" Yonk backhanded Nadus. "Say it again!" He punched Nadus on the back of his neck and sent him sprawling across the ground.

"I can't do it!" Nadus got on his knees and pled. "Papa will be upset."

"Do you think this is a bloody joke, uh? Answer!" The general gave the young boy another slap to the face. "Do you?"

"No, sir!" Nadus shook his mud-covered head and hands. "No, it's not a joke!"

"You think you can disrespect me in front of my men?" Yonk looked around at the faces of the rebels.

"No, sir!"

"You think this is a joke?"

"No, not at all, sir!"

"I'll show you, this isn't a game of choices!" The drug lord lifted the cuff of his cargo pants; from a concealed leather holster around his leg he pulled out a compact revolver. "When you're given orders," Yonk paused and stared at the handgun before opening the revolving chamber and letting the bullets drop to the dirt, "you do as you're told or you meet your death!" Yonk yelled and cracked his neck by swaying his head from left to right. The general then grabbed Nadus by his throat as he tried to get on his knees and shoved him back on the ground.

"No!" Nadus protested with a bloody lip. "I can't!" he said adamantly.

"Shut up!" the brigadier shouted.

"Shut up! You're making the general mad!" Ameduba added.

"When you're given a task," Yonk bent over and picked up one of the bullets from the ground, "you do it! No questions asked, real men listen to orders!" He wiped and dusted the slug on his khaki shirt before placing it into one of the six chambers of the revolving cylinder. He swung the cylinder back in place, spun it with his palm and pulled the hammer backwards. "Now, get up, you roach! I order you to get up!" Yonk grabbed Nadus by his neck and dragged up him to his knees. "You always do as you're told!" He placed the muzzle of the handgun on the side of the young boy's head. "You think this is a game, eh?"

"No, sir!" The young boy glanced at the revolver, shaking his head as he offered an inaudible response. "No, no, sir!"

"I'll play a game with you, as a matter of fact, I like games too!" Yonk laughed in a sadistic manner as he glanced at the other recruits who were herded a few feet away and expressing fear on their sweat-beaded faces. "There are six chambers in this gun for bullets and I have one bullet in here! You want to play games, right?" He blinked with force, sniffed and then bobbed his head. "I'll pull the trigger five times, let's see if you're lucky enough to receive my orders again, if you make it through, I'll let you live! Deal!" Straight away, the warlord squeezed the trigger and the hammer of the revolver snapped back to its original position. "One click, four to go!" Yonk laughed as he pulled on the hammer. The spectators, on the other hand, murmured in suspense and anticipation of the young boy's fate in "the game."

"It's not a joke!" A feeble, brief click emanated from the revolver for the second time, and Nadus closed his eyes as he wept and whispered his thoughts. "No, it's not a joke!"

"Three clicks!" Yonk yelled and Nadus shivered from the quick metallic snap.

I can't do it.

Please, please!

"Four click!" Yonk looked at the revolver and then at Nadus before chuckling. "You have some luck on your side today, boy! Last try, let's see if you're so lucky!"

"Papa, help me." Nadus listened to his heart sounds. "Please help me!"

I need to see Muotrahk again!

I need to see her again!

The warlord glanced at the viewers. "Five click!" He nudged the young boy's head with the muzzle as he pulled the trigger.

The hammer sprung back and the pistol clicked without firing.

"Well, well! Lucky you!" Yonk looked at Nadus. "Thank your shining stars! They must be working for you today, eh!" he scoffed. "You're the first I know to have survived this game." He sounded intrigued. "So you survived, a deal's a deal," he lowered the handgun, "you know! Right?" Yonk asked in a harsher tone. "Right?"

"Yes, yes sir!" Nadus was frazzled. He swallowed his saliva with added effort and he offered timid glances at the large man and noticed something sinister about his crooked smile. "Yessir!"

"Yes, a deal's a deal! I should let you live, you survived!" Yonk stared at the other insurgents. He switched his gaze from the masses and looked at Itto and Ameduba and then back at Nadus. "But, right now," he winked at his two officers, "I have the power of life and death in my hands, right here!" Yonk asserted with arrogance in his voice, "and I choose to end yours, just as you chose to disobey me!" he exclaimed. "Let this be a real warning to you roaches," he looked at the other recruits, "always, always follow orders, no questions asked!" Yonk pulled the hammer and cocked the gun. "To hell with you!"

Nadus closed his eyes and took in a deep breath and the world around him slowed once again. The hefty warlord snickered and blinked as he squeezed the trigger. The recruit heard a clink and momentary silence and the precious memories of his childhood flashed through his head.

Muotrahk!

Nadus saw himself by the stream with the love of his life.

"Say what?" Yonk yelled in a protracted fashion as he cocked the pistol again and pulled on the trigger. "What the…?"

"It can't be!" Itto said in a low voice with a look of bewilderment.

"Revolvers," Ameduba added, "never!"

The warlord vented his anger through his nostrils like a raging bull. He opened the cylinder of the revolver, pulled the frame closer to his face and briefly inspected the five empty chambers; he realigned the single bullet towards the short barrel and closed the cylinder. Then, he latched the revolver, cocked it and pointed it at the boy's forehead and pulled the trigger.

The hammer recoiled. The gun clicked but didn't discharge the round.

"What the hell!" Yonk yelled. "Impossible, it's jammed!"

"That's really strange, boss!" the brigadier chimed in.

"I just cleaned this piece of junk yesterday!" The warlord flung the revolver in dirt. "Hey, Itto!" Yonk turned towards his officer with his hand stretched out as though prepared to receive a baton. "Itto!" He snapped his fingers.

"Boss?"

"Give me!" Yonk beckoned. "Quick, pass me your dagger!"

"Yessir, boss!" Itto looked downwards; he unbuckled the sheath from around his waist in haste and tossed it towards the general.

"Enough with this nonsense!" Yonk exclaimed as he caught the leather sheath with his left hand and pulled out the black army knife with the other. "I'll get this done right! Good, old-fashioned way, death by stabbing!" The warlord glanced at the knife with intrigue and out of respect and admiration for its ability to snatch a life in minutes. "Jab a few times in the liver and the heart, it's all over, slow and painful!" Wasting no time, the stocky man pounced on Nadus and knocked him to the ground. Then, like a skilled butcher, he turned Nadus on his side and planted his knees on his arms. "I like this, stabbing doesn't jam!" Yonk laughed as he placed his hands over the young boy's face, covering his mouth and obstructing his breathing. "Yes! Never jams!"

The young boy widened his eyes as he began to choke and struggled for air and, hopelessly, for his life.

"Let this be a real warning, a warning to all of you!" Yonk yelled as he raised the dagger upwards. "You bloody roach!"

Although his current situation was dreadful and appalling, Nadus didn't wish to die; he wanted to see yet another sunrise and grow old enough to drink palm-wine with the farmers and fishermen. On the other hand, the young boy didn't believe he would realize any of his wishes; he felt he had already cheated death enough times for a day. With the corner of his eyes, he looked up at the warlord and focused all of his attention on the sharp, pointed blade. His boyish muscles tightened and his pupils dilated to let in more light.

"You disobey, you die like this cockroach!" Yonk grunted as he went for the kill.

Nadus held his breath and clenched his teeth together and closed his eyes as tight as he could. Immersed in pitch darkness, the young boy silently prayed and hoped that the agony wouldn't be too unbearable for his juvenile mind.

It can't be too bad!

It really can't be!

"Stop it, don't do it!" A deep, male voice echoed through the murmurs of the gregarious rebels. "Yonk, do not touch him, that lad!"

"Let go of me!" Yonk exclaimed. "The fool disobeyed, now, he deserves to die!"

"Don't do it."

"How about I cut his face so that he'll always remember to obey me?"

"Don't do it, I warn you!"

I'm still alive?

No pain?

With his eyes still closed shut, the young boy was amazed to still be breathing and not experiencing excruciating pain; he also didn't expect to hear any voices or dialogues rather the horrifying sounds of the blade churning through his gut.

I can't feel it!

"Why?" the general grumbled. "Why shouldn't I touch this roach?"

Nadus slowly opened his eyes and was greeted by a blur.

"He has a very special mark, this one!" the other man said.

"What mark do you talk about?" Yonk asked. "What mark, eh?"

"A divine one, from the heavens." the second man replied. "Please, put down the knife!" he tightened his grip around Yonk's wrist as he pulled his hand down.

"A divine mark?" The warlord lowered the dagger with reluctance. "I don't see any mark on him!" he shot out saliva from his mouth as he spoke. "Where is it?"

"In his spirit!" the second man said.

"Papa Agubak, you know, I have a lot of respect for you," Yonk stood to his feet, "but he disobeyed and deserves to be taught a serious lesson!" He kicked Nadus in the groin.

The young boy held his crotch and groaned as he turned over on his back.

"You're playing with fire!" Agubak warned in a more serious tone. "Listen to me!" he walked closer to the warlord and whispered in his ear. "You, listen to me, right now! Your little handgun didn't just jam for no apparent reason! It was a divine act; so I won't warn you a second time! Don't touch that boy again!"

"Or else what?" Yonk stepped on Nadus's thigh with his combat boots.

"Your worst nightmare," the second man raised his finger towards the face of the general and shook it slowly, "will come true!" He made a fist.

The warlord looked into the eyes of the second man and swallowed his saliva. "Is that so, huh?" he tried to hide his apparent fears.

"Yes, I warned you!"

"Nonsense!" Yonk turned around and faced the bonfire. His face and his eyes lit up in the reflection of the wavering flames. "Ameduba!" He cleared his throat.

"Yes, boss!" the colonel replied.

"Take that roach back to the others!" he pointed to the young boy's opponent who was squatting in dirt with his face hidden between his thighs.

"Yes, boss!" Ameduba smacked the recruit on the back of his head. "Get up! I said get up from the ground." The colonel grabbed the boy by his ear and pulled him up to his feet. "Over there, move it!" he pointed towards the other recruits.

"Itto!" the general called out.

"Yes, general!" the officer hollered.

"Assemble the recruits and continue to weed out the others, okay?"

"Yes, boss!" The officer saluted.

"That's nonsense! Take!" Yonk handed the dagger and the sheath back to his brigadier. "Nothing! Absolutely nothing, no divine mark or divine intervention or anything will stop me! I'm not going to lose this bloody war!" The warlord subtly expressed his fear. "Get to work!" He turned to the officers, clapping his hands as spoke.

"Yessir!" Itto marched towards the other recruits yelling out orders.

"No, I will not lose. I'm too meticulous!" Yonk cursed under his breath as he marched towards his throne. "I'm calculated. I always think ahead!"

"Get up, young lad!" Agubak looked at Nadus as he lay on the ground and then stretched out his hand. "Get up, you don't have to fear!"

Having gained back his vision and cognizance, Nadus looked up at the talker and tried to get a better view of him.

"It's okay!" the old man spoke softly. "Get up, you don't have to fear!"

Nadus coughed a few times, ejected the sputum from his mouth and then accepted the man's offer. The young boy warily grabbed on to the stretched-out hand and pulled himself up to his feet.

"Nadus!" the man bent his head sideways as though trying to get a different view of the young boy's face. "How are you feeling?"

He knows my name!

"Yes, I believe we've crossed paths before!"

We have?

"Yes, we have!" The man smiled. "Look at my face, do I look familiar?"

Nadus stared at the old man's face, straining his eyes in the process.

I don't know him!

"I don't," Nadus stuttered; he was anxious, scared and suffering from the symptoms of shock. "Sir, I don't believe we've met before."

"Yes, young lad!" The man nodded and smiled. "We've surely have!"

"No, sir!" Nadus shook his head. "I don't remember, sir!"

"Don't call me that." the old man replied.

"What is that, sir?"

"Sir! No, no!" The old man smiled again. "Don't call me that lad. I was proud of you, very proud of you! I see you've been practicing."

"Practicing?"

"Yes, you juggled in a 'perfect arc,' lad!" The old man winked.

"Perfect arc?" Nadus looked at the gentleman as he muttered. "You're the begg…"

"Yes, yes!" the old man interjected. "Indeed!"

"The marketplace, with all the oranges!"

"Excellent!" The man smiled, squinting as he revealed his teeth; they didn't look as crooked and brown as Nadus recalled. "Ha, you remember!" He patted the young boy on his cheeks.

"I remember!" Nadus was flooded with relief and tears formed in his eyes.

"Good, young lad!" Agubak wiped the tears on the young boy's dirt-covered cheeks with his aged hands. "No need to cry!"

"I've lost it all, I'm weak! My family's gone and my life is all over!"

"No, you haven't lost it all!" The old man held the young boy's shoulders with both hands. "You're still breathing and with life comes hope! Okay?"

The young boy nodded reluctantly.

"In your darkest moment of trial and tribulation, you've found courage from within to choose life over death and fulfill your heart's desire, your destiny!"

"My destiny?"

"Yes! You always wanted to juggle and perform in front of a crowd, right?"

"Yes," Nadus concurred, "but..."

"And you did it!" The old man looked over at the guerillas who were chanting as they watched two recruits battle for their lives. "Today, minutes ago, you did it! You've officially performed in front of a crowd!" He pointed to the rebels.

"But this isn't how I thought it will be like, this isn't what I wanted!"

"Yes, it is." Agubak nodded twice. "At times, we have different views of what we want in life and sometimes, in order for us to fulfill our destinies we have to go through the worst to get there! And in your case, you had to be dragged into the swamp to show your true talents as a juggler!"

"I don't know what to say!" Nadus looked up and noticed that the old fellow didn't look as frail as he had the last time they crossed paths. Agubak looked younger; his skin was smoother and his face was fuller and rounder.

"Don't say anything!"

"Okay, but how did you get here?" the young boy asked in a low voice. "How did you become part of them?" Curiosity crept into his mind and he began to itch for answers.

"Come with me!" the old man spoke with urgency lurking in his voice; he grabbed Nadus by his hand and led him a few yards away from the boisterous crowd. "It's a long story and I will not have enough time," he paused and looked in the direction of Yonk, "to go into it, how I got here!"

"Okay, sir!" Nadus replied.

"I was forced to do things and used my powers for selfish reasons!"

"I don't get what you're saying."

"Things that I'm not proud of! But I held on because the prophecy says that a 'boy with the mark' will bring an end to all of this!" The man stared at the young boy. "And you, Nadus, you bear the mark and will bring an end to all of this!"

"It's me?" Nadus was perplexed. "What mark do you talk about?" The young boy stared at his hands as though searching for a mosquito bite.

"Young lad, it is not visible to the sightless."

"What do you mean by that, sightless?"

"You have to be willing to see it," Agubak said. "But we don't have time now to discuss this in detail!" He sighed; he looked over his shoulders and caught Yonk eyeing both of them with malicious intentions.

"Nadus, listen to me," the man glanced at the sky, "you bear the mark and you're the one from the prophecy!" He looked at the young boy and shook him by his shoulders. "Do you hear me? It is you."

"Yes, sir!" Nadus replied. "I don't understand you."

"It's Papa Agubak, not sir!" The man sounded more pressed for time.

"Okay, Papa Agubak, I don't understand what you mean."

"Take, Nadus!" Agubak pulled out a ripe banana from the pocket of his robe and handed it to the young boy. "Take it." The old man forced the fruit into the hands of Nadus, "take it! This is my way of repaying you for the tuber of yam that you left in the market!" he smiled. "Besides, you'll need it soon, the strength!"

The young boy snatched the banana from the man, peeled it in haste and began to gulp it down. The brownish-yellow fruit was the first meal he had eaten since breakfast with his family earlier in the morning.

"Good, go ahead, eat it, eat it all! Quick!"

"Yes, Papa Agubak!" Nadus nodded as he chewed and smacked his lips together. "And how will I do it? How will I end this, the pain, the suffering?" the young boy spoke with a full mouth and a tongue laced with desperation. "I'm just the son of a farmer. How will I stop all of this kill-ing?" He looked around.

"To be honest," the man's voice was dry, "I have no foresight into your future nor do I know how you're going to do it! It's your fight, lad! It's your path and destiny! And only you possess the answer to the question you ask."

"Only me?" Nadus spoke in a low voice.

"Yes!" He bobbed his head. "Only you can answer that question."

"Papa Agubak!" Ameduba yelled from the distance. "Enough with the rat!"

Straight away, the old man looked in the direction of the voice and the young boy followed suit.

"What did you just say?" Agubak asked the colonel.

"General doesn't favor double standards!" Ameduba waved his hands as he spoke and approached the two. "And he demands that the boy im-mediately join the other recruits for training."

"Alright!" The old man scowled at the colonel. "He'll be right there!"

"General Yonk wants him. Recruit!" Ameduba shouted. "Join the line!"

"Nadus, I hope you heard what I said!" Agubak switched his attention to the young boy; he grabbed him by his shoulders and shook him again. "You bear the mark and only you have the willpower to end all of this!"

"Only me?" Nadus asked again; the young boy was baffled. "Me?"

"Yes, you, Nadus!"

"But how?" Nadus stared at his feet. "I'm only a boy, weak and tired!"

"No, don't you say that!" Agubak spoke in a hushed voice; he was cau-tious of Ameduba who was only a few steps away. "Nadus, you're a lot stronger than you know and appear. Believe in yourself!" The man shook the recruit. "Heavens have favored you. You just have faith, young-"

"That's enough talk, old man!" Ameduba interjected. "Let him join the others!" He grabbed Nadus by his wrist and pulled him away.

"Young lad, remember what I've told you!" Agubak winked at Nadus. "Listen and obey the orders from the higher authority!"

"That's right, listen to his wise words or next time you will be in the woods, lying with the other dead stinking rats!" Ameduba scuffed. "Let's go, move it!"

"Yes, Papa Agubak!" Nadus turned his head towards the old man who was standing a few feet away. "I'll try!"

"Shut up, recruit!" Ameduba struck Nadus on his cheek. "Didn't you hear my orders?" He looked at the young boy with a frown on his face. "I didn't give you permission to speak, you rat! Move it, before I change my mind."

"I warn you! Don't touch or hurt him!" Agubak shook his head in protest, watching as Nadus was dragged away. "The boy carries the mark."

"Whatever you say, old fool!" Ameduba cursed under his breath. "Why don't you go make us some more potion or something useful? You leave the muscle to us!" The colonel ignored Agubak and continued to proceed towards the crowd.

You bear the mark!

The heavens favor you!

The words of the old man replayed in the young boy's head.

What does he mean?

"Have faith? Believe in yourself!" Nadus whispered repeatedly as he was hauled towards the other recruits. "Have faith, believe!"

He must be mistaken.

I'm just a boy!

Nadus never thought of himself as the lucky type, surely not like his older brother. The young boy wasn't a good gambler, and he couldn't recall ever winning a game of checkers or cards. However, having faced and escaped death a few times in one day, he was beginning to believe his chances and the words of the old juggler.

I'm the boy from the prophecy?

"Alright!" Ameduba exclaimed. "Now, join those two rats!" the colonel tripped the young boy off his feet and onto the ground. "You get no special treatment, regardless of what that old drifter says!" He hawked and spat before walking away to "weed out more weak links."

Nadus fell on his rear with the back of his skull barely kissing the soil; then, almost as quick as a feline, he rolled over on his belly and crawled towards two boys who were sitting in the mud, away from the "unsorted roaches."

"On your heels!" Itto shouted from yards away as he signaled the colonel.

"Set!" Ameduba responded with a fleeting grin on his face. "Go!"

Without delay, two boys bolted towards the colonel and like frenzied jackals, they began to yelp and wrestle for survival. The rebels increased the sounds of their voices, clapping as they cheered and ranted.

"Idnurub!" Nadus whispered. "Idnurub!"

The schoolboy didn't respond; he sat in the mud and stared out towards the raging fire, frenzied spectators, and the two combatants.

"Idnurub!" Nadus nudged his friend with his elbow. "It's me."

The village boy turned towards Nadus with a bleak countenance; his face was smeared with blood droplets from his dead foe. "Yes, Nadus?" he asked in a listless manner. "It's good to see a familiar face again."

"Indeed, it is!" Nadus sounded more upbeat. "How are you?"

Idnurub was mute.

"Idnurub!" Nadus snapped his fingers and nudged his pal again. "How are you?"

"Is this a serious question?" Idnurub asked. "Seriously?"

"Yes!" Nadus whispered. "Yes!" He nodded. "How are you feeling?"

"Really?"

"Of course, Idnurub," Nadus replied. "Why do you sound so different?"

"Are you serious?" The boy looked at his friend with tearful eyes. "Are you?"

"I'm serious!" Nadus placed his hand on his friend's knee. "Yes!"

"I killed with both hands!" Idnurub looked at his bloodstained palms. "Nadus, I killed a boy. I'm a murderer!" He dropped his head and wept. "A killer!"

"No!" Nadus raised his brows, shaking his head in denial. "No!"

"I'm a murderer and his blood is on my hands!"

"No, don't say that." Nadus tightened his grip around his friend's knee.

"I am, Nadus!" Idnurub wept louder and his tears moistened the clay.

"No, you're not a killer or a murderer, you were forced!"

"I am!" Idnurub heaved aloud. "Yes, I am!"

"Besides," Nadus interjected, "it wasn't intentional!"

"It was intentional." Idnurub blew his nose. "I did it!"

"You defended yourself."

Idnurub wiped his fingers on his dirty shorts. "I did it!"

"I'm glad you're alive." Nadus continued to hold his friend's knee. "I don't know what I'd do without you alive."

"Please forgive me!" The pupil didn't respond to his friend's comment.

"Idnurub, it's okay!"

"I'm sorry, Adnawr!" Idnurub spilled out his consuming guilt. "Please forgive me, didn't mean…"

"It's okay!" Nadus butted in. "You didn't have a choice and did what you had to!"

"No! It's not!" Idnurub snapped a reply. "He's still alive and breathing. Isn't he?" He pointed to Adnagu who was sitting a few feet away in the mud, tired and with his head down. "Isn't he? Answer me!"

"Yes, you're right," the young boy stuttered. He was caught off guard as he wasn't expecting such an angry response. "I know how you feel."

"No, you don't, Nadus!" Idnurub coughed and rubbed the tip of his nose with the back of his hand. "You have no idea how awful I feel inside!" He sniffed. "You chose life!" Idnurub coughed and then wiped his tears. "There was a choice! You had a choice and I had a choice, but you made the right choice! And you chose not to kill, the right choice! Yes!" The village boy bobbed his head and tears formed in his eyes again. "You were brave enough to stand up against them. I'm a coward!" He shook his head; his tears left his eyes and rolled down his cheeks.

"Idnurub!" Nadus said. "You're right, Idnurub! But let's n…"

Before Nadus could complete his thought, the screams of yet another slain recruit echoed through the dark arena and stole the attention of the schoolboys.

"Get that bastard out of my sight!" Itto pointed to a village boy that was bleeding and lying lifelessly in the mud. "I said, right now!"

At the brigadier's command, two teenage guerillas darted towards the slain recruit. They both hunkered down in unison and lifted the boy by his arms and legs before dragging him away and smearing his blood on "the battleground."

"Alright, you little bastard, move! Move over there!" Itto shoved the winner of the scuffle in the direction of Nadus. "I said, move over, now!" He pointed.

Like an obstinate calf, the pupil didn't budge; he stood in the same spot and stared at his blood-stained hands with a horrified expression.

"You two!" the brigadier signaled to two other rebels, snapping his fingers as he spoke. "Get this bastard out of my sight before…" He paused and breathed in.

"Yessir!" Two teenagers hollered; they stepped out of the crowd and headed towards the recruit and began to push him towards Nadus, Idnurub and Adnagu.

"You!" The brigadier grabbed one of the recruits by his shoulders. "And you!" He pointed to another recruit. "Both of you, step out! I believe you two already know how it works…"

Nadus looked at Itto as he reiterated the sad "rules of engagement" and then locked eyes on his pal. "Idnurub!" He nudged the boy to gain his attention. "What I was trying to say," Nadus spoke in a lower voice, "is that it has already happened and we can't…" He paused and blinked as though fishing for the right words to say. "That's what they're trying to do, they want us all to feel terrible inside!"

"I'm a coward," Idnurub mumbled.

"Idnurub, listen to me!" Nadus nudged his friend again. "Listen to me! You're not a coward, they are!" He raised his voice a bit, speaking with vehemence and sounding a little aggravated. "We can't let them get into our heads and pull us down and make us feel like worthless trash! Listen to me. Trust me, Idnurub as I trusted you in that stinking hole! The only thing we have left is our minds and we truly can't let them get a hold of it!" Nadus raised his brows and puckered his face. "The worst they can do to us is beat us some more or take our lives, but we'll not let them use us any longer to kill one another. Now, we need to think clearly and find a way out of here, snap out of it!" Nadus spat in the dirt as though expelling a bitter taste from his mouth; he was starting to regain his strength and ever since he ate the banana he felt overcome by intense emotions and audacity. "Snap out of it, Idnurub!"

"Nadus!" The boy looked at his friend with awe; he was surprised and inspired by Nadus's passionate words. "You're right!" He concurred. "Yes, thank you!" His tears dried up and he looked more focused. "How do you imagine we'll get out of here?" He sniffed a few times.

"At this second," Nadus surveyed his surroundings, "I don't know how we're going to get out of here, but I know there's a way out!" he said with confidence.

"How do you know?' Idnurub asked, not out of mistrust, but curiosity.

"I just know it and I have a strong feeling inside!" Nadus looked at the rebels as they watched and cheered two fighting recruits. "Besides, the old man told me!"

Idnurub's face lit up. "What old man are you talking about?"

"Huh?" Nadus frowned. "Are you joking?"

"Old man?"

"How do you think I was saved from him? He was going to kill me!"

"Sorry Nadus, I didn't know that."

304

"It's okay!"

"I was upset and angry with myself that I didn't pay attention to what was going on around me. At least, what I recall last was you sitting on him and dropping the knife. The next thing I know, you and Adnagu were close to me. There was an old man?"

"Yes, there was!" Nadus offered his pal a momentary smile. "And he was standing over there." The young boy pointed towards one of the mud huts, "wearing a brownish robe, that general was about to stab me and he saved me."

"Oh sorry about that. I didn't see him."

"You didn't see him? He was the old market beggar that taug..." Nadus paused. "Never mind!"

"Never mind, what?"

"He said something about a prophecy and that I was the bearer of the mark." Nadus turned his head towards his friend as if trying to read his body language. "He told me that I had the power to stop all of this!"

"Really? How?" Idnurub was baffled, but his friend's newfound optimism was infectious. "Did he say how you would do it?"

"No, he didn't say how." Nadus took his time to respond. "No."

"He didn't say?" Idnurub sounded a little let down. "So how are we going to get out of here? Look around, they're all carrying guns and the place is well guarded. There's no getting out easy."

"Yes, I know that!" Nadus replied. "I asked him and he just said 'faith.'"

"Faith?"

"Yes, faith."

"What do you mean by faith?" Idnurub asked.

"The old man said that I should have faith and that the heavens ha-"

The impending sounds of a hand bell and the loud cries of a boy interrupted the chants of the rebels. "Boss! Boss!" A perspiring teenager ran towards Yonk, waving his free hand and ringing the bell simultaneously. "They're here! They're here!" he repeated as he approached the throne.

"Who's here?" The brigadier grabbed the boy by his arms and stopped him before he could reach Yonk. "Who's here?"

"The…" The teenage rebel uttered a few inaudible words as he tried to catch his breath.

"Speak up, boy!" Itto stood in front of the emaciated boy, holding him by his shoulders and shaking him. "Speak up!" The brigadier brought his ear closer to the boy's lip and appeared to be listening to his whispers.

Seconds later, Itto offered a nod, pulled his head backward and released his grip on the rebel's shoulders and the boy, as though suddenly tranquilized, collapsed to the ground. Itto then bent over and removed the hand bell from the teenager's hand before marching towards the general. As soon as Itto reached Yonk, who was still sitting on his improvised throne, he saluted him, walked over to his side and began to whisper in his ear. Yonk shook his head a few times and his facial expression turned from stoic to sour as Itto briefed him on the injured boy's message. Without warning, the general stood to his feet, snatched the hand bell from Itto and began to ring it.

"Shut up, shut up!" Yonk bellowed. "All of you, shut the hell up!"

At the general's demand, the sonorous swarm of boys and young men slowed their tempo and lowered their noise down to a few sneezes and coughs.

"All of you listen and listen good!" Yonk stopped ringing the bell and handed it to Itto. "The enemy is approaching fast, heading here to launch a surprise attack on us!" the general said. "Can you imagine?" he hissed.

"No!" the crowd murmured their surprise and anxiety. "No way!"

"Boss said, shut up!" Ameduba chastised the insurgents as he walked towards the general and the brigadier. "Shut up, pay attention!"

"At this moment," Yonk continued, "time isn't a friend, but an enemy, and as we can't afford to play with our enemies, we can't afford to play with time any longer! Do you hear me?" Yonk shouted.

"Yes, boss!" the rebels replied. "Yes, boss!"

"Those government forces, those infidels and devils are trying to rape our women and enslave our children." The general made a fist, gesturing as if he was choking his victim. "No!" he hawked and spat on the ground. "All those demons think that because it's getting dark we'll be scared and we'll let them defeat us! No!" Yonk spat and then laughed out. "They have no idea what's coming to them! Right, boys?"

"Yes, boss!" the crowd responded.

"We'll slaughter every one of them and piss on their bodies." Yonk unzipped his fly and began to urinate in the dirt. "Then, we'll storm the city and slaughter their women and children! Say it, slaughter…"

"Slaughter their women and children!" the rebels roared.

"They're not humans!" Yonk finished making water and zipped his fly. "They are all infidels. They belong to the devil and deserve to die! We'll show no mercy!" Yonk shrieked. "Absolutely no mercy! Do you hear me?"

"Yes, boss!"

"Good!" Yonk nodded as he stroked his goatee. "Ameduba!" He turned towards the tall officer. "Gather the recruits, all of them, weak and strong, and have them join the others in line! Okay?"

"Yes, boss!" The colonel saluted.

"We can use every able body right now!" Itto commented.

"Right away, boss!" Ameduba turned away from his superordinate.

"Wait there, one second!" Yonk snapped his fingers. "One more thing!"

"Boss?"

"Get all of them weapons and lots of khat to chew on!" Yonk smiled. "I want their heads to be focused on the target!"

"Yes, boss!" Ameduba nodded. "Was planning to do that!" He winked.

"Get to work!" Yonk clapped.

"Boss!" Ameduba marched away. "You, you, you and you," the colonel pointed to the rebels, "come with me!" he called out and four young men darted towards him.

"Itto!"

"Yes, general!" Itto faced Yonk who was staring out in space.

"You're familiar with the swamp, you know it fairly well. Correct?"

"Yes, boss!" the brigadier replied with little emotion in his voice. "Yes, I do."

"What parts of the swamp," Yonk placed his hand on the brigadier's shoulder, "would provide us with the best combat advantage over these infidels?"

"Really..." Itto glowered at Yonk. "The wet areas with quicksand!"

"Is that so?"

"Yes, general! If we lure them there, death trap!" Itto raised his tone. "It will be difficult for them to tell the difference and we'll be able to gun-"

"Fantastic!" the general interjected. "Map it, map it out for me." Yonk pulled out a small, black flashlight from his pocket and lit up the ground at their feet. "Quick! Show it to me, these areas of the swamp that you talk about, the wet areas with quicksand!" The general pulled out his dagger and hunkered down, grunting as he lowered his height. Then, holding the battery-powered lamp in one hand, he drew a large, crooked rectangle in the dirt with the tip of the oblong blade. "If this is the swamp and here's where we are," he drew a small square in the center of the box, "show me all the wet spots!" Yonk tapped the dirt with the blade. "Quick, time is our enemy!"

"Yes, boss!" Itto also whipped out his army dagger, crouched and began to add more shapes to the rectangle. "A couple yards from us," the brigadier drew a circle, "there is a large area with large amounts..."

"You over there!" Ameduba signaled to Nadus, Idnurub and Adnagu. "Get up!" he shouted. "And get your behinds over there, it's time to fight!"

The schoolboys like disquieted crickets leapt to their feet and darted towards the other recruits.

"You two," Ameduba signaled with his whip, "start handing out the rifles and the cutlasses!"

"Yessir!" the men who were each carrying a torch chorused; they then began to pick assault rifles and machetes from a rusty box and hand them out to the recruits. "Take! Take it!" they barked. "Place over your shoulders! One per person! Here, take!"

"You roaches are about to go out..." Ameduba stood in front of the boys and preached to them. "...Warfare isn't for the weak hearted..."

"Idnurub!" Nadus bumped his pal as they joined the recruits. "Hey!"

"What?" Idnurub glanced at Nadus furtively; they were in the front of the line and the schoolboy didn't want to draw attention to both of them.

"This might be our only chance," Nadus whispered, clinching the rifle around his shoulder and trying to converse without moving his lips. "This is it."

"You sure?" He looked at Nadus with the corner of his eye. "Are you sure?"

Yes!

Nadus nodded.

"...and because many of you haven't fired a weapon before," Ameduba yelled, "you'll have to be fast learners or else you'll all end up with bullets in your thick skulls! Do I make myself clear?"

"Yessir!" the recruits retorted.

"Alright," Ameduba signaled to the men that he had handpicked from the crowd, "start giving the stuff to chew on!"

"Yessir!" The rebels each picked a twine bag from the ground that contained piles of green leaves. Without delay, they began to serve each of the recruits a handful of khat leaves. "Chew on it! Suck it!" the young men demanded. "Don't spit it out!"

The recruits didn't hesitate and they began to devour the khat like famished goats.

"This tastes horrible!" Nadus murmured as he chewed the fairly fresh leaves.

It's so bitter!

"Now, I'll give you the basics! Basics will be all you'll need to stay alive and kill the devils that are out for your life!" The colonel frowned. "I'm not your mother so don't expect me to spoon-feed you." Ameduba shined his flashlight on the faces of the terrified recruits who were stuffing their mouths with the herbal stimulant. "Now, I want you all to listen up and memorize these four words like your daily prayers! One, aim, always aim before you shoot!" Amebuda waved his hand like a pistol. "Bullets in battle, they are your best friends and you need to use them sensibly, running out will bring you closer to death than anything else! Number two, the trigger!" The colonel revealed his index finger. "You need to be quick, pull the trigger of the rifle before your enemy gets a chance to drag you to your grave. Three, breathe! These firearms aren't toys or playthings and they'll show you this fact once you begin to fire them. You need to show who is boss, either you or the rifle! So control your breathing," Ameduba sighed, "and you'll control your weapon! Finally, proceed! Don't you ever, never turn your back in combat! Never! You always move forward until you've slaughtered all of the enemies in sight…"

What's going on?

My heart!

Focus, Nadus!

My chest.

Stomach burns!

The young boy felt funny inside. He couldn't keep still and he began to fidget and sweat; his heart rate increased and his breathing rose.

"Now to fire, put the magazine in like this," Ameduba inserted the cartridge clip into the automatic rifle and grabbed onto a metal bar that was on the top of the gun, "and then move the lever, the selector lever to the middle position and pull back," he tugged the bar backwards and released the charging handle, "aim," he pointed the firearm towards the recruits, "pull the trigger, fire!" Ameduba made a gunshot sound. "You're done! Bear in mind that the selector lever has to be in the middle," Ameduba showed the recruits the top part of the rifle, "for it to be in fully automatic mode!" he emphasized. "Then…"

"Colonel!" A rebel walked up to Ameduba and saluted. "Sorry to…"

"What do you want, lieutenant?" the colonel yelled at the young man.

"Sorry to bother," he stuttered, "but the general also wants you to give all of them brown-brown to jack them up." The man offered the tall officer a gourd.

Brown-brown?

"He wants me to hand it to them myself?" Ameduba frowned. "Is that right, uh?"

"Yes, yes, no!" the young man stuttered. "No, sir!"

"You must be a fool, can't you see I'm busy getting them ready, eh?"

"Yessir!" The lieutenant nodded. "Sorry to bother you, but I was just-"

"Shut up," Ameduba interjected, "and pass me the bloody pot!"

"Yes, yessir!" the rebel stuttered and handed the pot over. "Here!"

Ameduba handed his rifle to one of the rebels who were standing to his side with torches in their hands. The colonel looked into the pot before dipping his thumb into it and taking a pinch of the brownish powder.

"Aah, fire!" The colonel closed his eyes after snorting the powder and shook his head. "That's the right stuff!" He opened his watery eyes and handed the pot back to the rebel. "Remember, keep squeezing," he turned to the recruits and stuck out his index finger again, "until you've fired all your bullets and killed all the *devils*!" He turned towards the lieutenant. "I'm done with the rats. Give it to them!" Ameduba chuckled. He blocked one of his nostrils with his finger and shot out a chunk of opaque mucus from his nose.

"Yessir!" The rebel stomped his feet and saluted.

Without uttering a word, Ameduba turned away from the recruits and marched towards the other rebels who were a few yards away, chanting and smoking narcotics as they geared themselves up for battle.

I don't feel well.

My stomach hurts.

"I don't want it," Nadus mumbled as he pulled his head backwards.

"I told you to sniff it. Snort it!" the seemingly timid lieutenant yelled as he struck Nadus on his cheeks. "Don't let it drop again."

"No." The young boy shook his head again. "No."

"Take, snort!"

"No! I don't want it."

"Snort it!" The teenager planted another slap on the young boy's face.

Nadus, although hesitant, obliged without added resistance; he slowly leaned forward and inhaled the powdery substance off the back of the rebel's hand. "I don't want to…" he mumbled as he drew the drug into his lungs. Upon sniffing the acrid blend of gunpowder and cocaine, Nadus was instantly plunged into a sea of transitory disarray. With eyes closed, he tried to acquaint himself with the fiery sensation in his throat and the euphoric rush to his brain. He held the ridge of his nose, wobbling and shaking his head from side to side as though suffering from a seizure. The young boy lost his sense of time and space; his ears could only detect damped sounds of the insurgents' gabble and his perception of the world around him was a giant blur.

"Mo Ve Ov Er Th Er!"

Nadus opened his eyes in response to the loud, indistinct sound.

"Mo Ve Ov Er Th Er!"

He heard the sound again and looked in the direction of the lieutenant who appeared to be gesturing with his hands and yelling out orders. The young boy couldn't comprehend the words of the lieutenant; he blinked his teary eyes rapidly and stared at the lieutenant in an attempt to read his lips. The lieutenant, as though suddenly noticing Nadus, wore a frown and marched towards him.

"…DiD'nT I JuST tELL Ld YOu…" Waving his fist as he approached, the rebel lieutenant barked at Nadus with a voice that sounded distorted to the young boy as if it was traveling through running waters.

Nadus saw the rebel approaching, but he couldn't react; his throat was uncomfortably numb and a tingling sensation radiated from within his body. The young boy closed his eyes again and then placed his fingers over his eyelids and grunted.

Snap! snap!

He repeated in his mind as he tugged his cheeks twice for sensation.

Out

Of it, Nadus!

Yes, my name is Nadus.

Stop it, please.

The young boy was overwhelmed by the voices of his father and his brother and by a hodgepodge of everyday sounds: high-pitched laughter and yelps, touching cries, irksome sneezes, streaming waters, rattling leaves and dry coughs.

Snap out of it, Nadus!

What's he saying?

I don't understand you.

I need to get out of here.

Without warning, Nadus heeded the words of the guerilla with clarity. They were harsh and bitter and they rammed him so swiftly that he felt as though his face had been submerged into a tub of freezing water; with no buffering and at once, Nadus regained his sense of self and his awareness of his environment.

"...kill you if you don't move!" the lieutenant shouted as he cocked his high-powered rifle and pointed it straight at the young boy's chest. "Move over or I'll scatter you!"

"Yes, sir!" Nadus hollered as he staggered towards the rest of the recruits who were herded a yard away by the entrance of the fort.

20

CHAPTER TWENTY:

◎

"The rabbit that stays in a hole must be ready to face the hunter's fire."
African Proverb

The sun had finally retired and bestowed its watch over all of humanity to the full moon and the twinkling stars that lit up the night sky. A few nimbus clouds ruffled through the firmament above, weeping silently as they witnessed the decay of morality. Arisen by the scanty tears, the dank twilight breeze was vivacious as it sailed steadily across the swamp, cooling all in its path and swaying the quivering flames of the bonfires. Singing in loud, incoherent voices and dancing in eccentric motions with their rifles raised up in the air like newly acquired trophies, the enraged rebels geared themselves up for the eminent battle, firing warning shots as they prepared.

"Itto! Ameduba!" General Yonk beckoned to his officers in the distance as they rallied the rebels and primed them for war. "Over here!"

"Yes, boss!" the men chorused as they marched towards the general.

"This is it men!" Standing with both hands behind his back, the general spoke in a clear, deep and unusually calm voice. "This is what we've been training for all this time, to show the devils what we're made of."

"Yes, general!" the officers agreed. "This is it."

"Oh yes!" Yonk stared into the bonfire and the flames cast a shadow on one side of his stoic face, bestowing the burly man with a menacing visage. "They have no respect for us and we'll show them no mercy!"

"Yes, boss!" Ameduba replied and Itto followed.

"Listen," the general turned and looked at the faces of his men, "and listen carefully. In order for us to destroy them, we have to be quick, swift and unpredictable, we can't afford any mistakes. Understood?"

"Yes, boss!" the men responded.

"Excellent!" Yonk scratched his beard as though digging for lice. "This is what I want you two to do. Itto, you already know the game plan, stick with it! I want you to navigate the troops through the marshes and get those devils trapped right here in our swamp so that we can ambush and finish them off! Can you do that?"

"I'll make that happen!" Itto chuckled as he clasped his automatic rifle.

"Ameduba," Yonk continued, "I want you in charge of ammunition and make sure our men are armed and utilized to their fullest capacity, eh?"

"Boss!" The colonel gave a nod. "Yes boss!"

"We'll play this one like chess, pawns first. Then the men with the bigger guns will finish the job, okay?" The general ran his fist into his palm.

"Absolutely, boss!" Itto replied.

"Yes boss!" Ameduba added.

"Alright boys! Time is our enemy!" Yonk spat in the dirt and looked up towards the full moon and then at his officers. "Let's get to work and exterminate those devils." He pulled out his pistol, cocked it and began to march towards a wooden table that was canopied by an army tent and lit by a rusty hurricane lantern that rested on its wooden surface. "Yes, one more thing," Yonk turned around and glanced at the colonel, "I want you to hand whistles to all and any of the recruits who are too small to properly carry guns, have them at the frontline as 'whistleblowers' so that we know when those devils are getting close."

"You know it, boss!" Ameduba answered. "I was just about to do that before you called on me."

"Good to hear!" The general bobbed his head. "I'll be here at the fort. You two!" He pointed at the men. "Don't disappointment me." He waved his pistol in the air. "Finish them off!"

"Yes, boss!" the rebel officers retorted.

"Every last one of them!" Yonk saluted the men and they saluted back. The commandant turned around and headed towards the army tent that was surrounded and guarded by several trigger-happy youngsters.

"You're all child soldiers now!" the hefty colonel stood in front of the jaded recruits and announced. "Say it!"

"We're all child soldiers now!" the recruits gave a loud response.

"No, I'm a child solider now!" Ameduba scolded the schoolboys.

"I'm a child solider now!" they repeated.

I'm a child solider now?

Nadus looked at the rifle across his chest, staring at it and squeezing it as though it was a venomous creature.

"Louder! I can't hear you!"

"I'm a child soldier now!" the recruits shouted again.

"And you'll all fight, every single one of you wretched vagabonds will fight with the last breath in your lungs and strength in your bodies."

"Understood?"

"Yessir!"

"You, you and you, stand over there!" The colonel grabbed three boys by their necks and pulled them out of the herd of recruits. Then, he stood in front of the boys and barked. "All under the age of eight, step forward and position yourselves over here." Ameduba pointed to his side and towards the ground.

After his announcement, twelve scrawny boys crept out of the flock and walked timidly towards the colonel.

"Hey you!" Ameduba called on one of the rebels, snapping his fingers as he spoke. "Go get me the sac with the whistles."

"Yes sir!" A late teenager bowed his head before dashing towards one of the mud huts and entering it. Seconds later, he came out of the building and ran back to the colonel with a twine sac in his hand that clanked with each step he took. "Here sir!" The rebel bowed his head and with both hands, he offered the bag to the colonel.

Ameduba looked at the teenager as though appalled by his presence. "So what are you waiting for?" he asked. "Hand it to each of them!"

"Oh, yes sir!"

"Quick boy!" Ameduba shouted.

"I'm sorry sir!" the teenage rebel stuttered; he placed his hand into the bag and began to hand out rust-sullied chrome whistles to the boys.

"Place it around your neck!" Ameduba yelled at the younger boys as they stared at the whistles. "I said now!" he yelled again and the school-boys flinched as they slung the wind instruments around their slender necks. "As from now on," the hefty colonel looked at the boys, pointing as he spoke, "you'll be known as whistleblowers and your sole duty will be to protect your brothers in battle! Your lives depend on that whistle and the lives of the troops depend on your bravery and courage. You'll all be in the battlefront and your sole duty is to blow the whistle and signal to the troops as soon as you see the enemy in sight. Failure to do so will cost you your life. Do you hear me?"

"Yessir!" the fifteen boys moped as they offered hopeless responses.

"Your lives depend on the sounds of these whistles. Understood?"

"Yessir!" they chorused again. Most of the boys didn't understand the seriousness of their new mission and a hand full of them continued to peek at the whistles around their necks like they were newly-acquired charms.

"Very good!" Ameduba gave a nod and walked towards the brigadier who was a few yards away yelling out orders to the rebels.

"Brigadier Itto!" The colonel saluted.

"Colonel Ameduba!" Itto turned to his side with a firm, exasperated facial expression. "What is it?"

"They're ready for your orders!"

"Indeed!" Itto gave a nod. "I'll be there shortly." He placed his hand on the colonel's shoulders. "Thank you!" Without delay, the brigadier turned around and yelled at the battalion of rebels who were gathered a few feet away and itching for action. "As I have said before, you march behind the recruits. Do I make myself clear?"

"Yessir!" the rebels yelled, and a number of them stomped their feet on the ground. "Yessir!"

The brigadier and the colonel then marched towards the recruits who were in front, near the wooden gate that served as the entrance and exit to the hideout.

"Alright, all of you come with me!" Itto cocked his handgun and beckoned as he marched towards the gate. "Come with me now!" he spoke in a louder tone of voice. "Let's go! It's time for war!" he roared. "It's time to destroy those devils!"

Nadus, Idnurub and the recruits, along with the narcotized rebels who were clustered behind the recruits and chanting, marched out of the fort and into the marshland. The infantry, like a colony of termites burrowing through decaying forage, navigated their way through the labyrinth that was formed by the dense vegetation of the swamp.

"Stop!" the brigadier barked as he raised his pistol in the air, slowing the progression of the marchers. "Quiet and listen!" Itto turned his head to the side and looked upwards. "Hear that?" He looked at Ameduba.

"Yes I do." The colonel gave a hushed response, followed by a nod.

In the distance, multiple gunshots rang out and piercing screams of primates echoed through the marshes as the rebel sentries battled with the encroaching governmental forces.

"Whistleblowers!" the brigadier called out. "Step forward and assume your positions over here!" He pointed to his feet.

Without delay, fifteen juveniles stepped forward and flocked around Itto like hopeless sheep about to experience the butcher's sickle.

"Go ahead and get going!" Itto ordered. "Quick! Get going!" He clapped and made frantic sweeping motions with his hands towards the dark jungle ahead of them.

Confused, nervous and inexperienced with the dealings of a whistleblower, the young lads lurched towards the unfamiliar with terror shaking up their young, innocent minds.

"You're soldiers now!" Itto reaffirmed them. "Move your feet!"

"And don't forget to blow the whistle at the first sight of the devils." Ameduba added. "Remember that your lives depend on this simple task." The colonel ran his thumb across his neck as if slitting his own throat.

A number of the sweaty boys nodded, swallowed their saliva and began to trot into the darkness. With the backs of the whistleblowers barely visible in the dull luminance from the guerilla's torches and lanterns, the brigadier yelled another set of orders.

"Recruits set forward!" he yelled.

"Assume your positions!" Ameduba butted in.

Just as startled and perplexed as the whistleblowers, the schoolboys clutched their unacquainted weapons as they swarmed past the colonel and the brigadier.

"Fingers on the triggers, get ready to attack." Itto commanded.

In an uncoordinated fashion, Nadus and the other recruits drew their hands closer to the firing mechanisms of their respective automatic rifles.

"Do not pull the triggers! Do not!" Ameduba interjected. "Steady!"

"Move forward!" Itto ordered and the recruits began to march forward in the direction of the whistleblowers.

Afraid of being run over by the troops, a few of the recruits, especially those in the front of the line, sped up and jogged forward. "Hey, hey! Slow it, I didn't say run! Fools!" the brigadier yelled at the outliers and with a little ado, they controlled their strides and slowed down.

However, before the rebel officers could utter another degrading remark to the recruits, several shrill, high-pitched whistle sounds, gunshots and short-lived cries of "falling whistles" echoed through the swamp, calling the guerillas into a state of preparedness.

"They're close, those bastards are close by!" the colonel cursed.

"Kill all the lights now!" Itto turned around and yelled at his troops.

The rebels with the lanterns and the torches blew out the flames, bequeathing the luminosity of the night to the moon and the accompanying stars.

"Recruits!" Itto yelled. "Get ready!" He paused. "Attack!"

At the brigadier's declaration, all the recruits dashed forward, yelling as they began to fire their automatic rifles with the precision of a novice. In response, the governmental soldiers on the other side, who were hidden behind scrubs, opened fire on the recruits, instantly executing a number of them and ending their apparent misery. Stampeding through the muck and struggling to get a bearing of his surroundings, Nadus shouted with all of his lungs and then squeezed the trigger of the submachine gun that was strapped across his chest. In a split second, a few rounds spewed out from the barrel of the gun, jerking the young boy backwards and to his side. Although, terrified by the prospect of death and by the piercing cries of his injured mates, Nadus was bestowed with a weird sense of solace by the vibrations of his rifle along with the loud gunfire it produced. As a result, he squeezed the trigger harder with anger and let out some more of his frustration.

"Keep moving!" the brigadier yelled from the distance as he watched a few more boys drop to the ground. "Keep moving!"

"Destroy all in your path!" Ameduba yelled to the recruits. "Destroy!"

Like a demented chess game, the brigadier had sent out his "pawns" to weaken the enemy's offensive. As a large number of them were taken out of the equation, he decided to send in the "rooks" and "knights" to finish the job.

"Warriors prepare yourselves!" Itto faced the apprehensive boys and men that were clustered behind him with their guns drawn. "Brace yourselves! Get your weapons ready!"

Right away, the rebels began to tromp and chant "warrior songs."

The brigadier then turned to the colonel and spoke into his ear. "The recruits have done their part, we'll send in our trained men to eliminate them. The time is ripe, do you agree?"

"Brigadier Itto!" the colonel offered his response with a nod.

"Yes, those demons surprised us with this attack, but this is our element!" he hissed. "We run this place!"

"Yes, we do!" The hefty man nodded again.

"We'll storm over there, utilize guerilla tactics and finish them off!"

"Yes, boss!"

"Great!" He spat in the dirt. "Give the order. I'll be behind you."

"Will do, boss!" Ameduba immediately cocked his rifle. "Warriors!" He raised his hand upwards. "Remember all your trainings, be invisible in the elements and do not rest until you've finished off all the devils! Attack!" The muscular rebel dropped his hand to the ground, clasped his automatic rifle and dashed forward along with the rebel troops.

With the briefness of a second, ephemeral sparks of exploding gunpowder began to light up the hazy battlefront and scorching bullets from apathetic "killing machines" sailed through the air, piercing through the leaves and tree barks and the supple skin of young boys and young men.

"Idnurub!" Nadus called out to his pal who was a few yards away.

In shock and deafened by the gunshots, his friend didn't respond; he continued to fire rounds aimlessly into the dark.

"Hey Idnurub!" The young boy ran towards his pal, barely cautious of the injured and lifeless persons in the dirt. "Idnurub!"

"Move it boys!" Ameduba commanded. "Keep moving!" He knelt down and released a few more shells, pilfering the breath out of two of his foes.

The rebels continued to advance forward, utilizing the uneven terrain to their advantage as they combated and conquered the "enemy troops." Before long, many of the opposing armies began to yell. "Surrender!"

"That's right! Surrender!" Itto shouted and fired a few rounds from his pistol towards the sky. "Surrender now! You maggots!"

"Drop your weapons or else!" Ameduba, like an infuriated rhinoceros, dashed towards the soldiers who were kneeling in the dirt and clothed in green camouflage uniforms. "Put your hands on the ground!" he shrieked as he kicked a number of them in the gut. "Put your faces in the dirt!"

The "prisoners of war" obliged and they began to plant their faces in the mud. The guerillas rekindled the flames of their lanterns and torches. Nadus, Idnurub and the few surviving recruits stood in shock and confusion, staring at the carnage and watching as elated boys and men cheered for victory.

"Tie them up!" the colonel ordered. "Tie their hands!"

Like skilled cattlemen, a number of the rebels pulled out twine ropes from their pockets and began to bind their captives, physically abusing them with slaps and verbally assaulting them with curses in the process.

"Bastards!"

"I'll slaughter you!"

"Let me see your hands!"

"Face down!"

"Shut up!"

"Bloody swine!"

The rebels continued to yell as they gathered their foes and tied them up.

"Ha! Look at this! You're not even as tough as I had anticipated." the brigadier bragged as he patrolled the submissive men, laughing and willingly stepping on their backs and scalps. "Yes!" He spat on a few of them. "You devils!"

"Brigadier!" The colonel tapped his superior on his shoulder.

"Colonel Ameduba!" The brigadier turned to his side and looked at the rebel officer. "You did very well today! You fought like a true champion."

"Thank you, boss! It was an honor."

"I'll make sure I put in a word for you," Itto bobbed his head and spat some more, "with the general." He wiped his lips with his palms. "I'm confident that he'll be pleased to hear that you led us to victory today."

"I appreciate the kind words, sir!" Ameduba bowed his head slightly. "What do you want us to do with these rats?" He pointed to the ground.

"Well," the tall man paused, "we can use them as leverage, hostages!"

"Yes!" Ameduba drew out the word. "Good idea, boss!"

"Or we could simply get them to speak!" Itto gave out a sinister laugh.

"What do you mean?" Ameduba asked. "Get them to speak?"

"We'll torture every one of them until they spill the beans about their operations in the city!" The brigadier grabbed one of the prisoners by the collar. "Get up to your feet!" He dragged the teenage prisoner and pulled him up to his feet. "Get up, you fool!" Itto grabbed the boy's neck; he then pulled out a dagger from a leather sheath, fastened around his waist. "So, soldier!" Itto snickered. "Look at him!" He turned to the colonel. "He's not even a man, those fools sent boys to fight us?" He laughed again. "So tell me boy! Where's the main base for the governmental forces?"

The teenager mumbled a few words.

"What did you say?"

The soldier mumbled again.

"Speak up boy," Itto tightened his grip around the boy's throat, "or I'll pluck out your eyes!" He drew the blade close to the soldier's face.

The boy choked and attempted to let out a few words.

"Are you saying something?" Itto lessened his chokehold.

"I don't know anything!" The teenager gasped and coughed.

"I knew you'd say that!" He spat. "Let's see how much pain you're willing to endure before you start spilling all you know!"

The soldier closed his eyes and moved his lips inaudibly once again.

"Huh, what did you say?" Itto asked. "Better be saying your prayers!"

"Speak up, roach!" Ameduba commented. "Spill it out!"

"What did you say?" the brigadier asked again.

The soldier spoke in a stressed voice as he struggled to breathe, "and if I knew anything, I'll not tell you scum pigs!" He spat in Itto's face.

Upon hearing those words, Itto was consumed by unadulterated rage.

"How dare you!" Itto punched the soldier in his abdomen and multiple times on his face, knocking him off his feet. "Do you know what I can do to you? Do you?" He bent over and pulled the boy up by his collar.

The teenage soldier looked up at the brigadier with a bloody nose and made a very weak attempt to spit again.

"Okay, you're done!" The brigadier held the teenager firmly. "I'll personally pluck out your virgin eyes and feed them to your fellow mates!" Itto raised the dagger and went for the soldier's swollen eyelids.

Two gunshots rang out and the brigadier dropped his dagger and released his grip on the teenager. He staggered to his feet and then looked down at his chest, revealing a strained smile before slumping to his knees and collapsing in the dirt.

"Who was that?" Ameduba yelled as he looked around for the shooter. He then noticed the rebel officer on the ground and rushed towards him. "Itto?" He turned the brigadier over and was greeted by fresh blood and two lethal chest wounds, both close to the heart.

All of a sudden, the guerillas were welcomed from all sides by several impinging flashlight beams seeming to emerge from obscurity, followed by rapid gunfire.

"Ambush!" Ameduba shrieked as he let go of his comrade. "Open fire! Open fire on them!" He cocked his handgun and dove to find cover.

Thrown into a state of pandemonium, the befuddled rebels thrashed about and tried to gain their bearing back.

"Finish them all!" Ameduba yelled. Barely protected by a slender tree trunk, the colonel planted his knee in the dirt and fired a few shots from his pistol. "Finish them off! Move it!"

Several of the rebels and a few of the recruits reloaded their rifles and then opened fire to the surrounding forestry. However, their added efforts were no match to the aim and accuracy of the marksmen and the snipers that were stationed up in the trees; one by one, the rebel troops began to drop to the ground like almonds falling off on a windy day.

"Get down!" Nadus jumped on his pal and knocked him to the ground. "Get down, Idnurub!"

"Nadus!" Idnurub looked at his friend and spoke with joy in his voice. "You're still alive!"

"Yes," he responded. "It seems that way."

"What's going on?"

"Ambush!" Nadus replied. "I believe it's an ambush, it was all a trap!"

"What are we going to do?" Idnurub began to panic.

"We're going to get out of here, that's what we're going to do."

"Oh no! We're going to die!" Idnurub covered his ears with his hands, flinching as bullet flew pass their bald heads.

"No, we're not! Look, we're still alive." Nadus grabbed his pal by his forearm and shook him. "Remember what I explained to you earlier, the old man told me," the young boy paused and surveyed his dynamic surroundings, "that I have the ability to make all this stop! I don't know how yet, but I believe him and so I'm sure we're not going die here!"

"Yes we are!" the village boy sobbed louder as he observed the rising number of casualties around him. "Yes, we're all going to die like them!"

"We're going to get out here!" Nadus exclaimed in a hushed voice. "Get a hold of yourself, okay?" The young boy shook his friend again. "Okay?"

Idnurub went silent.

"Okay?" Nadus asked again. "Can you do that?"

"Okay." Idnurub sniffed. "Okay!"

"Now, just give me a minute to think," Nadus said with newfound assertiveness.

"Okay."

"Alright, just follow my lead," the young boy spoke a few seconds later. "See that over there." He pointed towards a section of the swamp. "There are no gunshots coming from over there!"

"Okay," Idnurub agreed. "Yes!"

"That's our way out of here."

"Are you sure about that?"

"Well, yes!" Nadus hesitated. "No, but we can give it a try. We're not any safer lying over here," he blurted out his frustration, "are we?"

"I'm not trying to question you, Nadus," Idnurub replied.

"Sure."

"Okay, how would we get there?"

Nadus paused. "We'll just have to crawl over there slowly and as soon as we're close we take to our feet."

"Okay, Nadus!"

"Let's do this." Nadus patted his friend on his back. "Good luck! I will see you over there." The young boy cracked a smile on his face and began to crawl through the gory battlefield like a snake in the grass.

Idnurub tailed behind and followed his friend's lead. In a short time, the piercing cries from injured rebels dampened and the gunfire ceased as the national army outnumbered and overpowered the few surviving rebels. The repetitive yelps of soldiers, containing their surroundings and the loud barks of working dogs sniffing through the marshes echoed through the still, drizzly night—replacing the prior battle reverberations.

"You're under arrest!" Flashing their torchlights into the faces of the remaining young rebel recruits, the soldiers yelled out commands.

"Kneel down now!"

"Put your hands above your head!"

"Where is your base?"

"You're all under arrest!"

With the soldiers busy searching the battleground for wounded survivors and interrogating Ameduba and his troops, Nadus and Idnurub in a stealthy fashion had reached their goal line. The village boys were three yards away from the thicket, camouflaged and sandwiched between the fallen soldiers.

"We're close," Nadus whispered to his friend.

"Yes!" Idnurub offered a furtive nod. "What do we do next?"

"We need to remove the guns off our shoulders." Nadus replied.

"Why?"

"Added weight to carry once we start to run!" Nadus wiped his sweaty forehead, smearing the few blood droplets on his face.

"Okay, but..."

"Besides, they're noisy things," Nadus grunted. Then, he slowly began to remove the strap of the automatic rifle from his shoulders.

"Okay! But how would we defend ourselves?" Idnurub asked.

"Let me see." Nadus paused for a few seconds. "I don't know, perhaps we wouldn't need to worry about that."

"Okay, Nadus. If you say so." Idnurub sighed in compliance as he began to take off the rifle from across his chest with added care.

"Alright!" Nadus responded, slightly propelled by guilt. "We could use this." The young boy crawled up to one of the deceased guerillas nearby. "I don't think you'll be needing this any time soon," Nadus whispered as he pulled away a dagger from the man's sheath. "Is this good for you?" He revealed the weapon to his friend.

"Sure," Idnurub replied. "It's better than having nothing."

"Fine!"

"I've taken it off." Idnurub carefully placed the firearm to his side and then looked up at Nadus. "What's next?"

"Alright!" Nadus turned to his friend. "This is what we're going to do," he spoke in a low voice, "at the count of ten we're both going to get up quietly and head over there," the young boy pointed towards the bushes that was a few feet away from their vantage point, "and as soon as we're hidden we'll both take to our feet and just keep running until we're far, far away. Does that sound like a plan to you?"

"Yes, yes." Idnurub nodded repeatedly. "Yes, it does!" The village boy was elated about the prospect of a successful getaway.

"That's great!" Nadus bit his lips nervously and then cleared his throat before wiping his moist palms on his shorts; his adolescent heart began to beat with excitement and fear. "You ready?"

"Yes, I'm ready."

"Good!"

"Are you ready?" Idnurub asked Nadus.

"Yes, I'm ready." Nadus took a deep breath. "Alright, let's do this. One, two," he raised his stomach up from the ground, "three. Wait, wait!"

"What's the matter?" Idnurub looked confused and a little frightened.

"You remember the time we were both chased by bees in the woods?"

Idnurub grimaced. "Yes, I remember. And? Why?"

"Remember how it hurt when they stung us?"

"Yes, I remember," Idnurub spoke in a hushed voice. "Your point?"

"Because I need you to run like we are being chased by lots of bees."

"Okay, I'll keep that in mind."

"No, promise me."

"Okay, okay! I promise you, Nadus."

"Alright, let's get out of here." Nadus spat to his side. "One, two, three," Nadus and Idnurub rose to their knees and began to crawl on their *genua* towards the thicket, "four, five…"

Three counts away from ten, the military dogs with their keen senses noticed the shadows of the boys in the distance and immediately became agitated, jumping and barking loudly.

"What's the matt…" One of the soldiers, who was restraining and guiding the dogs by their leashes, flashed his torchlight in the direction of the commotion. "Rebels!" he shouted.

"We've been discovered!" Nadus uttered, mumbling some curses as he jumped to his feet.

"Run, Nadus!" Idnurub hollered as he stood to his feet and headed for the bushes. "Run!"

The young boy rose to his feet and hit the ground running.

At once, the soldiers shined their flashlights towards the two surviving recruits. "Stop right there!" the soldiers yelled and began to release slugs in the direction of the village boys.

"Go get them!" the commanding officer lowered his pistol and yelled. "Don't let them get back to their base." He ordered two of his men to pursue the escapers. "We need the element of surprise! Go quick!"

"Yes, captain!"

"Don't come back without them, dead or alive!"

At the officer's command, two soldiers, one with a dog and the other without, bolted towards the bushes. They were both clothed in similar dark-green camouflage uniforms. Similar to the insurgents, they were each armed with a submachine gun strapped across their shoulders, and in their hands they both flaunted battery-powered flashlights. Terrified, jaded and disheveled, Nadus and his best friend scampered through the poorly lit marshland, lifting their feet as fast as they possibly could. Leaping over a few obstacles that hindered their path and running with no apparent plan or destination in mind, the boys quickly advanced deep into the wilderness. On the other hand, they were at a disadvantage because their pursuers were faster, stronger and better-trained. In a few short minutes, the dog barks grew louder and the boys began to observe impending rays of light from the distance.

"They're closing in on us!"

"Yes, yes, I see!" Nadus tried to catch his breath.

"I'm losing strength!" Idnurub gasped for air.

"Me too!" Nadus grunted.

"What are we-" Idnurub didn't finish his sentence; he placed his hand over his face, covering his eyes from several leaves that lashed them.

"Huh?" Nadus fought with the elements. "What did you say?"

"I wanted to know where we are going to."

"I honestly don't know. Just keep running like-" the young boy didn't complete his thought because he was somewhat preoccupied by his diminishing strides, "just keep moving like we're running from bees." He inhaled and struggled to run faster. "Bees!"

Unknowing to the sprinters, the soldiers had unleashed their military dog to hunt them down. Similar to a phantom in the night and relying on its predatory instincts, the large Doberman stopped barking and swiftly blended into the contiguous forestry; before long, the village boys were cornered in their tracks and attacked by the vicious canine.

"Haa! The dog! The dog!" Idnurub cried out as the Doberman leaped and knocked him to the ground. "Please, help me!" he yelled as he tried to fend off the growling beast. "Nadus! It's biting me!"

Nadus, heeding his friend's desperate cry for help, acted in response and ran towards him. The young boy quickly searched the moist earth for a crude bludgeon. To his good fortune, he found a sizeable stick near the scene, which he promptly picked up and proceeded to use to strike their attacker. Swinging the club with all his might, the young boy smacked the dog on its bony side, causing the animal to yelp. Angered by the twinge, the Doberman released its grip on Idnurub and then flipped around.

"Idnurub!" Nadus glanced at his pal as he took a few steps backwards. "Go, go! I'll take care of it!"

"No, Nadus!" The injured boy wobbled to his feet, holding the side of his stomach. "I will not leave you."

Diverting its attention to Nadus, the dog lowered its head slightly, revealed its sharp teeth and then barked a few times for reinforcement.

Don't fear.

He's like Dahc but just a little bigger.

Growling and slowly circling the young boy, the canine studied Nadus as he wielded the stick and swung it around. As though suddenly finding a window of opportunity, the Doberman commenced to take down the fugitive, galloping towards him before diving for his jugular.

The nose!

It's a weak spot!

Nadus stared at the approaching dog.

Steady!

Now!

The young boy gave the Doberman his best shot; the weathered stick landed on the dog's long snout before flying out of his hand and into the bushes. Whining and cringing from the agony, the army dog dropped to the ground, recoiled a little, and then covered its neb with its paw. Due to a transfer of the dog's momentum to Nadus, the young boy had lost his footing and had slipped in the dirt. With the passing of a few seconds, the docile but yet fairly aggressive beast reared its head to catch a glance at its opponent. Noticing that Nadus had been knocked to the basin of the forest and was attempting to stand up, the Doberman rose and garnered itself for another attack.

"Nadus, get up!" Idnurub yelled. "The dog is coming for you." The village boy made a weak attempt to throw a stone at the Doberman, but his efforts were futile; his arms were bruised and throbbing. "Nadus, get up!"

Acting on reflex, Nadus rolled on his back to face his attacker rather than risk having his back turned to the beast. He then began to kick in an erratic manner. The offensive watchdog suffered a few hits, but it wasn't deterred. The Doberman simply switched its position and then went for the young boy's face. Nadus responded promptly by placing his forearm over his face; as the schoolboy had predicted, the dog rammed its sharp teeth into his forearm and began to pull on it. From experience with his own dog, he knew not struggle because he would only further aggravate the beast and risk further damage to his skin and flesh. With his free hand, the young boy rummaged through the dirt, searching for a rock or a stick; there was nothing around. Then, just as he was about to give in, he remembered the dagger that he had salvaged from the battlefront. Wasting no time, Nadus withdrew the knife from his pocket and shoved the blade multiple times into the dog's ribcage, piercing its lungs and beating heart and snatching the life out of the canine soldier.

"Nadus!" The village boy reeled towards his pal. "Nadus?" He sounded more alarmed that before.

"Idnurub!" Nadus groaned.

"Are you okay?"

"I'm okay," he grunted as he pushed the dead weight off his chest.

"Gosh!" His friend noticed the gashes on Nadus's forearm. "I'm sorry."

"Why?" the young boy asked as he staggered to his feet.

"Your hand is worse than mine, it's bleeding badly!"

"What?"

"Your arm!"

"Oh, this?" Nadus looked at his forearm. "It's nothing!" He was fairly intoxicated by the adrenaline rush and all the endorphins that were flowing through his bloodstream.

"I'm such a coward!" Idnurub dropped his head in lamentation.

"No, you're not!" Nadus sniffed as he wiped the knife on his shorts and slid it back into his pocket.

"You've always been the brave one."

"You did well, Idnurub!" Nadus looked at his friend. "You did good!"

"I should have fought off that dog!"

"Stop worrying about the past, Idnurub." The young boy began to limp away. "We need to keep moving before those soldiers find us."

"That's true." The schoolboy caught up to his friend. "Nadus!"

"Yes?" The young boy looked at Idnurub as they both began to jog.

"You're courage is truly inspirational!"

"Thank you."

"I'm saying this from the bottom of my heart!"

"Thanks, Idnurub."

"Hopefully, I can someday be as brave as you."

"I'm honored." Nadus coughed and slowed his pace a little. "I'm honored!" The young boy coughed again.

"Nadus, how do you…" Before Idnurub could ask his question, the two villagers were greeted by bright beams of light on their heads and faces.

"You bastards!" one of the soldiers yelled from several yards away.

"Stop right there or you're dead!" the second soldier added.

"Put your hands on your heads and turn around, slowly!" the first soldier ordered.

"Do it now!"

CHAPTER TWENTY

"Don't you move or I'll shoot the both of you down."

The schoolboys obeyed; they stopped trotting and placed their hands on their heads.

"Good!"

"Now, turn around, very slowly!"

"You bloody rebels are both under arrest!" The soldiers began to walk towards the schoolboys.

"But we're not one of them!" Idnurub whispered to Nadus. "We're not rebels!"

"Yes, I know," Nadus retorted without moving his lips. "Maybe we can tell them all that happened."

"I have a bad feeling about this!"

"What do you mean?" Nadus asked in a hushed voice.

"We should run for it!" Idnurub suggested. "They're going to hurt us."

"Perhaps they'll hear us out."

"Don't think so!" Idnurub shook his head and his candid eyes revealed his intention. "Their voices don't sound honest."

"But what if..."

"Bees! Bees!" Idnurub screamed.

"What in the...?" The soldiers were momentarily perplexed.

"Run, Nadus!"

Before the young boy could reason with his comrade, Idnurub altered the sequence of events. Straight away, the boys took to their feet and the soldiers responded by opening fire on them. The boys ducked and then nosedived into the thick bushes, sprinting with their last surge of energy.

"Stop!" the soldiers hollered as they chased after the schoolboys.

The barefooted boys blazed through the swampy habitat with all they had in them, but it just wasn't good enough; their feet were sinking into the soil with each step they took and the soldiers were closing in.

"Keep following the blood trail!" the militiamen exclaimed. "They're close by!"

"I see you!" the other man bluffed, flashing his torchlight through the thicket and yelling. "Stop right there!" He fired some more shots.

The schoolboys ducked again at the sounds of exploding gunpowder and continued to run for their lives.

"I can't!" Nadus struggled for breath. "I can't do it."

"Can't do what?" Idnurub asked.

"I can't keep running!" The young boy had lost a significant amount of blood from his injuries and he was becoming lightheaded. "I give up!"

"No, Nadus!"

"I can't!" He began to reduce his speed. "I can't"

"Yes, you can." Idnurub grabbed Nadus by his hand and pulled him as he progressed. "You can't just give in now, remember what the old man told you. You can make all of this to stop!"

"No, I'm finished." Nadus looked up to the full moon and exhaled.

Unfamiliar with the terrain and blinded by the fairly dense vegetation, the village boys ran into a steep slope and without warning, they found themselves tumbling downwardly towards the lower aspect of the forest.

"Arrgh!" Nadus groaned as he landed on his back. "Arrgh! My head!"

"Ouch!" Idnurub gnashed his teeth in pain as he attempted to rise to his feet. "Ouch! It hurts! I think I've sprained my ankle! Oooh, it hurts!"

"What just happened?" Nadus sat up and asked with earnestness; he was temporarily dazed.

"We're being chased by soldiers," Idnurub replied.

"Well!" Nadus coughed. "I know that!" He stretched out his unharmed arm to his friend. "Please help me up!"

"We fell!" Idnurub grabbed onto Nadus's hand, grunting as he pulled his friend up to his feet. "That's what happened, we both rolled down the hill." Idnurub pointed towards the apex of the slope.

"I don't feel well at all!" Nadus shook his head; he had a headache and his vision was blurry. "I need to rest."

"Me too!" Idnurub bounced on his left leg with his right ankle elevated from the ground. "We need to find somewhere safe to hide." The schoolboy took a step followed and immediately fell on his knee. "Ouch!"

"What's the matter?" Nadus lent a helping hand to his friend.

"I think I've hurt my ankle really bad."

"How bad?"

"I don't know if can walk." Idnurub pulled himself up.

"Crap!" Nadus exclaimed. "You can lean on me till we find somewhere safe to hide and rest."

"Thank you!" Idnurub wrapped his arm across his friend's shoulder.

"They're over there!" one of the soldiers flashed his light on the boys from above and shouted. "I see them down there!"

"Yes!" the second soldier hollered. "Get them!"

As once, the trigger-happy men opened fire on the schoolboys.

Like wild game and driven by survival instincts, the defenseless boys dispersed at the loud bangs and scrambled for refuge behind the few scrubs and trees in their vicinity. Ten seconds later, the soldiers ceased the one-sided shootout and like experienced hunters, they both shined their flashlights on the hazy marshland; they briefly surveyed the region from above for any movements before venturing out to claim their prizes.

"Idnurub!" Nadus crawled in the dirt. "Where are you?"

The young boy waited for a few seconds, but didn't get a response.

"Idnurub?" he whispered again. "Answer me!"

The young boy heard rustling from the bushes to his left.

"You there?" Nadus crawled towards the sound.

"Nadus," Idnurub called out in a low voice. "I'm over here."

"Where are you?"

"I'm over here." Idnurub was sitting in the dirt with his back against a tree trunk. "Over here!" he beckoned to his friend.

"You're not dead?" Nadus teased his friend as he crept towards him.

"Yes!" He snickered and then coughed. "I suppose so."

"I told you we weren't going-" Nadus reached the trunk and caught a clearer view of his friend. "No!" The young boy's half-smile vanished.

"What?" Idnurub asked.

The young boy's eyes became heavier as it filled with warm tears.

"What is it, Nadus?"

"You've been shot!" Nadus blinked and tears rolled down his eyes.

"This?" The schoolboy dropped his head and looked down at his abdomen; it was smeared with blood and two inches below his right nipple, a circular wound hemorrhaged. "Oh, it's nothing." Idnurub smiled as he attempted to imitate Nadus's previous response to his injuries.

"You're bleeding!" Nadus didn't know what to do; he placed his hand over the wound and pressed on it. "You're bleeding a lot." Nadus sobbed.

"It's nothing," Idnurub gasped. "Guess you were wrong this time?"

"How?"

"That I wasn't going to die." The schoolboy slurred his speech.

"No!" Nadus pressed harder. "Don't say that! You're not going to die."

"I just wanted to," Idnurub coughed up blood, "be as brave as you, Nadus."

"You're the bravest boy I've ever met."

"Thank you!" Idnurub held his friend's hand.

"Don't talk."

"You leave, get going while you still have time."

"No, I'm not going to leave you here." Nadus replied.

"Remember the old man's words, this is your destiny!"

"Don't say this!"

"Now, leave before it's too late."

"No, don't leave me!" Nadus cried.

"I'll distract them." Idnurub tightened his grip on his friend's hand.

"Don't leave me."

"Go, now!" Idnurub pushed Nadus's hand away from the wound.

"No, please don't do that!"

"I'm so proud to have known you as a friend, a brother." Idnurub inhaled deeply and then cried out with his last breath of life. "I give up!"

Already positioned nearby, the unrelenting searchers reacted to the call. Beaming their flashlights towards the tree trunk, they marched with caution towards the young boy and his departed best friend. Nadus heard the treads of the approaching soldiers, but he was too upset and stupefied to react; the young boy stared at Idnurub, sobbing as he recollected some of their cherished moments together: dancing at the festival, running to school in the mornings, hunting birds in the forest and being chased by angry bees. Suddenly, he felt very incomplete, like the last remaining sane part of his existence had been stripped away. In that moment, he came to the daunting realization that in the course of just one day he had lost everything he owned, including his family, his friend and his true love. As the soldiers drew near, the young boy began to contemplate his actions and his next moves. He was weak, exhausted and had been robbed of a peaceful youth. A part of him wanted to surrender to be arrested or even executed by the soldiers. Another part of him wanted to stay with Idnurub to ensure that he received a proper burial and wasn't just left in the wilderness to rot alone or be eaten by scavengers. But then, the optimistic side of him, wanted to believe in the man's fable about "the one from the prophecy" and "the bearer of the mark."

The heavens favor you!

You bear the mark!

Young lad, it is not visible to the sightless.

Nadus recalled bits of his conversation with Agubak.

What do you mean by that, sightless?

You have to be willing to see it.

"I bear the mark?"

The young boy whispered as he stared at his palms. Then, his heart almost skipped a beat because he suddenly saw "the mark." The gashes from the dog had formed a shape on his left forearm that resembled the *Aya*, the leaf of a fern, which according to the natives symbolizes defiance and endurance.

You bear the mark!

You're the one from the prophecy!

You have the power to end all of this.

The young boy heard the old man's voice repeatedly in his head.

This is your destiny!

He recalled Agubak and Idnurub repeating the phrase to him.

"They both said it!" Nadus's faith was rekindled. "How did he know?"

The young boy looked at his best friend and his tears dried up.

"Thank you, Idnurub!" He rose from his knees and stood to his feet. "I'll endure for this is my destiny!" he professed as he began to stagger towards the bushes, further away from his past.

"We've got one 'dead on arrival' here!" One of the soldiers flashed his torchlight on Idnurub's face, squatting as he inspected the deceased boy.

"He's just a boy!" The second soldier glanced at Idnurub and responded with a hint of remorse in his voice. "Where's his partner?"

"The heck should I know!" The first soldier replied.

"We need to find him and bring both of them in, dead or alive. Those are our orders!"

"Alright!" The first soldier sighed and stood to a more erect position.

"Let's split up, you search over there," he pointed to his left, "and I'll search over there." The man pointed to the opposite side. "Converge here in fifteen."

"Okay!"

The two men separated and went hunting for the last fugitive.

The second soldier hiked through the wooded area, listening for unusual sounds and inspecting the integrity of the flora; he didn't notice anything unusual except for a faint trail of blood on a few of the leaves. Following the lead with his flashlight and increasing the pace and length of his strides, the vigilant hunter neared his prey. Then, suddenly the blood trail disappeared. From a distance away, the young boy had seen the approaching light rays and had veiled himself behind a few shrubs. Hoping to avoid detection and capture, Nadus lay on his stomach and exploited the natural surroundings for disguise by covering himself with several dead leaves. Respiring at a curbed rate, the young boy clenched his teeth together and then stiffened his muscles and tightened his entire body. The soldier was perplexed by the sudden disappearance of his lead and reasoned that the fugitive was in close proximity; he squatted and in a circular fashion, he examined his surroundings for any oddities, but he didn't find any potential leads. The hunter, however, didn't immediately give up; he turned on and turned off his flashlight rapidly for a few seconds as he continued to scan his vicinity. Straight ahead from where he was hunkered down, he noticed something that caught his interest, a heap of leaves and dirt that appeared to have been recently tilled. He beamed his flashlight on the region and studied it with caution. Then, he scuffed and smiled.

"You think you're so smart, eh?" the soldier whispered. "You're messing with the wrong man here!" He rose to his feet and proceeded towards the peculiar sight.

Still hidden under the compost, the young boy heard the approaching footsteps of the soldier and his physiology reacted to the possibility of danger. His heart beat shot up and his stomach tightened, causing him to flinch a little. The soldier noticed a flicker in the pile of leaves and responded by removing the strap of his rifle from across his shoulders. Holding the butt of the gun in one hand and placing the flashlight under his armpit, the corporal stretched out his rifle and used the barrel to clear away the leaves from around the young boy.

"I see you!" the soldier exclaimed. "You're under arrest, rebel!"

Nadus didn't budge, trying to play dead.

"Are you deaf?" The soldier shook the young boy again.

There was still no movement.

"Alright!" the corporal hissed. "I'm just going to have to beat you up!"

The soldier turned his rifle over to use the handle as a bludgeon. Just as he was about to produce the first thud, Nadus sprang to his feet and with a stick in hand, he struck the corporal hard on his shoulder, causing his rifle and his flashlight to fly off in different directions. Nadus then hit his attacker once more on the head, causing him to slump in the dirt. Noticing that the man had dropped and was attempting to rise, the young boy rushed forward to deliver a third blow.

"I'm not one of them!" Nadus darted forward. "I'm not a rebel!"

Inches before the blow could do damage, the corporal ducked and the stick missed his face. He then leaped towards the young boy and knocked him to the ground. Nadus tried to struggle his way out of the jam but he was too fatigued. Responding swiftly to the situation, the man pulled out an army knife from around his thigh and cursed.

"You little bastard!" He slapped Nadus. "You take people's lives at will, rape innocent women and destroy villages. Not on our watch! I thought you could be saved, but you're all the same! You deserve to die here!" The corporal went for the young boy's liver.

"No!" Nadus garnered all his strength and held onto the man's hand before the blade reached his skin. "Oh, please! I'm not one of them. I'm the son of the land!" He exhaled with his dwindling breaths. "Nadus."

"What did you just say?" The soldier scrunched his face.

"I'm the son of the land," Nadus replied in a lower voice.

"Where did you learn that?" the corporal lowered the knife and asked in an angry tone. "Answer me!" He grabbed Nadus by his neck. "Answer!"

"My father," Nadus wheezed. "My father used to call me that."

"You say your father used to call you that?" The man's eyes were shadowed with anger. "Answer me!"

"Yes, my father," Nadus said, weakly.

Still holding on to Nadus's neck with one hand, the man inspected the young boy as though looking for clues on his body; he saw the leather bracelet around the boy's wrist that instantly made his throat burn.

"Your father!" The soldier looked at Nadus. "What is his name?"

The young boy didn't respond; he just stared at the soldier.

"I said," the man shook Nadus again, "what's his name? Answer me!"

"Nineb." The young boy coughed. "Nineb, my father's name is Nineb."

The man looked away for a fleeting moment. "Where is he now?"

He didn't get a response from the young boy.

"Where is your father?" The man asked with a sudden lack of malice.

"He's dead," the young boy said bluntly; he wanted to cry but he was too dehydrated and anemic to produce tears. "Everyone is dead!"

"Dead?" The soldier let go of the young boy and stood up. "Your father is dead?" He looked at Nadus.

"Yes." The young boy nodded as he sat up with caution.

"How did he die, your father?"

"He was killed earlier today on his farm."

"No!" The man looked down to his feet and wept. "What have I done?" Shaking his head from side to side in disbelief, the grieving man dropped the army knife to the ground and then raised his head towards the sky and wept some more. "This isn't it! This isn't why I signed up. I've turned into a fellow monster. I'm no better!"

The young boy was bewildered by the man's absurd behavior.

"Nadus?" The soldier asked with teary eyes. "Is that your name or is it Tpgye?"

Nadus was stunned to hear the soldier utter his brother's name.

This evil man knows my name and brother's name.

"Which is it?" He looked at the young boy.

"Yes, it's Nadus!" the young boy responded. "Tpgye was taken away by the rebels to fight in the big city."

"No!" The man sounded more upset and displeased than before. "No!" He dropped to his knees and touched the young boy's face. "Nadus! What have I done? I'm sorry!" He sobbed. "You're my nephew. I'm your uncle."

"My uncle?"

"Yes, your uncle, Anahg!"

"Uncle?" The young boy repeated the word as though it were a foreign concept. "You're my uncle?" He was too fatigued to elicit any emotion.

"Yes!" The man pulled Nadus's head closer to his chest.

"My uncle?" Nadus didn't resist.

"Yes, I'm your uncle. Your father Nineb is my brother."

"Why did you…?"

"Forgive me, Nadus!" Anahg interjected. "Please forgive me! Heaven is my witness that I joined the army to stop the rebels from hurting others and destroying lives, not to kill the innocent. I just wanted to protect our village and family, not to kill my blood!" He looked down at his injured nephew.

"Uncle Anahg!" Nadus finally recalled his "favorite Papa's brother."

"Yes, Nadus!"

"I'm in so much pain!" the young boy said feebly.

"I'm sure you are!" Anahg gave a nod. "Let me see wha…"

His uncle halted his statement and looked away, turning his head towards the direction of the impending footsteps and light rays. He then rushed to his feet and picked his rifle and his flashlight from the dirt.

"Nadus!" Anahg turned to his nephew and spoke in a hurried manner. "You need to get up!" He held the young boy by his shoulders and pulled him up to his feet. "Look at me, Nadus! Look at me." He tapped him on his cheeks. "Listen to me carefully," he spoke in a low voice, "the other soldier is on his way and he can't find me talking to you. We both have strict orders to bring you in, dead or alive. I can't let that happen to you! Do you understand me?"

Nadus gave a frail nod and licked his chapped lips.

"He's going to arrest you! Perhaps the other soldiers will torture you as well and it can take forever, months for your innocence to be proved. Nadus, do understand what I'm saying?"

"Yessir," he responded on impulse. "Yes, uncle."

"Very good!" Anahg blinked and kept his eyes closed for two seconds. "So you need to follow my instructions carefully if you want to get out of here and survive. Hey, take this!" He placed his hand in his breast pocket, pulled out a small green booklet and placed it in his nephew's hand. "This is a refugee pass card, it will enable you to get into Édujtnias."

"What's Édujtnias?" the young boy asked candidly as he struggled to pronounce the foreign name.

"Édujtnias, is a refugee camp on the other side of the forest. The card will allow you to get in without questions. They'll help take care of you and your injuries and protect you from all this evil." He looked around. "Just show it to them," he pointed to the card in the young boy's hand, "and they'll know that you're not a rebel and they'll let you in. Okay?"

"Yes uncle."

"Alright," Anahg looked out for the approaching soldier, "to get to the camp from here." He pulled out a pocket compass from his belt pack and looked at it. "The refugee camp will be over in this direction." He pointed towards the northern part of the forest. "Just keep running this way and you would be there in about an hour or so."

"Okay." Nadus murmured. "Thank you."

"Look at this!" Anahg looked at his nephew's arm with pity. "You need to have this looked at as soon as you get to the camp. Okay? But for now, I'll give you something that will help to reduce the pain you're suffering right now. Hold on." The corporal unzipped his belt pack again and pulled out an autoinjector with faded inscriptions on its surface. With his teeth, he unscrewed the cap and exposed the needle to the air. "This is going to prick a bit, but then you will be feeling a lot better." The man grabbed the young boy by his thigh and jabbed him with the autoinjector, releasing the intramuscular dose of morphine into his system.

The young boy felt the pressure of the medication seeping through his thigh muscles as his uncle injected him with the analgesic. Within a few seconds, Nadus felt some relief from the pain that he was suffering.

"You need to leave now!" Anahg placed the used autoinjector back into his belt pack. "Remember what I said, just keep heading that way!" His uncle pointed north.

"Thank you." Nadus glanced at the pass card and then at his uncle.

"Get going now!" He patted the young boy on his head. "Watch out for wild beasts out there and may the spirit of our ancestors be with you!"

"I will." Nadus began to walk to his left.

"Wait, Nadus!" Anahg walked towards the young boy. "Take this!" He handed him his flashlight and compass. "You'll need these more than I do."

"You're too kind, uncle." The effects of the opiate were kicking in and the young boy sounded clearer and a lot more comfortable.

"Use it only when you need it," his uncle warned. "You don't want to draw unnecessary attention to yourself."

"Yes uncle." Nadus turned on the flashlight briefly to look at the compass before hiding away both gadgets in the pocket of his shorts.

"I hope you can forgive me for my actions towards you." Anahg pulled his nephew's cheeks. "I don't know if I'll ever be able to forgive myself."

"It's okay, uncle."

"Get down! Get down," Anahg said in hushed voice as he shoved Nadus towards the bushes. "Hide here for a bit and get going fast!"

"What are you doing there?" Puffing on a hand-wrapped cigarette, the first soldier walked up to Anahg and beamed his flashlight in the vicinity.

"What's your business, eh?" Anahg rubbed his eyes to hide his tears, coughing and sniffing in the process

"Are you alright?" The soldier shined his light on Anahg and stared at him with suspicion. "Are you?"

"Will you take that light off my face?" Anahg spoke with forced anger.

"What happened to your face?"

"Huh? What?" Anahg looked at the soldier with disgust. "What are you talking about?"

"What happened to your face, it's swollen on the side."

"Oh!" He touched his cheeks and it was a little tender. "It's nothing."

"Are you sure?"

"Of course, I'm good! I'm alright." Anahg hawked and spewed yellowish sputum on some leaves.

"What happened?" The other soldier was prying for answers.

"What is it with you now? So you all of a sudden care about me? Are you my mother now? I tripped and fell when I went looking for that little bastard and lost my flashlight in the process."

"Is that so?" the first soldier asked.

Anahg didn't answer and simply shook his head and hissed.

"What were you doing before I came?"

"You're beginning to get on my nerves." Anahg raised his tone. "I was just taking a leak." He fuddled with his zippers.

"Alright! Alright! Calm down!"

"So any trace of his partner, the rebel?" Anahg asked expressionless.

"I was just about to ask you that question," the man replied.

"Oh really?" Anahg sounded surprised. "Nothing on your end?"

"Yes nothing!" The soldier took a long drag on his cigarette.

"I haven't seen any sight of that little bastard either," Anahg said with a straight face. "I suppose he got away or has died somewhere in the forest."

"I guess so!" the first soldier retorted with a pinch of relief and fury. "Not my lucky day!" He blew out smoke from his nostril. "I really wanted to catch those snakes alive so that I could teach them a lesson, give them a few slaps and kicks for making us chase them deep into this disgusting swamp and yes, for killing the dog!" He hawked and spat. "She was a good dog too!"

"Well, alright then!" Anahg interjected as though uninterested in his associate's rants. "Well, I guess today wasn't your lucky day, eh? Say, we both go grab that dead boy for the captain." He began to walk away from the other man. "Come on!" Anahg beckoned. "Let's get going before we're both left behind by the others!"

"Sounds good to me!" The soldier tossed his exhausted cigarette towards the patch of bushes that sheltered Nadus from him.

The burning cigarette filter dropped to the ground beside Nadus and he was arrested by the fear of discovery. To his relief, however, the man just rubbed his palms together and coughed before turning around and joining Nadus's uncle in the distance. With the two men out of sight, the young boy crawled out from behind the bushes like a cautious rabbit emerging from a hole in the ground and began to run in the direction that he had been assigned. Entertained by the distant howling of wild dogs and jackals and the gloomy hooting of owls, Nadus continued to progress through the strange landscape, one step at a time with no room for fear. Although the shot of morphine had conferred him with a reduced sense of pain and had curbed his anxieties, the sedative effects of the drug coupled with his acute blood loss and the interactions of the prior toxins in his system caused him to be lightheaded and fatigued by the minute. Challenging his will to survive and struggling to distract himself from his predicament, Nadus continued to replay the old man's divinations over and over again in his head.

You bear the mark!

This is your destiny!

You're the one from the prophecy!

You have the power to end all of this.

The more Nadus sprinted through the forest and the more he chanted in his mind, the more he believed that he indeed possessed the mark and that it was his prophesied destiny to live through the day's ordeal. Nevertheless, the last statement was hard to swallow; he couldn't comprehend the idea that he alone had "the power" to end everything: all the suffering, the agony, claimed lives and lost ambitions.

"How can I possibly stop this?" Nadus whispered. "I'm just an orphan boy from a small village." He acknowledged his new status. "How will I?"

Then, just as suddenly as the appearance of rain on a bright cloudless morning, the young boy lost his vigor and collapsed to the ground. As his kneecaps made contact with the dirt and his head was jerked backwards, Nadus looked upwards and caught a candid glimpse of the true magnificence of his surroundings. The trees and scrubs were all unusually tall in height and their leaves were seductively green in hue. Complementing the bright moonlight, iridescent fireflies danced without worry and lightened up the misty ambience. Smelling like and resembling an exquisite bouquet, the forest floor was adorned with several colorful arrangements of large, exotic flowers that were foreign to Nadus; it was a truly remarkable sight and he couldn't understand how he had initially failed to notice the grandeur and the drastic change in scenery.

What a bizarre transition!

When did I get here?

As the young boy kneeled in the earth with hardly enough strength to maintain an erect posture, he looked ahead and saw a faint light source in the far distance, glowing at timed intervals.

"Édujtnias, the refugee camp!" Nadus whispered as he pulled out the compass with added effort and peeked at the oscillating needle; the readings of the navigational instrument confirmed his prior conjecture. "I'm so close and yet so far away!" Nadus took a long and deep breath that became a visible fog as he exhaled into the oddly cold jungle. "Is this how my life ends?" Nadus murmured. He felt like a shriveling frog in a desert that was on its way to an oasis only to pass away in the heat, a yard before it could leap into the water and moisten its desiccated skin.

"Muotrahk!" Nadus spoke softly as he looked up to the sky and caught two closely apposed stars blinking and conversing. "Muotrahk!"

I'm so sorry.

I failed to protect you.

The young boy's head drooped towards the earth in resignation and a few drops of saliva slipped out from his chapped lips and onto the mud. Shortly after, his ears detected some strange activities to his side, rapidly impending vibrations mixed with the sounds of ruffling leaves. In hopes of reveling his last moments, the young boy strained his neck and turned his head to his right to catch the perpetrators in action. Yards away from where he was kneeling and running towards his direction, Nadus saw a growling leopard chasing a hare that resembled the one in his barn. Hop-skipping from side to side, the long-eared animal dashed for safety while the wild cat with its sharp teeth and ferocious appearance closed in.

What?

The young boy couldn't believe his eyes. Then, just as sudden as the two runners had appeared, Nadus saw the prey leap high into the bushes and watched the large predator trip in its own tracks and collapse into a hole in the earth.

What?

"Just like Papa's story!" Nadus could barely mumble out his thoughts. "Papa! Mama! I truly miss you bo..." Scanty tears filled his eyes and rolled down the side of his cheeks. "I hope to see..." The young boy blinked with added effort before collapsing on his side.

Grasping onto the seed of hope that the old beggar had planted in his mind, Nadus didn't let go; the young boy clinged onto the last drops of life with vehemence. As he lay on the ground, he tuned his mind towards his final destination. Then, he opened his puffy eyes and was instantly afflicted with mild diplopia. Nadus began to lose his peripheral vision and the lights in the distance slowly ebbed away.

I have the mark.

I have the Aya.

I'll endure.

In the middle of his mantra, a cool breeze swept across the woods and embraced Nadus like a mother's love. Seconds after, the young boy was roused from his sleepiness by heavy thumps in the underlying flora. With his head resting on moist leaves, Nadus moved his eyes to the approaching sounds; he looked up and was taken aback by what he saw. Growling in a low tone and licking its lips, the leopard with a scar on its side hovered over Nadus and stared at him with bright greenish-yellow eyes. The young boy was overpowered by fear and he wanted to flee. However, he didn't have the strength to materialize his desire. The cat revealed its teeth to Nadus, sniffing him like a foreign object before growling louder.

"I'm so weak and sad!" Nadus moved his lips and spoke in whispers. "I lost everything I own and love. You remind me of Papa's story!"

Only a few have faced the great leopard in the forest and survived.

You're favored by your ancestor and by Mother-nature.

Nadus recalled his father's account of his leopard encounter. At that moment, unlike most people whose heartbeats rise in the face of danger, the young boy's heart rate began to drop. "I'm supposed to end this." Nadus heaved. "I'm supposed to get to the camp and save her! I beg you."

As if listening to the young boy's pleads, the great leopard roared and then opened its large mouth and went for Nadus's pelvis. "Is this how it ends?" Nadus looked at the approaching beast. "So be it!" He passed out.

Actuated by the heavens and the young boy's intercession, the great leopard picked Nadus by his belt and began to dash through the woods in the direction of the light. For a fleeting second, the young boy opened his eyes and upon realizing that he was being carried towards the light, he smiled and was thankful for his destiny. Shortly afterwards, Nadus was surrounded by bright lights and in a blur, he saw two hefty men carrying him away by his flaccid extremities. Then, smiling at him, he saw the face of a beautiful woman.

"You're saved, kid!" the lady said in a motherly voice. "You're saved!"

Nadus smiled back at her before losing consciousness.

The young boy was at peace.

21

EPILOGUE:

◎

"A chick that will grow into a cock can be spotted the very day it hatches."
African Proverb

A steady, high-pitched beeping woke the young man from his uncomfortable sleep. For a moment he lay still with his eyes shut. Despite the pain he felt from several points within the tightly packed organs of his emaciated body, he managed to let his thoughts wander to the plans he was making for himself. He had survived the horrors of being a child soldier and he was going to do his best to make sure that other children wouldn't have to endure them. However agonizing some of the experiences had been, he was relieved just to be alive. He slowly became more aware of his surroundings, and the first thing he noticed over the din of electronic humming and pulsing was the smooth, even tone of a man narrating the familiar events in the day of an sub-Saharan African village.

At the village market, a person can buy the ingredients for the next morning's meal, catch an impromptu performance, or even hire a ride.

The boy was still confused as to his exact situation, and he warily opened one eye to see two faces above his, smiling down upon him. A middle-aged man with a receding hairline and silver-streaked ponytail darted his eyes back and forth from the boy's to some of the instrumentation set up around the bed. The boy turned his head to get a better look at the other person at his bedside. She was a soft-featured, short woman whose attire and general demeanor betrayed her as a westerner, but nevertheless her smooth, dark complexion and the subtle upward tilt of the outside cusp of her eyes reminded him of Muotrahk. The memory of her caused him to open his eyes and fix his gaze upon the woman's face.

"Muotrahk," he said, struggling to utter her name through his parched and burning throat. Now that his eyes were open and he was more conscious, he quickly recognized that he was in a modern, if somewhat bare, hospital. Behind the faces, an old television showed scenes of the African savannah.

"Is that a friend of yours?" the woman asked.

She doesn't know Muotrahk?

This is Édujtnias?

"Muotrahk?" the boy asked.

Despite the boy's feeble demeanor, the woman sensed his desperation and reached for his hand. She placed the boy's palm on hers and slowly ran her fingers over the top of his hand. When the boy looked down to see her comforting hands, he was astonished to see his pale complexion. Small, overlapping blood-colored circles of purpura were spread out over his forearm where the soldiers' Doberman had bitten him.

"How much do you remember?" the woman asked. "Can you tell me your name?"

"I'm Nadus," the boy replied. "I'm a refugee and I have my papers."

"Oh, Victor. You've been through so much. You're just a little confused from all of it."

"Victor?"

"Yes, Victor." the woman replied in a warm motherly voice.

"My name is not Victor. It's Nadus."

"Oh dear," the woman smiled again, "your name is Victor Shenglizhe."

Victor Shenglizhe.

Victor Shenglizhe.

The bare mention of the boy's name summoned a stream of memories that began to intrude on his most recent adventures. Almost in an instant, he remembered his quiet suburban neighborhood, being home-schooled by his parents, playing with friends in the woods behind his subdivision and imagining all sorts of dangerous and perilous adventures. Sunday mornings were spent in church, learning Bible stories, and the evenings were spent drinking hot chocolate and listening to his parents philosophize and discuss future mission trips and whether or not to take him along. He recalled his few trips to New Orleans to observe Mardi Gras with his mother's side of the family and the tasty meals he ate with his father's relatives during the Chinese New Year celebrations. Then there were his early teenage years where his family packed up and went with "Uncle." Victor remembered flying for the first time in his life, seeing the patchwork of his neighborhood, his city, his home state slowly grow smaller and smaller below and eventually disappear beneath a gentle cumulus blanket as the plane took him to New York City and then Paris and then on to Cairo. There was the shock of stepping out into the heavy, dry Sahara heat and then half-consciously lugging his share of the family's luggage into a dingy bus for the long ride to the Sudanese border. He remembered dozing off in the tattered chair of the miserable government office as his parents and Uncle haggled with men in drab green clothing for hours over the arbitrary bureaucratic procedures and necessary bribes they would need to secure safe passage into southern Sudan.

He remembered the friends he quickly made in the Sudanese village and how, despite the overwhelming language barrier, they could still enjoy playing "futball" and taking their meals together. He remembered the summer he went to Burundi to enjoy a "vacation" at a small resort with some more modern conveniences while his parents and Uncle went up to Khartoum to help the victims of some recent civil strife. He remembered the last day of carefree happiness he enjoyed, swimming in the small hotel swimming pool and then sneaking out of his room that night to watch the revelers at the shore of Lake Tanganyika. And then, with the sudden but familiar rush of grief, he recalled the hotel manager knocking frantically on his door in the early hours of the morning and explaining through sobs in broken English that Joseph Kony's army had swept through Khartoum and slaughtered everyone in their path, including his parents and Uncle. He recalled the confusion of the ensuing days, the bizarre funeral ceremony held right there on the hotel grounds, the thousands of things he wished he could have said to and learned from his parents. He recalled wallowing in his sorrow without making a sound and occupying his time with the few books that were left behind by previous guests. He also recalled watching a long documentary about African politics over and over again on the black-and-white television in the hotel lobby. He remembered waking up each morning and seeing the salmon-colored walls of his room, and how much he hated that bright color for the suddenness with which it always gave him that painful reminder that he was no longer an innocent child.

And then, while staying in the same hotel with the manager's family through a miserable dry season while the countless official procedures were underway to repatriate the "newly-orphaned American boy," that sudden pain hit Victor when he awoke one morning. He kept quiet and tried to ignore the awful spasms that sometimes caused him to buckle in agony, until one day a few weeks later when he noticed a bruise that wouldn't go away and kept getting larger and more discolored. Arduous bus rides to run-down hospitals ensued, where doctors poked and prodded him and talked furiously amongst themselves in their inscrutable native language. Right there in front of Victor, they would open up thick, black leather-bound volumes and mutter in frustration as they snapped through the endless pages. But he never got an answer and the pain only got worse, as did the feeling of something ominous lurking inside of him that shouldn't be there, growing and taking from him what it wanted.

Right after the rainy season subsided and the heat rushed in, Victor found himself on a plane and then another and another, until finally he arrived, in a haze of agony and bewilderment, back in the United States at a charity children's hospital, Saint Jude. *Éduj tnias!* He remembered conferences at a table full of doctors, with them trying their best to explain to him in their uneasy professional manner that his condition was grave, very grave indeed, as he was in the advanced stages of cancer, and that he was going to need to be strong, like he had been in Africa, so that they could help him get better. In those few seconds, Victor reconciled reality with Nadus's odyssey and the truth found its proper place among the fantasies. Victor had reconstructed an elaborate, substitute reality to escape his agony. He made up names of people and places in his adventures by reversing the names of actual places that he had visited or knew in Africa; he also included the names of the rebel leaders who killed his parents as well as the names of the people he saw in the "old documentary."

Nadus! Sudan, that's where I lived with step-mum and dad!

Idnurub! Burundi, the hotel where I found comfort.

Nineb! Benin, mum and dad's first mission trip!

Yonk! Joseph Kony, the evil man who killed my parents.

Ameduba! Abudema, he's one of Joseph Kony's officers and killers.

Muotrahk! Khartoum, that's where my parents and Uncle got killed!!

Victor knew he had been through a series of brutal surgical operations that he had somehow incorporated into his fantasies: the throbbing bee-stinging effects of chemotherapy, the smell and sounds of cauterizing flesh, harvesting of organs, the sharp knives and the bloodsheds. The orphaned boy had no idea of their number or how long he had spent at St. Jude Children's Hospital since arriving from Africa.

"Congratulations, Victor, you survived an especially difficult surgery," said the doctor. "We couldn't get you to wake up for quite some time afterwards, but you showed real progress today. We've all been pulling for you these past few weeks." Dr. Presbury offered Victor a nod. "Given the progression of your cancer, not too many people would have made it as far as you. We've still got some tough odds to overcome, but we have confidence that you can pull through."

The woman began to speak, but her voice was so soft that it caused Victor, who was already weary in body and spirit, to fall back into sleep. The voice on the television droned.

Many legends, of varying levels of truth, exist about the man-eating crocodile Gustave, who patrols the shallows of Lake Tanganyika…

Victor's hands trembled as he held the crumpled paper in his left and the crooked pencil in his right. Sweat was trickling down his forehead as he began to write his final legacy – "Five things I will do differently."

Wake: I will wake up every morning and smile at the world. I will be glad for the chance to see yet another day, and most especially I will be grateful for the "gift of life."

Eat: I will cherish every meal I receive. I will eat healthy, delicious meals and I will take my time to savor the complex flavors of each meal. My body is divine and it surely deserves the finest of foods.

Love: I will develop my innate ability to Love myself and to Love others, as Love is the universal language that all humans understand.

Work: I will establish my identity at work and I will let my purpose of positively improving humanity fuel my creativity. I will view success not through the eyes of an epicurean, but through the eyes of a famished person who has been fed and empowered with the wisdom of life.

Sleep: At the end of each day, I will lie in my bed and I will sleep like a baby because if life is worth living then it must be worth dreaming as well. Furthermore, I cannot dream without sleep!

Upon writing these words, Victor carefully folded the piece of paper and thrust it into the waiting hands in front of him. He smiled and felt calm. He was at peace with himself because he realized that he had lived a great life and completed his legacy. It was now time to celebrate!

NOTE TO MY READERS:

"Do good because of tomorrow."

African Proverb

M y Dear Reader,

How are you today? I hope my note meets you in good spirit! First off I'd like to thank you for reading my novel and I hope that you've found it just as entertaining as it is enlightening to some of the plights that are faced by millions of people around the world. In this novel, I especially want to demonstrate that certain qualities in life like love, happiness, pain, suffering and the feelings of dejection are common to every race and color of peoples, regardless of our positions in life. Losing a loved one to diseases like cancer, financial difficulties, pain of a lost dream, depression and many more are real issues that affect every one of us in different forms. I'd like to stress the fact that although this is solely a work of fiction, the underlying themes and events as well as the atrocities to humanity described are very real—just as real as the beating of your own heart. Sadly, many children, especially in Africa, have been snatched away from their families and forced to live in deplorable conditions and commit atrocities against innocent people. The notorious and evil Joseph Kony is a real man and the fictional exploits of the character he inspired are not so far from Kony's own. He is the head of the Lord's Resistance Army (LRA), a guerilla group that exploits the Bible and uses their bizarre interpretations of it to engage in widespread violence. Through the actions of his LRA, Kony is responsible for the abductions of thousands of children, who are forced to fight in his campaign of murder, rape, mutilation and sexual slavery. Joseph Kony is also infamous for forcing young children to murder their own parents as part of the initiation process into his group. He's currently wanted by the International Criminal Court for thirty-three charges, including war crimes and crimes against humanity. He's still at large and is on the top ten Most Wanted list by the FBI and he is considered a Specially Designated Global Terrorist by the U.S. Treasury Department.

As a young African, deplorable characters like Joseph Kony and his deputies like Vincent Otti make me sick to my stomach and bring shame to the face of Africa. In this work of fiction, I hope that I have been able to transport my readers into a unique world and reveal not only some of the suffering of Africans but also some of the rich culture and the joyful moments that are shared with family and friends. Not to sound cliché, but the truth is that I'm very fortunate to have been born in Nigeria. Although Nigeria is plighted with unique political problems, it is probably one of the most stable countries in Africa. As a result of my upbringing and having been granted the golden opportunity to receive a stellar education, I continually ponder on the other side of reality. With a different stroke of luck, I could have been born in one of the war-torn regions of the beautiful continent and I could have been abducted at a young age and forced to become a Child Solider with no prospects of a bright future. I know for a fact that I'm not smarter, more athletic or more handsome than many of the innocent boys that have been used as pawns and lost their lives in wars in which they had no business or desire to participate. I'm just fortunate to have been raised under different circumstances! I've heard many people say that our lives are predestined and things in life happen to us for a reason. However, I sometimes find it hard to fathom the idea that an eleven year old boy had been predestined to become a soldier and die in the woods or a young girl deserves to be enslaved to a tyrant and pedophile. Did they really have a choice or was it all predestined to happen? Anyway, I'm not trying to arouse your emotions or bore you with my spiel on morality but I just want to thank you again for reading my first novel and I hope that in reading this book you've found at least a bit of inspiration to continue to persevere through many of life's difficulties. Please spread the story of this young boy and help someone else in need because I believe it's the right thing to do as we're all connected in one way or another.

Warm Regards,

Sheg Aranmolate

FEATURED ORGANIZATIONS:

"He who forgives ends the argument."

African Proverb

ST. JUDE CHILDREN'S HOSPITAL:

The mission of St. Jude Children's Research Hospital is to advance cures, and means of prevention, for pediatric catastrophic diseases through research and treatment. Consistent with the vision of [their] founder Danny Thomas, no child is denied treatment based on race, religion or a family's ability to pay.

(RED) / GLOBAL FUND:

(RED) is a business model designed to create awareness and a sustainable flow of money from the private sector into the Global Fund, to help eliminate AIDS in Africa. Consumers buy (PRODUCT)^{RED} items, and at no cost to them, a portion of the profits is sent directly to the Global Fund. The Global Fund is the organization that (RED) works with to put the money generated from (PRODUCT)^{RED} products and events, directly on the ground in Africa. The Global Fund is the world's leading financer of programs to fight AIDS, tuberculosis and malaria. The Global Fund invests 100% of (RED) dollars in AIDS programs in Africa with a focus on women and children. Programs supported by (RED) and the Global Fund have reached over 7.5 million people to date.

NOT ON OUR WATCH:

The mission is to focus global attention and resources towards putting an end to mass atrocities around the world. Drawing upon the powerful voices of artists, activists, and cultural leaders, Not On Our Watch generates lifesaving humanitarian assistance and protection for the vulnerable, marginalized, and displaced. [They] encourage governing bodies to take meaningful, immediate action to protect those in harm's way. Where governments remain complacent, Not On Our Watch is committed to stopping mass atrocities and giving voice to their victims.

FALLING WHISTLES:

Falling Whistles gives a small window into [one of]our world's largest war. Originally just a journal written about boys sent to the frontlines of war armed with only a whistle, readers forwarded it with the same kind of urgency in which it was written and demanded to know.

Disclaimer: The author and his publishers are not in any way or form affiliated with the above named organizations. The author, *Sheg Aranmolate*, is only a firm supporter of their humanitarian efforts towards helping indigent children and decided to incorporate them into the story to further spread their message. Please make a monetary donation to these organizations or show your support by learning more about their works and spreading their message to others.